An Element of
MYSTERY

An Element of

MYSTERY

Sweet, Funny, and Strange

Tales of Intrigue

Editors
Marianne H. Donley and *Carol L. Wright*

Bethlehem Writers Group, LLC
Bethlehem, Pennsylvania, USA

An Element of Mystery
Sweet, Funny, and Strange® Tales of Intrigue

Published by Bethlehem Writers Group, LLC
https://bethlehemwritersgroup.com

Cover design by Marianne H. Donley and Carol L. Wright
Cover and interior images licensed from Depositphotos.com

"Method for Murder" by Carol L. Wright was first published in *Ellen Hart Presents Malice Domestic 15: Mystery Most Theatrical,* Wildside Press (2020)

ISBN: 978-1-954675-00-1
Ebook: 978-1-954675-01-8

Library of Congress Control Number: 2022942305

Printed in the United States of America

In appreciation of
all the mysteries
we've encountered . . .
in fiction and in our lives

Also from the
Bethlehem Writers Group, LLC

Sweet, Funny, and Strange® Anthologies

A Christmas Sampler:
Sweet, Funny, and Strange Holiday Tales (2009)
Winner of two 2010 Next Generation Indie Book Awards

*

Once Around the Sun: Sweet, Funny, and Strange
Tales for All Seasons (2013)
Finalist, 2014 Next Generation Indie Book Award

*

A Readable Feast: Sweet, Funny, and Strange
Tales for Every Taste (2015)
Finalist, 2016 Next Generation Indie Book Award

*

Once Upon a Time: Sweet, Funny, and Strange
Tales for All Ages (2016)

*

Untethered: Sweet, Funny, and Strange
Tales of the Paranormal (2018)
Finalist, 2019 Killer Nashville Silver Falchion Award

*

Fur, Feathers, and Scales: Sweet, Funny, and
Strange Animal Tales (2020)
Winner of two 2021 Next Generation Indie Book Awards

Other Publications

Off the Rails: A Collection of Weird, Wicked,
and Wacky Stories (2019) by Jerome W. McFadden
Finalist, 2020 Next Generation Indie Book Award

*

Let it Snow: The Best of Bethlehem Writers Roundtable
Winter 2015 Collection (2015)

*

Bethlehem Writers Roundtable
https://bwgwritersroundtable.com
Since 2011

TABLE OF CONTENTS

Acknowledgments

The Bethlehem Writers Group acknowledges with gratitude the contributions of the Guest Judges for our 2021 and 2022 Bethlehem Writers Roundtable Short Story Award competitions. Charlaine Harris, international best-selling author of the *Aurora Teagarden, Lily Bard (Shakespeare), Harper Connelly, Gunnie Rose, Southern Vampire,* and *Midnight Texas* mystery series served as judge for our 2021 competition, selecting "Good Cop/Bad Cop" by Trey Dowell. Kate Carlisle, the New York Times best-selling author of the *Bibliophile Mysteries* and the *Fixer-Upper Mysteries* series served as judge for our 2022 competition, selecting "The Tabac Man" by Eleanor Ingbretson. Both stories appear in this volume.

Editors' Note

Since you've chosen a volume entitled *An Element of Mystery,* it should come as no surprise that it contains some stories that involve crimes or attempted crimes, including murder. Some of these stories involve the use of firearms, poisons, bludgeons, knives, or other weapons. Some involve domestic violence, sexual harassment, reference to torture, or allusions to suicide. Nonetheless, we only publish stories that would be rated G, PG, or PG-13 if using the MPAA rating system. We sincerely hope that, being forewarned, you enjoy this collection of stories.

Marital Problems

Jerome W. McFadden

He walked into my office, locked the door, and switched off the light. A finger to his lips told me to be quiet. He had a gun in the other hand and casually sat down in front of my desk, laying it in his lap. My instincts told me there was no way I'd be quick enough to grab my Glock out of my drawer if he attempted to shoot.

So we sat in silence, neither of us moving, although my mind was racing a mile a minute trying to figure out what the hell was going on. Footsteps in the hallway approached my door. Most offices on this floor were empty this late on a Saturday.

The footsteps stopped. A woman's shapely silhouette pressed against the frosted glass on the top half of my office door. The woman held a hand to her forehead trying to peek in. She tapped on the window with an object that gave a metallic *tink, tink, tink,* which I assumed was a gun barrel. She rattled the door handle, then peered in again before moving on.

My new friend and I continued to sit in silence. My office is an oversized closet with a small desk, two chairs (currently occupied), a filing cabinet on the left, a coffee stand on the right, and a back wall that gave just enough room for me to move my chair a few feet back and forth. A tight fit, but cheap for a downtown office. If we were going to have a gunfight we'd both end up with flash burns on our dead bodies and still be sitting straight up.

"She's gone," the man whispered.

"Can we turn on the light?" I whispered in return.

"Too soon. She might wander back."

"So we just sit here in the dark?"

"You're catching on."

I dropped back into silence. Nothing much new to say.

He broke the quiet. "You're a private detective?"

I smiled. A new trend in the conversation. "Says so on the door."

"I want to hire you."

"To find your wife? I think I just saw her shadow loitering in the hall-way. Can I bill you for these few minutes?"

"To kill her."

"Ah, yes. But that is, uh, not in my job description. But I could walk down the hall and bring her back. Then you could shoot her. Just don't do it in my office or mention my name. Ever. And, of course, in this case, I would charge you a finder's fee and would prefer to be paid in cash, in advance. No checks or bank transfers, Western Union. Know what I mean?"

The man stood up to turn on the light. A decent-looking guy. In his forties, I guessed. Thinning hair, a slight paunch, blue tie, white shirt, nice gray suit. Might have been a prized customer if his demands were a little less *demanding*.

"I am serious," he said.

"Maybe you should hire a lawyer? One of those scumbags who devour angry wives?"

He pulled out his billfold to lay out five one-hundred-dollar bills on the desk. A good start for a search project. But I assumed your average kill-for-hire guys charged a bit more. "You do realize she has a gun, too? I think she was tapping on the window with it," I said.

"You want more money?"

"Maybe you should try marriage counseling. Sitting on a nice sofa in front of a pleasant shrink who might talk you into an armistice, a conversa-tion without guns. A verbal firefight instead, so to speak. I could help find you find a good counselor. No charge. I have a phone book. And internet."

"Too late for that."

"Never too late not to shoot someone."

"She's gonna get me if I don't arrange for someone to get her first."

I shrugged. "Private detectives are not allowed to kill people except in self-defense. It's a legal thing, you know? And I'm definitely not going to murder anyone for five hundred dollars."

"You're bargaining with me, right? I got more money. I can cover it. How much . . .?"

I stood up, cutting him off, and reached into my desk drawer for my Glock. "Get out," I said.

"Jesus, no need to get violent."

"Get the hell out of my office."

He shoved the gun into the back of his belt and held out the palm of his other hand as if to ward off my anger. "I'm going. I'm going, but could you steer me to some sleaze bag on the street who might—"

"Out," I said, waving my Glock.

"Come out of there, Harold," a woman's voice shouted from the hallway.

"I think she found you, Harold," I said. "I won't charge her for that, I promise."

He turned to yell back at her through the door, "Go to hell." Apparently, I was no longer part of the conversation.

A shot shattered our eardrums, showering us with the glass from my frosted window, I was too stunned to duck. Harold wasn't. He was already squatting between the wall and the front of my desk, pushing the chair in front of him. Great reaction time from a slightly overweight, middle-aged man. A second shot whizzed two inches past my ear. I dropped behind my desk, deciding that hiding behind my chair was not a bad idea.

"How many guns do you two have in your family, for chrissakes?" I asked, not really wanting to know.

"That's my gun," Harold said angrily. "She took it from my vault. That's how I knew she was out to get me."

"I know what you're doing in there, Harold!" she yelled. "You were trying to set me up, take me out with some gun for hire." She emphasized her outburst with another shot that plowed into the wall above my head.

"Jennifer, stop this nonsense," Harold yelled at the door.

I cringed inwardly. I was going to have a hard time explaining all these bullet holes to my hard-ass landlord.

After taking a deep breath, I decided to enter the conversation. "I was telling Harold to see a lawyer, Jennifer. Or a counselor. You guys can work this out. It's not too late."

"It's too late for him," Jennifer answered, emphasizing it with another shot.

This time the bullet came through the bottom half of the door. I scrunched a little bit further back.

"He's telling the truth, Jennifer. We were talking about lawyers and counselors," Harold shouted.

"My ass," Jennifer bellowed back.

"You have a nice ass, Jennifer. A very nice ass," Harold retorted.

"So does your new girlfriend, right? The young blonde chick?"

"A mistake. It's over now. We can talk this out."

"I'm gonna make you pay for that, whether it's over or not."

"Shooting him is not the answer," I yelled. "It really isn't. Make him pay through a lawyer. They know how to do that. They're good at that."

Harold nodded his head and smiled at me as if he was suddenly in agreement with a little non-violent negotiation.

That encouraged me to say, "Slide your gun along the floor, Jennifer, so we can hear it. Then I'll bring Harold out and we can talk. It would be better this way. Really. We can work something out."

Harold leaned toward me to whisper, "Great idea. When she comes forward, you can step out and shoot her. Piece of cake. Good thinking."

"That's not gonna happen."

"You want more money? You take a check?"

"Forget it, Harold," I said. "We're done. You try anything funny, I will shoot *you*, not her."

Harold ignored me, standing up to smash out what was left of my frosted window with his gun, firing two shots down the hallway. I was sad to see my own beautiful window, with my name and title on it, completely smashed.

Harold wasn't looking my way. I reached up to snatch one of the hundred-dollar bills he had left on the desk as reimbursement for a new window.

"Why don't I take you on, too, Jennifer?" I yelled out. "Then whoever wins this gunfight can pay me. But no double billing, I promise."

She shouted in response, "Bastard." But I wasn't sure if she was referring to me or Harold.

Harold replied, "Bitch."

These two were obviously meant for each other. But I noticed Harold did not fire back this time. Maybe getting worried about how much ammunition he had.

"I am calling the police, folks. They should be here in a flash. If I were you, I'd call a truce for the moment while both of you get the hell out of here. Then you can kill each other later, somewhere else. Well away from my office."

"Who's the jerk in there with you?" the wife yelled.

"My private eye. He's gonna find you and put you out of your misery."

"I am not going to shoot anyone," I said. "But if I see either of you again, I might change my mind." Of course, I had no clue of what she looked like, but I might just chance it by shooting any woman I saw standing near him.

"We'd better get out of here, Jennifer," Harold finally said. "We don't want to get involved with the police."

He thinks of that now?

Jennifer fired one last round. With no reaction from Harold, she said, "Okay, I'm leaving."

Harold turned to me. "How do I know she won't be waiting for me outside the building?"

I held up the phone. "Cops. They're gonna be all over this building and around the perimeter, too. I'll assume Jennifer isn't dumb enough to wait for them."

"Oh, okay, I guess you're right. I'll be leaving then."

"You may not want to go home. She might be waiting there."

"Good advice," he said, wedging the pistol back into his belt and walking out of my office, not looking back.

"Good luck," I called after him, watching him walk down the hallway. When it was clear he was not coming back, I picked up the remaining hundred-dollar bills that he had apparently forgotten about. Not bad for a late Saturday afternoon.

FUNGI

Dianna Sinovic

The mushrooms frying in the camp skillet gave off an earthy aroma that blended with the butter sizzling beneath them. Cassie's mouth watered as she watched them cooking, their edges beginning to curl. As delicious as they smelled, she couldn't bring herself to eat them and knew that would set Rayna off, even after such a perfect day at the lake.

"Almost done," Rayna said, stirring the skillet's contents. "So's the curry." She checked the pot bubbling alongside.

To put off the inevitable argument over dinner, Cassie opened a bottle of merlot and offered her sister a cup. "To our annual backwoods adventure," she said, and they clinked camp cups. Rayna drained hers quickly and added more wood to the campfire.

"Do we really need a bigger fire?" Cassie said.

Rayna pulled the mushrooms off the flames and covered the skillet with a lid. "We've been coming here for twelve years, and I haven't burned down the forest yet."

Cassie relaxed a little—Rayna was right. She loved their June retreat at the remote lake in the Poconos, the chance to reconnect as sisters when their lives were so busy and not all that much in sync. The woods, the water, the same campsite on a family friend's vacation property—it was all familiar and yet exotic by her daily suburban Bucks County standards. And that year, especially, it felt like a needed escape.

Rayna poured another cup of wine and sat near the fire. She checked her cell phone and sighed. "No bars. I can't reach Todd."

"And you're surprised? When have we ever had cell reception here?" Cassie said. "Todd's fine without you. And if you really need to talk to him, there's always the Gas and Go." The gas station/bait shop was a half mile away, but it still had a land line.

Rayna kept fiddling with her phone. "He just likes to know where I am. Maybe if you'd stayed in touch with Pete a little more, you'd still be married like me." Her tone was kidding, and Cassie felt her face flush.

"Touché," Cassie said. "I'll shut up now." She got out the plates and forks for dinner. Pete had filed for divorce three months ago, saying he felt tied down by their marriage. What he really meant, she found out, was that he lusted after a coworker, a blonde with a size thirty-eight bust.

Rayna ladled the curry onto two plates and raised an eyebrow at Cassie before dipping into the mushrooms.

Cassie took a deep breath. "None for me. Just the curry."

She had reluctantly hunted for mushrooms with Rayna earlier that day. Her sister was studying medicinal mushrooms with a local herbalist, and bold in her newfound knowledge, she'd pointed out what to watch for and what to avoid. They had brought back a handful of wild fungi, Rayna's first forage without her teacher, and Cassie knew her sister was eager to show that she knew what she was doing.

Rayna half smiled. "You're chicken," she said, scooping them onto her plate. "You don't know what you're missing."

They sat on their camp chairs and ate, watching the sun set over the lake, scattering red and gold on the still water. The fireflies winked in the gathering dusk; a screech owl called in the distance.

"See?" Rayna said, sopping up the last of the juices on her plate with a piece of bread. "I've eaten them all, and I feel just fine." Her tone was once again kidding.

Cassie had to acknowledge that she was impressed with her sister's foraging skills. "You're right," she said. "But I'm still not eating any wild mushrooms."

They cleaned up after the meal, washing up pots and plates, and tidying up the site.

"So, how *are* you doing?" Rayna said, stirring the embers in the now inky evening. A sprinkle of stars glazed the sky. "How soon is the divorce final?"

Cassie dug for a tissue and dabbed at her eyes. *Damn it.* She didn't want to cry. "It's tough, I'll be honest. Some days are great, and others, I hurt so bad. Not that I want him back after what he did."

"Oh, honey," Rayna said, giving her a hug. "Of course, it's tough." But then she grimaced and quickly went into their tent. Emerging with a small, droppered bottle, she flashed Cassie a woeful smile. "Keep talking. A migraine is ramping up. Red wine strikes again." She opened the tiny bottle and put several drops from it under her tongue.

"We're both hurting, you and I," Cassie said with a chuckle, dry-eyed once more. "Your head, my heart."

They sat in silence for a while, listening to the crackle and pop of the fire. Cassie, lost in thoughts about the divorce, at first didn't notice Rayna's whimpers. Then Rayna threw up, vomiting her dinner, and just missing her sneakers.

Oh, no, Cassie groaned inwardly. *Here we go again.* "How much wine did you *have?*"

Rayna closed her eyes and groaned, bent over, her arms wrapped around her waist. "Just two cups." She rocked back and forth. "My stomach." Then she slid off her camp chair onto the ground, her moans louder and more insistent.

"Rayna?" Cassie was at her sister's side, feeling her forehead, watching her face contort in pain. *It's the mushrooms.* "Let me get you to the tent." She helped Rayna up, and they stumbled the five feet to the tent flap. Her sister shivered violently as Cassie zipped open the screen. *Inside, inside,* Cassie repeated to herself. *If I can just get her inside the tent, everything will be all right.* She helped Rayna into her sleeping bag and laid her own bag on top. Switching an electric lantern on low, she pulled out her cell phone to call for help. No bars. They were probably miles from the nearest cell tower. *Unplugged,* they had joked. That remoteness had been the charm of the place.

"Shit!" Cassie muttered and scrambled out of the tent. Still no bars. In her frustration, she nearly flung her phone into the darkness but caught herself. Losing the phone wouldn't help.

Rayna was panting shallowly. "It's hard to breathe," she said.

"I hate to leave you alone here, but I've got to get help." Cassie blinked back tears. "I'm heading to the gas station to call an ambulance. Back in just a bit."

Was it only an hour or two ago that they had been laughing at dinner? If she could only rewind the scene, to the part where Rayna moved the first forkful of mushrooms to her mouth. Cassie slipped on her daypack and ran up the path toward the road.

The ambulance arrived more quickly than Cassie hoped, and the crew began working on Rayna. Cassie followed the emergency van to the small county hospital and sagged into a chair in the ER waiting room. The ambulance bay had been bustling, with injuries from a multicar wreck, but the waiting area was almost desolate. She needed to call Todd, to let him know, but she hesitated. *I don't want him here.* Then she scolded herself. *Todd isn't Pete, and he has a right to know what's happening.*

She was scrolling through her contact list when the ER doctor found her.

"We did our best," he said. His eyes spoke of a tiredness steeped in emotion.

Hand to her mouth, Cassie gave a cry. "But she's . . ."

He shook his head. "Your sister passed away as they were wheeling her in." He paused. "We tried again and again to resuscitate her."

"No," Cassie almost shouted. "She can't be dead!" She lowered her voice. "She was very much alive in the ambulance."

"I'm very sorry," the doctor repeated.

"Those *damn* mushrooms," Cassie said. *If only, if only, if only,* she repeated silently. "I've got to call her husband, to let him know."

Todd answered on the second ring. Steeling herself, Cassie gave him the details of the mushroom hunt, their dinner, its aftermath.

She had always known Todd to be outgoing and charming, ever the salesman. This time, he spoke so fiercely, she was taken aback. "How could you?" he snarled. "You know how flaky she can be, to trust her to pick safe mushrooms—no wonder you didn't want any of them."

"But, Todd, she's as stubborn as they come—"

He cut her off. "I'm driving up. I'll be there in about two hours."

If only, if only, if only.

By the time Todd arrived at the hospital, Cassie had spoken with a grief counselor on duty. She was awash in guilt, but she had no more tears.

"Cassie," Todd said. This time there was no snarl, but no charm either. His eyes were red, and he moved with a slowness, almost as though he were on automatic. He hugged her, and then stepped back. "I'm still angry, but I realize I can't blame you for this. Where is she?"

Cassie waited for Todd to return from the hospital morgue, wondering if Pete would have been as sensible had the situation been reversed. She chided herself: *You're getting a divorce. He would be celebrating to have you out of the way.*

"Cass, thanks," Todd said, returning to the ER waiting room. "You don't need to stay. I've got it from here." His somberness was painful to watch.

What a good man Rayna picked, Cassie thought. *Why couldn't I have been so lucky?*

Back at home, Cassie dumped the camping gear in the basement and went back to work. But she felt adrift. It wasn't as though she and Rayna talked every day, or even had that much in common. But now it seemed that she needed to ask her sister about some detail in their past life or get her opinion on something she would never have bothered Rayna with before.

Cassie, the librarian, needed order in her world. She enjoyed the structure of the stacks and the challenge of the reference desk, hunting down the answers to patrons' questions. Rayna eschewed order imposed by the outside world, willing to let life lead the way. Cassie tried to recall the complete list of her sister's zigzagging interests. Ray had passed up college to hitchhike around Europe. She had been a waitress, a cashier, and a telemarketer. Most recently she had been teaching yoga and studying with the herbalist.

If Cassie embraced the work ethic, Rayna avoided it. How many times had they argued about the way their lives were going? "When are you going to settle down?" Cassie would say, realizing how like their mother she sounded. "Maybe never," was Rayna's defiant reply.

And now Rayna was beyond help, and Cassie would live with the guilt that she hadn't been able to save her.

Despite the vocal objections from Cassie's mother, instead of a funeral, Todd had Rayna cremated. A memorial service would follow, he said, when he had recovered from the initial shock of her death. Todd said the decision had been made jointly. "She and I had talked about what we wanted, and now that it's a reality, I want to remember Rayna the way she was—full of life."

Cassie had always liked Todd and appreciated his willingness to put up with her sister's unpredictability. He worked as a salesman for a line of computer software and seemed at ease in any situation. He helped steer Rayna through the turbulence of her personal battles with a calm that Cassie admired.

Todd scattered Rayna's ashes and asked Cassie if she would help organize the memorial.

Cassie realized she had nothing that belonged to her sister to hold on to and cherish. She remembered a framed photograph of Rayna and her that hung in the hallway near their guest room. She stopped by their house one night after work to ask about it, but he didn't answer her knock or the doorbell. A "For Sale" sign swung back and forth from its post in the front lawn.

With a shrug, she got back in her car and drove home. She found a large potted plant on her porch, a sympathy gift from her coworkers. From the mailbox, she pulled three sympathy cards from friends. Her home phone flashed with a new voicemail from her mother. She was complaining once again about Rayna's cremation.

Geez, Mom, let it go.

Rayna, despite her rudderless life, had been her mother's favorite. Cassie was expected to provide the adult support and assistance their mother needed, but Rayna was the one who had given their mother a reason to live.

Instead of calling her mother back, Cassie tried phoning Todd. Both his home line and cell went to voicemail, and she felt a twinge of guilt. Why was she bothering a grief-stricken widower? If she was broken up by her sister's death, she could only imagine the depth of his sorrow.

To her surprise, though, he called her back while she was fixing dinner. He had seen her missed call, he said.

"I just wondered," she said gently, "if I could have the photo of Rayna and me, the one with the gold frame? No rush, but it would mean a lot to have it. I stopped by earlier to ask you and saw the 'For Sale' sign."

Todd sighed. "Don't hate me, Cass, but I can't stay here . . ."

"I understand. Too many memories. I'd feel the same way." When Todd said nothing more, she added, "And the photograph? Can I stop by to get it?"

"Everything's going to auction next Saturday," he said. "But I'll set it aside for you."

"Auction?" Cassie was puzzled. She had imagined spending the next several months helping Todd sort through Rayna's belongings.

"Well, the house will sell faster if I auction it," he said, his tone now almost pleading. "To be honest, I really need this sale. Our money situation was getting pretty serious. I wasn't thinking—I haven't been thinking straight since . . ."

Cassie choked up. "It's okay, Todd. Neither have I."

Over the next few days, Cassie jotted down ideas for Rayna's memorial service. She had photos of her sister growing up that she would lend Todd. Rayna would have had a collection of her own. They could make a slide deck that rotated through Rayna's ever-changing interests—except for the mushroom hunts. No one, especially Cassie, needed a reminder of the unfortunate circumstances of her death.

She tried calling Todd several times to discuss the memorial, but his phones still went to voicemail, so on a whim she decided to try his work number.

"I'm Todd King's sister-in-law," Cassie said. "I need to ask him a question about my sister's—his wife's—memorial service."

"He's in a sales meeting right now," the cheerful receptionist said. "I tell you, talk about ups and downs. Todd takes the prize."

"Oh?" Cassie said.

"I mean, you lose your wife and then you win the lottery. The Fates must be toying with him." The receptionist laughed. "He must not know whether to cry or to laugh."

"Are you sure about the lottery?"

"Hon, he's given his two weeks' notice. I can't blame him. Raked in a cool million, heading to the Bahamas."

Cassie hung up without leaving a message. Something seemed off. If he'd won the lottery, why was he so desperate for money? Did Rayna's death have something to do with it? She tried to remember the specifics of that day in the woods.

She and Rayna had hunted for mushrooms. Rayna had cooked them. She alone had eaten them, and then she had died.

Cassie looked up the herbalist's website and called him. Yes, the herbalist said, it was possible that Rayna could have mistaken a poisonous mushroom for a benign one, but he didn't think that had happened.

"Your sister was an excellent student," he said. "She grasped the nuances that other students have taken several years to master."

Cassie savored this bittersweet revelation—her sister an excellent student?

"Let's suppose she did accidentally choose something like an Amanita muscaria," the herbalist said. "She would have gone into a coma—but it wouldn't have been fatal. She absolutely would not have harvested an Amanita bisporigera, the Destroying Angel. She was too smart for that."

"Then what killed her?" It was futile to ask, but she was grasping for reasons, any reason.

"I'd pretty much stake my reputation that it wasn't a mushroom," he said.

It was on Friday afternoon, the day before the auction, that Cassie ran across Rayna's migraine bottle in her backpack. She had stashed it there the night of her sister's death, after finding it on the ground next to her sister's camp seat. The small, brown, glass bottle came from a local homeopathy store and was fitted with a dropper to dispense the liquid within. Rayna's migraines put her in bed for several days when they hit, and she had been using the homeopathic remedy for several years.

Cassie held the bottle up to the light, but the brown of the glass was too opaque to allow her to see much beyond a faint line of liquid. She called a chemist friend, who recommended a lab that could run a diagnostic on the liquid. Maybe the store had mislabeled the contents, selling a solution that was either toxic to take orally or one that had caused a fatal reaction.

At the house auction on Saturday, Cassie sobbed her way through her sister's belongings, picking out a jacket she knew her sister had liked, a series of pamphlets on herbs, and a coral necklace that she'd given Rayna. She also picked up the framed photograph that Todd had promised her. She'd planned to ask Todd about the lottery money, but he was busy the entire time she was there, almost as though he was avoiding her. The crowd that filled the house for the auction milled around him and bought item after item.

She returned to the house late in the afternoon, just as the auctioneer pounded a "Sold" sign into the front lawn. Todd, who had been smiling goodbyes to the auctioneer, frowned when Cassie came up the walk. He seemed to be reading her mind.

"You've heard about the lottery, haven't you?" When she nodded, he went on, as though he'd been rehearsing. "That's just something I made up. Rayna and I wanted to make sure each of us was well protected. A million for her, a million for me. Believe me, this isn't how I meant to collect."

"Why the lie about the lottery?" she countered.

He sighed, his frown relaxing into a slight smile. She felt his charisma reaching out to suck her in, just the way it had Rayna and so many others.

"She was your sister. She was my wife. Those relationships are different, you know."

"So, you're running away, and a lie was easier?"

"Not exactly."

"How much did you get for the house?"

"Enough."

She knew he would never tell her the real reasons for his move.

"The herbalist says she didn't eat a poison mushroom."

She sensed a momentary recalculation in Todd's demeanor, but he quickly recovered. He shrugged.

"He wasn't there."

"What did you do to her, Todd? I want to know the truth."

"The truth is that Rayna's dead. She made a mistake, and it cost her her life. I'd give anything to have her back, but that's not going to happen."

He walked inside the house and shut the door, leaving her alone on the porch. It seemed especially empty now—the bank of wind chimes that Rayna had collected was gone, as were the porch chairs and the ceramic frog she had made in a long-ago pottery class. Rayna's things were scattered across town now, just as her ashes were. How would she ever find her again?

By the following Wednesday, Todd had moved out of the house. Cassie heard he was living temporarily with an old college friend until he left town. She got the lab results in the mail that same day and ripped open the envelope. Her hands were shaking; she wanted to know but was almost afraid to look.

Digitalis. She Googled the details: a potentially fatal drug. Originally from the foxglove plant. Not a migraine remedy. The concentration of the sample went far beyond any homeopathic drug concentration. Rayna had been poisoned. Had it been a tragic error by the homeopathy supplier or had Todd tampered with it? Cassie had the proof but no body to corroborate this piece of evidence.

"It was so easy."

Cassie started at the voice. Todd was behind her, his voice low and seductive. She quickly closed the browser window, and he laughed.

"It will be so easy now."

She slid her cell phone off the desk onto her lap. Thinking quickly, she pulled up her contact list, typed *Help Me*, and sent the text. She slid the phone into her pocket and hoped for the best, that whomever she reached might realize that she needed the police. Now.

Todd grabbed her arm and pulled it behind her, then before she could free herself, he had her other arm, securing them together with a zip tie.

"No!" Cassie screamed and tried to stand up.

Todd pushed her back down, pinning her to the chair. "Stop fighting me." His face was flushed, and his eyes bored into hers. After a moment, he dropped his gaze. "She was a piece of work."

"Let me go." Cassie tried to calm herself. If she were quiet, it might mollify him, make him forget what he came to do.

Todd pulled a small bottle from his shirt pocket. It was dark brown, much like Rayna's bottle. "She was never going to grow up," he said. "I just got tired of it."

"'Til death do us part." Cassie murmured the words, her eyes blurred with tears, seeing Rayna's contorted body, hearing her moans.

Todd laughed again, this time hollowly. He shook the bottle, as if to feel how much liquid was in it. "Stay here while I get a glass." He turned toward the kitchen and then turned back. "If you get up, it will just be that much more painful."

When he was gone from the room, Cassie stood up, wrenching her arms up from behind the chair, biting her lip so she wouldn't groan from the pain. *I've got to get out of the house.* She knew this: Todd would kill her by poison or by force if she stayed.

She made it through the laundry room and was almost to the back door before he found her. Her arms ached from the angle that they were held in by the tie, and her head pounded from panic.

"Neither of you Meyer girls ever listened to me," he said. He pulled her back into the laundry room, then pushed her against the washer, forcing her head back. With a sneer, he held up the shot glass of amber liquid. "To your health."

Using every bit of her strength, Cassie butted her head against the shot glass as it came toward her. The glass and Todd's hand flew back, and the liquid, with exquisite slowness, arced in the air before it splashed onto Todd's face, into his eyes and mouth.

THE LOST GOLD OF RHYOLITE

DT Krippene

It took Nathanial three days to make the cross-country trip and a couple more to find an apartment before he arrived for his first day on the job. The one license plate in the parking lot of Pahrump's new museum wing read "Home Means Nevada." From what he'd read about the town, it was close to the aptly named Death Valley National Park—home to big ass spiders, snakes, lizards, and scrawny coyotes.

"God, I hope they installed the air conditioner," Nathanial grumbled in the triple-digit Nevada heat. *If I hear one more "it's a dry heat," I'm heading straight back to Connecticut.*

Older outbuildings behind the new wing featured a slat-wood supply store from the early 1900s, Native American artifacts, ranching exhibits, and railroad history. It even had an authentic re-creation of a small mine, complete with a bearded prospector mannequin.

Nathanial sighed. After a thirty-year professional career as a historical archivist for several of New England's oldest institutions, he was now relegated to an Old West folk museum at a fraction of what he used to make. But the death of his wife left him empty and in desperate need to leave the New England area.

He adjusted his tie, buttoned his midnight-blue blazer, and entered the front door to scents of sawdust, drywall paint, and fresh varnish. Thirsting for a drink of water, he gave silent thanks for the blissful coolness of the air conditioning system, accentuated by empty shelves and display cases.

He wandered to the back storage room and found a chair, cardboard file boxes four layers deep stacked to the ceiling, and a set of keys on the desk—but no desktop computer or laptop. A white envelope addressed to "Dr. Nathanial Beekman" was taped to a box at eye level.

Handwritten below the letterhead of the Pahrump Historical Society President, it began with, "Welcome Nate."

He uttered a groan. *Only Pam called me Nate.*

> We're so happy you've joined our team. Apologies that I can't be there to greet you. A family emergency popped up, and I won't be back until next week. In the meantime, Hector will be around if you have any questions. He manages the self-guided tour area and locks up the place at five. Volunteers handle any requests for group tours through our website. The museum is open on weekends and closed on Monday, but as agreed, you make your own hours. A society member who retired from the Bureau of Land Management might stop by to drop off research he's collected on a 1907 train robbery.
>
> We plan to have a soft opening in three weeks. As you can see, you've got your work cut out for you. I listed a few ideas on where to start on the next page.
>
> Valerie

Train robbery? His knowledge base of vintage Western culture was limited to TV reruns of *Gunsmoke* and old cowboy movies on a rainy Saturday afternoon as a kid—because it was the only thing on besides roller derby.

Nathanial regarded the file boxes with dread and a parched throat. The damned place sucked water out of his pores like an industrial-grade dehumidifier. He located a faux-wood Formica sink in a bathroom the size of a coat closet—with no toilet paper. Brown water spit from the faucet and splashed his white button-down shirt.

Trudging back to his car, Nathanial flinched when the door handle burned his hand and had to use his blazer sleeve to access an interior hot enough to bake bread. He gagged on his first sip from an equally hot water bottle. Tossing his blazer on the passenger seat, he went back inside.

A few minutes later, an elderly woman in tan shorts, a flower-embroidered denim shirt, and a wide-brimmed gardening hat burst through the door.

"Hi," she chirped. "I was wondering if the society would be interested in an old watch that belonged to my father for your new exhibit."

"Um, I'm Dr. Nathanial Beekman, the new archivist. Antiquities have to first be examined by the Historical Society Board."

"Here," she insisted. "Tell me what you think." She proffered a stained jewelry box containing a scratched vintage timepiece missing the hour hand. "Belonged to his uncle who worked in the mines."

Nathanial left a career surrounded by documents and letters from before the Revolutionary War, and this little biddy thought a beat-up timepiece she'd found in a closet worthy of a historical exhibit. "As I've said, I don't handle these things."

"What do you mean you don't?" she said with indignance. "Isn't that what you archivists are supposed to do?"

Unwilling to debate the difference between a curator and archivist with garden club Calamity Jane, Nathanial attempted diplomacy. "The Historical Society President will be back next week. She may be more qualified to help you in this matter."

"Guess I don't have much of a choice, Nate."

"It's Nathanial."

She harumphed, turning toward the door. "Archivist, my foot."

Where is that Hector fellow when you need him?

That afternoon, with less than half a file box sorted, Nathnial heard the sounds of heavy boot clomps coming from the front room. He dropped a folder with regrets that he hadn't lock the door.

A man who personified cowboys on the covers of cheap Western pulp novels scrutinized the bare shelves. Sporting a white brushy mustache with a few days of beard stubble on a sun-weathered face, he wore scuffed, faded blue jeans, a beige double-pocketed, long-sleeved shirt, and a tan cowboy hat.

"You must be the new archivist Valerie spoke of," he said in a deep, Sam Elliot-like voice. "Monty Contreras."

"Nathanial Beekman. What can I do for you, Mr. Contreras?"

"My father was Mr. Contreras. Call me Monty." Calloused hands nearly crushed Nathanial's fingers in a handshake. "I came by to drop off research I have on the 1907 Train Robbery."

Please don't let it be a collection of Wild West comic books. "Valerie mentioned you might stop by."

"Yep. It's all here, copies of everything I've found about the theft of gold bullion south of Rhyolite. Probably not known back East, but it's the stuff of legend around here."

Nathanial suppressed the urge to say *now is not a good time for Roy Rogers tales* when Monty hitched thumbs in his front pants pockets and began reciting the tale like a carnival storyteller.

"Almost succeeded. Three company mine guards were killed in the shootout, along with four of the bandits. The sheriff at the time, John Simmons, had to back a locomotive with a passenger car to recover the gold and haul it back to Rhyolite." Monty paused for dramatic effect. "When the recovery train returned to the station, ten of the sixty-four gold bars on board were missing. By the time Sheriff Simmons whittled it down to one of his deputies as the prime suspect, the miscreant had vamoosed during the confusion before anyone noticed him gone."

Against his better judgment, Nathanial asked, "Is there a happy ending to it?"

Monty grinned like a rancher who got top dollar for his steers. "That's where the *real* mystery comes in. The gold thief, Chipper Daniels—he's the deputy I mentioned—was found dead inside an unregistered miner hole a few days later, crushed by a cave-in with only his feet sticking out."

Nathanial figured there'd be no stopping Hopalong Cassidy until he finished his nail-biting tale with the obvious ending. "Let me guess. The gold wasn't in the mine."

Monty nodded. "You're firing on all cylinders there, Nate."

"It's Nathanial." He glanced at his watch. *Four-thirty.* "Did you want me to help you bring the records in?"

"Thanks. Won't take but a minute."

Monty's concept of a minute was off by ten to transfer six heavy boxes from his road-dusty white Ford F250. Nathanial sat on the desk to rest a moment, wondering if the faucet sludge was poisonous. Monty came in with the last box and four chilled water bottles.

Nathanial downed the first in seconds and opened a second. "Thank you. The water from the new sink might be sourced from one of those mines you mentioned."

"If you remember nothing else, always have water on hand and stay hydrated." Monty tipped the brim of his hat up with his water bottle. "What do you say you and I grab a beer and a taco at Inez's?"

Personal space alarms went up, and tacos weren't on Nathanial's list of preferred cuisine. "I should get back . . ."

"My treat," Monty insisted. "Kind of a welcome to Nye County. Get a primer of sorts on your new home."

Nathanial assumed the joint was peppered with folksy Western lore, but the idea of a frosty adult beverage had merit. He locked up, scanned the outbuildings one more time for the elusive Hector, then headed for his car. A hairdryer set on the highest setting blasted from the vents when he started it. Trailing behind the whiny buzz of Monty's off-road tires, the car's aircon achieved lukewarm when they arrived at a rectangular strip mall with a blinking neon billboard for Mama Inez's Mexican Cuisine.

The place was crowded with no visible open seating. Monty led the way toward the only available, burgundy-colored, vinyl bench seat with a reserved sign. The waitress appeared in less than a minute, greeted Monty with a toothy grin, a basket of corn chips, and two chilled bottles of beer.

You'd never see service like that in a Connecticut restaurant. "I take it you're a regular."

Monty guzzled half his beer before answering. "Been a resident of Pahrump since it was patched together from several ranches in 1970. The town name's a Southern Paiute word for Water Rock because of the artesian wells here. A fairly important resource in these parts."

Nathanial remembered its current reputation of having two famous licensed brothels. *Think I'll leave that one alone.*

"It's changed a lot over the years. Got all modernized," Monty reflected. "Sort of miss the old days when the streets were quieter, less crowded."

Nathanial couldn't help himself. "Did you ride a horse to work?"

Monty chuckled. "Drove an old 1969 Mustang, if that counts."

A plate of tacos and two more beers magically appeared. Nathanial's first bite nearly cauterized his tongue, and against guidance to not drink when dehydrated, he downed the beer for fire suppressant purposes. The day's rigid tension eased when the alcohol highway to his brain raised the speed limit. "Tell me more about this Rhyolite place."

"A classic gold rush boom to bust," Monty began. "About eighty miles north of here, Rhyolite's been a ghost town for nigh on a hundred years."

He rattled off a timeline like memorized bullet points from a college student's notebook. "Guy by the name of Shorty Harris discovered a rich vein of gold ore near the Bullfrog settlement in 1904, which triggered the gold rush. By the end of 1906, the town had electricity to serve a population of ten thousand, with banks, post office, town board, schools, churches, you name it. Even had its own newspaper. Three competing railroads tied Rhyolite to Tonopah's ore processing for over two thousand mining claims.

But the gold ran out in 1909. Town went bust four years later. The place was mostly deserted when the last train left Rhyolite Station in 1914."

More familiar with New England historical sites dating to the 1600s, Nathanial found the concept of a town's birth and death in less than a decade hard to comprehend. "So, you're saying when the town died, evidence of where the gold went died with it," Nathanial surmised. "I gather you've been looking a long time for it."

Monty wiped hot sauce from his lips. "I started dabbling in it not long after starting with the Bureau of Land Management, gathering bits and pieces about prospector mines in my spare time. Before I knew it, I was hooked."

"What makes you think the gold is still here? Do your records have any more details? Like, what evidence pointed to Chipper Daniels as the thief other than that he disappeared shortly after the theft?"

"Forgot to mention they found one of the gold bars near Daniels' body." Monty reached for a chip and winked. "Going theory is he was getting ready to abscond from the territory, had it on him for expenses. With the location of that miner hole less than a day's horse ride from Rhyolite, stands to reason he stashed the rest not far from him." He drained his beer and raised a finger to order another. "Ah. If only the hills could talk."

They'd be singing "Imaginary Needle in a Haystack." "I'm going to guess there've been other treasure seekers interested in finding it."

"More *others* than a fifty-gallon drum filled with Hershey Kisses," Monty said with a chuckle.

"Does your gathered information include shared data?"

"I have some comparative info, but most of it is mine. We treasure hunters can be a secretive lot."

And I'm supposed to verify enough research to support an exhibit for this Western fairytale based on one man's assortment of suppositions and a century of hearsay? Perhaps Monty's collection held more details, like evidence of a gold bar he forgot to mention. "It's a noble gesture that you're willing to donate your files to the museum. Does that mean you've . . ." *Don't say hung up your spurs.* "Lost interest?"

"Don't think I'll ever lose the passion, but I'm not getting any younger and the frustration is growing harder to bear. The story itself is a Nevada legend. I just thought it should be memorialized for future generations. Inspire some young person to look at it from a different viewpoint."

Monty exchanged smiles with the waitress when she set two fresh beers down. The bottle halfway to his lips, he turned to Nathanial. "How about we take a ride out to Rhyolite tomorrow? A site survey to give you a sense of the place."

Nathanial's New Englander reserve raised caution flags on the idea. The second beer countered with, *why not? Could be more entertaining than locals showing up at the museum with stuff they found in the attic.* "Sure."

"Great. That Honda Accord of yours isn't suited to handle the back roads out there. I'll pick you up first thing in the morning." Monty tapped his bottle on Nathanial's untouched third brew and squinted. "You going to drink that or wait for it to evaporate?"

Nathanial drove below the speed limit to his rented apartment in fear of being pulled over for DUI. He sullenly regarded the floor mattress of the supposedly furnished one-bedroom apartment while a category-three taco storm raged in his belly. After popping an antacid and preemptive ibuprofen for the expected morning headache, he sat at the secondhand desk and fired up his laptop for a map of Rhyolite.

"Dammit." No internet.

A rude awakening came from the shrill ring of his smartphone skittering across the desktop. Nathanial's fogged brain debated answering it. *Better not be a spam call from the East Coast.* He rolled out of bed and clambered on all fours to grab it before it went to voicemail.

"You have got to be kidding me." Nathanial punched the screen with Monty Contreras' name on it.

"You ready to roll?" Monty's voice said.

"It's five in the morning."

"Unless you like hanging with a bunch of tourists in the midday heat, best we get an early start. We can grab a burrito when we reach Beatty."

For breakfast? Nathanial switched on the desk lamp. "How much time before you arrive?"

"I'm in your driveway, so hop to it."

Adherence to rancher's hours was not part of my job description. No time to shower, Nathanial hung up and stumbled to the bathroom for a quick face scrub, pit wipe, and mouthwash gargle. After guzzling two eight-ounce tumblers of water, he grabbed a clean shirt and socks, then realized his travel pants were still at the dry cleaners. No choice but to slip on the same eau-de-taco permeated slacks from yesterday, he grabbed his blazer off a kitchen stool and dashed for the idling pickup.

Monty squinted at Nathanial's attire and business shoes. "You always dress up for a hike?"

A boring day at the museum might have been a better option. Nathanial grabbed a water bottle. "Let's . . . just go."

Monty filled in the first half-hour's drive north with unsolicited snippets about Nevada's geology. The eastern horizon transformed from light purple to brilliant reddish-orange more stunning than any Connecticut sunrise in recent memory. They entered the small town of Beatty when the sun rose above distant mountains.

The air temperature was already in the low nineties. "Going to be a hot one," Monty said, pulling into a local fast-food joint with pickups lined up at the drive-through.

What a shocker. Nathanial turned down the offer of a breakfast gut grenade.

Monty ambled over to a shack next door that offered fresh homemade jerky. He set a paper bag on the center console, ripped off a jerky section with his teeth, and hit the gas in a gravel-flaying spinout. "Prospector's breakfast. Help yourself."

After a peek at the mummified strips smelling of months-old, desiccated meat that might have been accidentally dropped behind a cabinet, Nathanial cracked open the window.

Ten minutes later, Monty pulled onto a northbound access road. A cloud of dust kicked up by the tires rivaled a Sahara sandstorm. Nathanial wished he'd peed in Beatty when the road narrowed with the truck inches from a sheer drop without guardrails. Monty slowed to a stop by a wood-slatted train caboose without wheels.

The dust storm caught up to Nathanial's open window, and he ripped three nose-burning sneezes into his blazer sleeve. *The damned place is dustier than a warehouse of used vacuum cleaner filters.*

Monty pointed to a two-story, mostly intact building across the road. "That's the old railroad station where our story of the stolen gold began."

Nathanial left the blazer on his car seat. "Do you think anybody would mind if I stepped behind the caboose to relieve myself?"

Monty dipped his head toward a brick shack with two vent stacks. "Vault toilet right over there." He reached into the truck cab and tossed Nathanial a small bottle of hand sanitizer. "Here. Take this."

The sharp stench of fermented sewage wafted from fifty yards away. Nathanial looked skyward for a sign that he might be caught in a bad dream but found only heat-striated air. A tree would have been preferable, but the closest one was probably in the next state.

Scrubbing his hands afterward like a surgeon, Nathanial took in the desolation of a desert landscape. Although the train station was still in decent condition, all that remained of Rhyolite's past were a half-dozen crumbling brick and stone structures that brought to mind a nuclear bomb test site from the forties.

Monty drove a couple of miles to the Bullfrog-Rhyolite Cemetery. In the middle of a forsaken landscape, a few plots bore headstones. Some were surrounded by rusted metal fencing or dry-rotted planks, or bordered by a simple ring of pebbles.

Nathanial wandered toward a coffee-brown, dry-roasted, cracked-wood marker. Any wording had long been eroded by a century of wind-swept sand. He spotted a plot nearby marked by a primitive cross of two sticks held together by petrified twine and jammed upright by a stack of rocks like a scene from a Clint Eastwood spaghetti Western.

Monty sidled up alongside. "Not much of a memorial to a man's existence on this earth." He readjusted the set of his cowboy hat. "They're the lucky ones, I guess. A lot of lost souls dreaming of riches died alone in the desert, their bodies buried in a mine hole, or claimed by the sand after the buzzards were done with them."

Despite the heat, Nathanial shivered. "Considering the thousands that once lived in Rhyolite, you'd think there'd be more graves."

"If you walk around and pay attention, most are nothing more than faint outlines in the dirt. I counted over two hundred, but I'm sure others were swept flat over time. The USGenWeb archives listed sixteen with markers. Seven of them unknown, like this poor fellow."

Intimately familiar with the USGW genealogy project, Nathanial often used the archives from restorations of headstones going back hundreds of years. "Who takes care of the place?"

"Volunteers, mostly. The ghost town and this cemetery are protected historic sites and managed by the Bureau." He scratched an ear and shook his head. "Do you even own a hat?" Without waiting for an answer, he strode back to his truck.

Of the nine still readable tombstones, only three were dated before 1916. James Cauthorn, died 1905. Donald Kentzler the same year. A woman whose name sounded like a character from a Harry Potter story, Fanny Fitz, died in 1907. The remaining memorials were interred decades later, the latest as recent as 1991. He stooped to examine a rock from the mound covering the Fitz plot. Ingrained silver flecks sparkled in the early morning sun.

With Monty still rummaging through the back seat of his truck, Nathanial meandered toward the stone monument at the cemetery entrance bearing a plaque dated 1959.

> This enduring bronze is placed here to the blessed memory of those who sleep herein and to the remembrance of all others who came this way and opened up the great Nevada desert mining world—by those who cared.

Nathanial swallowed a lump in his throat. Sparked by the silence in this hallowed place, a festering hurt arose from a dark place in his heart from the memory of Pam's funeral. The sound of dirt dropping on her coffin from his shaking hand still haunted him in nightmares, after which he'd awaken weeping like a lost child. If it hadn't been for people who cared, he would never have been able to cope.

Monty wandered over, clutching a white straw cowboy hat that had seen better days. "Unless you want to turn redder than a ripe tomato, put this on." He must have noticed the blush of reddened eyes. "You okay?"

Nathanial brushed off his slacks and donned the hat. "I was thinking of my wife. Being here conjured up some sad memories."

"Yeah. Valerie mentioned it." Monty stared at his feet. "The desert can bare a man's soul out here, challenge one's reasoning and purpose, but I have a feeling her passing is what brought you out here." He adjusted his hat over thinning gray hair. "An educated man with your credentials pulling up stakes to be fish out of water? You'd have to be both crazy and brave."

"I was laid off last June, and the opportunities for archivists are few and far between during a recession."

"Well, ain't that timing a barrel of horse manure."

"Did me a favor, I think. We lived in the same town for over twenty years. Everywhere I went reminded me of her."

Monty hitched thumbs in his pockets, a sure sign of a Will Rogers witticism to come. "Only way to handle it in my view is feet forward. Never look back because there's nothing to see."

Nathanial pinched his lips to keep from smiling. The man might be corny as hell, but his Dr. John Wayne psychology was just the tonic he needed. "So, what's next?"

"Head up that ridge over there to see what a real prospector mine looks like."

When they turned onto an uphill road, unpaved took on a new definition. They slalomed past half-buried boulders jutting from hard-packed dirt, wash erosion deep enough to swallow them whole, and thorny brambles scraping the sides of the truck.

They waited to let the dust settle before stepping out on a sloping hill. If it weren't for scrub brush pocking the ground like withered pricker bushes, the place could pass for a lunar landscape. *The only green this place ever sees might be a side order of broccoli from a Chinese take-out box.*

Rancher's wire fencing cordoned off a cave entrance no bigger than a hobbit hole. "You think the gold has to be hidden in one of these holes, based on . . . the deputy's body found a day's horse ride from Rhyolite?" Nathanial asked. "What is that, twenty miles?"

"Closer to thirty at a steady pace in these mountain areas. Less if leading a pack mule."

Nathanial mulled it over to himself. Anything within a mile of Daniels' mine like this one had likely been excavated to bedrock. "Metal detectors haven't been much help?"

Monty harumphed. "Metal detecting is a blood sport in this state, most of which unearth beer cans. Rocks around here are loaded with metal-bearing ore. Makes even the newer models squeal like a poked pig."

A century passed with treasure seekers and nothing to show for it. *Forget the needle in a haystack concept. It was like searching for a single grain of sand in the desert.*

Nathanial approached the wire fence and peered into the mine's seemingly endless black. To chip at solid rock with a pickaxe, armed with little else but grit and the fever of becoming rich, spoke of a blind determination that bordered on the manic. He thought of a deputy called to duty with others to recover gold bars from a derailed train, who cleverly came up with a plan on the fly to toss a few bars out a window without anyone seeing it, yet quickly found by a sheriff's posse that finds him dead from a cave-in with incriminating evidence near his body, the location of the remaining gold lost to the ages. It sounded more like a Western folktale passed down by old ranch hands to tell at a Boy Scout camping trip. The story had more holes than a salad spinner, like why would Deputy Daniels, whose name sounded like a cartoon animal character, hide in the most obvious of places so close to the crime scene?

Yet, Monty spent the better part of his free time investigating abandoned mine sites to find the gold, along with many others following a legend believed to be real. He might come across as folksy, but Nathanial didn't sense him to be stupid.

"Your head appears to be a thousand miles away," Monty said.

Though Nathanial's archivist experience flagged it as not worthy of his time, something in his bones felt pieces of the hundred-year-old story got lost in the translation. "I'm thinking I should take a closer look at the files you brought in."

Monty flicked the brim of his hat and grinned. "Got a better idea. How about we head back to my hacienda, where you can check out the original copies. I make a mean brunch omelet with hash browns."

Monty's ranch-style house on the outskirts of Pahrump consisted of old Western furniture, cowboy collectibles, and Navajo-style rugs.

"I gather you're not married," Nathanial observed.

"I'm too ornery for a live-in partner." Monty hung his hat on a mounted bighorn sheep head in a converted bedroom office wallpapered with Nevada topographical maps. "If I get a hankerin', I have a few lady friends in town."

Why did I bring it up?

He cringed inwardly at an archivist's nightmare. Reams of printed documents covered the surface of a vintage hardwood desk. Folders protruded from overstuffed, four-drawer file cabinets. Wastebaskets overflowed with crumpled paper and crushed beer cans. *Man needs to hire a housekeeper.*

Atop the desktop flotsam, Monty set an accordion file with a bullet-pointed sequence of the crime, then went to the kitchen to make lunch. Nathanial gave him credit for his detailed typewritten notes.

A private, southbound train owned by the Goldfield Mining Company loaded with fifteen hundred troy pounds in gold bars, stopped in Rhyolite for water and coal. Twenty miles out, robbers lay in wait to derail it, followed by a shootout with company mine guards that ended with seven dead including four bandits. Two of the robbers escaped. The surviving three guards sent the train engineer hoofing it back for help. He got lucky and flagged a wagon back to Rhyolite. It was dark before Sheriff Simmons organized a volunteer posse to include Chipper Daniels and one other deputy, the town undertaker, and eleven volunteers. No turntable in Rhyolite, a locomotive and passenger car had to be driven in reverse to rescue the gold and three mine company guards who remained at the derailed train. The undertaker supervised the loading of seven bodies on one end of the car. Gold bullion was stacked on the end closest to the locomotive firebox, verified all accounted for by Sheriff Simmons, then covered with canvas before heading back. Upon arrival at Rhyolite station, ten gold bars were found missing, presumed tossed off the train in the dark. Sheriff Simmons went after the deputy and found him dead in the mine cave with one bar of gold, the rest missing.

"What's the source of the information in your notes?" Nathanial called out.

Monty came to the door wearing a frilly apron that Aunt Bea would be proud of from an episode of *The Andy Griffith Show*. "A few court records and archived copies of the 1907 *Rhyolite Daily Bulletin*. It was headline news for months."

And triggered many decades of treasure seekers. Nathanial perused topographical maps pasted to the walls. Sites ruled out were checked off, candidate sites circled in red for further examination, and way too many verified collapsed holes were highlighted in yellow.

"Come and get it," came a call from the kitchen.

For a hardcore, grizzled bachelor, Monty did indeed make a delicious omelet loaded with sauteed tomatoes, onions, mild green chilies, and just enough chorizo to spice it up. Satiated, Nathanial sipped his second cup of dark-roasted coffee and let the subtle chocolaty bitterness draw him into thoughts of what he'd just read.

"Gets under your skin, doesn't it?" Monty said to break the silent musing.

"Have to admit it intrigues me." Nathanial set his cup down. "But when I study the historical accounts based on newspaper articles, it reads like a romanticized Wild West story to capture reader's interest. People in the Midwest and East gobbled up sensationalized tales of the Old West in those days."

Monty leaned back. "Not catching your meaning."

"I'm suggesting that over a hundred years, the incident became a legend of lost gold hidden in the hills. As an archivist, I first consider the accuracy of data regarding the people who made it historical. In this case, all that is recorded came from basically one source—a newspaper that printed whatever Sheriff Simmons told them."

"Interesting." Monty scratched his chin. "After finding Chipper Daniels, the mining company posted a bounty for half the gold's value of forty-eight thousand dollars if found and returned. It became national news for a while."

"What's it worth today?"

"Little over five million."

"If found, do you get to keep it?" Nathanial asked.

"With the mining company no longer in existence, it's considered finders-keepers." Monty waved the air when Nathanial smiled. "Okay, maybe it was my initial incentive—like everyone else trying to find it."

Monty leaned forward with elbows on the table. "Didn't take a hammer to the hand to know you weren't buying it until now. What piqued your interest?"

Nathanial took a deep breath and slowly exhaled. *Do I want to go down this rabbit hole?* "I'm having trouble believing one man planned it with nobody else noticing, only to be found conveniently dead with one of the gold bars. My first suspect is the sheriff. He orchestrated the recovery. It was his deputy."

"You're not the first one to suspect his involvement. Simmons stayed on as sheriff for another few months until the hype settled down, then got hired by the mining company as chief of security. While visiting family in Wisconsin a year later, he suddenly died of a heart attack. The Rhyolite newspaper ran a nice feature on his life. Doesn't sound like a man who orchestrated stealing the gold, only to go on with life without it."

Nathanial wasn't so sure, but he went down the list of other candidates. "You said two robbers involved in the derailment got away. Any possible connection?"

"They were caught soon after the incident and swore they didn't know Daniels. Can't see why they'd lie when facing a noose for murder."

"The company mine guards who remained behind until rescued?"

"Oh, they went through a serious grilling by Sheriff Simmons and the mining company authorities. They were eventually cleared."

That left the undertaker. "I wasn't aware mortuary guys made house calls back then as part of a posse."

"Bartholomew Stumpf was one of the town fathers, a church-going man, a real upright citizen. Wasn't a bad word said about him by anybody. Decided to get himself ordained and left Rhyolite in 1908 to start a church in San Francisco. He, too, was celebrated in the paper when he left."

Again, the newspaper. "How long did the *Rhyolite Daily Bulletin* stay in publication?"

"Ran from early 1907 to 1909. After that, the only papers that still followed mining news were the *Goldfield News* and *Tonopah Daily Bonanza.*"

Nathanial glanced at Monty's grandfather clock at two thirty-five and failed to stifle a mouth-gaping yawn. "Sorry. Guess I'm still adjusting to the Western time zone."

"Tromping around Nevada mountains can take the steam out of anyone not used it. Let's get you on home." Monty fetched his hat. "You'll find copies of most everything here in the files I left at the museum."

"The new wing doesn't have internet access yet. If I'm connected at the apartment, think I'll work there in the morning."

And research the data available. In this case, checking the journalistic integrity of the local newspaper.

Nathanial tried to sleep but couldn't shut down his mind. He gave up and switched on his laptop. *All give praise, the internet is working.*

He accessed the Library of Congress online to locate where digital copies of the 1907 *Rhyolite Daily Bulletin* were housed. His professional credentials got him into the University of Nevada's archives for articles before and after the gold robbery. For good measure, he also accessed the *Goldfield* and *Tonopah* archives the weeks before and following the gold robbery on March 14. As expected, Chipper Daniels' name didn't appear until after the sheriff disclosed him as the suspect. Articles waxed on about his former life as a washed-up prospector who did odd jobs in town to feed himself before becoming a lawman. In the following weeks, the headlines switched to where the deputy might have hidden the gold, the bounty posted, and a mad rush to find it. *Stuff that sells papers.*

He then focused on Sheriff John Simmons and discovered plenty with his name in articles describing his arrests, murder investigations, jailing drunk prospectors who passed out in the street, and breaking up fights in the saloons, usually over a woman—all written with a pulp novel voice to encourage wagging tongues. He found the issue where Simmons presided over the hanging of two bandits who were part of the train derailment, gruesomely displayed on the front page for optimum shock value. Judging by the grainy black-and-white photos in multiple issues, Simmons was a VIP regular with various ladies' social groups. A two-page article venerated his service to Rhyolite when Simmons went to work for the mining company.

The only person left—Bartholomew "Bart" Stumpf, the undertaker. Articles abounded that included Stumpf's officiation at funeral services, church bazaars, town hall meetings, and another special feature in reference to his selfless contributions to Rhyolite's population. Using his professional access to sites unavailable to the general public, Nathanial quickly located an archive link that mentioned the "Sanctuary of God's Holy Presence" in San Francisco, run by pastor Dr. Bartholomew Stumpf.

At first, Nathanial thought it odd that two people present on the gold recovery effort left within months of each other. With little else to go on, he had to assume them to be smart men who bailed when they recognized signs of Rhyolite's future collapse.

About to give up for the night, Nathanial tried one last search that led him to the obituary of John Simmons. Nathanial's blood pressure kicked up a notch when a Wisconsin newspaper, the *Neenah Times,* claimed the former sheriff died not of a heart attack as was reported in the Rhyolite paper, but from food poisoning from eating a tainted sausage.

A history professor's advice while Nate was attending Yale for his Ph.D. came to mind. *If you're searching for a specific tree and reach the end of the woods, you might be looking in the wrong forest.*

He typed in keywords and was rewarded with another lengthy obituary written by admirers. Several intense searches later, Nathanial uncovered a missing tree from a completely different forest.

His next thought was, *how early does Monty get up in the morning?*

The dawn light had brightened enough to see without headlights when Monty parked at the cemetery entrance. "Over an hour drive without a hint of what's on your mind. You going to finally tell me why we're here?"

"Thought a little show might help the telling," Nathanial replied. "Most of those files you have were primarily sourced from the *Rhyolite Daily Bul-*

letin and a few other Nevada sources—which primarily had articles about the lost gold."

"That's about right. What are you getting at?"

"In the science of archiving, relying on one source runs the risk of not finding pertinent details that might be found elsewhere. Add journalism to the issue, accurate reporting and sensationalizing to attract higher readership is often a porous boundary, which might also include editorial modifications to protect the legacy of a famous citizen."

Nathanial opened a briefcase and handed Monty a printout from the *Neenah Times*. "Case in point, former Sheriff Simmons died of food poisoning, not a heart attack." Another printout from a San Francisco paper had the obit of an undertaker turned church pastor. He held up a finger to stop Monty from interrupting, then pointed to a highlighted paragraph.

> Known to be a faithful servant of God to his parishioners,
> a brief visit to his family in the Midwest was the only time
> Pastor Stumpf was absent from his church.

Monty scratched his head. "How'd you find this?"

"Same as you. Internet. But I have access to sites only a professional historian would know about. I was amazed to find there were more Stumpfs than Smiths in Oshkosh, Wisconsin—only thirteen miles from Neenah."

Monty's eyes widened. "You're thinking they knew each other before coming west."

"The odds of two men involved with the incident hailing from the same area of Wisconsin makes it highly suggestive, but without more to go on, it's only speculation. What caught my eye was the approximate date Pastor Stumpf wasn't at his church—which was about the same time as Simmon's death."

"Go on," Monty said. "Stumpf poisoned him?"

"Undertakers by trade used toxic chemicals. Stumpf had proximity, but still circumstantial evidence without proof. But to me, it strongly suggests Chipper Daniels, Bartholomew Stumpf, and John Simmons were all in on a last-minute plan to steal a few of the gold bars. With the sheriff's hero-like community standing and larger-than-life persona that sold papers, how hard would it be for him to orchestrate Daniels' killing as a one-man caper."

"You sound more like a detective than a historical archivist," Monty observed.

"Much of what we do is investigative work, connecting dots, resolving discrepancies."

Monty scratched the side of his head. "Okay. Let's say Simmons and Stumpf both knew where the gold was hidden. Stumpf knocks off Simmons so he can keep it all and bides his time playing preacher man until the coast is clear. Guess he kicked the bucket before he could get back here?"

"Take a look at the date of his obituary."

Monty put on reading glasses to read the printout. "Well, I'll be damned. He died less than a year from when Simmons did. Doesn't say how."

Another newspaper article appeared in Nathanial's hand. "Buried in the crime section a few days earlier, a certain Bart Stumpf was shot in a bar for cheating at cards," he said. "I'm guessing that San Francisco crime events were all too common to warrant headline news unless it was someone important. It appears the good pastor didn't quite live up to his professed pious principles, but devoted parishioners left his scandalous demise unstated in the obit."

"Damnation," Monty uttered.

Nathanial popped the door open. "Let's take a stroll. I want to check out another theory I have." They stopped at the grave marked with a petrified stick cross jutting from the ground. "I revisited an article that described Chipper Daniels, specifically his odd jobs before becoming a lawman. Gravedigger was one of them."

As if to interpret the lightbulb that went off in his head, Monty went still for a moment, then let out a long whistle. "You . . . think the gold is buried in one of these unknown graves?"

"Certainly not beyond the capabilities of an undertaker."

"This graveyard is considered a historical monument. I doubt the Bureau, not to mention historical societies who tend the site, will give permission to exhume close to two hundred graves of the unknown on a theory."

"Actually, the one over there is most interesting." Nathanial pointed to a cement marker. *Fanny Fitz—Died April 14, 1907*—a couple of weeks after the heist. "When I checked copies of the Rhyolite paper, there was no obituary for the woman. You'd think someone worthy of a fancy headstone might be a well-known, upstanding citizen—have a flowery frontpage feature with her picture in the paper."

Monty removed his hat and inspected the inside band. "Got to admit, you connected some interesting dots, but even with your superior credentials, I don't know if it'll be enough to convince government authorities."

Nathanial scraped his shoe on the flat ground of an unmarked plot. "One of the activities you get used to in New England is spending time in cemeteries. Old graves concave when a wood coffin deteriorates to the point of collapse and fills with burial dirt." He spun in a circle, pointing with his finger. "Every grave here is either flat or a bit sunken. Wind-borne dust over the past century likely filled over the oldest ones until they're as level as the landscape."

He turned to Fanny Fitz's plot. "Except for that one. The rocks are still mounded like she was recently buried." Nathanial picked up a rock from the mound. "Only reason I can think of why the ground didn't eventually sink is that the coffin didn't collapse, either because there's no coffin, or what's buried is solid." He dropped the stone. "Don't modern mining methods use borehole probes with a camera or upscale metal detector attached to the end?"

"Damn, son, you do have one hell of an analytical mind. But it's government land. If by some miracle the authorities consider investigating it, you do know that all proceeds will go to the federal government." Monty chuckled and rested his hand on Nathanial's shoulder. "But there might be a finder's fee for you."

"Us," Nathanial corrected. "It was you who brought me into it, and you should receive a bigger share for all the years you've spent searching."

"No use counting chickens while they're still inside the shell." Monty patted Nathanial's back. "But I might have a few friends in the Bureau."

Five months later

His brow shaded by a straw cowboy hat, Nathanial zipped his jacket in the blustery chill to admire Amargosa Valley's grandeur. Monty had found him a 1997 Toyota 4Runner with more dents than not, but it was cheap with a trade-in and had off-road tires capable of scaling dirt roads to awe-inspiring heights like this.

It took a lot of negotiating, even with Nathanial's superior credentials, to approve a camera borehole for examining Fanny Fitz's grave under the watchful eyes of the Bureau of Land Management archivists and Nevada Historic Preservation Office archeologists. The coffin was filled with rocks—and the missing bars of gold. After considerable debate regarding heaviness, it was agreed by committee decision that the casket was most likely empty when lowered into the hole and loaded before burying it. Unless someone rummaging through great-grandma's belongings comes up with a century-old letter bearing new data, no one will ever know what really happened. In the end, it was always about finding the lost gold.

Accolades poured in from people all over the country when the disinterment was broadcast on national news. Congratulatory notes came nonstop from ex-colleagues. His old employer offered his old job back. The Pahrump Historical Society bestowed him the title of Archivist and Curator of Collections and made sure he and Monty were featured in Nevada papers.

Although visitation at the museum reached an all-time high, tourist interest for the "The Lost Gold of Rhyolite" display was less popular than obtaining autographed brochures by Pahrump's famed archivist. Nathanial dodged questions of what he'd do with the finders' fee if the slow wheels of the government bureaucracy deemed it worthy of consideration. *Unhatched chickens.*

Monty relentlessly teased him about multiple museum visits by women laden with cookies, cakes, and baked casseroles when word got out that Nathanial Beekman was a widower. He handled it with smiling discretion, suspecting Monty might have encouraged a few of his acquaintances.

A student wandered up. "Mr. Beekman? Are we going to the cemetery soon?"

Though still adjusting to his newfound fame, Nathanial loved participating in school class field trips and the energetic curiosity the kids brought with them.

Nathanial smiled. "My father was Mr. Beekman. Call me Nate."

RINGING THE NEIGHBORHOOD WATCHDOG

Emily P. W. Murphy

On Saturday, June first, Cam celebrated the first day of Pride Month by raising a brand-new Progress Pride Flag. Standing barefoot in the dew-covered grass outside hir tiny gambrel colonial, Cam admired the way the cheerful pride rainbow emanated from the white, pink, blue, brown, and black triangle.

"What do you think, Wolfgang?" Cam asked the enormous mutt who had just finished watering the base of the flagpole. Wolfgang appeared unimpressed. "Well, if you weren't colorblind, you'd agree it's a beauty." The flag snapped in the wind, as if in appreciation of the praise.

Cam picked up a suet feeder and large wrought-iron hook—Hanukkah gifts that had been on the to-do list for months, now. "I bet this will be more your speed." Cam drove the base of the hook into the soft ground near the front door, where it should be visible from the home office. "Just need the suet." Wolfgang huffed and watered the base of the hook.

The suet was slimy once it was out of the packaging. "Gross." Cam slid the suet cake into the feeder. "This better work."

Wolfgang whined and pressed against Cam's leg. "It's not that bad—" Cam looked down at the dog. Wolfgang was focused on the recently sold house next door. Cam turned to see the new neighbor scowling from their driveway. Cam raised a hand in greeting, but the neighbor was already disappearing into a red sedan with dark tinted glass. They gunned the engine and peeled out of the driveway.

"Hi," Cam said to the empty yard. "Happy Pride." Xe turned and continued the conversation in hir head. "I'm Cam. Your new neighbor. My pronouns are xe/hir/hirs/hirself. They're called neopronouns. I use an x when I spell xe. Some people use a z, but the x is more me. You can use they/them if it's easier, but xe/hir is the best fit. What pronouns should I use when I talk about you? What's your name? Ugh! Awkward!" Xe imagined the neighbor growling *so are you a boy or a girl?* Cam rolled hir eyes and looked at Wolfgang. "This is why I don't *people*."

Cam pulled the dog's leash out of hir back pocket. "Want a W. A. L. K?" Wolfgang's tail flapped in excitement. Cam had learned early on that Wolfgang would happily pee on anything—and everything, ugh—but preferred to poop under the trees in the public space halfway to the local Dollar Store. So, three times a day they left Cam's bubble of comfort (hir yard) and walked two tenths of a mile away from home into The World to give the dog the opportunity to poo in its happy place. "The things we do for love," Cam growled at the dog as xe avoided the eyes of the strangers they passed on the sidewalk.

Cam hated the way people looked at hir. Not in an unfriendly way, but in a confused way. Xe knew what they were thinking. *Boy or girl?*

"Why can't I just be me?" xe'd asked once. But people were confused. Hir height read "male," hir delicate, hairless facial features read "female." Hir clothes—jeans, t-shirt, bare feet (or boots when it was chilly out)—and hairstyle—a soft curly fade—could read either way. Most of the time Cam felt euphoria with hir unique gender expression, but with other people . . . well, Cam didn't want to deal.

As soon as Wolfgang finished, Cam hurried back home. The red sedan was back in the neighbor's driveway, but there wasn't any sign of life. "It's for the best," Cam muttered. "Stay inside, scowly neighbor. I don't need your drama."

On Tuesday at noon, the doorbell chimed. Wolfgang answered the sudden noise with a barrage of barking. It was Tina, Cam's twin, here for their traditional Twin Takeout Tuesday. Tina's moniker. Cam called it lunch.

Tina let herself in. "Hi, Wolfie," she said, dropping to her knees to embrace the dog. Wolfgang's barks had morphed into happy whines and grunts. "How's my sweet boy?"

Cam rolled hir eyes. "The dog's gender is TBD," xe grumbled.

Tina laughed in that easy, unselfconscious way she had. "Nope, I asked him, and he said he's a good, good, gooooood boyo!" She kissed the dog's nose. "Aren't you, Mr. Wolfie McWolferson?" Wolfgang rolled onto its back, slapping the floor with its tail.

"Gross," Cam muttered under hir breath as xe retreated into the kitchen to get Tina a cup of tea. Hir twin was so predictable.

"I see you finally put up the feeder I gave you," Tina called from the front hall. "I saw a new neighbor checking it out."

"What is with them?" Cam placed the kettle on the burner and went back into the hall where Tina was slipping out of her annoyingly adorable flats. "What are they doing now? Were they in my yard?" Cam asked. "I get a weird vibe from them."

Tina lowered one eyebrow and tilted her head. "You get a weird vibe from . . . a bird? That's antisocial even for you. You're bordering on curmudgeonhood."

"What?"

Tina smirked. "I was talking about the catbird I saw at the feeder. What were you talking about?"

"Oh . . . that kind of new neighbor." Cam glanced out the front window, but the feeder was empty. "I haven't seen any birds at the feeder yet." Xe turned and went back into the kitchen to finish brewing tea. Tina followed hir.

"What were you talking about? Who—or what—gives you a weird vibe?"

"The new human neighbor," Cam said, pointing toward the blue house. "They were scowling at me when I put up my pride flag. Happy Pride, by the way."

"Oh please, every month is pride month for me," Tina said, flicking her long individual braids over her shoulder before studying her perfectly manicured pink, white, and blue fingernails.

Cam had to admit that Tina was right. She'd been authentically herself since they were seven years old. Born three minutes before Cam, Tina had paved the way with everything in their lives. She'd shattered their parents' identities as "Boy-Moms" long before Cam found the words to articulate hir own unique place in the world. Tina had chosen the town where they would settle as young adults—pointing out that she could live downtown, and Cam could have a house to hirself within walking distance. She'd tried to get Cam to work at the pride center with her, but Cam had to draw the line. Tina loved people. Cam loved numbers. And quiet. And Tina. And Wolfgang. And the absence of people, *thankyouverymuch*.

Now, Tina was networking, and helping, and changing the world while being unabashedly loud and proud in every aspect of her life, while Cam, a dedicated introvert, worked from home as an actuary and avoided . . . well, everyone.

"Why would they scowl at your gorgeous flag?" Tina asked, breaking Cam from hir reverie.

Cam shrugged as the kettle began to whistle. Xe poured the steaming water into Tina's mug and watched the teabag float gently to the surface.

Just then, the doorbell rang again. Wolfgang rose from the floor near Tina's feet and exploded toward the door, barking. Cam jumped. Tina smiled. "That must be lunch. I'll get it."

Cam followed hir sister into the hall. Tina grabbed Wolfgang's collar and opened the door. "Oh," she said. "Not what I expected." She reached outside and brought in a large box. "Your paper towels have arrived." She said *paper towels* as if it the words were a question.

"Close," Cam said, taking the box as Tina closed the door. "Toilet paper." Xe opened the box and pulled out the bundles of Charmin.

"Don't tell me you'll use all that." Tina laughed, grabbing a bundle, and putting it on the floor next to her purse. "I'm nearly out, thanks."

Cam scowled. "Hey!" xe said in mock protest. "I'll use it. Eventually. It doesn't go bad." Xe carried the remaining rolls upstairs to put them away under the bathroom sink. Tina followed, talking nonstop. Cam had learned to tune her out half the time. It was one of hir twin survival mechanisms.

Downstairs, Wolfgang exploded in another bout of barking. "No doorbell," Tina said. "What's he barking at this time?"

"Probably someone at the door," Cam said. "Maybe lunch?"

"I'll check," Tina said. Cam heard her jog down the stairs. "Shhhh, Wolfie. That's a good boy." The front door opened and closed. "It's lunch," Tina called.

Cam went down the stairs and took the bag from hir sister. "Burritos?" xe asked, sniffing the bag.

"Noooo," Tina said. "Tacos. We're having Twin Takeout Tuesday Tacos. It will be . . . terrific." She frowned. "I can't believe they didn't ring the bell, though. What if we'd let our food sit outside and spoil? It would be a tragedy. A terrible Twin Takeout Tuesday Taco Tragedy."

Cam shrugged and ignored hir sister's alliterative humor. "That's why I have a dog. Doorbell or not, Wolfgang always lets me know when someone's outside."

That evening, Cam thought back to hir conversation with Tina when Wolfgang again exploded in barks, this time in response to a doorbell ringing on TV. Xe glared at the dog. "You always let me know someone's outside . . . even if that someone is fictional."

The next morning Cam woke to another torrent of barks shortly after dawn. "Now what?" xe groaned, peeling back the covers. Xe padded downstairs in boxers and a t-shirt. No doorbell, but Wolfgang was barking at the door. "What's up, pup?" Cam peeked through the peep hole in the door. Nothing. Xe grabbed Wolfgang's collar and opened the door a crack. No packages. Wolfgang stopped barking, and the neighborhood was silent except for some birds singing in the trees. The morning air felt cool and damp. Everything was quiet.

Cam closed the door and faced the dog, arms crossed in front of hir chest. "What do you have to say for yourself?"

Wolfgang sat at hir feet, looking up with eyes full of anticipation. Cam knew that look. "Did you just wake me up for breakfast?"

At the word breakfast, Wolfgang sprang into motion, racing to the kitchen. Cam followed, bare feet padding across the cool hardwood floor. "Fine, but I'm getting coffee."

In the kitchen, Cam set about hir morning routine, making coffee, and preparing Wolfgang's food. While the dog ate, xe ran upstairs and pulled on a t-shirt and jeans. Remembering the cool air, xe considered adding a jacket to the ensemble but opted instead for socks and boots. Wolfgang met hir by the door and sat while xe attached leash to collar. "Come on, bonehead," Cam said as they left the comfortable safety of their house.

The neighbors were stirring. Somewhere far off, a lawnmower was droning. There were cars passing on the street. Cam heard a neighbor a few doors down yelling something about being late to school.

As they left the house, a gray bird flew away from the suet feeder. Wolfgang watched it fly past before watering the base of the hook. Waiting for the dog, Cam looked around. Hir dew-damp flag hung limply in the still, humid air. As xe waited, the red sedan passed in front of hir house and pulled into the driveway next door. Cam saw the outline of a driver through the tinted windows and waited for them to emerge, but the car sat motionless in the driveway. Cam debated walking over to say hello, but hir introverted tendencies won out. Wolfgang pulled at the leash, and they set off down the sidewalk.

They'd been home less than an hour before Wolfgang alerted Cam to someone outside. No doorbell. "I didn't order anything," Cam growled, turning away from hir spreadsheets to meet the dog at the door. Xe peeked out the peep hole. No one. Xe opened the door a crack. No package. Xe closed the door and turned to the dog. "What was that about?" Wolfgang yawned and lay down. "Did you have a bad dream?" Wolfgang stretched out across the floor. Cam glanced outside at the pride flag, which fluttered cheerfully in the breeze, a gray bird perched on top of the pole. Cam sighed and returned to work.

Wolfgang dozed until lunchtime, at which point the dog considered it a sacred duty to supervise all food consumption. No Tina today, so Cam made a peanut butter sandwich. Despite having two moms, Cam had never learned to cook. Xe existed on takeout with Tina, sandwiches, and if xe was feeling adventurous, cans of Campbell's soup. On Wednesdays, lunch was always a peanut butter sandwich, never takeout with Tina, because Wednesday nights were, according to Tina, "Twin TV Time." Cam called it dinner. Every Wednesday evening, Tina brought over something she'd cooked, and they put on a movie and ate in front of the television.

Wolfgang's eyes were glued to the sandwich, as usual, as Cam pretended to ignore the dog—as usual. Xe nearly choked on a bite of chunky peanut butter when Wolfgang's head snapped toward the front door. The dog burst up and ran to the door, barking. No doorbell.

Cam followed the dog. Nothing through the peep hole. Nothing through the cracked door. Nothing.

Cam studied the dog. "Well, you were awake, so it wasn't a dream. And you're not asking for food." Cam stepped out on the front stoop and looked around. The neighborhood was quiet. The lawnmower had stopped, and the neighbors were mostly at work or school at this time of day. Cam felt hir skin crawl and turned toward the blue house. The red sedan, now empty, sat in the driveway. Everything was quiet except for the pride flag flapping in the breeze. Xe went back inside.

Wolfgang barked at the door four more times throughout the afternoon before finally announcing Tina's arrival. By the time hir sister arrived,

Cam had abandoned hir work and was pacing from window to window trying to catch a glimpse of whatever was triggering Wolfgang's alarms.

"Get inside" xe said, grabbing Tina's hand and pulling her across the threshold.

"Why was your door locked? What's going on?" Tina said, as Cam stared at the blue house before closing the door. The red sedan was still there.

"I think my new neighbor is stalking me."

"The catbird?" Tina slipped out of her heels and held out a casserole dish. "Careful, it's still hot."

"Not the bird neighbor," Cam said, taking the dish in hir bare hands. "The human neigh—ow! This is hot!" Xe ran to the kitchen to put the dish on the counter. "Why didn't you warn me?"

"You think your new neighbor is stalking you? Explain." Tina crossed her arms in front of her ample chest. Her face took on an expression Cam recognized from the mirror. Despite the different paths their bodies had taken, and the very different ways the twins expressed their gender, Cam could still see hirself in hir sister. Xe was reminded of the time they'd switched places for April Fool's Day. Their kindergarten teachers had been fooled, but their moms had known instantly who was who.

Cam sighed. "It's Wolfgang he—" but xe stopped short when Wolfgang burst out barking. Again.

Cam raced to the door and didn't bother checking the peep hole. Xe tore the door open and looked outside. Nothing. Xe stepped outside. Tina, right behind hir, shut the now-quiet Wolfgang into the house.

"Cam. Explain." Tina said, furrowing her brow.

"Look," Cam said, gesturing to the front yard.

"I don't see anything."

"Exactly." Cam lowered hir voice. "Wolfgang keeps barking that 'there's someone outside' bark. But when I look, no one is there. Just that red car in the neighbor's driveway."

"Cam . . ." Tina paused as if considering how best to word what she was about to say. "Neighbors are allowed to have cars in their driveway. There's one in yours right now."

"No, you don't understand." Cam grabbed hir sister by her shoulders. "Wolfgang keeps barking—"

"Hi," Tina called over Cam's shoulder. Cam snapped around and saw the neighbor standing in front of the blue house. "Welcome to the neighborhood."

The neighbor's eyes widened. They looked around as if about to cross a busy street, then walked toward them. "Hey," they said. "Um. Hi."

Cam didn't have to look at hir sister to know she was flashing her "I know you're gonna love me" grin. Cam felt immobilized as the neighbor approached, studying their face for clues of bigotry.

"I'm Tina," she said, holding out her hand. "Pronouns she/her/hers. It's a pleasure to meet you."

The neighbor reached out and took her perfectly manicured hand. "I'm Phil. He/him."

He looked at Cam. Cam looked at him. Tina elbowed hir in the ribs. "This is my sibling," Tina said. "Xe actually lives here. I live a few blocks that way." She pointed in the direction of downtown.

"Hey," Phil said, extending a hand. "I'm Phil. He/him."

"Hey," Cam said, ignoring the hand. "Cam. Xe/hir/hirs/hirself. They're neopronouns." Xe recited, looking at the grass past Phil's shoulder. "Nonbinary pronouns for ... people. Um—"

"Cool," Phil said. "Hey, I love your flag." He moved his hand closer to Cam.

Cam glanced at him from the corner of hir eye. "You were scowling," xe muttered.

"Huh?" Phil withdrew the hand, cocking his head to the side.

"When I saw you the other day, you were scowling."

"Oh. Um. Sorry." He clasped his hands in front of his belt buckle. "I'm just really afraid of dogs, and you have a big one."

Cam turned this information over in hir brain. Phil seemed genuine, friendly, and honestly rather attractive. But if he wasn't stalking hir then why—

At that moment Cam heard hir doorbell ring. But it wasn't hir doorbell. Inside the house, Wolfgang burst out barking. Phil jumped as if he'd been electrocuted.

"What the?" Cam searched the yard for the source of the sound.

"It's the catbird," Tina cried, pointing.

Phil clapped his hand to his chest. "Is that dog going to stay inside?"

Cam, frozen in place, looked back and forth between hir twin and hir neighbor. The doorbell rang again from the yard. Cam whipped around to the source of sound and found hirself facing the bird feeder. A sleek grey bird opened its mouth, and the sound of Cam's doorbell chimed again.

"Your dog is going nuts," Phil said, edging back toward the blue house.

"This is so cool," Tina said, jumping up and down. "I've heard that catbirds are related to mockingbirds, but I've never seen one in action before."

"Oh!" Cam's brain suddenly switched back on. "Wolfgang thinks someone is ringing the doorbell. I bet that's been happening all day."

"You should meet him," Tina said, opening the door. "He's the sweetest little boyo."

"No, that's oka—" Phil tried to protest, but it was too late. Wolfgang was already out the door. The dog barked once at the birdfeeder, inspiring the cat bird to fly to the top of the flagpole. Then Wolfgang hurried over to Phil, sniffing his legs, and flopping down at his feet.

"See?" Tina said. "He likes you."

"Wolfgang's gender is T—never mind," Cam said, giving up.

"Hey, boy," Phil said, giving the dog a little wave.

"He wants you to rub his belly," Tina said.

"Um. Maybe next time." Phil took a step back. "It was a pleasure to meet you, Tina." He stepped back again. Wolfgang sat up but didn't follow. "Cam," Phil said, with a small smile. "See you around?" He locked eyes with hir a beat longer than was socially required.

Cam nodded.

"Ooooooh," Tina said under her breath as Phil returned to his house. "I think he likes you."

Cam rolled hir eyes. "Shut up."

"No, I really think he does. Did you see that smile? He might as well have winked."

"Come on, Wolfgang," Cam said with a sigh.

"I wonder if he can cook," Tina mused as Cam opened the door.

Behind them, the catbird chimed from the top of the flagpole. Wolfgang looked at the bird and gave out a single huff, before following her humans back into the house.

Death in the Hand of the Tongue

Debra H. Goldstein

hat do you get when the rabbi, priest, and police chief of Wahoo, Alabama get together on Tuesday mornings? Easy answer—a golf game. Not today, though. Instead, as I offered up a little prayer while I teed my ball up, a cell phone interrupted my concentration. You'd have thought "When the Saints Go Marching In" would be my ringtone, but it belongs to Chief Tom Johnson. Before Tom could pull his phone out of his pocket, Rabbi Eddie Greenberg's phone began ringing, too.

"We got to go?" I didn't wait for a response before I picked up my ball, thrust my club back into my bag, and jumped, as fast as the few pounds I've gained allowed, into the cart next to far younger and more slender Eddie. Whatever had disturbed our game had to be important. Tom was already heading his cart back to the clubhouse. "What's up?"

"They found a body at the Temple. My stuff is in your car. Would you drop me off at the Temple instead of taking me home?"

"Of course." Because a body necessitating pulling the chief of police off the golf course isn't often found in a small town like Wahoo, let alone in our houses of worship, I refrained from observing I was glad to have a reason to accompany Eddie to what had to be a suspicious death scene. Besides, with our golf game canceled, my schedule was open until a pastoral counseling session at three.

At the Temple, Eddie led Tom and me down the stairwell that led to the Temple's reception hall and kitchen. At the base of the steps was an alcove and a double doorway opening into the large room used for events. As Eddie walked briskly through the reception room to the kitchen, which was on the far side of the hall, we passed two tables filled with women. Although I only glanced at them, I could feel their eyes following me to the kitchen doorway, which was completely blocked off by yellow crime-scene tape.

A young officer stood guard in front of the taped door; a dark-haired woman waited a few feet away. When Eddie and I moved aside to watch the confrontation between the smooth-faced officer and Tom, she joined us.

"Robinson," Chief Johnson said, "what's going on here?" Tom gestured toward the yellow tape.

Rather than answering the question addressed to him, the officer pulled a pad from his pocket and glanced at his notes. "Chief, our dispatcher received a call at nine twenty-seven a.m. that a group of Sisterhood women and the Temple's cantor found Sylvia Horowitz dead in the Temple's kitchen. I immediately responded to the call. When I arrived, I learned the women were supposed to be part of a matzah ball making session that Mrs. Horowitz was chairing."

Officer Robinson consulted his notes again. "In case you don't know, a matzah ball is a Jewish dumpling made from matzah meal, eggs, and oil."

"I'm aware of that," Chief Johnson said. "Get on it with it, Robinson."

"Yes, sir. Apparently, on entering the kitchen, the group found Mrs. Horowitz lying on the floor and called 911." He pointed to two men standing on the far side of the room. "It was too late by the time the EMTs arrived, so we were called."

Eddie looked toward the dark-haired woman, who nodded her head affirmatively. I assumed she was the Temple's new cantor, Joyce Silberman. I hadn't met her yet. All I knew about her from Eddie was that she was about forty, had a melodious voice, was a transplant from the East, and he repeatedly teased her about the difference between New York and Southern bagels.

Before Officer Robinson could continue his recitation, Eddie interrupted him. He stretched his hands wide, pointing one at Chief Johnson and me while gesturing with the other to the dark-haired woman. "This is Cantor Silberman. Cantor Silberman, this is Wahoo's Chief of Police, Tom Johnson, and Father Brendon O'Reilly. We acknowledged each other, but then directed our attention back to Officer Robinson.

Consulting his notes again, Officer Robinson said, "I responded, checked the body, confirmed she was dead, and sealed off the area. I found no sign of a weapon. Considering her age, which the other women indicated is somewhere between sixty and seventy-five, the EMTs and I figured she had some kind of seizure or heart attack, fell, and hit her head about an hour before she was found. Still, I thought you'd want me to treat it as a crime scene until you and the coroner knew for sure."

Tom peered through the tape and then back at the women seated in the reception hall. "Did you do anything else, Robinson?"

"No, I mean, yes. I turned off the stove. Ms. Horowitz apparently was waiting for a giant pot of liquid to boil when the incident happened. It was boiling, so I turned off the heat. I also knew you'd want to talk to the people who found her, so I had them sit out there. The first table has the group who found the body, while the second is people who came in later. To keep everything quiet until you got here, I made all of them give me their cell phones."

Great police technique, I thought, observing the women speaking in hushed tones to each other. I guessed Robinson never heard about keeping witnesses separated until after they gave their statements.

A noise attracted my attention to the right of the door, where a small table was piled with cellphones. Two women stood next to it. The first thought that went through my mind was that I was looking at Mutt and Jeff. One was small, but solid. Her hair matched the red of her lipstick and nail polish. The other was tall with a curvaceous physique and sun-kissed skin. I assumed they sidled up to us during Tom's exchange with Officer Robinson.

The redhead spoke first. "I'm Ellen Levy, president of the Sisterhood. This is our secretary, Mitzi Katz. She helped give Mrs. Horowitz CPR."

"But to no avail." Mitzi Katz shook her head sadly.

Mrs. Levy patted Mrs. Katz's shoulder. She then focused attention back on Tom and Eddie. "When you get this ridiculous tape down and get into the kitchen, you'll see Sylvia was murdered. She didn't just face plant herself next to the chicken soup. I've seen plenty of heart attacks at the retirement home where I live. If Sylvia had one, she'd either have knocked the pot from the stove with the big spoon she was stirring the soup with, fallen differently, or gotten herself to one of the chairs in this room."

Mitzi ignored both Ellen and the sputtering sounds coming from Officer Robinson that reminded me of how Barney Fife got upset during every episode of *The Andy Griffith Show*. She addressed her remarks to Tom. "Chief Johnson, I'm so glad you're finally here. Officer Babyface keeps insisting the chicken soup, the ladle in Sylvia's hand, and everything else in the kitchen is evidence relevant to his crime scene. That may be, but the Sisterhood needs our kitchen and its contents back immediately."

When Tom didn't respond right away, she turned toward Eddie. "Rabbi Greenburg, explain it to them. The girls and I have a lot of matzah balls to make for the Temple Seders."

"I'm afraid the kitchen will have to stay closed until we figure out exactly what happened." Rabbi Greenburg gently took Mrs. Katz by the arm and escorted her back to the nearest table, with Mrs. Levy two steps behind them.

He returned and stood next to Cantor Silberman while Tom pulled the crime tape off the doorway. Once Tom was done, he walked into the kitchen toward where Mrs. Horowitz lay. The rest of us just poked our heads into the kitchen to evaluate the crime scene for ourselves.

There was a gigantic pot on the stove. The counter next to the stove had crates of eggs stacked and an industrial-sized container of matzah meal. The table behind Mrs. Horowitz had been divided into individual work-spaces denoted by torn pieces of waxed paper. Eddie and I couldn't help but move further into the room, but Cantor Silberman didn't follow us. Sensing she wasn't with us, I looked back and saw her standing by the door, her gaze riveted on the body.

"Cantor?" Rabbi Greenburg said. "What were you doing down in the kitchen area today?"

"Saying 'hello.' I knew Sylvia came in early to get all the ingredients and stations set up for the volunteers and to start the soup base. Because the rest of the Sisterhood women were going to be in the kitchen around nine, I thought it would be a good idea to be in the lobby to open the door when they arrived. You know how Sylvia complained last week that the Sisterhood does so much for the Temple, but the members often feel ignored by the clergy and staff?"

Rabbi Greenburg nodded in agreement. I understood perfectly. Volunteers want to be appreciated when they're not being martyrs.

"Once I let them in, I thought it was the perfect time for me to come downstairs with them and stay ten minutes as a goodwill gesture. We were laughing and kibbitzing as we came into the kitchen. That all stopped when we saw Sylvia. I yelled for someone to call 911, while two of us tried to give her CPR."

My attention focused on the Cantor, I could see blood dotting her clothing and shoes. I thought about something Ellen had said. "Did you move Mrs. Horowitz?"

"Yes, we turned her over. It was the only way we could give her CPR. Sadly, we were too late." She followed my gaze to her skirt. "I must have gotten blood on me when we turned her over. I'm sure the woman who helped me did, too."

Chief Johnson knelt next to Mrs. Horowitz, carefully out of the way of where blood had pooled from a wound on the back of her head. "Did she have any enemies?"

"Oh, no." Rabbi Greenburg wrung his hands. "Everyone loves, I mean, loved Sylvia. When she moved here three years ago, she immediately became such a Temple super-volunteer that she's slated to be the next Sisterhood president."

"Nobody else wants the job?" I couldn't help myself. My quip was rewarded by a gasp from the Cantor and a smile that Eddie quickly wiped from his face. I caught it, but I don't think Tom saw it as he stood up.

"Being a volunteer was a calling for Sylvia and a blessing for the Temple," Eddie said

"That type of volunteer always is," Tom said. He moved next to me, and together we peered into the oversized pot. It was filled with a green and orange-tinged liquid that I presumed from its smell was chicken soup. The orange I attributed to the sliced carrots floating alongside chunks of chicken, but I had no idea what added the green tint. The chief and I quickly stepped back from the stove.

"Today's Tuesday," Tom said. "If I remember correctly, your services are usually on Friday night and Saturday morning. Isn't it unusual to have so many people here on a Tuesday morning?"

"Not before Passover. Our Sisterhood does yeoman work making matzah balls for our three Temple Seders," Eddie said.

"Three?"

"Yes, we offer a congregational, women's, and children's Seder. All told, we use five to six hundred matzah balls, so you can imagine what a project it is preparing them. For the past two years, Sylvia has coordinated our Passover efforts. I guess I should tell everyone we won't be cooking today."

"Let me," Cantor Silberman said. When she left, Tom turned his gaze back to Eddie.

"Super volunteers sometimes get on people's nerves. Is there anything you can tell me about Mrs. Horowitz that might have irked someone?"

"If you weren't the one asking, Tom, I wouldn't say this. I don't believe in talking badly about a member of my congregation, especially a dedicated volunteer like Sylvia Horowitz, but you know how it is. Some volunteer to serve, others to also gossip."

I knew exactly the type of woman about whom he was talking. "In my church, we call those folks 'pillars of the parish,' and we watch our step around them because they're the ones who know everything about everybody and love to share what they know."

Tom smothered a laugh. "So, everyone tries to stay on their good side and out of the way of their mouths?"

Eddie and I agreed.

Tom motioned to two men, one with a camera, who'd just arrived and stood by the door. Eddie and I stepped aside so the crime scene techs could get into the room. Before we could leave, Tom put his hand on Eddie's arm. Removing it, he pointed toward the reception hall where Babyface had finally separated most of the women by moving them to different tables and was now taking statements. "What can you tell me about them?"

"The ones still sitting at the first table are the cantor and mainly Sisterhood officers. You already met Ellen and Mitzi, who helped give Sylvia CPR. The one in the aqua polyester pantsuit is Sylvia's best friend and the vice-president of the Sisterhood, Candy Feldman. The woman in pink is the Sisterhood treasurer, while the one in jeans is our newest temple member, Terry Reed."

"Reed doesn't sound Jewish. If she's new, what's she doing with the officers?"

"She recently converted. Mitzi and Sylvia adopted her to make her feel comfortable. In our faith, we don't seek converts, but once someone converts, that's it. We welcome them and don't mention it again."

"Well, she seems pretty broken up about what's happened." We all looked in Terry Reed's direction. She was sobbing on Cantor's Silberman's shoulder.

"I'm sure she is. Sylvia has been a mentor and a quasi-mother to Terry," Eddie said.

"What do you mean?" I asked.

Eddie lowered his voice. "Terry moved here from New Jersey when she got engaged to a young man who was a member of our congregation. She found a job and started her conversion classes in anticipation of her wedding. Then, her fiancé dumped her. He left our Temple and moved out of state, leaving her here alone. The Sisterhood women circled their wagons around her, especially Sylvia, who also was a transplant from New Jersey.

Coming from the East, Sylvia felt a kinship with someone thrust into our southern culture and then deserted."

I watched Cantor Silberman smooth Terry's hair and whisper in her ear. Whatever she said apparently was comforting because Terry slowly straightened up, pulled away, and wiped her eyes. She stood and moved to an empty table. For a moment, I thought Cantor Silberman was going to follow her, but instead she turned in our direction. "Looks like you eased a rough moment," I said, when she neared me.

"Hope so. Apparently, they had words the other day and Terry hadn't seen her to apologize."

"Was it over something important?" Tom said.

"Probably not. Terry's the type who hears something and blows it out of context."

Eddie gave Cantor Silberman one of the semi-stern looks clergy of all faiths use to make members of our congregations pause and hopefully have a moment of self-inflicted internal guilt. It beats giving them a formal scolding. The cantor must have gotten his message. She pressed her lips together before asking Tom, "Chief Johnson, would it be okay if I wait in my office in case you need to ask me anything beyond what I told Officer Robinson? I must prep for some students coming in this afternoon."

Tom acquiesced. As she left, he turned to say something to Eddie, but stopped when Ellen and Mitzi left the table and joined us. I hadn't noticed it earlier, but Mitzi had a dark stain on the left knee of her pants.

"We see you let the Cantor leave," Ellen said. "May we go too? As we told Babyface in our statements, everything is as you see it except that when we came in, Sylvia was clutching the soup ladle."

"It must have fallen out of her hand when the Cantor and I turned her over and gave her CPR," Mitzi said. "That's all we can tell you, so can we go?"

Tom blessed their departure. He then walked over to those sitting at the other tables and one by one dismissed them, too. As the women were leaving, all having retrieved their cell phones, Tom came back to where Eddie and I waited.

"Don't you think you should caution them to not say anything?" I knew immediately Eddie had his Rabbi hat back on. "You know how it is. The last thing my congregation needs is for them to spread any gossip about what happened or our reaction to this tragedy."

"We can't shut them up."

"Besides," I said, "asking that group to be quiet would only backfire. What are you so worried about?"

"The Temple's reputation. Tradition teaches: 'Gossip kills three people: he who speaks it, he who listens, and he about whom it is said.' The analysis equates gossip with murder."

"If I remember right," I said, "it's a discussion interpreting the meaning of the Biblical verse, 'Death and life are in the hand of the tongue'." The quizzical expression on Tom's face amused me. From things said on the golf course, I bet he couldn't remember the last time he crossed the threshold of any house of worship in a non-working context. "Guess you aren't familiar with this Talmud passage."

"No, I am," Tom said. "If I recall, it continues 'that just as the hand can kill, so too can the tongue.' One might suggest that unlike the hand, which can kill only one near it, the tongue can kill he who is far away. Therefore, the text states, 'The tongue is a sharpened arrow'."

Every now and then, our police chief astounds me. This was one of those times. I couldn't believe he pulled this passage out of the recesses of his brain. I stared at him.

"My philosophy class." Tom smiled. "Appreciate you guys reminding me of it."

Slowly, it dawned on me. He didn't need the yellow tape, any test results, or to question more witnesses—he'd figured out who killed Sylvia Horowitz.

"How? Who?" I asked.

"Can't talk now," Chief Johnson said. "I need to get upstairs and confiscate the murder weapon—probably the big can of oil missing from the matzah ball prep table—before Cantor Silberman disposes of it."

"But . . ." I said, as I followed him to the steps.

"Simple. Sylvia Horowitz was a gossip who learned things and then used them against others. While she was killed by a hand near her, I think we'll find the gossip Sylvia got from Terry concerned something that happened on the East coast that the Cantor didn't want shared here."

"You figured it out from the quote?"

"I only wish I were that smart. It was the blood spatter pattern. When you hit someone in the head, there will be a spatter. The only blood on the floor was the pool from where Mrs. Horowitz bled after the Cantor and Mitzi turned her over. I was careful to stay away from the puddle when I knelt next to Mrs. Horowitz. Mitzi obviously put one knee in it, the only place she got blood on her, when she administered CPR. That means the spray at the time of the murder had to go somewhere else.

Cantor Silberman probably wiped some of it away when she went upstairs to hide the weapon. She thought she eliminated being considered a suspect by opening the door for the matzah ball makers and then going downstairs and finding the body with them. After you noticed how the telltale spatter marked her skirt and shoes, she told us other women had blood on them, too, but when I went to each table, I realized that except for the knee of Mitzi's pants, everyone's clothing was spotless.

Good Cop/Bad Cop

Trey Dowell
2021 Short Story Award winner

Only one word came to Florence Standish's mind after the haze cleared, and it applied to everything about her situation. *Dreadful.*

The chilly room, the unyielding metal chair beneath her bottom, but most of all, the nonsense being spouted by the two simpletons—one woman, one man—sitting across the empty table from her. Both of whom had chairs with cushions.

"I understand this is a lot to digest, Mrs. Standish."

Florence eyed the middle-aged woman's sensible brown suit and ten-dollar manicure before snorting. "That I'm dead? That I have to justify my existence to the two of . . . you?" She snarled "you" with a vitriol usually reserved for "Ebola" or "ready-to-wear."

The man chuckled. "This ain't gonna take long." Garish fluorescent light reflected off his slick black hair.

"Don't be so glib, young man," Florence snapped. *Fool reminds me of a used car salesman.*

"Dial the indignation down a notch or two, Flo." Saliva glistened on Salesman's teeth. "Also, I'm more than two thousand years old, so ditch the 'young man' bullshit."

Florence shrank back. "You can't . . . no one talks to me like th—"

He shook his head. "No wonder you had an aneurysm. Your arterial walls are as thin as your skin."

Brown Suit waved a calming hand. "Mrs. Standish, are you thirsty? Perhaps you could use some caffeine." She pointed to the corner of the table at a large cardboard cup, steam curling up from the lid opening.

Was that cup there before? Wait, where was I before . . . here? A fog lingered over her thoughts, making it difficult to recall anything beyond the last thirty seconds.

I was walking, I know that. To the car? Then . . . what? Death? Is that how the end comes?

A flutter in her chest made her reach for the coffee. She needed to feel the warmth of the container, the smooth cardboard surface—anything to make her feel . . . rooted . . . in this strange place. "But if I'm dead, why would I be thirsty?" she asked. "Does caffeine even work on me?"

Brown Suit smiled. "The freshly deceased often carry over the pangs of their physical selves. They'll fade over time. Your 'body' certainly doesn't need the coffee, but you'll enjoy the taste all the same. See for yourself."

Florence put her nose to the slit, inhaled. A bittersweet tang filled her nostrils. "Smells like a Point Café double macchiato. My favorite." She took a small sip and the smile it brought forth quickly morphed into shock. "This *is* Point Café macchiato. But how . . ."

Good Lord, this is real. I'm . . . dead.

Brown Suit ignored the question, withdrew a computer tablet from her lap, and placed it on the table. She punched a red button in the middle of the display. "Recording. Florence Standish of Boulder, Colorado. Deceased, age seventy-two years, thirty-seven days." Salesman pulled out a tablet of his own to reference.

Brown Suit continued, "This is intake—where we examine each individual case. When you're approv—"

"*If,*" Salesman interrupted.

Brown Suit rolled her eyes. "Thank you. *If* approved, you'll be promoted upstairs, where a more, um, traditional afterlife awaits. Heaven, joy, etc."

Florence perked up, nervous now. "What happens if I'm not approved? Do I go . . . downstairs?"

Salesman's alligator grin spread wide. "Yes. And they're *traditional* down there, too."

Brown Suit spoke to Florence in a soothing tone. "Don't worry. Your position in the afterlife is based on one thing."

Florence's eyebrows knit together. "What's that?"

"The one true currency. But based on a cursory glance at your file . . ." She flicked a finger, scrolling through a long list. ". . . I think you're going to be fine."

"What one thing?" Florence squeaked.

"Mrs. Standish, are you familiar with the term 'altruism'?"

"I don't understand," Florence said, twenty contentious minutes later. "I donated two million dollars to the Mayo Clinic last year alone."

Brown Suit tapped the tablet, nodded. "Admirable . . ."

". . . out of a fortune valued over seven-hundred and fifty million," Salesman said. "How many times do I have to tell you—charity is *not* what we're looking for. Altruism is about *selflessness*. Giving while gaining nothing in return."

"I didn't get anything from them."

Salesman thumped an unseen link on his screen. "Except your name on a new hospital wing. And you threw a party to celebrate. Classy. And the thirty years of donations to Rochester University."

"A healthy pattern," Brown Suit added.

Salesman scoffed. "Five hundred bucks a year. Except for 1999, when the donation jumped to fifty thousand. The year her nephew got accepted. Yep, that's healthy."

"That money was to refurbish Adams Hall! Billy's acceptance was just a coincidence, I swear!"

"Be careful what you swear to in here," Salesman said, tapping away.

Florence shivered, rubbed her own arms. "I'm very chilly . . . would it be poss—"

"Not your biggest long-term problem," he deadpanned.

Brown Suit hit "pause" and glared at her co-worker. He raised hands in mock surrender until she started the recording. "Mrs. Standish, childhood memories often reveal remarkably altruistic behavior. Think back, to the beginning—the first street. Your first house."

Florence closed her eyes, pictured the old clapboard ranch. "On Galveston."

"Perfect," Brown Suit purred, drawing the memories out. "Your family. Friends. You did favors for them, helped out around the house."

"Yes! Weekly chores . . ."

Salesman stared at the ceiling. "Lemme guess, you cleaned the cat's litter box."

"A dog, actually. And yes, I helped take care of Muffin."

Salesman bent over and hit "pause" himself. "Muffin? Seriously?" he whined at his co-worker. "Ten-year-old Genghis Khan kept a tidy room and loved his puppy, too—that means *nothing*. How much more of this garbage do we need to listen to?"

Brown Suit wagged a single finger. "Mrs. Standish has a long record of charitable giving . . . the sheer amount has to count for—"

Salesman slapped the table with enough force to make Florence recoil. "Look at the damn file! She's not a philanthropist . . . she's a freaking *actress*. The generosity is a façade. White paint over rotten wood. And it's not even a thick coat."

Fluorescent lights buzzed in the wake of his outburst. Florence whimpered.

Eventually, Brown Suit gathered herself enough to hit "record." She bent over, spoke to Florence in a low voice.

"There's a final part of the file we haven't discussed. Your daughter."

Florence cocked her head. "I don't understand. I don't have any children."

Brown Suit locked her gaze. "Mrs. Standish, I need a selfless act. Tell us about your daughter. The one you gave away."

A wave spread over Florence's face. The eyes clouded; frown lines deepened.

They know. Of course, they know.

"I was seventeen. My boyfriend left me. A single mother in those days . . . life would have been hell."

"Whose life?" Brown Suit's eyes widened just a hair.

Florence understood. "The baby's. I was poor before I met Edward. I never could've provided for her.

"You saved your daughter. Gave her a better life for nothing in return, then?"

Florence sniffled, dabbed her eyes with a sleeve. "Yes."

"Tell me her name."

The old woman shook her head. "I don't know her name. She was delivered via C-section . . . adopted the day after I delivered."

Brown Suit shook her head. "I don't mean the name she got after. The name you picked before. The name you never shared with anyone."

"I . . . I don't know what . . ." Florence stammered.

"The name you can't bear to speak," Brown Suit said, leaning closer. Her voice was almost a whisper. "That name has power. Value. Prove to us you have the selflessness, the strength. Prove you belong upstairs."

Florence dropped her head. The soft word echoed through the small room. "Julianna."

Brown Suit looked to Salesman, who only nodded in return. Both co-workers stood and gathered their tablets.

Florence's pinched throat said, "What happens now?"

"Transport will be down in an hour or so. They'll process you . . . upstairs," Salesman said, sounding a little disappointed. "Wait here."

The old woman nodded so vigorously her neck hurt.

Before the pair left, Brown Suit turned. "Just so you know, Julianna is fine. She did have a good life. I believe her name is . . ." She referenced the tablet a final time. ". . . Elizabeth. Good luck to you, Mrs. Standish."

Florence squeaked out, "Thank you," just as the door closed.

The co-workers tapped away at their screens as they walked down the hall together.

"Long day, eh?" he said.

She didn't respond.

At the end of the hall, they pushed open the outer doors and emerged into bright sunlight. Both took a deep inhale in the afternoon sun. They walked together through the parking lot, down Thirteenth Street, past the Point Café, and headed north.

"To the bank, then?" she asked.

"Hell, yeah. Transfer's already complete. Security questions, my ass. College dorm, childhood pet, street she grew up on, we got *everything*. And of course, the crown jewel, daughter's name—a name no one on the *planet* knew except her." He chuckled softly. "'*You're dead, Mrs. Standish.*' God, you were brilliant. She bought it completely."

The woman nodded. "The benzodiazepine probably had more to do with it than my performance."

"Don't sell yourself short. And nice sleight of hand getting the coffee on the table while she was focused on me, by the way."

She looked back at the empty industrial court with the "For Lease" sign—a nice private place to interrogate a drugged heiress.

He followed her gaze. "How long you think she'll wait?"

She shrugged. "Doesn't matter."

"You are something else, Lizzie. You really want me to wire your share to Greenpeace?"

She laughed. "Fifty million dollars of an industrialist's wife's inheritance to an environmental group? A selfish bitch who never bothered to even *find* her daughter, let alone give her a dime? You bet your sweet ass."

He tapped the necessary instructions. "Done."

A block farther he asked, "So is this altruism? Or revenge?"

Elizabeth stuffed her hands in her pockets and shrugged again. This time, though, a hard smile spread across her features.

"Can't it be both?"

THE HAIR OF THE DOG

Peter J Barbour

I lay on the call room bed waiting for the next shoe to drop, unable to sleep, just two days into my turn as chief resident, my final year of training. My stomach knotted. I thought about my new responsibilities. How would I measure up functioning mostly independently? Dr. John Sanders, our supervising staff neurologist for the month, had my back while I managed the Neurology Department's in-patient service.

The hands of the clock moved steadily around the dial when the siren ring tone on my phone, set on maximum volume so I wouldn't sleep through it, propelled me to a sitting position. I did not have to wait for the caller to identify himself.

"Gordie, it's Dr. Sanders. I was just informed by a friend that her husband, Michael Johnston, suddenly became ill. I expect he will need to be admitted. Sounds serious. Please meet him in the ER and take care of the admission."

"Sure, Dr. Sanders, I'll take care of it. Do you have any information about what happened?"

"Not much. Apparently, he has not been himself lately, off-balance. He deteriorated suddenly tonight. He's disoriented, vomited, and seems in pain."

I called Neal, my first-year resident, expecting him to be out on the floor checking on our patients, but his hazy voice sounded like he had just awakened from a sound sleep. My message was succinct. "Meet me in the ER. VIP Michael Johnston is ours. He's a personal friend of Dr. Sanders."

Upon entering the ER from the back door, I zig-zagged past residents and nurses, all of them moving about in different directions as if in a choreographed dance, each on a mission. At the end of the hall, I spied the ER Chief, Dr. Matthews, who stood outside bay twelve. He was handing a laptop computer to Neal, who then pulled back the curtain and entered.

Neal immediately popped back out and shouted, "I need assistance. I think he's seizing!"

I sprinted up the hall to join the crowd that quickly gathered. We placed Mr. Johnston on his side, I pulled his jaw forward to protect his airway, made sure he was secure on the litter, and loosened any tight clothing. We struggled to hold him as he stiffened and shook. His face contorted as he arched his back, arms and legs extended. The seizure lasted less than a minute, although it seemed to go on forever. We secured his airway, started an IV, drew blood for laboratory evaluation, and administered anticonvulsant medication.

I pulled Neal aside and suggested we observe our patient before starting our formal exam. Mr. Johnston had started to come around, moving all four extremities randomly. He moaned but said nothing intelligible. The ER team finished their assessment, ordered labs, including blood count and chemistries. I asked Neal to be sure they included B-12 and folate levels, and a toxicology screen. Then, they whisked our patient off for a chest x-ray and a CAT scan of the brain. Neal tried to hold back the transport people so he could more fully examine the patient. I stopped him.

"What's more important, the exam or his history? He's stable. Let's go talk to the family and find out what happened. We shouldn't hold up the studies," I said.

In the ER waiting room, we found Dr. Sanders with a cluster of two young women and a man I assumed to be the children of our patient. Dr. Sanders waved us over.

"This is Dr. Gordon Edwards and Dr. Neal Stevens, our resident house officers. They will be taking care of Michael with me," Dr. Sanders said, then turned to us. "And this is Evie, Mr. Johnston's wife, Chester, his son, and Arda, his daughter."

I wanted to kick Neal, whose eyes were glued to the very attractive Mrs. Johnston as she extended her hand to me, then to Neal. She smiled at Neal, raised her eyebrows, and patted his arm, no doubt fully aware of his attention. The chart said Michael Johnston was sixty-seven years old. Mrs. Johnston had to be no more than half her husband's age.

"Well, Gordie, how's Mr. Johnston doing?" Dr. Sanders asked.

"Settled for the moment," I said. "He's getting a CAT scan of the brain and chest x-ray as we speak. I'd like to get some history from the family to find out what's been going on."

"Is he going to live?" Mrs. Johnston asked Neal as she stared into his eyes and drew out each word.

"He was already coming around when we left him," I said. "I need to ask you some questions."

"I hope he dies," Chester Johnston muttered, turning away. Arda Johnston grabbed his arm, but he pulled away and just kept walking. He paced, staring into space, with a furrowed brow and downturned mouth. Arda started to go to him but stayed. I wanted to distract Neal from staring at Mrs. Johnston, so I sent him back to the ER to see if our patient was back from the Radiology Department so he could finish his exam.

I told the family what happened in the ER. Arda stepped back, eyes wide while Mrs. Johnston said, "Michael has never had any seizures before." I heard skepticism and denial in her tone.

Dr. Sanders looked on with a blank expression, listening carefully. *He's just being a senior attending,* I decided. *Evaluating my care and bedside manner dealing with the family.*

In answer to my questioning, Arda volunteered, "My father has mild diabetes and hypertension, and he is a long-time smoker."

Mrs. Johnston frowned as if Arda were revealing family secrets that should be left hidden.

"He also likes his scotch," Arda added. Mrs. Johnston scoffed.

After asking about his prescriptions and over-the-counter medications, I inquired about illicit drugs. Mrs. Johnston looked up. Her lips pursed. I felt challenged. *How dare I ask? Do I assume the answer is no?* I already asked for a tox screen for drugs, so I let it slide. If he were a big drinker, I would be worried about his diet, but Mrs. Johnston assured me his diet was fine. The ER team ordered B-12 and folate levels, and they had given him folic acid and thiamin empirically per protocol in case his diet had been inadequate.

"After dinner, Dad complained of an upset stomach," Arda continued, despite her stepmother's obvious disapproval. "His speech was slurred, and he argued with me that he had to go to the club to play golf. I think he was confused. It was late in the day, and he hasn't played golf for years."

I considered diagnostic possibilities as she spoke. *Elderly patient with risk factors for stroke, first seizure is most likely due to stroke.*

After gathering his medical history, including past illnesses, social history, and review of systems, I went to meet Neal who was still waiting in the ER. From there, we made our way to Radiology to see the CAT scan and chest x-ray. Both were negative. The CAT scan ruled out a large brain mass or hemorrhage.

I sent Neal back to Mr. Johnston's bedside while I stopped by the ER waiting room to ask permission to do a spinal tap, an appropriate procedure in the setting of the first seizure. Mrs. Johnston looked at Dr. Sanders, who responded for her. "I don't think that will be necessary." That surprised me, but I could re-address that with him in the morning when Neal and I met with him after we finished our early rounds. Besides, we'd already checked Mr. Johnston for a fever and neck stiffness that might signify spinal infection or indicate a bleed. Arda didn't mention any complaint of headache. Perhaps Dr. Sanders was right: the patient did not need a spinal tap tonight.

I entered bay twelve. Neal was shining a light into the patient's eyes.

"Mr. Johnston, stay awake," Neal shouted, trying to get him to sustain attention. Johnston's eyes opened, then his lids fell slowly like shades. "Level of consciousness, barely able to stay alert, somnolent," Neal said. "He has a pretty big bite mark on his tongue from the seizure. He's going to feel that when he awakens. His eyes and facial strength are symmetrical and appear intact. Gordie, could you check his neck for me. I think it's supple, still no sign of meningitis, but I want to be sure."

Neal stepped aside, and I rotated and flexed his neck. "I agree, it's supple."

"I'm unable to evaluate his muscle strength," Neil continued. "He can't cooperate with that part of the exam, but he seems to move everything well. There were no muscle stretch reflexes at his ankles or knees. When I poke his feet with a pin, he doesn't react. I guess he isn't with it enough to respond. I think it's a post-seizure state or medication effect."

I raised my eyebrows, not convinced by Neal's assessment. His examination was superficial and incomplete. I took out my reflex hammer and checked ankle, knee, and finger reflexes myself. All gone. Elbow and jaw jerks present, however. I poked his feet with a sharp object and then moved up his leg. He reacted when I got to the thigh. I did the same to the arm and got a reaction above the elbow.

I looked at Neal waiting for a response. "What do you think now?" I said after a sufficient pause.

Neal looked at me blankly.

"He's got a neuropathy," I said. "His nerve endings are affected. Looks symmetrical. Glove-stocking distribution. Maybe sensory-motor. Given his history, he could have a neuropathy due to diabetes, alcohol, or some deficiency, like B-12, assuming these findings are chronic. Acute neuropathies are less common. What else do we have to look for?"

"Infection, an inflammatory problem, cancer, toxins?"

"Good. We have to think of something that gives our patient seizures and confusion plus neuropathy. Something that affects the brain and nerves. When the lab results are available, we may have more clues."

That afternoon, Neal and I met to do chart rounds. We sat in front of the computer and reviewed each of our cases, checking the results of the studies we'd ordered earlier. I had argued again for the spinal tap, but Dr. Sanders asked we continue to defer that study. Neal pouted. I knew he wanted to check off having done a spinal tap in his procedure book. We ordered an MRI of the brain to rule out a small stroke or other abnormality beyond the resolution of the CAT scan. The blood sugar was elevated, as were the liver enzymes, but B-12 and folate levels were normal, as was the toxicology screen for drugs. In the context of Johnston's history of alcohol and diabetes, we felt these labs were adequately explained.

"What do we need to do next?" I asked Neal.

"Mr. Johnston hasn't seized again, and his confusion is clearing. His neuropathy is severe but hasn't progressed in the last twenty-four hours. We can give him a few more days here to recover, then send him to a rehab center."

"Don't you want to know his diagnosis?" I said and frowned at the first-year resident's lack of curiosity.

Neal looked at the ceiling, at me, then, as if a light went on. "More tests?" he responded.

"What do you want to know?" I reminded myself that he was in his first year, just starting, new to neurology, and tried to be patient.

"We could get a sed rate looking for inflammation, some kind of autoimmune disease or chronic infection," Neal said pausing to read my expression for approval. I looked at him deadpan. "But I don't really think it's an infection," he added, again looking at me as if trying to discern what I was thinking. "We haven't looked for toxins," he finally said.

I smiled. "Let's go back to the patient and ask some more questions," I suggested.

We found Mrs. Johnston sitting at the bedside across from Arda. Chester sat in a corner. Arda stood as she helped her father sip water from a cup.

Mrs. Johnston uncrossed and re-crossed her legs, then, sat up taller in her chair and reached out to touch Neal's arm. Neal tried to ignore the gesture; but, when he looked back, Mrs. Johnston raised her eyebrow and winked.

"Any news, Dr. Edwards?" Arda asked.

Mr. Johnston scowled turning toward Neal and me. "What do you want now? When can I go home?" He demanded and struggled to sit up in bed, fumbling with his utensils as he attempted to feed himself. A small dog stuck its head out from under the sheets and snapped a morsel of food out of Mr. Johnston's hand.

"If we could please have a moment, we have some questions," I said. The dog looked at me with slitted eyes and emitted a low menacing snarl. *I hope that is a therapy dog, properly credentialled to be here. I'll have to bring this to Dr. Sanders' attention later. I'll let him inform his VIP patient about the hospital rules.* The dog stared at me, teeth bared, matching its master's expression.

We learned that the Johnston family lived on a farm, a gentleman's farm, managed by tenant farmers. They had two horses and some sheep. Looking for possible exposure to toxins, we asked about their water source, battery disposals, factories, lumber yards, or smelters nearby. He had no hobbies.

As we peppered him with questions, Mr. Johnston knitted his brow and held his mouth in a down-turned scowl. I sensed he was about to throw us out of the room when a tall gentleman dressed in a fitted, dark, three-piece suit entered. He walked over to Mrs. Johnston and bent down to kiss her on the cheek, causing Mr. Johnston's grimace to grow more menacing. The gentleman greeted Arda but avoided Chester.

"What are you doing here?" Mr. Johnston barked. "I didn't think we were speaking." The dog growled with its tail down, poised to attack.

"I heard rumors that you were ill. I wanted to see for myself. You are still alive."

"So, you've seen, now leave. I'm still not going to cede any shares of the company to you."

"So be it. Have a pleasant day. May you rest in peace," he said and left abruptly.

Arda looked at me and started to explain, not that Neal or I deserved an explanation, but the interaction did make me curious. "That's George Victor," Arda began. "Dad's one-time business partner. They had a falling out. My father bought him out for a fraction of what the company is worth."

Mrs. Johnston sat quietly. Chester smiled seeming to enjoy the animosity displayed by George toward his father.

"Stop right there," Johnston shouted. "That cheap son of a bitch got what he deserved. Don't let him in here again. Do you hear me? Why are you smiling, Chester, you parasite?"

I turned to Neal. "Tell security, George Victor is not allowed to visit," I said in a calm, reassuring voice.

We walked out of the room. I told Neal to order a heavy metal screen and sed rate and headed to the library to read up on how each of the heavy metal intoxications presented clinically. I discovered that lead possibly contributed to the fall of Rome, but probably not the fall of Mr. Johnston. Mercury produced mad hatter's disease, but our patient did not make felt hats. Armed with new knowledge, I headed to Dr. Sanders to tell him what I found.

I knocked on Dr. Sanders' office door and started to walk in. I hesitated. He and Mrs. Johnson were standing in the middle of the room and quickly stepped apart. Dr. Sanders looked surprised. Mrs. Johnston looked like the cat that swallowed the canary, adjusted her skirt with a wiggle, and walked out of the room, head erect, smirking.

"Dr. Edwards," she said and tipped her head as she passed me.

"I'm sure Michael will continue to improve. A couple of weeks in the rehab center will do him wonders. I'll stop by his room later," Dr. Sanders called after her before switching his attention to me. "Now, Gordie, what can I do for you?"

"I ordered a heavy metal screen on Mr. Johnston."

"Do you really think that is necessary?"

"His presentation included confusion, seizures, liver dysfunction, and neuropathy. I think he could have arsenic poisoning."

"Really? I don't see where he would have been exposed. Arsenic would be highly unlikely, but satisfy your curiosity if you must."

The following day, before returning to the resident's workroom to look for Neal, I stopped by Mr. Johnston's room. He was watching the financial channel on TV. As I attempted to examine him, he snapped at me when I held up his arms to check his axillae. He had dark patches of skin in his armpits, stigmata of arsenic poisoning. I jumped back when the fox terrier reappeared from beneath the sheets and bared its teeth, ever vigilant.

"Don't let Beau bother you," Arda said, as she walked into the room. She greeted her father, then pulled me into the hall to talk. Arda was always present. She asked me to give her an update on any further insight we had gained into her dad's illness.

"I think we are on to something. I'm waiting for some additional tests." I didn't want to tell her about my concern regarding arsenic without more proof, given the implications. Arsenic poisoning might be accidental. That seemed unlikely without an obvious source. I doubted poison had been self-inflicted. He hadn't left a note, and his behavior was rife with anger, not depression. That left arsenic as a well-regarded murder weapon, having no odor or taste. I was curious about the family dynamics, and I felt Arda was likely my best source of information.

"Tell me, is everyone holding up okay? For instance, Chester always seems so angry," I said.

"I shouldn't talk, but he's been upset since Dad married Evie. He is concerned that she just wants his money. When Chester protested to Dad about their plan to wed, Dad threatened to change his will and leave Chester out, but I don't think Dad has changed it yet."

"Do you think Chester would try to kill your father?" I blurted out.

"No way," Arda responded, her eyebrows arched, mouth agape. "I can't imagine it. Why would you think that?"

"He said he hoped your father would die," I said, surprised at Arda's response. "What do you think of Mrs. Johnston, your stepmother?"

"I don't trust her," Arda said, a little calmer. "That is why I stay close to my father. It wouldn't surprise me if she were cheating on him the way she dallies with every man she meets." Arda crossed her arms in front of her and gazed at the floor. "You are upsetting me, Dr. Edwards. I want to see my father, now. Can we meet later to talk about this?"

"You can call me Gordie," I said. *Was that too familiar?* The last thing I wanted to do was upset her, and I knew I had. I wanted to console her, but I snapped back to the task at hand. If there were people with motive, I had to prove arsenic was the agent. "We'll talk later. Maybe I'll have more definite information then," I said.

I wondered what my legal obligations were regarding a possible attempted murder if I truly thought someone was trying to kill Michael Johnston. Was it like child abuse with mandatory reporting if just suspected? I went to my supervising physician, Dr. Sanders, for advice.

"You have an active imagination, Gordie," Dr. Sanders said. "You don't know that he has arsenic poisoning, or that there is some nefarious plot to kill Michael Johnston. Let it lie."

That didn't satisfy me, so I contacted an old friend from college who was just out of law school.

"Interesting," Judy said, "but you need probable cause that a crime has been committed before the police will do anything. Sounds like you just have a hunch. Prove that arsenic is the culprit here and I think that might get their attention."

I returned to the library, sat down at a computer, and searched, Arsenic Acute Poisoning. I found an article, in the New England Journal of Medicine, "The Mechanism of Arsenic Intoxication, a Case Report, and Review of the Literature," by John Sanders, our John Sanders. I knit my brow and stroked my chin. *Dr. Sanders is an expert on Arsenic poisoning. Yet, he appears aloof, even disinterested in Johnston's case.* Late for our afternoon chart rounds, I returned to the ward to meet Neal.

"George Victor tried to see Mr. Johnston, again," Neal said. "I called security, and they escorted him out. He was yelling about getting revenge. By the way, Mrs. Johnston looks at me like I'm a piece of candy, the dog wants to bite me, and I'm tired of Mr. Johnston abusing me. I'm not going back into that room alone."

"He'll be gone soon," I said. "His renal and liver functions have normalized, and there's been no recurrence of seizures. He's ready for rehab."

I was disappointed but not surprised when his heavy metal screen came back negative. We tested him days after admission and the toxin might have already cleared from his body. I had Neal arrange transportation with social services to Good Samaritan Rehab for a short stay, anticipating he'd be walking safely in another week or two.

At the end of the day, I saw Dr. Sanders walking to his car. "Dr. Sanders," I called. "We are planning to transfer Mr. Johnston to rehab tomorrow. I was going to let you know in the morning."

He stopped walking. "Okay, but do you have a diagnosis yet?"

"No, I haven't proven anything. I still think it could be an acute intoxication, perhaps arsenic. Do you think someone wants to harm Mr. Johnston?"

"You have been reading too many detective stories. The heavy metal screen was negative. Look elsewhere. I'm late for a dinner meeting. See you in the morning." As he walked to his car, I caught a glimpse of a woman sitting in the front seat.

That evening, I re-read the literature on arsenic poisoning. We could send off a sample of hair or nails to test for arsenic; if the intoxication were chronic, maybe we'd find it there. I called Neal. He'd already left the hospital but promised that he'd get the samples in the morning.

The next day Neal reported to me that he went back to Mr. Johnston's room after morning rounds to get the hair and nails samples himself, but transport had already gotten Mr. Johnston who was on his way to the rehab center. I realized I also missed my opportunity to follow up with Arda.

I called Becky, our clinic administrator, to schedule Mr. Johnston for my clinic post-discharge from the rehab center.

"He's already scheduled to see Dr. Sanders," she said.

No problem, I'll ask Dr. Sanders to order the testing on hair and nails.

But when I approached him, he said, "I think that would be a waste of resources, not worth the money," and he dismissed me.

My focus returned to managing the ward, supervising Neal and six third-year medical students who showed up three weeks into the month. I delegated responsibilities, managed the daily routine but remained unsettled about Mr. Johnston's case. I kept a record of interesting patients and those with unresolved diagnoses. I added Johnston's name to the list.

"Have you asked Dr. Sanders how Michael Johnston is doing?" Neal asked me one day. "I believe Dr. Sanders sees him in clinic. It's almost two months since we said goodbye to the man. Did you ever get the results from the hair and nail samples?"

"I tried to approach Dr. Sanders about it, but he didn't think the tests were warranted. I checked the chart later and found they had never been ordered," I said.

"That's too bad. We may never know what happened."

Two months later, at two a.m., I got a call from Mark, the second-year resident stationed in the ER. "Looks like Michael Johnston is back. Will your service take him?"

"Of course. What's happening?" I replied.

"I looked at the old records. Same presentation. Seizure, confusion, abdominal pain. He's weak and complaining of burning hands and feet. I have a message here from Dr. Sanders that Johnston will be his private patient, even though Dr. Sanders is off service now. We suggest you put him into the intensive care unit tonight. Looks like he has a little congestive heart failure going on as well. I already put in for a cardiology consult." Mark said.

On my way to the ER, I stopped at Neal's call room and rousted him out of bed to join me. Given Johnston's original presentation, I was more certain than ever. *Someone is trying to kill him.*

Neal and I met Mr. Johnston in the intensive care unit, then stopped in the waiting room to talk with the family. Mrs. Johnston fidgeted in her seat. Chester stood off to the side, his mouth perpetually turned down, eyes dark, unfocused. Arda smiled as I approached.

"It was just like the last time, only worse," Arda said. "After dinner, he started to complain about pain in his belly. He's also been complaining of burning in his feet and hands, and he's been falling. He had been doing so well. I don't understand why it's suddenly happened again."

I approached the patient, fully expecting the dog to jump out from under the covers, ready to attack. I remembered we were in the ICU and safe, with no dogs allowed.

"Where's Beau?" I said as a joke.

"Poor Beau," Mrs. Johnston said with a sad voice. "The little dear has gone on to his maker."

"I'm sorry for your loss," I said.

"Nasty animal, not to be missed," Chester muttered in an audible whisper.

"I'll miss him," Arda said.

We finished our examination and stepped out to the nursing station to discuss testing. A CAT scan of the brain, obtained in the ER, was negative. The chest x-ray confirmed mild congestive heart failure. Urine showed elevated protein. His liver function was abnormal, and his blood count demonstrated anemia. Results that were all compatible with arsenic poisoning. We were about to enter orders for additional testing when Dr. Sanders arrived.

"You can go," he said. "I'm taking over this case."

"Sir, if it's okay with you, we know Mr. Johnston well, and we'd like to participate in his care," I replied. I doubted Dr. Sanders would repeat the tox screen or send off hair or nails as I suggested if we weren't on the case.

"No. At the special request of the family, they'd prefer you not be involved."

Neal tugged at my sleeve. "If they don't want us, let's go. One less patient to care for."

I allowed Neal to pull me away, but I didn't want to give up one more opportunity to make a definitive diagnosis for Mr. Johnston. Neal and I walked down the hallway when I heard someone call my name. I turned. Arda walked briskly toward me. Her dark hair bounced with each stride, her eyes desperate.

"Gordie, where are you going?"

"We've been taken off your dad's case. Dr. Sanders said it was at the request of your family."

"Not by my request. I want you involved. There is something strange in all of this."

"I can't just butt in. Dr. Sanders is a senior attending. If he removes us from a case, we are done."

Her longing look captivated me and lowered any will to resist.

"Okay, how can I help?" I said and paused for a moment. "Maybe we can meet outside the hospital and finish the conversation we started during the last admission. I can't be involved here. Once I'm off the case, I can have nothing to do with your dad or family. I no longer have access to his records. You can do something for me, though. When we examined your dad, I noticed a white line in his nail bed. Could you measure how far it is from the base of the nail?"

Arda paused, looked at me as if about to question why, then agreed to do what I asked.

Arda and I met in a park across from the hospital once visiting hours were over. We found a bench and sat in the cool moonlight. The scent of flowers floated on the evening breezes.

"Well, did you get the measurement?"

"About half an inch."

"How long ago was Mr. Johnston's first admission?"

"About four months," Arda said.

I took out my phone and looked up nail growth, then opened the calculator function.

"I bet, based on how fast nails grow, I could tell when those lines started. Nails grow 3.47 millimeters per month. Those lines on the nails are called Mees' lines, a finding seen in heavy metal intoxication. It's been four months, and that's 13.88 millimeters of growth, about half an inch. Just what you found. I'd like more definitive evidence that arsenic is the cause of your dad's illness. Can you get some hair or nail clippings?"

The next day, I bumped into Arda in the hospital cafeteria. She was wearing a skirt and a tight sweater. Close to her, I could smell a faint hint of perfume. Her hair cascaded over her shoulders. She wore a frown.

"His nails were cut to the quick, and his head is shaved," she whispered. "Why did they do that?"

"I doubt it was a plan to send off samples for testing. Do you know who ordered that to be done?"

"It had to be Dr. Sanders," Arda said.

How else can I make the diagnosis of arsenic poisoning? We could test his food. I bet their water comes from a well, but no one else was sick. Then, it came to me.

"Your father always fed Beau from his plate, right? Do you know if they buried Beau or had him cremated?"

"He was buried, not cremated," she said, eyes narrowed, but she asked no further questions.

I returned to the ward and went directly to the nursing station to talk to Johnston's nurse. I had to be discreet.

"Joanne, can I ask what happened to Mr. Johnston?"

"I'm embarrassed to say that we prepped Mr. Johnston for neurosurgery by mistake. A long strip of hair was shaved from his scalp by the neurosurgery resident before we realized it and could stop him." Joanne wrinkled her forehead and clenched her fists. "Boy, was Mr. Johnston pissed. He argued with the neurosurgical resident before the resident started the prep, but the resident kept insisting that the OR was waiting and started despite Johnston's protests." She gazed up at the ceiling and rolled her eyes.

"Did he check the chart first?" I asked.

"He said he reviewed the order, but I don't think he reviewed the whole chart to see if the prep made sense."

"He could get fired," I said. "You know the family."

"When Mrs. Johnston saw him with a strip of hair missing, she talked the resident into finishing the job."

How convenient, I thought.

"The daughter expressed concern and wants an explanation for how something like this could happen."

"Does Dr. Sanders know?"

"He was surprisingly calm about it, especially since the incident involved his patient. Somehow, the order for the prep found its way onto Mr. Johnston's chart. Information Services will be looking into that. I'm sure we will know who entered that order sooner rather than later. The patient advocate is on her way up here to try to placate the patient. Knowing that family, they'll probably sue."

My phone rang as I left the floor. Information Service wanted to know if I had accessed Mr. Johnston's records. They said my log-in was linked to orders on his chart.

"You need to report to the Chief of Medicine immediately," the Information Service officer demanded.

"I'm out of the hospital right now." I lied to buy time. "I'll get to the Chief as soon as I can," I said, hung up abruptly, and headed to the parking lot. My career was on the line. I wondered how they'd set me up. Only the Neurology Administrative Office and Information Services knew my log-in information. I needed to get to Johnston's farm. I called Arda.

When Arda answered, she was cold and distant. I detected an edge. The Chief Executive Officer of the hospital spoke to her and implied that I wrote the orders for the prep in her father's chart. When I presented my theory about what happened, Arda relaxed.

"Can I meet you at your farm?" I said. "I bet Beau was poisoned when your father shared his food with him." Arda listened silently. "If Beau died of arsenic poisoning, that would suggest someone is trying to poison your father. Do you know if there is arsenic on the farm?"

"We use insecticides from time to time, but I don't know if any contain arsenic. I'm still at the hospital, but I will leave soon."

Arda met me at the entrance to the farm and led me immediately to the barn. We entered and walked to the back where shelves housed boxes and cans of varying ages. I had brought us each a pair of surgical gloves so we wouldn't disturb any fingerprints if we found what we were looking for. We looked at a dozen containers before I found a box behind a canister that looked ancient although the thick dust around it appeared disturbed. Among the ingredients listed on the package was copper arsenate.

"Can I help you?" someone called from the barn entrance. Arda and I turned together as Chester walked toward us.

"I saw two people walk into the barn, I didn't realize it was you," Chester said.

"Gordie thinks someone is trying to poison Dad with arsenic. We found a box of insecticide with copper arsenate. It's probably fifty years old."

"I suppose you're going to dig up Beau next," Chester said, his suggestion laced with sarcasm. I looked at Arda. *Why would Chester say that?*

"Gordie? What the hell are you doing here?" Arda, Chester, and I looked in the direction of the voice. "What are you looking for?"

Silhouetted against the entrance to the barn was Dr. Sanders, his brow furrowed, lips tight, eyes laser focused on me. "You are already in enough trouble. Information Service and the Chief of Medicine are looking for you. Accessing a medical record without authorization is a big HIPPA violation, a dismissible offense. Now, you're here at my patient's home. I demand an explanation."

"I think Mr. Johnston is being poisoned," I said.

"Really. With what?" Sanders shouted, his face red, eyes bulging.

"Arsenic," I said, pointing to the shelf where we found the insecticide. "Johnston used to share his food with the dog. I bet we find arsenic in samples of the dog's hair."

I grabbed a shovel, and Arda led us to the place where they buried Beau. I dug into the shallow grave. Arda, Chester, and Dr. Sanders watched as I tossed aside shovelful after shovelful of dirt. Chester paced while Sanders stood by, arms crossed, a smug expression on his face. Arda kept her eyes on Chester.

Three feet down, the shovel hit something hard. I reached down and cleared dirt from the top of a wooden box. I pried open the lid. Beau's partially decomposed body lay on his dog pillow. I pulled my shirt up over my nose to protect me from the foul odor of decay, then reached down to snip some fur, and placed the sample into a small plastic zip-lock bag I'd brought with me.

"So, what are you planning to do now?" Dr. Sander's shouted at me.

"I will get this tested for arsenic," I responded.

Before Dr. Sanders could continue, I saw someone go into the barn behind us. I replaced the lid on Beau's casket, stuck the shovel in the dirt, and led Arda, Chester, and Dr. Sanders back to the barn to see who had entered. We found Mrs. Johnston rooting through the shelves in the back of the barn.

"Looking for something?" Chester said. Our eyes were wide as we waited for an answer.

"Dr. Sanders mentioned that he suspected someone is trying to poison Michael with arsenic. I was curious to see if there was any arsenic on the farm," Mrs. Johnston said, as she reached for the nearest carton on the shelf.

"Don't touch anything," Arda shouted, and Mrs. Johnston stepped back. "Your prints are probably already on them."

Mrs. Johnston frowned and glared at Arda. "How dare you imply such a thing. If anyone wants Michael dead, it's Chester."

"You're the one who married him for his money. How convenient if he were to die," Chester snarled.

Mrs. Johnston grabbed the tool nearest to her and started to swing it at Chester. Dr. Sanders grabbed her before she could land a blow and hugged her until she dropped the weapon. *He seems awfully comfortable with his arms wrapped around her.* I glanced at the barn entrance. Standing in the doorway was a woman I had not seen before. She turned and ran. I took off after her. She headed for the house but stumbled. At the back door, I caught her

"Who are you, and why did you run?" I demanded as I gasped for air.

"I'm Berta, the cook. I ran when I saw Dr. Sanders," she responded, panting, as she tried to catch her breath. "He used to give me medicine for Mr. Johnston. I sprinkled it on his food. When Mr. Johnston got sick, I began to wonder about that." She studied me, her eyes darting back and forth. "I saw everyone by the barn and thought I'd better take a look to see what was happening. I did nothing wrong. I only did what the doctor ordered."

When Arda caught up to us, Berta ran into the house. I turned to Arda.

"Go back to Dr. Sanders," I said. "We need to keep him here. I'll go into the house, make sure Berta doesn't leave, and call the police."

As I entered the house, I found Berta at the front door. She was speaking to someone, but I couldn't see who. They conversed in soft tones, so I hid behind a wall and listened.

"Good work. You gave them Sanders' name as I told you."

"Yes, yes, just like you said. I told them I thought it was the medicine he was giving me to put on the old man's food. My money, please." Berta extended her hand.

I stepped out from behind the wall. Our eyes met. George Victor, Johnston's ex-partner, pulled out a gun, pointed it in my direction, and fired, then turned and ran. The bullet missed me. Berta stuffed a wad of bills into her apron pocket as she scurried away. I let her go and trailed after George.

I pulled my cell phone out of my pocket and dialed 911 to give them his license number as he pulled away.

The police put out a BOLO to apprehend George Victor and Berta. Their pictures were everywhere. It took a few days, but George was pulled over and arrested on the interstate when he was stopped for speeding as he tried to leave the state. The police apprehended Berta at the bus terminal when she attempted to purchase a bus ticket to Topeka, Kansas, with a Michael Johnston credit card.

Beau's hair proved that his cause of death was arsenic poisoning, and by association, so was Mr. Johnston's illness. We eventually proved that through samples of his hair and nails, once both grew back. Mr. Johnston eventually recovered, too slowly for his care team, who couldn't wait to see him go. He barked at the nurses and other caregivers right up to discharge.

The Chief of Medicine gave me a reprieve from the chart mix up. I wondered who was to blame for the error. I suspected Sanders, who mysteriously resigned from the medical staff within days of George's capture. He gave up his family and career to move abroad with Mrs. Johnston. Surprised everyone. Who knows how long that relationship will last?

He wrote me a letter six months after the whole affair. In it, he admitted to using my log-in to put the bogus order into Mr. Johnston's chart to have his head shaved and nails clipped. He explained that he recognized arsenic was the potential cause of Michael Johnston's illness from the start. He worried that Mrs. Johnston was behind it and wanted to keep me off the scent to protect her. I guess the letter was an attempt at an apology from him. Perhaps he felt remorse, as well he should. He almost ruined my career and should lose his own license to practice medicine for what he did.

Chester got what he wanted, to be rid of Evie and back in his father's good graces. I'm not sure what "in Mr. Johnston's good graces" means, though. Mr. Johnston is just as nasty and every bit as verbally abusive well as he was when he was ill.

Chester smiles whenever I see him, and I see him a lot. I have continued to visit Arda regularly. When I arrive at the farm, she greets me with a hug and kisses me on my cheek as I take in the honeyed fragrance of her hair. When she steps back, I see the sparkle in her eyes, a smile on her lips. I hope our friendship continues to grow.

THE TABAC MAN

Eleanor Ingbretson
2022 Short Story Award winner

I adore this little neighborhood café on the *Place de la Musée:* its food, the locale, even the young servers, primarily students, shy boys, and girls with bobbed hair and black tights. I usually arrive as they open, maybe waiting a minute or two as they bring out the tables, positioning a vase with a flower on each. Two or three chairs to a table. Or singles, if you like to breakfast alone. I do, and near the garden railing where the view is best. As I have nowhere to which I must rush, I can loiter over breakfast, enjoying the morning as befits a semi-retired grandmother nursing a bad knee.

For the past month, I've loitered with a purpose. Early today I learned from Victoire that the café's upper room had been reserved for this morning. I did not recognize the name on the reservation, but maybe we'll be lucky.

I watch as the *Tabac* man rolls his kiosk onto the *Place.*

I buy the paper from him, shake it out at my seat, and regard the *Tabac* man over the top of the news. Early in the day, he is busy with tourists eager to do as I am doing or waiting to enter the museum. But when his business slows, the *Tabac* man becomes a study.

He will lounge against the yellow-grey, sun-warmed stone of the museum, bending his knee to rest the sole of his boot against the wall. He'll dig in his apron's large pocket and bring out a handful of change, searching with a forefinger for the correct coin.

This morning, over my tea and croissant, I watch him. He's not far away, only across the narrow street from the corner of the café's railed garden where I sit. It's an excellent place to park a kiosk; the café has a circular stairway in the street leading to the second floor and the roof. The *Tabac* man has WC privileges on the second floor. His days are long.

My server, Victoire, asks if I would care for more tea. She is the grand-daughter of an old friend, a colleague at my *bureau*. Victoire has always called me *grand-mère* also, which pleases me. She hopes to work with us when she is older. She is quite capable.

I tell Victoire that as there is a nip in the air, I would like a hot chocolate with rum while finishing my croissant. The *Tabac* man raises his head and watches her reenter the café; he's sweet on Victoire.

He sees me glance at him, smiles and looks back down at his palm, chooses his coin, and begins to flip it with a fillip of his thumb. It winks in the sun; it lands this way or that on the back of his hand; a yes or no, a do or don't. What does he calculate so faithfully with that coin?

I regard the *Tabac* man, my hot chocolate, and the crows which peck the crumbs I've scattered for them.

Victoire returns to remove my plate. She kisses me and asks me to pass the kiss on to her grandmother at the *bureau* and tell her she will visit this weekend. Her message is necessarily quick as the café tables have filled up.

She turns to take an order but is interrupted by the owner. He talks fast and gesticulates rapidly. I certainly hadn't forgotten, but Victoire has; it's been an increasingly busy morning. Half a dozen businessmen will have breakfast today in the café's upper room, and she will be their server. The room is only one flight up, but the ceilings are doubly high in this reno-vated stone granary, with many stairs. Victoire scowls. I squeeze her hand; she is fretting, remembering a previous breakfast.

The businessmen fancy the waitresses with their long legs in black tights. I looked like that once, but it seems to have been a bothersome, con-fusing time when one looks back. I prefer my meals and semi-retirement, and these occasional forays for the *bureau* are sufficient for me now.

I take up my paper and watch the *Place* over the top of the news. I watch the *Tabac* man flip his coin; we both watch as, by ones and twos, beautifully clad men approach the café for their breakfast. It is the group I've been waiting for, loitering as I have over breakfasts for the past month.

One individual is particularly unsavory. I've had my eye on him for quite a while, and I raise my paper to avoid his glance. Another man buys a cigar before entering the café. The owner hails each by name, ushering them in. I hear the clatter of their smart shoes on the metal steps leading to the high upper room. Looking up, I see the backs of two well-groomed heads at the French window through the low ironwork of the balcony. The disreputable one I have long waited to detain. Today?

The *Tabac* man shifts his feet, first his right foot, then his left braces against the museum wall. His coin resumes its rising and falling.

I order a quiche, though I am no longer hungry. The crows become impatient with me.

I look up at a sound. Victoire is opening wide the tall glass doors to the French window. The cigar's sweet scent wafts down to my table, together with bantering voices protesting the smoke in the room. Victoire looks down at me and nods.

She doesn't like this particular job, but today it is her job.

Resting my paper alongside my plate, I do a semblance of justice to my quiche. I take a bite or two, a delightful mélange on my tongue, the memory of which I will save for another breakfast.

I set my knife and fork across my plate and regard the *Tabac* man who catches my eye. Victoire admires him, she has seen him often enough this past month, and they've spoken. She has mentioned that perhaps she will invite him to her grandmother's.

He wheels his kiosk into a shadier corner. He leans against the wall, and he, too, becomes shade. I see the glint of his coin as it flips in and out of the shadows. Looking upward, I see Victoire and the despised businessman whose searching glance examines her. His sleek head a pale profile against the room's dimness, his tongue a swift snake across his lips. I've grown to hate this man.

I shake out my paper and resume reading. I assume an attitude of interest. The crows move along to other tables.

A young man buys a paper and leans against the wall around the corner from the kiosk. He hides his face in what I know is the sports section.

Another server, not Victoire, as she is busy upstairs, asks could he bring me something different? Was there anything wrong with the quiche?

I assure him that my eyes were bigger than my stomach when I ordered. Would he get me a glass of water, perhaps? He hurries off and hurries back. I am a regular here and treated royally.

Chairs grate on the terrazzo floor of the room upstairs. Have they finished so soon? I glance at my watch; not so soon, it seems. I dab my lips and fingers with my napkin, wipe up some spilled hot chocolate and nudge my plate away from me. I upset the vase. It rolls to the table's edge and drops, breaking with an indifferent sound. I shove my chair back; it topples, and I utter a plaintive cry loud enough to bring the server back to my table and turn the eyes of the other patrons toward me.

In the shadows, the *Tabac* man removes his apron and lays it across his wares.

The server consoles me; it is only an inexpensive piece of glass, he says as I apologize, and the *Tabac* man crosses the narrow street to access the stairway to the second floor. The young man reading the sports section slips behind the kiosk and ties the apron around his middle.

There is a small cry from above. I hear the *Tabac* man's rapid steps up the outside circular stair and the tread of many feet descending the staircase inside.

The café owner comes out; he confirms the vase is a piece of junk; it deserved to fall. I am a good customer, break this one also, he insists, handing me another vase. We both laugh; the tension breaks.

All but one of the businessmen leave the café, none glancing toward my small commotion but dispersing to their businesses. The *Place* is full and clamorous now, but I hear other sounds from the room above, sounds only someone listening for them would notice: angry words, a thud, a moan.

"He has him," I say to myself. We'll have done a good day's work when he brings him down.

"The window! He's losing his balance!" the owner suddenly shouts, looking up.

He thrusts me away from my table. I stumble when my knee gives way, and a man, falling from the window lands too close to where I had been standing.

"*Mon Dieu!*" the owner cries. "He hit his head on the railing when he fell. Call the ambulance, someone."

Amid the chaos of servers and patrons, Victoire runs to me from the café, her hair, and clothing in disarray. "*Grand-mère,*" she calls to me, loud enough to be heard over the din. "He," she points at the man lying motionless. "that man, he came at me! I ran, he tripped and fell. Is he, is he dead?"

"Hush," I soothe her and press her face against me. "He's gotten away, yes?" I whisper.

"Yes, by the roof," she whispers back, relief in her voice that this job is done.

My *Tabac* man is safe, but what has he done? A simple sting to finally apprehend this monster has now become a *merde*-load of paperwork for the *bureau.* I look at the body.

"*Madame,*" the owner pleads, his arms like windmills, "do not look; it is terrible."

Sirens wail; I surprise the cafe owner with my credentials, dismiss him, and kneel to check the body. I roll it to its side and contemplate the eyes protruding from their sockets, a textbook result of a massive blow to the skull. I study the face of this elusive offender whose mind was so foul, his eyes always searching. For a very brief moment, I ache to pluck out those offensive eyes and throw them to the crows. Instead, I toss my soiled table napkin across his face.

A hand under my elbow helps me stand, my knee now past semi-retirement. I turn and see my re-aproned *Tabac* man. He shrugs, an expressive Gallic shrug, and I believe him.

Some people don't go quietly.

ICED

Marianne H. Donley

Detective Eleanor Reed pushed open the back gate to Roxana Pine's home. Rusty hinges squealed in protest, as if they hadn't moved since the last time Eleanor visited, way back in school when she and Roxana were friends.

The changes to the garden inside stunned her. Vines choked the uncut hedge along the fence and climbed the dead branches of two small trees.

"Are you sure about this?" asked her partner, Detective Stan Bailey. The path had once been wide enough for three people to walk abreast. Now the two of them rubbed shoulders as they navigated the debris-littered flagstones.

"Yes, I'm sure. Used to come here all the time in high school." She pointed toward the back of the house. "Leads to the side door."

Stan grumbled something Eleanor decided she didn't want to hear.

"Look," she said, "I called ahead, and Chad Pine said to use the garden gate. This is the garden gate." Pushing a branch out of her way, she added, "Watch your step. The path isn't level."

"Should have grabbed our flashlights. Even in broad daylight, this place looks haunted."

Eleanor laughed. Only she knew that, at the moment, the garden *was* haunted. She looked up at the eyes, glowing an unholy pink, of Regina Virtue's ghost. The familiar specter hovered just between a purple-leafed weigela bush and a towering rhododendron, then drifted to sit on the top of a dead rose bush. She crossed her legs and bounced a foot, making her fancy, kitten-heeled shoe with the pom-pom at the toes wiggle. One fisted hand rested on her black negligee-clad hip. The other held an elegant cigarette holder, complete with a smoldering cigarette, which she inhaled, as if she were alive, then blew a cloud of smoke in Eleanor's face.

"A little late, kiddo," she whispered as Eleanor walked by. "Roxana needed your help last night."

Eleanor held her breath and disregarded the ghost. Stan did not. Oh, he couldn't see the ghost, but she knew he could smell the cigarette. And her partner wasn't the only one. Everyone—everyone—from her mother to her priest to her captain, could smell Mrs. Virtue's cigarettes. Only Eleanor was *charmed* and got the ghost's full show—sight, sounds, smells.

Stan glanced her direction. "Have you taken up smoking?"

"No." She shook her head and continued along the zigzagging walkway. The heavy scents of roses, Asian lilies, and elder flowers clogged the blistering still air, making it hard for Eleanor to catch a decent breath.

Maybe Stan would think of flowers instead of smoking. Maybe her suspect would confess. Maybe Mrs. Virtue would stop haunting her.

Yeah, and maybe the moon was made of fresh cheese.

Finally, the vegetation gave way to an expanse of grass surrounding an Olympic-sized pool. Smack in the center of the pool, Chad Pine reclined on a floating lounge chair, sunglasses on his face, a tumbler half full of amber liquid in his hand.

Stan announced their arrival. In response, Chad Pine waved in the general direction of the round table, tucked in the shadow of a red and white cantilevered umbrella. "Iced tea, Detectives? Or something stronger?"

"No thank you, Mr. Pine." Eleanor felt beads of sweat running races down her back and puddle just below the waistband of her green linen dress. "If you don't mind, we have a few more questions."

"Does he appear sad?" Mrs. Virtue demanded as she floated next to the pool, puffing smoke as she spoke. "Why isn't he heartsick? Roxana was his wife, for damn sake. Poor lamb was *just* my godchild. I'm heartsick, and my heart isn't even beating. He should be wailing and weeping."

Eleanor longed to tell Mrs. Virtue to go away but chatting to ghosts—with witnesses—horrible idea. Stan waved his hand in front of his nose. "Seriously? Eleanor, you *have* started smoking."

Instead of answering either the ghost or her partner, she flipped open a notepad and fished in her blazer pocket for a pencil. *The sun is blazing, and she has on a blazer. At least it's white cotton. Stan must be melting in his dark navy-blue polyester suit.*

Stan crooked his finger at Chad. "This might be easier if you exited the pool, Mr. Pine."

Without spilling his drink, Chad rolled off the lounge and into the water. Stan muttered in Eleanor's ear. "Oh my, little black swim trunks. Are we in mourning?"

She flashed Stan a warning glance; he raised one eyebrow in response. Mrs. Virtue puffed her cigarette. Eleanor sighed. Stan wanted Chad Pine to be guilty. The ghost wanted the guy to be guilty. Eleanor wanted him to be guilty, but the back of her neck itched.

Chad set his drink on the deck and pulled himself from the swimming pool. Snatching a beach towel from a patio chair on his way to the table, he dried off his hair, then draped the towel around his shoulders. More a gracious host than a grieving husband, he suggested they sit. Eleanor and Stan remained standing. Mrs. Virtue glided up to Chad and shoved, but instead of moving Chad she floated right through him.

The man shivered, then pushed his sunglasses on his head and scanned the yard. Frowning, he lifted a Waterford pitcher of, *hopefully*, tea. Despite the drink waiting on the side of the pool, he grabbed another tumbler, added a few cubes of ice, and poured. The ice jingled and cracked. Eleanor shook her head. The crystal pitcher, the ice, the small round table. They pricked at her memory of the last time she had seen Roxana.

The occasion had been a few weeks ago at that new restaurant Stan insisted they try. Empty plates littered the table as they had just finished lunch. Eleanor pushed back her chair when a woman whirled through the entryway.

All conversation stopped and focused on Roxana Pine.

She looked so different that for several seconds Eleanor hadn't recognized her. Roxana's hair was a wild tangle of very red curls instead of her typical neat, proper auburn plaits. Her usually quiet brown eyes flashed green with—Eleanor decided—great contacts and a good deal of rage. A rage directed at the table behind theirs.

Eleanor twisted in her chair to see who had caused Roxana's startling transformation. At a cozy bistro table for two sat her husband Chad, head-to-head with a lovely blonde.

The scene looked damning. A cozy lunch. The discarded wife.

Chad had the wide-eyed, open-mouthed look of a surprised husband. But his companion . . . her reaction puzzled Eleanor. Instead of shock or stunned horror, a tiny smug expression flashed across her face. Eleanor wondered if the woman had planned this encounter.

Roxana slapped a bundle of papers on Chad's table. "I'm divorcing you. And your pathetic attempts on my life haven't worked. You have to do more than tamper with my car to frighten me. Now, you've just made me furious."

"Honey, I'm so worried about you." Chad tried to grab Roxana's hand. She slapped his away.

"Honey," she purred, "go to hell." The pitcher of iced tea from the middle of Chad's table proved too tempting to ignore; Roxana emptied it all over his head.

A server appeared at Roxana's side, whispering in her ear. Without glancing at him, she thrust the young man aside and left. Chad wiped the iced tea from his face and raced after her, leaving the blonde sitting at the table with that smug smile.

"I'm going to check—" Eleanor tilted her head toward the doorway. "She's a friend."

Stan waved her out. "I'll pay for lunch."

Outside, Eleanor stopped without approaching the couple.

While Roxana cried on Chad's shoulder, he stroked her back and speaking low. "Honey, I'm not trying to kill you. I'm not. Why would I?"

Roxana mumbled something that Eleanor couldn't hear, to which Chad replied, "I am so worried about you."

Eleanor had been worried, too; but not for Roxana. Roxana was freaking smart and could take care of herself. She wasn't so sure about her friend's husband.

"Iced tea?"

Chad's voice brought her back to the present. Eleanor blinked and focused on the man holding the pitcher of tea. Chad smiled at Stan. But when he turned to her, she noticed his smile appeared tight and didn't reach his glacial blue eyes.

"Ask him where he got the ice," the ghost said. "Ask him how long it takes ice to melt in this heat."

"Mr. Pine, last night, when—"

"Please, I answered all your questions. When can I see Roxana?"

"Mr. Pine, we need to ask some questions," Eleanor said, hoping she sounded polite and patient.

"I don't understand. Why can't I see my wife? How do I know it's really her?" Chad rubbed his face. His eyes went wide, then narrowed. "Wait. Do you think this is murder?"

"Just need you to answer a few questions," Stan said.

"Of course, you think it's murder. Do I need an attorney? I was at dinner with several unimpeachable witnesses. That's an airtight and unshakable alibi."

"If you have an airtight, unshakable alibi, why would you need an attorney?" Eleanor looked straight into his icy eyes. The man blinked, turned, and marched into the house.

"Well," Stan muttered, "Doesn't Mr. Pine seem worried—even with his airtight, unshakable alibi?"

"Yes," Eleanor answered. "Yes, he does." While she admitted his alibi was a stroke of genius, it worried her. Chad Pine didn't strike her as that smart. "Let's head to the sunroom while we wait for the lawyer to show up."

The sunroom was empty of furniture or fixtures. A faint set of concentric rings graced the middle of the floor, as if someone had dumped a huge bucket of dirty water and forgot to mop it. To the side of the rings, a vague outline of a blob. Eleanor knew that was where Roxana had been found, and if she squinted hard, it did look body-ish.

"Come on Eleanor. Figure this out." Mrs. Virtue hovered over the rings while focusing her spooky gaze on the ceiling. Eleanor glanced at the glass panes supported by metal rods meeting at the peak. The reason for the ghost's fascination eluded her.

"Smells like stale cigarettes in here. Why is it hotter than hell?" Stan loosened his tie and unbuttoned his collar.

"Sunrooms are like greenhouses. All that glass traps the warmth." Eleanor lifted her hair from the back of her neck. The heat dragged at her like a thick, wet, wool blanket. Pulling off her blazer, she twisted the sleeves around her waist, then nodded toward the thermostat. "The HVAC has been shut off."

"Why would anyone want a sunroom attached to their house?" Stan asked.

Eleanor shrugged. "Roxana and I went to high school together. The room was pleasant, especially in the winter when the snow's falling. There used to be wonderful potted plants and wicker furniture." Pointing at the windows, she said, "Supposed to have automatic shades in between the panes of glass that detect the sun and close or open as necessary."

"So, someone shut off the air-conditioner and the fancy blinds. Then why didn't the heat kill her?" Stan asked.

"Wait," Mrs. Virtue said, pointing the glowing tip of her cigarette at Eleanor. "Roxana was murdered, so you should see her ghost. That's your deal, right? So, where's her ghost?"

"Or the humidity . . ." A sharp rapping interrupted Eleanor. Chad Pine, now dressed in a cream polo shirt, cream pants, and cream deck shoes, stood at the closed solarium door. He motioned for them to come out. When they did, Eleanor asked. "Has your lawyer arrived?"

"Not yet." Chad handed Stan a business card, then tapped it. "But you need to call Roxana's doctor. Roxana had been unwell, depressed. This is no mystery. My wife killed herself."

"But she didn't—"

Eleanor interrupted Stan with a tap on his arm. "Now why would she do that, Mr. Pine?"

"Told you she was unwell. Stressed. Wasn't sleeping. Roxana imagined all sorts of weird things. I can't tell you how relieved I was when she agreed to counseling. Talk to the doctor." Chad gestured toward the card in Stan's hand. "Police are always trying to pin it on the husband. Why?" He shoved his hair back from his forehead. "Why would I want to kill Roxana?"

"Divorce, she was going to divorce you," Stan stated.

"Which gives you a motive," Eleanor said.

"What motive?" the man shouted; veins stood out on either side of his neck.

"Pre-nup in a divorce," Stan said, "But if she died. All her green, green money. You inherit—"

"Nothing. Absolutely. Nothing."

"Mr. Pine, we have a copy of Roxana's will, and you inherit her entire estate," Eleanor said.

Chad Pine's eyes went wide. His tanned face turned a ghostly white, and then he hit the ground, hard.

"Did not see that coming," Mrs. Virtue said.

Stan summoned an ambulance, but Mr. Pine refused to go to the hospital. Eleanor and Stan followed as the medics helped Pine across the wide patio, through a set of French doors, into his formal living room. The paramedics left, but Chad didn't seem to notice. He sat on the huge, blue sofa, staring off into space.

"Mr. Pine, we still have questions," Eleanor said.

Pine startled, then pointed to the corner where a snazzy bar was arranged. "Can I have a drink, please?"

Mrs. Virtue floated over and settled on the corner of that snazzy bar and grinned. "Pretty Boy wants you to pour him a drink."

"Not your maid. Not serving you a drink." Eleanor tapped her pencil on her notepad.

"Then I'm waiting for my lawyer," Pine said just as the doorbell rang.

Before she or Stan or Pine could move, the door opened, and a couple walked inside. The older bald man in a conservative dark suit introduced himself. "Wayne Swanson, Attorney at Law."

"And you are?" Eleanor asked the second half of the couple, a woman, blonde, and stylishly dressed. Eleanor couldn't figure out why she looked so familiar. The woman remained silent, gaze trained on the floor.

Attorney Swanson marched over to the bar and helped himself to some alcohol. "All of you need to leave while I consult with my client."

The blonde jumped as if someone had poked her with a cattle prod. "Oh, yes. Of course. Of course. Chad, I'll call you later." Then she scurried toward the front door.

"Don't leave, Nadine," Chad said. "Go wait out by the pool."

"Good idea. We'll go with you," Eleanor said.

Mrs. Virtue blew a ring of smoke. "This should be interesting."

The lovely, stylish blonde turned out to be Nadine Brennan and claimed to be Roxana's cousin. Mrs. Virtue snorted. "A shirttail relative. Second stepdaughter of a third cousin."

Nadine sat on the edge of a lawn chair under the umbrella and glanced back at the French doors. The woman shifted her feet and stared at the grass. When Stan handed her what must now be lukewarm tea, Eleanor's memory clicked. "Nadine, you were with Mr. Pine when Roxana gave him the divorce papers."

"What?" she asked, shaking her head no.

"Detective Bailey," Eleanor pointed at Stan and then herself, "and I were having lunch at the restaurant that day."

Stan snapped his fingers. "Right, I remember that. So, are you and Mr. Pine having an affair? Kissing cousins and all that?"

Mrs. Virtue floated next to Stan and winked. "The fuzz is sharper than he looks."

"No, it wasn't like that." Nadine sounded defensive, but she flashed a small, smug smile, as if it were exactly like that.

"So, what . . ." Eleanor let her words trail off. The silence stretched and stretched and stretched.

"Chad was worried about her. He called me. Wanted my help."

"Why would Mr. Pine call you to help with his wife?" Stan asked.

"Roxana made all these wild accusations about Chad and was becoming more and more unhinged," Nadine said.

"Again, why would Mr. Pine call you about it?" Stan raised his eyebrow.

"I was Roxana's friend."

"You set up the lunch or he set up the lunch?" Eleanor asked.

"Honestly, I don't remember. It may have been me. She was imagining things. I wish I had called him *sooner*. We should have gotten her to a doctor."

"But she wasn't imagining anything. Roxana's car *was* tampered with. She was lucky the accident wasn't fatal." Eleanor pulled her notebook out of her pocket and flipped through a few pages. "A few weeks before, she was pushed in front of a speeding truck."

"Oh my god." Nadine put a shaky hand over her mouth. "I . . . I didn't believe her. I believed him. Chad said she was delusional. Do you think . . . oh my god. This can't be happening. Was he really having an affair? Did he kill her?" Without waiting for an answer, she lurched out of the lawn chair. The chair smashed into the round table. Both chair and table wobbled and crashed to the ground. "Oh, my god. I failed her. I think I'm going to be sick." She ran toward the house.

"Why do I feel like applauding?" Stan asked.

"That time we saw them at the restaurant, I thought the same thing. Nadine had a look on her face—like she had arranged the entire scene."

"Blondie took acting lessons," Mrs. Virtue said between puffs of her cigarette. "Told Freddie, that's her father. Told Freddie acting lessons were a waste of money. But did he listen to me? Nope."

"Well, Stan?" Eleanor asked as they stepped back into the sunroom. Mrs. Virtue floated right through the glass.

Stan shrugged. "If Chad Pine knew about the will, he gets an Oscar. Nadine Brennan, no way did I buy her 'I was just helping Chad.' Not at all. Either they're having an affair, or she wants us to think they are."

"Agreed," Eleanor said. "This whole thing is making me crazy. Murder? Suicide?"

"Roxana's wrists and ankles were bruised as if they had been bound. And the preliminary toxicology indicates she was most likely drugged." Stan nodded toward the metal rod that supported the peak of the ceiling. "If Roxana's hands were tied, how did she get the rope over that rod? Must be at least fifteen feet from the ground. What did she stand on?" Gesturing around the empty room, he frowned at Eleanor as if the lack of chairs or ladders was her fault.

"Something is very wrong here." Mrs. Virtue materialized at the ceiling, and then inch by inch she floated to the floor. "Come on, kiddo, where's Roxana's ghost?"

Eleanor said, "Not the first attempt . . ."

"Yeah. Yeah." Stan interrupted with a wave of his hand. "And Pretty Boy has an alibi for every single one of them. Could the blonde have helped him? Was Roxana alone during the car deal?"

"I'll find out." Eleanor rubbed her face. "Inheriting everything sure gives him motive, but if he was acting when we told him . . ."

"Wait," Mrs. Virtue said. "Pretty Boy gets everything if she dies? That can't be correct. Roxana's lawyers would not allow that. No way her mother would allow that. Hell's bells, her grandfathers are rolling over in their graves."

"Roxana was smart, right?" Stan asked.

Eleanor nodded. Mrs. Virtue nodded.

"If she's so smart, why didn't she change the will? Almost like she was daring him to kill her," Stan said. "Would she do that?"

"Well," the ghost said, tapping her cigarette holder as if an ashtray floated in the air beside her, "that is an excellent question. Especially with Blondie hanging around. Don't you agree, Eleanor?"

Eleanor agreed but had no intention of telling that to Mrs. Virtue. So, she said, "Let's go see if Chad will talk. Then we can hit up Nadine after."

The ninety-degree heat outside the sunroom felt delightfully cool. Eleanor paused before locking the door. "Why is it so humid in there?"

"Don't know." Stan raked both hands through his damp hair before turning to Eleanor. "And it's bugging me. Something else is too. Red feet. Almost like she had frostbite. Sure wish she could tell . . ." Stan shook his head. "But she's not talking, is she?"

Eleanor looked across the patio through the French doors. Chad Pine waved his arms as he paced toward the bar. Even as agitated as he appeared, he poured two drinks. *Bet the amber liquid was stronger than tea.* And she fancied she heard the ice as it jingled and cracked.

Ice, of course. She grabbed Stan's arm. "How long, Stan? How long does it take for ice to melt?

This was too easy, way too easy. Eleanor rubbed her eyes. In less than four hours she had located the icehouse that had delivered a four-foot block of ice to the Pine estate. All that melting ice sure explained the humidity in Roxana's sunroom. Stan had taken even less time to locate a discarded rope and syringe in the trash cans behind the restaurant where Chad dined with two ministers, a U.S. Senator, and Fred Cotter, the chief of police. Crime scene investigators did not expect any trouble in matching the rope with the one found around her neck. No one was surprised that the syringe contained the same drug that showed up in Roxana's toxicology report. The empty bottle of her anxiety meds sealed the deal.

But it bothered Eleanor. Those tidy pieces of evidence. Mrs. Virtue sat on the edge of Eleanor's desk. With her legs crossed, she bounced her foot, making one of her fancy, kitten-heeled shoes with the pom-poms at the toes wiggle. "Pretty Boy was framed."

Eleanor sighed, then glanced at Stan, who frowned at her.

"Sorry, Stan. Pine isn't a genius, but he must be smarter than leaving all this evidence pointing directly at him. Plus, the will shocked him."

"Look, Eleanor. Chad played us with the will. That man drugged his wife, then he tied her up, stood her on the block of ice, and slipped the hanging noose over her head. Figured the ice would melt, and his wife would die while he and his buddies had dinner. Now, what's your problem?"

"Why the ice?" she asked.

"He wanted to make sure she died when he wasn't home."

"Why didn't he put a chair or a ladder or a stool in the room? So we wouldn't question suicide."

"You said it yourself. He's no Einstein. And. That's." Stan spoke each word slow and quiet. "Why. It. Was. Easy. To. Figure. Out."

"I don't know," Eleanor said.

Then the icehouse delivery driver arrived for his routine interview. He had been pretty steamed not to receive a tip after lugging that huge hunk of ice to the Pine sunroom. He was positive Chad Pine hadn't accepted the block of ice. "Witchy woman was as snooty as she was cheap," he said.

Eleanor watched the driver walk away. "Where's that copy of Roxana's will? Who would inherit if Chad could not?"

Stan rifled through the files on his computer. He whistled and turned the screen toward Eleanor. "Think they were in it together? Think we can get one of them to flip?"

"Who's going to flip? If Pretty Boy didn't do it . . . Well, I'll be damned." Mrs. Virtue puffed out an impressive set of smoke rings. "That's why Roxana's ghost is missing. She's not dead, is she?"

Roxana finally agreed to talk—but only to Eleanor.

Eleanor headed off to the hospital without her partner but with Mrs. Virtue's ghost still wearing those pom-pom shoes, that black negligee, and carrying her elegant cigarette holder.

Once she arrived, she exchanged greetings with the patrol officer guarding the hospital room.

After opening the door, Eleanor paused a moment to watch Roxana. Nothing of the wild woman from the restaurant remained. Covered in a long pink bathrobe and those odd hospital socks with the grips on the soles, she sat sedately in a beige hospital recliner. Her hair was properly auburn and braided; her eyes, when they turned toward Eleanor, were calmly brown. She rubbed the bruises on her throat.

"Last time I saw you, your hair looked quite red," Eleanor said.

"When was the last time . . ."

"At the restaurant, when you dumped iced tea all over Chad."

"A temporary rinse. I wanted to be noticed for once. I was so tired of being that foolish woman being duped by a charming man," Roxana said, then frowned. "Have you arrested him?"

"Who?" Eleanor leaned on the bed and folded her arms to prevent herself from waving at the smoke Mrs. Virtue blew in her face.

"Chad. He tried to kill me. Several times. You know he did."

"Why would he?" Eleanor asked.

Roxana sniffed the air. "Did you start smoking?"

Mrs. Virtue smirked.

"Roxana. Why would Chad want to kill you?"

"I suppose he thought it was easier than a divorce. He was having an affair."

Eleanor asked, "Why did you change your will?"

"I didn't change my will."

Eleanor handed her the document.

"No. No." Roxana shook her head. "This is fake. This isn't my will. Even if I wanted to leave all my money to Chad, I couldn't. My grandfathers had everything tightly tied up in trusts. And I mean tight."

"So, if you didn't do this . . ." Eleanor tapped the papers in Roxana's hands. "Chad?"

"No, he knows all about the trusts. He has his own trust. His own money. This can't be about money. It was convenience."

"That doesn't make sense," Eleanor said. "How is death more convenient than divorce?"

"Have you met our lawyers?"

"Let's pretend we accepted this will at face value. If Chad was convicted of killing you, he couldn't inherit even with this will. Who would?" She flipped the pages so Roxana could read it herself.

"This is ridic—" Roxana stopped talking and rubbed her neck.

"What are you thinking, Roxana? Look, Nadine may be your cousin," Eleanor said. "But she wasn't such a brilliant partner in crime."

"Nadine is not my partner in anything. She's a friend." Roxana looked down at the papers on her lap. "We're not related."

"I heard she was your cousin's stepdaughter. Is that wrong?"

"That's not really related," Roxana said. "And it doesn't matter. She's my friend."

"Shirttail relative," Mrs. Virtue said, floating just behind Roxana's chair. She tapped her cigarette in the air and ash drifted to the floor before winking out of existence. "Don't think Blondie is her friend."

"I don't think Nadine is your friend." Eleanor echoed Mrs. Virtue. "Let me guess. She told you about Chad cheating . . ."

Roxana interrupted. "No, it wasn't like that."

"Sure, it was." Eleanor plugged on. "Nadine figured she could talk you into staging your death to punish Chad for the affair. But she planned for you to die. Chad would get convicted, and she would get all your money."

"No, I didn't try to stage my death. Neither did Nadine. That's nuts. She was driving my car when it failed. If she hadn't acted so quickly we would have died."

"Was she?" Eleanor asked. "Now that's interesting."

"No. No. It was Chad. He was having an affair and wasn't even discreet about it. People saw him." Roxana's voice rose with each word.

"Roxana . . ."

"I found an earring in our bed. I don't wear earrings. I found local hotel receipts for days he was supposed to be visiting his grandmother. When I confronted him, the attempts on my life started. To solve that problem, I filed for divorce," she shouted.

"Only two people suggested Chad was having an affair. Nadine and you. So where are the earring and the receipts."

Roxana looked away. Her face tight. Her shoulders rigid. "They're locked in my safe at home."

"Okay, good. Do I have permission to go get them?"

"Yes, of course." She once again rubbed her neck. "Nadine wouldn't do this."

"Yet, you believe Chad would? So why was he still living with you?"

"He wouldn't leave. He insisted he wasn't having an affair or trying to kill me. He insisted we go to a marriage counselor. In the moment, I believed him. Look where that got me." Roxana rubbed her bruised neck, again.

"I don't know," Mrs. Virtue said as Eleanor stood up to leave. "I don't think Roxana was in on this. I think Blondie acted alone."

By the time Eleanor (and Mrs. Virtue) got back to the station, Stan had fetched the earring and the receipts from Roxana's safe. He held them, encased in their evidence bags, for Eleanor to see.

"Called the hotels." He shook the papers. "These are fake. The Inn on the Square closed for business two months before the date on those receipts. I got Cooper trying to trace the earring. It looks expensive . . . and there's Nadine."

Eleanor turned toward the woman. Her blonde hair was scraped into a severe knot on the top of her head. She wore a deep black pantsuit and carried a handkerchief that she used to dab at her eyes.

"Why does she look like she's playing a grieving widow?" Mrs. Virtue asked. She had exchanged her smoldering cigarette for a martini glass and sipped as she spoke. Eleanor wasn't sure what would happen if she became intoxicated. But at least people stopped asking Eleanor if she was smoking.

Stan led Nadine into the interview room and offered to bring her something to drink. She shook her head, no. He shut the door as soon as Eleanor entered.

"Please take a seat, Ms. Brennan," Eleanor said. She pulled out her own chair. Nadine remained standing. Mrs. Virtue sat on the edge of the table. Stan leaned against the wall.

"Wait. What's going on here? Have you arrested Chad? Surely, you have enough evidence."

Eleanor nodded. "We do have enough evidence, but not any pointing toward Chad."

"What?" Nadine said, sitting down with a thud. "You must have . . ." She stopped talking as if she realized she couldn't reveal what she knew.

Eleanor let the silence grow when Nadine looked ready to bolt, she said, "You didn't tip the ice truck driver enough when he delivered the ice."

"I didn't tip him at all."

Eleanor smiled.

"Oh, well done," Mrs. Virtue said.

METHOD FOR MURDER

Carol L. Wright

"You know, I really never could stand the woman," she said, fumbling to pull a cigarette out of the pack I'd brought her and lighting up. "It's been that way since college. Me versus Ivy Mason, as she was known then. She only became 'Kara Alexander' after graduation. We two were always up for the same parts in the school's theater productions, and she nearly always got the lead." My client exhaled smoke, creating a cloud between us.

I coughed, but she didn't seem to notice. My only reason for being there was to tell her what to expect during arraignment—a quick in and out—but she clearly wanted to make her moments out of the cell last as long as possible.

"I'm sure she was sleeping with the director even back then," she said, locking her eyes on mine. I looked away first, as she continued. "But she always pretended this . . ." She shook her head, waving her cigarette in a circle, searching for the right word. "This doe-eyed innocence and mock surprise when the casting lists were posted." She flung her hand, spraying ashes into the air. "Ridiculous. No one bought it. We all knew the fix was in. That *I* was the more talented of the two." A bit of an accent had crept into her speech, and I wondered if she was channeling a character she'd once played.

"Well, nonetheless—" I began, but she cut me off.

"I was always prettier, too. Okay—not beautiful, but better looking than she was even then. I should have had the starring roles." She shivered. "I mean, with that horse-face of hers. No wonder she did all her work on Broadway."

I must have looked confused because she clarified.

"No close ups."

I couldn't stop my eyeroll in time, but fortunately she wasn't looking at me. I leaned back in the hard chair. It was nice to get away from the stress of the office for a change, even if the change of scenery was a consultation room at the local jail. I thought I might as well let her talk.

She gazed off into the distance and continued her monologue. "I always should have been the star, but I ended up playing her mother or her best friend. That was no way to showcase my talent."

I shifted my position and pretended to take notes. Who knew? Maybe some of this would be interesting to my boss. As an associate at my law firm, I would normally never have a chance to talk to a high-profile client, but my supervising partner, "Iron Lady," had even bigger fish to fry that day, and Glinda, her other senior associate, was tied up in court. So here I was, across the table from a delusional, washed-up, second-banana actress.

"So anyway," I began, "Judge James is on arraignments tomorrow, and . . ." I could see she wasn't listening. When your client is a "creative," you can't always be sure you're getting through to them, but I was supposed to try.

"It's not my fault, you know," she said as if I hadn't spoken. "I just finally had enough." It sounded like she was quoting from a play. "Enough of getting the scraps from her table. Enough of playing second fiddle. I knew this play was my ticket. Two leading female roles. Finally, it would be clear to everyone that she and I were at least equals, right?"

She expected me to fuel her delusion, but that wasn't my job. "I'm afraid I don't know much about the play."

"Then how can you possibly defend me?" She squinted at me, appraising me, and I didn't come out well.

I didn't dodge her stare this time, nor did I think I needed to go into the office politics that put me in this seat today instead of the high-priced counsel she expected. Actors are so self-centered. They think the whole world pays attention only to them. Who had time for Broadway shows when trying to make partner, anyway?

Still, helping to get a famous actress off a murder charge should help my chances for advancement—but Glinda and I were both up for partner this year, and the firm had said they'd only elevate one of us. I closed my eyes. I knew I was the better lawyer, but Glinda was better at office politics. Still, I had more billable hours, and a law firm runs on its billables. Maybe spending a little more time listening to a well-heeled client couldn't hurt.

"Why don't you tell me about the play. I'd like to learn about it from your point of view," I said in my practiced "I'm in control here, not you" voice.

"Well then," she began, leaning forward. "The director contacted my agent about it. Said they really wanted me to star in this new play, 'Jackie and Jill,' by that wonderful young playwright, Sarah Townsend. You know her?"

I looked up from my legal pad and shook my head. I got another disdainful look that said, "plebeian."

"Well, she's wonderful. Writes women particularly well. Great, meaty roles that get to the heart of a woman's passions. Obviously, I was very interested."

"Of course," I said, trying to be encouraging, but I got another look from her that told me I had best not interrupt again. "Go on," I urged.

She flicked a cigarette ash across the gray, metal table that separated us and looked out the barred window.

"Anyway, they had me read both parts, Jackie and Jill. They were fairly equal in importance, so I didn't much care which one I played." She looked at me through narrowed eyes. "I really didn't care."

By then, I knew better than to respond, so I simply nodded.

"Then they brought us both in to see us together." She paused, apparently to let me know that this was when the trouble started. "As I said, I didn't care which part I played, but *Ivy* had set her heart on the Jill role." An arched eyebrow said this was all part of an evil plot.

"But if you didn't care . . ."

"Well, I didn't want *her* to get first choice and leave me with her leftovers again, so I said I preferred to play Jackie." She stubbed out her cigarette and folded her hands, staring at them. "Top billing," she said, *sotto voce*. "That means I'm the star."

"So, you read both parts together?" I asked, trying to draw her back to her narrative.

"Yes. It went perfectly well no matter which part either of us played. You see, Jackie and Jill are supposed to be best friends, but they secretly hate each other. It's a very complex play."

"I see," I said, hoping I hadn't said too much.

"Yes, so our natural antagonism toward each other really worked in those scenes. I could say things to her that I had wanted to say for years, but of course could not. I wouldn't want to appear petty. It wouldn't look good, and I wouldn't do anything to hurt my career."

I took in the stale room, the bars, the gray furniture, the locked door with a reinforced window and wondered how much good *this* would do for her career.

"Anyway," she continued, "I got the part of Jackie, and she got Jill. We pretended to be happy to be working together, but I knew it bothered her as much as it did me." She pulled out another cigarette but didn't light it. "But before all the world, it would finally be clear that I was the better actress."

She opened her arms as if embracing the globe—or perhaps "her public." Wasn't that what actors called it?

"Together we made great box office. Tickets were snapped up as soon as they were made available." She tapped the end of the unlit cigarette on the tabletop. "In fact, if you want to know the truth, Jackie really was the better part. It demanded that I plumb the depths of human angst in a way that the Jill part just didn't allow."

"Good for you then," I said. She looked at me quizzically, so I added, "That they trusted you with the tougher role."

"Yes, you're right," she said. "It was a tougher role. All through rehearsal, the director kept giving me lots of notes. Of course, the great Ivy hardly got anything but praise. But her role was easier. Anyone could have played Jill."

"So, what turned things nasty?"

She lit the cigarette and took a drag. Smoke puffed out as she spoke, "Well, clearly the actor playing Jackie should have gotten top billing, but when the marquee went up, *her* name was first."

"Well, her name comes first alphabetically—"

"That's not the point!"

I tried to keep my look steady and again pretended to take notes.

"So, in the play, Jackie stabs Jill, you know?"

I couldn't help arching my brow, but I looked down so she might not notice.

"It actually helped to unleash some of those feelings that one tries to suppress. And I was magnificent." She took another drag and let out a long stream of smoke. "You see, I'm a Method actor."

I looked up, afraid to ask for an explanation of what that meant. She must have understood my expression as confusion.

"Stanislavski? Strasberg? Meisner? Adler? Haven't you ever heard of The Method?"

I shrugged. I'd heard the term, but if pressed, I couldn't define it.

"It's about experiencing your character's life by re-experiencing things from your past, immersing yourself in your emotional memory. Some of the best actors use it: Olivier, Brando, DeNiro, Pacino, Day-Lewis, Jack-Freakin' Nicholson?"

I nodded to indicate I got it. I *sort of* did. I had heard about actors starving themselves, breaking their bones, or pulling their own teeth without anesthesia so they could appreciate what their characters were going through. Some, I'd heard, stayed in character the whole time they were filming, refusing to talk to their coworkers except as their character while involved in a project.

"Those are mostly movie actors," I ventured. I couldn't imagine an actor staying in character for months on end in a successful Broadway show.

"Good acting is good acting, whether on stage or screen," she said, a self-satisfied smile on her lips.

"You mean your character plotted to kill Jill, so you started to plot to kill the actress who played her?"

She looked at me as if I were insane. "Of course not. That would be crazy. Without her, the show would close, and I would be out of a job." She shook her head as if she doubted my intelligence. "I wouldn't do *anything* to hurt my career."

"Sorry," I said. "Go on."

"Well, the set was being built in the theater, so we had to rehearse in a different space. All perfectly normal." She stubbed out her cigarette, then reached for another. "Rehearsals went well. The playwright tweaked the story, gave us new lines, cut others. The director played with the blocking. We were getting some really good stuff to work with. It was, you know, therapeutic I think, to finally get out some of those long-held emotions. I could tell her what I thought of her without anyone knowing it was the real me talking to the real her. I was having a pretty good time of it, actually."

"So, what changed?"

She shifted in her chair, turning away from me to look toward the window. I waited.

"It came time for tech rehearsals—you know—when the set is ready, and we move into the theater to work on all the sound and lighting cues. Tech is a long, laborious process. You say a line and wait while the crew figures out how to light you and checks your mic balance."

"Sounds like a drag," I said, more to have something to say than because I cared. I didn't. This little break from the office was getting old. I wished for a more comfortable chair, better smelling air, a fresh cup of coffee, and gentle music in the background. Here, the chairs were straight and hard, the air reeked of smoke and sweat, and the background music was muted voices, shuffling feet, and the occasional clanging of cell doors.

"These are the longest rehearsal days. Tiring—no exhausting. The only bright side is that we get to go to our dressing rooms when there's a break."

I put my pen down. I was ready to leave.

"But what should happen when we went for our first break?" she asked rhetorically.

Okay—she had my interest. "What?"

"I found out that Ivy's dresser had moved her into the largest dressing room."

I knew the client well enough by now to realize this must be a big deal. "What do you mean her 'dresser'?" I asked. Wasn't that a piece of furniture?

She gave me another impatient look. "In a play, we need to make quick costume changes, and our dressers help us do it. I always get one assigned to me for each play—not that they're ever any good. I've had to fire so many of them, I can't even . . ." She drifted off for a moment, as if lost in the memory of dressers she had fired. Then, refocusing, she continued.

"But Ivy is such a diva that she insists on having the same dresser for every show she's in. They've been together for years and, they say, the two were as close as sisters. I never much liked my sister, so I was never sure whether that was a good thing or bad." She snickered, then continued. "But in this case, her dresser just wedged her into *my* dressing room, and had it all set up just the way she likes it before Ivy ever set eyes on it. Soft chairs, a thick carpet, a Tiffany lamp, roses on the make-up counter, a box of imported chocolates, a mini-fridge, and a coffee bar. It was . . ." She spat out the last word. "Elegant."

"What did your dresser say about that?"

"*My* dresser was the usual incompetent staffer provided by the theater. She hadn't done a thing to protect my rightful territory. Not a single thing. She'd let Ivy's dresser steal the bigger room without so much as an argument. Here I was, the star, and my room was at least a foot narrower than Ivy's. Unacceptable."

"Had she at least gotten it set up nicely?"

She stood and loomed over me. "Of course not. The idiot." She threw down the cigarette and started pacing. "She hadn't put anything more in my room than a single, rolling clothes rack. That was it. One metal chair, a wall mirror surrounded by bare bulbs, and an empty clothes rack."

She was shrieking, and I noticed a guard peer in through the meshed window in the door. I nodded to show I was okay, and he disappeared again despite the continuing rant.

"Not even a pitcher of ice water was there when I went in during the break. It was intolerable, and I told her so. 'I didn't know how you'd like it,' she said in a whiny voice. 'Well, not like this,' I told her. But at least this one was smart enough to quit that day before I had a chance to fire her. I told her she would never work in this town again."

I was beginning to wonder about an insanity defense when she took her seat and continued.

"But I am a pro," she said in a manufactured calm. "I don't let such things get in the way of an excellent performance. Previews were only a few days away. Reviewers would start coming so they could write their reviews and release them on our official opening night. And, after all, the show must go on despite such hardships."

"So, you'd had a couple of weeks of shows before the incident, right?"

"Yes, and I knew I was wonderful in the part. 'Magic! Yes, yes, magic! I try to give that to people'."

The way she said it, I was pretty sure *that* was a quote from a play—or maybe a film. With my job, I didn't get to watch any movies either.

"So that's when you decided to kill Miss Alexan—er Ivy?"

"No. You haven't been listening. If I killed her, the show would close, and what good would that do? I would be out of work, and . . ." She waggled an eyebrow. "I wouldn't do *anything* to hurt my career, remember?"

"But, you . . ."

"I didn't want her *dead.* I just wanted her to *look* bad. More to the point, I wanted her *reviews* to be bad. That way, everyone would have to acknowledge that without *me,* the show would fold. *I* am the *star.*"

"Okay, but you substituted a real knife for the prop knife in the scene where your character tried to kill hers."

"Ah yes, but I didn't use it in the scene, did I?"

"But, you . . ."

"I threw it off stage where I knew her dresser always stood. I have great aim. I once played a knife thrower, you know. Got her right in the heart." Her smirk was a mix of evil and bloodlust. "I knew without her precious dresser, Ivy would be too distraught to go on—or if she did, she'd give a bad performance. Either way, the reviewers would crucify her." She laughed deep in her throat. "A perfect crime." She laughed again.

"But it wasn't perfect," I said. "You didn't get away with it. You're going to be arraigned for murder tomorrow."

"So what?" she said, with a flip of her hand. "It was an accident, as anyone could plainly see. You will make sure they know that, won't you?"

I winced. At least I wouldn't be the one standing up in court trying to make that argument. Iron Lady would—if it ever got to court.

"And, best of all, Ivy will never be the same. Jackie killed Jill after all." The smirk returned—more smug than evil this time.

I'd had enough and stood to go. After getting the guard's attention, I gave her one last bit of advice. "Remember not to talk to anyone. Not the guards, not your cellmate, no one. No matter how proud you are of what you've done, just act like a nun. You ever play a nun?"

"Oh sure," she said. "Mother Superior in *The Sound of Music.* Wise, strict, compassionate. I can do that."

"Great, but this nun has taken a vow of silence."

She flashed an "okay" sign, and, without another word, left with the guard, her cuffed hands pressed together as if in prayer. I hoped she was as good an actor as she thought she was.

As I left the jail and descended the concrete stairs, I had to shake my head. I couldn't believe how deeply into her delusion she had sunk. The lady was batshit crazy, that was certain, but not in a legal sense. She was lucky New York no longer had a death penalty.

On one level, though, I could understand her desire to promote her career. Don't we all want to do that? But all she had accomplished was to make her play notorious and to give her understudy her big break—to co-star with Kara Alexander. As Iron Lady says, they're not in jail because they're smart. Nope. Not smart at all.

Now if she were *really* smart, I thought, as I took the subway back to the office, she would have gotten rid of the competition. She could have arranged an "accident." Like maybe a piece of scenery falling at the right time. Or maybe an assisted stumble in front of a moving bus. Tragic accidents happen every day.

I turned it over in my head as I reached the crosswalk near our mid-town office building. With a glance at my phone, I realized Glinda should come by any minute. Maybe I should wait in the corner Starbucks and help her across the street. Her balance is bound to be compromised by the five-inch heels she always wears to court.

But it must look like an accident.

After all, I wouldn't do anything to hurt my career.

All In

A. E. Decker

To top off the night, it appeared she was about to get mugged.

"Lady Fortune's flatulent fanny," muttered Sonata, slipping her tiny pistol out of her sleeve and palming it. Gambling held its dangers, particularly for a young woman, and a few painful incidents had taught her the virtue of being prepared. But to be robbed for a miserable sixty-two pennecs—an amateur's take—was more ill-luck than she was prepared to swallow in one evening.

Rain dribbled out of the sooty sky, dripping off the tips of her short hair as she scanned Haymaker Lane. The man-shaped shadow she'd glimpsed had been large, in a lump-in-the-throat, instant-sense-of-menace sort of way. Too large to be hiding behind the rotting crates piled beside the pawn shop or lurking in the abandoned hostel's recessed doorway. *Has to be the alley leading to the old livery stable,* she decided, eyeing the gap between the crumbling storefronts.

Kicking a heap of rags aside, she advanced, pistol leveled, on the alley's mouth. The lingering stink of old horse sweat clogged her nose. Her cheap boots slopped through the puddles collected between the gritty cobbles. "Don't keep me waiting," she called into the alley's depths.

The shadow appeared first, that too-large shadow, stroking along the dirty brick wall. Ancient straw crunched as a man flowed out of the cloaking darkness. His boots—supple, hand-tooled leather—made soft spongy noises against the stones.

Black clothes. Masked features. Not good signs. Sonata stood fast as his broad-shouldered form, topping her by better than a head, approached.

Better than two heads, she amended, staring up at him. Could her little pistol even penetrate his skull? A dying sparklamp across the street picked out silver highlights on his mask. How odd, that mask. A simple bandana would serve for concealment, but this was hand-carved and shaped like a—wolf's head. Sonata's jaw tightened. The wolf was the lowest-value face card in a standard deck. *Some game's being played with me, and I don't recall asking to be dealt in.*

"Well?" she asked, sharply.

He stopped. The rain continued to fall with the soft patter of coins dropping from a torn pocket.

Sonata cocked her pistol. "Either rob me or run. I'm getting soaked."

Very slowly, the masked man extended his right arm. The sparklamp's glow caught a buttery shine off the gilded borders of a pasteboard card lying in his palm.

Sonata's breath checked. As if drawn, she stepped forward, pistol forgotten.

Her eyes hadn't lied. The card's curling gold inscription gleamed like a smile hiding a wicked secret.

Acheron Aldis Lordstar Sincail
The Lucky Dragon

They'd said his agent would be at the Anvil Tavern, but they said that of every two-pennec game played in every dive in the city of Bellweather. And her performance tonight hadn't impressed. After Alan Portois drove his fist into Marc Fennerel's gut, all the energy had gone out of the game.

The man flipped the card over with a flick of his thumb. Edging closer, Sonata read the words written on its back in dark blue ink: *Sonata Kiel. You are invited to Play. Fourthday, the hour of the dove. A carriage will wait at the Ruined Tower.*

Play. A squeak escaped her throat. The Grand Deal, in the Dragon's own chateau.

With another flick, the man held the card out, offering it between the tips of his fingers. Sonata snatched it away and cupped it to her breast.

"I'll be there," she said, caressing the smooth gold filigree with her thumbs.

The wolf-masked man bowed. Darting past his lowered head, Sonata jogged the rest of the way home, her feet drumming an exultant staccato against the cobblestones.

Three years ago, as a prank, a pair of aristocrats slammed a piano's fallboard on Sonata's father's fingers as he played an impromptu during one of their soirees. The clucking hostess sent her own doctor to tend the Maestro's injuries, but her compassion did not extend to covering the medical fee. The Maestro's hands, already troubled with arthritis, never fully recovered. Besides, the aristos were bored of him.

"Won't anyone do anything?" Sonata remembered asking Nocturne as they perched on the stone railing outside their house—the old, nice one, with climbing roses covering its brownstone walls. Angry tears burned her cheeks. *"Won't they be punished?"*

"No," replied her brother, staring at nothing. *"The aristos make the laws. They own the guards. No one will do anything."*

He began meeting with radicals in secret clubs. A year later, riots erupted in Ventiver Square. Swiftly quashed. Nocturne vanished.

What happened to you, Nocturne? Sonata stared out her bedroom window, running the Dragon's card through her fingers. Dusk grayed the pockmarked street as the hour of the dove approached. *Were you killed, as that grim-faced guardsman said, or are you in prison?*

She'd never have won this invitation without Nocturne. He'd played cards before her. Taught her to watch, to count. To figure the odds.

A cough rose up from the parlor below, where her mother and the twins, Cantata and Fantasia, sat ruining their eyes making lace.

Sonata crumpled the Dragon's card. She met her reflection's gaze in the splotchy wall mirror. "I'll take the money when I win."

There, she'd said it. It was sense, not avarice. Five thousand filles meant rest and medicine for her mother. Gowns for Cantata and Fantasia, so they could shine in society. Her father could quit teaching music for a pittance and return to composing.

Snatching up her comb, Sonata ran it through her hair, short-cropped as a blonde helmet. With every stroke, her pewter star pendant—Nocturne's gift for her sixteenth birthday—tapped her breastbone. *When I win, when I win, when—*

Another cough from downstairs; wet and shallow. Sonata hesitated in mid-stroke. And if she didn't win?

She remembered Danvis Elbron, found dead on the road beside an abandoned coach. Artor Bracewell, crumpled at the base of the Ruined Tower. Jay Rees, dragged from the depths of the Wending River. All presumed to have challenged the Dragon. All presumed to have lost.

I should tell Mother. Say goodbye.

The hall's floorboards squeaked as she crept downstairs and slipped, unnoticed, out the front door. Its hinges hardly squeaked at all.

The Lucky Dragon's carriage practically flowed up Drake Mountain, pulled by a perfectly matched pair of sapient crystal horses. Their faintly glowing forms cast a blue gleam over the winding road.

Almost halfway up already, thought Sonata, poking her head out the carriage's window. Cold air glazed her cheeks. This high above Bellweather, safe from its stench of cheap liquor and urine, she could admire the elegant spiral of the Ruined Tower and Bellamy Cathedral's vibrant stained-glass windows.

The driver, the same large man who'd delivered the Dragon's card three days prior, turned his head inquiringly, eyes glinting through the slits of his wolf mask. He still hadn't spoken.

"Beautiful view," she called. Damned if she'd have him thinking she was staring longingly back at the city and suffering doubts.

Nodding, he jerked his thumb over his right shoulder, toward the mountain's side. Unwillingly, Sonata's gaze followed, climbing up and up until it alighted upon the jagged silhouette perched atop a steep crag.

The Castle of Mont Fere. The rays of cloud-slimed moonlight seemed reluctant to touch its stone towers. *King Alcore is mad,* whispered the rumors. Dangerous-mad, not crazy-mad. Iron cages hung over the front gate; not all empty. They said Alcore bred saber vultures specifically to pluck the flesh off the prisoners inside.

She could've sworn a low growl trickled out of the driver's throat. *Does he know someone imprisoned there?* A hideous thought to contemplate.

If only I had a pair of giant shears. She pictured their huge, snapping blades cutting the cages' chains so they fell and smashed the castle's walls.

Defy a king? Ridiculous! With a contemptuous snort, Sonata yanked the drapes closed. Her family was all she could hope to save. Best to concentrate on the coming game; not childish fantasies of toppling the Castle of Mont Fere.

The crystal horses' canter was so gentle that only the cessation of their hoofbeats told Sonata they'd stopped. She sat up. At almost the same instant, the door opened. White light spilled into the compartment, fracturing into prismatic sparkles. A hand—the silent driver's by the size of it—guided her down the carriage steps.

"Welcome, Miss Kiel," greeted a sunny male voice. "Pleased you could join us."

"Lord Sincail?" she asked, wincing, arm flung up against the brightness.

"Only under duress," replied the sunny voice. "Oh, your pardon." At a snap of fingers, the light receded to a tolerable level. "Didn't mean to dazzle you. Yet."

Sonata heard his smile before her vision cleared enough to see it: a white crescent framed by a pair of dimples. Then, the rest of him; the Lucky Dragon in the flesh, clad in embroidered silk and a not-quite-foppish long coat. Eyes an old-water green. His hair, golden as his card's filigree, spilled over his shoulders.

"Your servant," she managed as he bent to kiss her hand. Light winked off a gold ring on his left forefinger.

"And yours." The smile was still in place when he straightened. And the dimples. "Come now."

Tucking her hand under his arm, the Dragon led her across a vast courtyard, toward a chateau composed mostly of tall, graceful archways and latticed windows. Each step they took across the flagstones, cut from some smooth, golden-brown substance, released spicy aromas into the air.

The driver paced behind them, walking between two robed attendants, each of whom carried a glass globe filled with daystar crystals—the source of the prismatic light. Depending on their size and purity, daystar crystals cost as much as ten filles apiece.

Sourness twisted Sonata's insides. Even the aristos who crushed her father's hands had never flaunted such wealth. *He'll never miss the five thousand filles I'll win from him tonight,* she thought, glancing at her companion.

He smiled. "Shall we discuss the terms of the Grand Deal?" he asked, drawing her into the chateau's spacious interior. Carved pillars supported high ceilings. Sonata's boots clicked against the white jade floor tiles; the Dragon's long coat whisked over them. Silky red draperies rippled in the breeze, seeming to have been placed about the chateau for no other purpose than to billow artistically.

"Please do," said Sonata. His ring, shaped like a coiled dragon, caught the light again. Its tiny emerald eyes seemed to scrutinize her. "I know cards. I'll stake my life, if the game's honest."

"Oh, it's an honest game, to be sure." Something dark entered the Dragon's voice. "No one would dare cheat at my table."

"Good," she said. "I despise cheaters." All aristos were cheaters, acting like their birthright allowed them to take whatever they wanted.

"We're in accord, then," said the Dragon. His dimples returned. "The game's Dragon's Keep. No ante, full deck."

"That's fine." Sonata wetted her lips. All sixty-two cards. Many games discarded the two wilds.

They turned down a narrow hall. The attendants with the daystar crystals fell back, leaving only the silent driver for an escort.

"Everyone starts with five hundred filles," the Dragon continued.

Sonata's heart glugged. The sound echoed down the hall, repeating and fading. Perhaps it was only her ears, for the Dragon kept talking.

"I know you haven't the money. I'll lend it to you. Don't worry about repaying it if—"

"Everyone?" she interrupted. She'd already weighed the risks of losing. Discarded them.

"Everyone." The Dragon opened a door at the corridor's end, revealing a rectangular room with somber, dark-paneled walls. An oval table covered with thick red felt dominated its center. Three black-cloaked figures waited behind chairs, their faces concealed by stylized masks, each representing one of the five face cards. The Knight. The Huntress. The Prince. The wolf-masked coachman circled to an empty seat, making it four. The fifth face card was, of course—

Smiling, the Dragon strolled to the table's head, where a chair upholstered in green brocade awaited. Another chair stood at the table's foot, pulled back in clear invitation.

Sonata's hands knotted. *I thought I'd be playing just the Dragon.* With five players ranged against her, all sorts of agreements could be in place.

"Last chance to turn back," he said, hooking a leg over his chair's arm. "Once you sit, you are committed."

The masked figures waited motionless beside their chairs; waxworks whose blank gazes fixed upon her. Sonata had seen something like the overall effect in her nightmares.

Perhaps I'm in a nightmare.

Yes. Ever since the aristos crushed her father's hands. Yes.
She sat.

As the game progressed, a rhythm emerged, an understated melody.
Copper chips came and went in painful increments.

"Professional gamblers don't play comrades." Sonata remembered the
dry slap of card against card as Nocturne shuffled, his eyes on hers. *"Professional gamblers . . ."* He'd paused. Smiled grimly. *". . . seek out players they
have a chance of defeating."*

I didn't seek out these players, thought Sonata. And she wasn't sure she
could defeat them.

The Prince bid seemingly on whim, while the Huntress only played
good hands. The Wolf, Sonata found almost unreadable; he handled
his cards with great indifference but much skill. Most irritating was the
Knight, who enjoyed driving up the bid until everyone folded. The single
time Sonata called (as she thought) his bluff, he'd revealed a full house.

Down a hundred and sixty filles.

"Have some refreshments," said the Dragon as the Knight shuffled.
Sonata's eyes went to him across the expanse of red felt. He lounged, one leg
dangling over his chair's arm, the picture of serenity. Of all her opponents,
he gave her the most unease. She'd swear his pile hadn't varied by a single
chip since they sat down. She couldn't shake the notion that he had but to
choose, and the right cards would simply fall into his hand.

People have beaten the Dragon, she reminded herself. "Thank you," she
said, accepting a glass of white wine from a server in a domino mask. One
sip sent bursts of tangy citrus and floral sweetness over her tongue. Her
mouth watered for a second taste, but she set the glass aside.

"Nothing else?" asked the Dragon.

The server tilted the tray to display the dainties arranged upon it. Fresh
fruit, creamy cheese, pickled lesquel eggs, and fallownuts dusted with sweet
spices.

Sonata swallowed a rush of saliva. Candied fallownuts had been her
favorite treat back when her family could afford such indulgences. How
could he have known?

He couldn't have. Coincidence. "Nothing else," she said, waving the tray
away.

Smiling, the Dragon lifted his goblet. The intensely alcoholic, somehow purple-black fragrance of the richly colored liquid inside reached across the table, almost crisping the hairs in Sonata's nostrils. Robber plum whiskey. *The Dragon must possess a stomach of pure iron as well as bottomless coffers.*

"Perhaps you find it crass," said the Prince.

Sonata started. Aside from the Dragon and herself, no one had spoken a word beyond those necessary to raise or fold. The Wolf didn't even say that much, indicating his decisions with gestures.

"Crass?" she asked guardedly. Something in the Prince's tone suggested tight control: a dark and seemingly calm pool with angry biting things swimming just beneath the surface.

"You do not strike me as a mere thrill-seeker," said the Prince. He glanced down as the Knight dealt a card onto the felt before him. "Therefore, you must have accepted this invitation because you are desperate. To come here and witness such sheer opulence . . ."

The ring coiled around the Dragon's forefinger flashed as he raised his goblet again.

"Perhaps," she said. *Yes,* she thought. But despite the Prince's words, his accent was highborn enough to set her teeth on edge. No cheating at cards, perhaps, but what other traps might spring on her if she misspoke?

They make the laws. They own the guards.

She forced a light tone. "It's not for me to say how people should spend their money."

A look passed between the Huntress and the Prince.

The Knight dealt the "horns," the first three community cards, into the center. The six of stars, then the seven. The nine of rings. Sonata picked up her hand. The eight of blades and the wolf of stars. Potential for a straight or flush.

"Ten," she bid.

Everyone checked. "Have you decided whether you'll ask a question if you win or take the five thousand filles?" inquired the Dragon, his posture a study in nonchalance.

Rumor said the Dragon could answer any question, any question at all. If she won, she could discover what happened to—

Her hand twitched toward the pewter star hanging around her neck. She forced it to settle on the red felt. "No."

She almost missed the Wolf's tiny snort.

The fourth card, the "wing," turned out to be the deuce of cups. *Of all the bloody, useless*—Sonata forced calm. A straight was still possible. Her opponents could be hoping for a flush, or possibly three of a kind.

"Twenty," she said, pushing the chip forward.

The Wolf hesitated. Sonata held her breath. He had an uncanny ability for sensing bluffs. But he folded. The Prince checked.

The Dragon gestured the bid on. "Surely the question option opens more possibilities," he said.

"The money's more certain," Sonata countered. True; she could ask the Dragon where to find treasure worth more than five thousand filles—but how would she reach it? Bring it back to Bellweather unmolested by the brigands who prowled the mountain roads? A laughable prospect.

The Huntress folded. The Knight—

He's going to do it again, Sonata thought, an instant before he did it again.

"Forty," he rasped, as if his throat were terribly sore—or perhaps damaged. A diagonal scar ran perilously close to his jugular vein.

Sonata always gave herself three seconds to respond, so any hesitations would go unnoticed. Her lips pressed against her teeth. Double her bid or fold? She needed the "tail" to be a five or ten for a straight. Unless—

She glanced at the card that had been lying face-down by her left elbow since the opening deal: the "keep" card that gave Dragon's Keep its name. She couldn't look at it unless she used it, and if she used it, she'd have to play out the hand—no matter how high the bidding went. Thus far, only the Knight had used his keep—the knight of stars—in the third hand. Since then, Sonata hadn't seen the wolf of cups, the nine or prince of rings, the huntress of blades, the gold dragon, the four of stars, or either of the wilds. Two of those had to be that odd coincidence of cards; that some simply didn't appear as often as the others. The other six were lying face-down on the table right now, waiting to be unleashed.

Her three seconds was up. *See what the tail is first*, she decided. "Call."

The Prince also called. Taking up the deck, the Knight dealt the tail. The ten of stars.

She'd gotten it! A wolf-high straight!

Outwardly, she remained perfectly still. Inwardly, her heart raced. She could win big this round. Of course, if either the Prince or the Knight held two stars, their flush would beat her straight. But flushes were rare; about a three percent chance per hand.

"Fifty," she said.

"Call." The Prince pushed his chips into the center. Sonata envisioned a cynical grin spreading beneath his mask.

The bid came to the Knight. He ran his thumb along his jawline. Sonata's breath hitched. She looked up as the dim room seemed to brighten, but the candles in the brass chandelier burned as stolidly as ever. Something impossible and heartbreaking had just occurred . . . but she couldn't say what it was.

Dropping his hand, the Knight tapped a forefinger against the felt twice. For an instant, she imagined he'd fold. Then he pushed two large chips into the center. "One hundred," he said.

Sonata willed a bead of sweat not to run down her face. Was he bluffing this time?

Again, she contemplated her keep. The four of stars would give her a nigh-unbeatable flush, as would the changeling, which could mimic any card in the deck. The other wild, the mask, was played offensively. If one of her opponents had a flush, she could use it to steal one of his stars.

But the last five potential keep cards wouldn't help her. *Poor odds*, she decided. She held a strong straight. It should be enough.

"Call," she said.

"One-fifty," said the Prince, again with that sense of a grin.

Aristo. He didn't care. Why should he? He'd sleep on silk sheets and wake to a truffled omelet served on a gilded tray.

"Call," rasped the Knight.

She hated them. Hated them all, in their fancy carved masks and velvet cloaks. The Dragon's lazy smile was the most despicable thing she'd ever seen.

"Call." She shoved her chips into the center.

The Prince showed his hand. "Three deuces."

"Straight, wolf-high," countered Sonata. Her blood pounded in her ears as she looked to the Knight.

Slowly, he set down his cards. And said the word she'd dreaded. "Flush."

There they lay, the four of stars—finally—and that gods-damned knight again. His first keep, returning to him like a demon settling in to roost.

Down another two hundred chips.

Sonata kept her face slack as the Knight raked in his winning. Her mother's cough echoed in her mind. *I didn't even say goodbye.*

Sonata shook herself. She still had a hundred and forty chips. *Not finished yet.* But when she picked up the deck, its edges bit into her flesh, as if her skin had grown as thin as paper.

She dealt: two cards to each player, then the three horns in the center. The wolf of rings. The silver dragon. The ten of rings. She picked up her hand.

The five and huntress of rings.

Her heart knocked her ribs so hard she winced. Four rings already. Dammit; she had to play conservatively. The last thing she needed was to give in to the temptation to try for a flush. *"The odds, sis. Never forget the odds."* Nocturne could have been sitting beside her, whispering in her ear. Two flushes in succession were vastly against the odds.

Liquid glugged against glass. Looking up, Sonata met the Dragon's eyes. Robber plum whiskey swirled against the sides of his goblet.

Shaking his head, the Wolf set aside his cards.

"Fold," said the Prince.

"Thirty," said the Dragon. A great, creamy smile of satisfaction broadened his face.

Thirty. With two rounds of bidding yet to come.

"I will fold." Bitten-off words. With sharp, precise movements, the Huntress squared and dropped her cards. A crisp accent, more educated than high-bred. The Knight glanced at her before folding as well.

Never forget the odds. Sonata stared at her cards. Four rings already. So deceptively alluring. She should fold too. Let the Dragon win this round with his bluff, if bluff it was.

Capitulate. Like her family capitulated. Never seeking redress against the aristos who'd maimed her father. Never demanding to know what really happened to Nocturne.

Like the whole of Haymaker Lane capitulated, accepting squalor, disease, and heavy taxes as the aristos reveled in their mansions.

Like all of gods-damned Bellweather capitulated, averting their eyes while King Alcore hung prisoners over his castle gates for the vultures to strip.

Her head burned. Thunder mixed with quicksilver roared through her veins. "Call," she said, sliding the chips into the center.

The Dragon unhooked his leg from his chair's arm. Leaning forward, he pressed his elbows against the red felt.

Sonata dealt the wing—

The red dragon settled next to the ten of rings. Sonata's hand remained flung out, foolishly hovering over the line of cards, as if to call it back. Two dragons showing now.

Forty," said the Dragon. Chips clinked. His old-water green eyes speared Sonata.

Did the Dragon hold dragons? Sonata couldn't have laughed, even if it had been funny.

Fold, her brain, or perhaps it was Nocturne, screeched. *You can still battle back with a hundred and ten chips.*

Seemingly of their own accord, her fingers selected two chips from her dwindling stack.

"Call," she said.

The Huntress made a small, angry grunt, like a prodded cat. Utter stillness from the Wolf; he could have been a piece of scenery. The air crackled around the Prince. From the Knight she sensed anticipation, more galling than the Dragon's smile. Sonata slapped the tail into the center. The nine of rings.

She'd gotten her flush.

Elation failed to ignite in the pit of her stomach. Too easy. Too easy, and too—

"Fifty." The Dragon's chip clinked into the table's center.

—beatable.

Figure the odds? The odds said she should've won the last round. The Knight shouldn't have had a flush the same time she had a straight. And by all the gods-damned odds, the Dragon shouldn't be holding two dragons now.

Four dragons would beat her flush.

Sweat glued her palm creases together. Air—why was there no air in this room? She had to decide *now.* Fold? Try to hang on with seventy chips—near-hopeless in this company? Call *draco, draco* and use her keep?

Her keep . . .

A soft thump made Sonata jump. The room had grown so quiet the merest whisper would've sounded like a scream. But the Huntress had just dropped her hand to rest on the table; that was all. Surely it was only coincidence that her index finger angled toward the nine of rings.

The hitherto *missing* nine of rings.

Three seconds had passed, but Sonata kept staring at the nine. Only six cards unaccounted for now; six possibilities remaining for the hidden keeps.

And those six . . .

She looked up into the expressionless masks. "You bastards," she said.

No reaction. She realized the words had choked off in her chest before they reached her throat. She tried again, slamming both palms down onto the tabletop. "Bastards!"

The Wolf shied back. The Prince and the Huntress leaned forward. Beside her, the Knight tensed.

The Dragon . . . smiled.

Sonata spoke to him alone. "You said there'd be no cheating."

"So I did." Dimples deepened. Flash of a gold ring and matching green eyes.

"You want to play a game with me? *You want to play a game with me?*"

The Dragon raised a brow. "That's why I invited you here."

"All right." Sonata swallowed the boil of bile. "All right." Her hands didn't shake as she pushed her remaining chips into the table's center. "Draco, draco," she said and discarded her five of rings.

"Ah." The Dragon set down his goblet. "Draco, draco. I'll match you."

"Don't bother," said Sonata. "You can't beat a straight flush." She reached for her keep. If she was wrong, this was the end for her. Her body would be found in some gutter tomorrow.

But I'm not wrong. She turned over her keep.

It was the changeling.

His expression utterly blank, the Dragon flipped over his own keep. The gold dragon.

Sonata pointed around the table. "The wolf of cups. The prince of rings. The huntress of blades."

As she named them, the Wolf, the Prince, and the Huntress revealed their keeps. Only one card remained hidden, lying face-down on the table by the Knight's left wrist. Slowly, Sonata faced him. "The mask," she said.

He turned it over.

"But originally, it was the knight of stars," she said. She tried to gauge the color of his eyes through the narrow slits of his gilded mask. "The knight of stars, masked." She touched her pendant to her breastbone. "My brother Nocturne gave me this pendant."

"So he did," said the Knight. Gloved hands reached up to fumble with a clasp at the back of his head. A snick, and pale, silvery-blond hair tumbled free. "So he did," he repeated, no hint of a rasp now, and in accents once very familiar, very dear.

She belted him, full in the jaw. "Bastard," she screamed. "You *bastard*. For two years, we've thought you were *dead*. For two years—"

Two years of her father's mournful sighs. Two years of her mother wandering the creaking hallways at night, occasionally pressing her forehead to the darkened windowpanes, as if in hope of spotting her missing child. Two years of an intangible hole through which poured her family's energy, ambitions, and joy.

Nocturne's head snapped around at the blow and came back again. No sound of pain or reproach escaped him. Gathering her in his arms, he pressed her head to his shoulder. "I know," he murmured as a billion hot, needlelike tears swarmed from under her eyelids. "I know."

Eventually, she ran dry. Eventually, the feel of his soaked shoulder beneath her cheek became a fact, something that wouldn't vanish the moment she released it. Hiccoughing, she straightened, scrubbing a sleeve across her face. "Why did you leave us?" she asked.

No reply. The last of the tears cleared her eyes. Three unfamiliar faces came into focus. Her fellow players, unmasked.

Freed of their covering, the Wolf's hair shone creamy silver and his eyes amber with oval pupils—a Lycaen from the Caravan Mountains. No wonder he never spoke; the were-folk lacked the power of speech. Rumor said the Lycaen leader's head hung over King Alcore's throne. Next to the Wolf sat—

"Prince Luccan," Sonata gasped, recognizing the aquiline nose and brooding profile from royal portraits. King Alcore's second son inclined his head.

The scarred woman to the Dragon's left could only be Captain Davri, commander of the royal guards.

Such an unlikely group, here, together. Why? Sonata's brain spun.

The Dragon smiled. "As you've all unmasked, it would be rude for me not to do likewise." Before Sonata could protest that he wasn't masked, his smiled stretched. His ring flashed, then began melting. Gold spread over his hand and up his arm. Horns sprouted while his neck and torso elongated. A fringed tail wrapped around his chair's arm, reaching up to lazily brush the felt-covered tabletop.

Sonata stared up into the face of the Dragon, now a dragon in truth. Delicately, he lifted his goblet with a clawed hand. Sipped.

"The game was never about the cards," she said.

"No," said the Dragon, his voice as sunny as ever. "But perhaps you could choose your prize: the money or the question."

Her prize; she'd almost forgotten. *The money, of course. Mother's still sick, Father still poor.* And now she knew, at least in part, what had happened to Nocturne. She opened her mouth, but nothing came out.

If she took the money now, would she ever learn why these five had gathered?

The game was never about the cards. And we're still playing.

"No," she said, and stopped a moment, shocked by her own harshness. "I won't choose until I know what's at stake."

The Huntress—Captain Davri—smiled.

"You know what's at stake," said Prince Luccan. "The future of Bellweather." He waved a hand, indicating the world beyond the paneled walls. "My brother Alvring? He's worse than my father." The angry, biting passion in his voice resurfaced. "If he becomes king—"

"You're revolutionaries," said Sonata.

"Yes," said Nocturne. "As are Danvis Elbron and Artor Bracewell."

Two of the men who had challenged the Dragon and—as she thought— lost.

"And Jay Rees?" she asked.

Nocturne's dark eyes clouded. "He was."

"Until my father hung him over gates of Castle Mont Fere," added Prince Luccan.

Sonata's stomach iced. The real game was even more dangerous than the one she'd come to play.

Something slid over her shoulders: a gold wing, warm as a cloak, shining like a new-polished coin. She looked up into the Dragon's great, leonine face. Years, perhaps centuries, of wisdom swam in his green eyes.

"They won, but they didn't take the money," he said gently. "Not that money, at any rate. My race is not allowed to intervene in human affairs directly, but anything necessary for the cause, I supply." His wing curled her closer as he added, "I had to make it look as if they died. Their families would never have been safe from Alcore's wrath otherwise."

So that's why you vanished, thought Sonata, looking at Nocturne. Silently, he nodded, and in that moment, she forgave him. Now she understood why the Dragon had given her the changeling card. The true prize of the Grand Deal was neither money nor a question but being granted the power to help transform the world.

"Mother's sick," she said. It burst from her chest like a spasm.

Nocturne's stricken expression told her he hadn't known. She gripped his arm then looked up at the Dragon. "If I vanished too, it would kill her. I want to join you. I'd cut out my liver for a chance to kick back at the aristos. But I won't."

She paused. "Unless you tell my family I'm alive."

"That's not part of the deal," said Prince Luccan, but Captain Davri shook her head.

"Sometimes we have to trust people," she said. "What's the point of fighting for them if we can't?"

"Thank you," Sonata told her full-heartedly. If Captain Davri hadn't tapped her finger, she might never have considered the incongruous nine.

The Wolf grunted and turned a hand palm-up toward the ceiling.

"Symbur agrees," said Captain Davri.

The Dragon nibbled his tail thoughtfully. "The guards will still have to believe you're dead, for the safety of your family. But I could get a message through, assuring them you're alive."

"And Nocturne as well," Sonata added quickly.

"And Nocturne as well," the Dragon agreed. Crinkles appeared at the corners of his mouth. Dimples still, apparently. "In return—"

"And Mother needs medicine."

The Dragon broke into a peal of golden laughter. "Medicine too, and I'll add a hundred filles to the bargain; enough to buy them a little peace. What say you, Sonata Kiel? Will you join our cause?"

Sonata hesitated. Agreeing meant she couldn't go home. No more teasing Fantasia and Cantata about suitors. She'd seen her mother's last smile, heard her father whistle his last composition.

Nocturne squeezed her shoulders, perhaps guessing her thoughts. Probably they were his as well; he too had spent evenings nibbling candied fallownuts and listening to their parents singing duets over the piano. "It's not necessarily forever. We'll get it all back if we succeed."

"And so very much more," said the Dragon, smiling down on her.

Sonata looked around at the faces of her new comrades, considering the possibilities of a world without classes or cages. One in which people no longer capitulated.

"All right." She took a breath. "I'm all in."

Car Wash

Jerome W. McFadden

Tina sensed the two men were up to no good. They parked their battered Toyota Camry on the far edge of the lot, in the dark, away from the lights at the gas pumps. They sat for a long time, talking. They finally climbed out. One man approached the cashier's window while the other scurried into the obscurity at the end of the shed. Tina assumed he was positioning himself as the lookout for the holdup they were about to pull on her.

She had been afraid this was going to happen ever since she took this job. The car wash closed at six p.m. in the winter and the gas pump business slowed to almost nothing an hour later. She was alone, stationed at the small window in front of the pumps to accept payments for gas and to sell cigarettes, soda, candy, gum, motor oil, windshield wipers, and any other nickel-dime thing that the owner thought someone might purchase. The shed was locked, and she was by herself, sitting on a stool behind the high counter next to the cash register in the brightly lit window. It would be midnight before the owner would come to close and take the cash receipts.

She loved the hours, despite her boyfriend's complaints. It gave her the whole day to get her two kids off to school, nap a little, run errands, take care of things, and clean the apartment a little before picking up the kids in the afternoon to take them over to her mother to babysit them until she got home after work. But there was always the suppressed fear of being alone at night in a mini-convenience store/gas station. It was always there in the back of her mind.

"Not very busy tonight, are you, hon?" the man said as he stepped up to the window.

"Busy enough," Tina replied nervously. "There is always a steady stream of cars coming in right up to when we close," she said, adding a little defensive white lie.

"That so? I heard you guys weren't very busy in the evening."

"Where'd you hear that?" Tina asked.

"Never mind," the man said.

"What can I do for you? You wanna pay for your gas before you pump?"

"No. Not really. I want a carton of Winstons and all the money that you got in that there cash register."

Tina said nothing, frozen that her worse fear was happening. He was a big, mean, rough-looking man with a two-day stubble of beard. He looked like he wouldn't worry too much about hurting her.

She finally broke out of her fear to timidly tap the sign on the window that said the cash register never contained more than fifty dollars in the evenings. "You…You ain't going to get much," she said. "We have even less than that. It ain't worth the effort."

"Don't bullshit me, girl," the man said, raising a gun to the window, but not pointing it at her, more like making sure she knew he had it. "Just do what I tell you, you hear?"

What she heard was someone banging on the door of the shed.

"Your friend ain't gonna get in, you know. That door is bolted and barred on the inside. Just for this kind of thing."

"I'm getting tired of talking to you, hon. I want this done before some asshole drives in here for gas."

Tina climbed off the stool to cross the small room to fetch a carton of Winstons. She placed the carton on the counter and then deliberately shoved it hard out the window, causing it to sail past the man's arm to bounce on the driveway. She used the instant of distraction to duck under the high counter to hide. She scrunched up against the wall, out of sight, tucking her legs up tightly. She was a small woman and knew he wouldn't be able to see her.

The man picked up the carton of cigarettes and came back to the window. "What the hell you doing?"

"Hiding."

"Get out from under there and give me the money!"

"I'm scared."

"You damn well should be."

"And I don't like you calling me hon or girl."

"Do you like bitch any better?"

"I'm gonna call the cops."

"How you gonna do that? The phone is on the back wall. I can see it. You reach for it, and I'll cap your ass."

Tina looked across the room and realized he was right. She would have to expose herself to reach the phone and she had no doubt he would shoot her. Even worse, her purse was sitting next to the phone. Her cell phone was in the handbag. She was at a total loss about what to do, until she saw a long-handled mop propped in the corner. She inched over to grab it, then slowly stretched the long handle out to try to hook the strap of her bag.

"What the hell you doing now?"

"What does it look like?"

"Trying to find your cell phone in your purse?"

Tina didn't bother to answer, concentrating on sliding the heavy purse down the mop handle back to her under the counter. The man surprised her by shooting at the purse and the mop handle. He missed both but Tina jumped at the sound of the shot and yelled, "Shit!" as she banged her head against the bottom of the counter, causing her to drop the mop and the purse. She thought her eardrums were broken. She waited for a moment for her heart to calm down, taking deep breaths. then dared to sweep out her foot to hook the purse strap with her toes. She was terrified that he was going to shoot her foot, but nothing happened.

"I hear you tapping on your cell phone, I'm gonna shoot right through this wall and kill you."

"I gotta gun in my purse," Tina said. Which was true. Her boyfriend gave it to her a month ago as a precaution for coming home late at night all by herself.

The man said, "Ah, shit," and Tina heard him walking away from the window. She heard his footsteps along the side of the shed, walking to where the other man was, and heard them talking but she couldn't make out what was being said.

The man came back to the window "I'm gonna reach in and stretch over to open the cash register. You just stay down there and be quiet and we'll be outta here."

"I hear you reaching across that counter, I will shoot up at you."

"What is your problem, bitch? It ain't your money."

"It ain't yours, either," Tina said.

"I need the money."

"And I need this job."

"It ain't worth being shot for."

"The money ain't worth going to jail for."

The man sighed, "Well, it don't matter none." She heard his weight leaning on the counter as he stretched in toward the cash register. She pulled the .38 Smith and Wesson out of her purse, cocked the hammer, and fired up through the counter. Her boyfriend had told her that the .38 had a two-inch barrel so it would fit in her purse, but he said she probably couldn't hit anyone even if she aimed. But with a little luck, it might scare the hell out of somebody. She had never fired it before, and the noise and violence stunned her.

"Son of a bitch!" the man screamed.

"Go away!" Tina yelled.

The man shot a hole through the thin wooden wall, missing her head by inches. Tina thought her heart was going to come out through her mouth. She scrunched up even tighter, her heart pounding, but she fired over her shoulder, back through the wall. She heard a metallic plink and shattering glass in the distance, across the parking lot.

"Damn, you just shot the side-view mirror off my car!"

If she wasn't so scared she would have smiled in satisfaction.

"Who's gonna pay for that?"

"Call your insurance agent. Tell him that you were pulling a holdup, and somebody shot the mirror off. I'll stand as a witness for that."

"You got a smart mouth, woman! And it is going to get you hurt!"

Tina was trembling too much to tap 911 on her cell phone. Instead, she hit the speed dial button for her boyfriend. It rang and rang and rang with no response. She could also hear the second hold-up man's cell phone ringing at the far end of the shed. She hung up quickly to see if she could hear what was being said on the phone outside. But his phone stopped ringing, too.

She tried her cell phone again. Again, there was ringing outside the shed. The man with the gun yelled, "Answer your damn phone, Johnson, or turn it off."

Her boyfriend's voice came over her cell phone in a low quiet whisper, "Tina?"

"Johnson," Tina said, barely able to control herself, "Is that you out there by the shed door?"

"Yeah, it's me."

"What the hell do you think you are doing?"

"I need the money, Tina."

"Everybody seems to need the money tonight."

"Just give him the money and we're outta here."

"And then what happens next week when you need the money again? You gonna come back? The week after that, too? They're gonna get suspicious real quick, you know, if you hit this place every time I'm working. The cops ain't that stupid."

"It ain't like that, Tina. I promise."

Tina closed her eyes, nearly too tired to speak. "You're damn straight that it ain't like that! Your clothes and whatever else you got in my apartment better be out of there by the time I get home tonight. I never want to see your sorry ass again. And I'm bringing this gun home with me."

The man at the window was yelling, "She gonna give us the money or not, Johnson? She's your bitch, so make her get with it. You said she was going to roll over and this was gonna be a piece of cake."

Tina threw the cell phone across the room and yelled out at the top of her voice, "Piss off, both of you!" then fired two more random shots through the front wall.

She heard the two men hurrying back to their car, the other man saying, "What in the hell is wrong with that woman?"

She stood up as she heard them drive off. She was tempted to take another shot. Instead, she said to herself, "Goodbye, Johnson," while crossing the room to pick up the telephone to dial 911.

SENSE MEMORY

Paula Gail Benson

Chip didn't know which he loved more: the story or Zoe's telling it.
Who was he kidding? Zoe's telling it would always win.

They sat in the most secluded and intimate corner of The Norse Star Restaurant, where Chip was primary assistant to Idonia Dunn, Owner and Chef, known as "Idunn." Chip had meticulously organized their three-course dinner in advance, leaving detailed instructions for its preparation. After finishing the last bite and watching their server clear away their plates. Chip placed his elbow on the edge of the table, rested his chin on his palm, and gazed across at Zoe.

"Now, tell it again," he urged Zoe.

She rolled her eyes. "It's a story only a method actor could love."

He wiggled his eyebrows. "Or a foodie."

She sighed. "Okay, Chef Boyardee."

"Make that Wolfgang Puck."

She shook her head, but she wore that fetching, irresistible smile, so like the one in the portrait of Madame Mole Reymond they had seen in the Louvre. "Very well, Wolfgang. In *Acting: The First Six Lessons,* Richard Boleslavski presents a series of discussions between a young actress and her mentor."

Leaning more heavily into his palm, he remembered the first time she had told him about Boleslavski's book. They had just arrived in Paris as interns in separate programs, hers acting and his culinary. They went on a picnic with an excellent, reasonably priced bottle of wine, a block of camembert, and a crusty-on-the-outside, soft-on-the-inside baguette.

As they lounged on their blanket in the bright sunshine, Zoe told how Boleslavski's professorial character, the mentor, explained using the concept of sense memory to the actress. The story so entranced Chip that, as Zoe finished, he leaned across the picnic blanket to kiss her. Their first kiss. In that moment, he knew he would love her forever.

On subsequent picnics, he and Zoe had taken the book along and read it together. Leaning close, their heads touching, they each held a cover while Chip took the mentor's lines and Zoe voiced the actress.

He would always picture her as the actress. If the book were made into the movie, he would concede the mentor's role to a mature actor with a distinguished career, but for their private readings, the part remained forever his.

And, tonight, at their table in the restaurant, after he coaxed her into telling him the cucumber story one more time, he would get down on one knee and produce the ring.

He began the prompting. "So, the mentor described how the actress could use sense memory to enhance a performance. What's sense memory?"

She rolled her eyes. "I've only told you a million times."

"Once more. Pretty please?"

Zoe shook her head. "Suppose the actress wants to know how to play a person with whom she shares no experience."

"Like a murderer."

Zoe's smile broadened. She repeated the mentor's line from the book, "Why do actors always want to play murderers?"

He mugged, trying to look adorable.

She smirked at his attempt. "Anyway, the actor approaches the role by analyzing the character's focus at any given moment and drawing upon a similar memory the actor had."

Chip repeated the mentor's suggestion. "Like, for a murderer, a relentlessly buzzing mosquito, that becomes so irritating its victim must swat it into oblivion!"

Zoe leaned toward him, taking his right hand in both of hers. "Exactly. The actor immerses himself in his own memory and begins playing the scene to produce the same sensation on the stage. That's all there is to it."

Not quite. "Tell the cucumber story," he begged.

She sighed.

"Please!" His eyes locked upon hers.

Zoe opened her lovely mouth. "Once a young couple walked through a summer garden, stopping at intervals to pick and eat a cucumber as they got to know each other better."

Literally sitting on the edge of his seat, he now grasped both of Zoe's hands as he listened and watched her beautiful face and glistening eyes.

"In time, the couple married and had children. They dealt with adversity and occasionally argued. When that happened, their daughter discovered she could restore peace by serving cucumbers."

"Because cucumbers symbolized their love."

Zoe smiled. "Possibly, but the cucumbers certainly triggered subconscious memories of their courting ritual in the summer garden, and that made them happy again."

Chip's knee had been sliding toward the floor. He reached into his pocket for the ring box. "Happiness. That's what I want for . . ."

Another voice halted his proposal. "Ah, here you are! I've been searching everywhere for you."

They looked up to see Tate Riddle, son of the producer for the off-Broadway show where Zoe now prepared to play the lead. In two weeks, the show would open. Tate was the publicist.

"Look, I know I promised you the night off, and I wouldn't bother you, except that one of the major backers is in town. We were hoping to show him the new scene you rehearsed today."

Zoe looked at Chip. The light still shown in her eyes, but he could tell her attention had shifted. This was her big break. He needed to be supportive.

"Of course," he said without enthusiasm.

Zoe looked at Tate. "It will take thirty minutes at most, wouldn't you say?"

Tate checked his watch. "Well . . ."

Tossing his napkin on the table, Chip gave her a break. "We'll get together another night." He leaned over meaning to kiss her lips but connected with her cheek instead as she looked at Tate.

"And I'll promise no interruptions then." Tate raised his hand solemnly and smiled.

But you're no boy scout, Chip thought as he watched Tate curve his arm behind Zoe's back to escort her out. Then Tate used his free hand to slap the back of his neck.

"Finally got that annoying gnat that's been buzzing around my ear!" Tate laughed and held the door so Zoe could exit.

If only Chip could smash Tate away as Tate had done with the gnat.

Like a wistful pet watching its masters leave home, Chip followed them to the sidewalk where a chauffeur stood holding the limo's back door for Zoe and Tate. After Zoe slid in, Tate said something to the chauffeur before scooting into the backseat next to Zoe. The chauffeur looked back at Chip before departing.

Chip returned to the restaurant. Heading into the kitchen, he found his boss working at a counter.

At almost six feet, Idunn's definitively straight posture gave her a striking appearance. She looked ready to be cast in stone as the Norse goddess Idunn whose apples ensured youth. She wore tie-died gowns like a new age healer. Her long purple and gray braid coiled around the back of her head while the bangs in front remained spiky, creating an unexpected halo effect. All illusion. When she spoke, she emerged as a shrewd, no nonsense, cut-to-the-chase businesswoman.

"So," Idunn asked. "How did Zoe answer?"

"I didn't get to ask the question."

Reaching into a wooden box stocked with her preferred Golden Delicious apples, Idunn took out and rinsed two, then began chopping them into inch-sized pieces. "What stopped you?

"Tate showed up to take her to a meeting with a backer."

Shaking her head, she waved aside a server who had appeared with a champagne bottle in an ice bucket. "Just put it back in the fridge," she said. Returning her attention to the apple, she completed the last slice with a *thunk* before sticking the tip of the knife into the board. She picked up a chunk of apple and chewed it thoughtfully. "You have to commit to action. Otherwise, Zoe will always slip through your fingers."

He shrugged. "How can I stand in the way of her career?"

Idunn took up the knife and made a few more strategic whacks. "Then, let her go."

"But I love her!"

"Then ask her to marry you."

"I want the setting to be right."

"You want her to tell that damned cucumber story, which, by the way, means more to you than to her. By the time she gets around to it, something always intervenes."

He smiled. "She loves that story."

"But does she love you?"

He had to think about that a moment. "I hope so."

Idunn smirked. "Why don't you use her precious sense memory to conjure up a moment when she was totally devoted to you?"

As he left that night, munching on one of the Golden Delicious apples, Chip looked up at the restaurant's roof. At the top of a long pole, an electric star, composed of rows of tiny bulbs, remained lit and glistening against the night sky. "Loki's Torch," Idunn's poet husband had called it. Idunn explained that the phrase referred to the actual star, Sirius, which had been her inspiration for the roof design.

Chip took another bite of his apple as he gazed at the twinkling fixture. Slowly, its shape became taller, more like a giant tower reaching into the night sky toward the moon. He felt as if he were transported back in time, to an evening in Paris when he and Zoe strolled along the *Champ de Mars*, watching the lights of the Eiffel Tower, taking in the sights and aromas of the River Seine.

He felt someone grab his elbow and pull him back toward the restaurant. A car screeched past them hurtling down the street.

A voice intruded. "Wow! You are one lucky dude!"

Still focused on his memory, Chip agreed. "I am."

"No, man. I mean to be alive."

Chip blinked. A co-worker, the one who had the bottle of champagne on ice, stood beside him.

"That car came out of nowhere and almost mowed you down. Didn't you see it?"

Chip shook his head. "I was lost in thought, I guess."

"Take it easy, man," the co-worker warned him, patting him on the shoulder. "Don't leave me to face our knife-toting boss alone."

"I'll try not to," Chip promised laughing. "Thanks for the assist." He took one last look at the star on the roof just as its lights went dark.

The driver had sped a few blocks beyond the designated spot and jerked into an empty park. *How could I have missed? The guy, with attention on the sky and taking no notice of surroundings, had been right in the middle of the car's headlights. An easy hit and run. I'm just not cut out for this.*

When the phone rang, he snapped it up. "Yeah?"

"Is it done?"

The driver sighed. "No."

"What happened?"

"That's the crazy thing. I had him in my sights, bearing down on him. Then, suddenly, he was gone, just disappeared."

"Look, you've been paid well. The job needs to be done. By tomorrow night at the latest. Other things are depending upon it."

"I'm doing my best, Mr. Riddle."

"Well, you've got to do more. Finish it. Tomorrow night."

Throughout the next day, Chip thought about Idunn's challenge to use sense memory to ensure Zoe accepted his proposal. He kept remembering the times he and Zoe went on picnics in Paris, with baskets of bread and butter, salt and radishes, and an affordable fine wine. After patronizing a number of bakeries, they discovered the most delectable baguettes came from a place by the theater where Zoe interned.

Arriving early for his shift at The Norse Star the next evening, Chip told Idunn how heavenly the bread had been. Crispy on the outside, soft inside, and slathered with butter.

"Then, make some bread," Idunn advised.

"I could never duplicate it."

"Order a shipment. If it's that good, we'll serve it here."

He shook his head. "The shop went out of business."

She gave him the look of a whaler ready to throw the harpoon. He figured he was the target.

"I'm sorry," he said. "I've been trying your patience with my personal problems . . ."

"You'll assist me serving the Hollowells' anniversary dinner tonight," she told him.

A welcome surprise he interpreted as her vote of confidence in his skills. She had always been extremely protective of Earl and Mollie Hollowell, her first clients and great patrons of The Norse Star. The rest of the staff laughingly referred to them as Thurston and Lovey, from *Gilligan's Island*, but no one would use those names within Idunn's hearing.

When the Hollowells arrived, Chip followed Idunn to their table, remaining completely solicitous and in the background. Although the Hollowells looked a bit like the television couple, they had kind, generous, and courteous natures.

"Dear Idunn," Mollie said, looking up at her. "Have you prepared our special dessert?"

"How could I not?" Idunn replied, gesturing for Chip to follow her.

They returned to the kitchen. She stopped to place an apple from the bin in her apron pocket and handed one to Chip.

"Stay close, put this in your pocket, don't speak, and do your best not to come into contact with anyone you see."

He did as she requested and followed her.

Entering the pantry, they passed by its shelves to the back wall covered in aprons hanging from pegs. On one side, there was a small fuse box Idunn reached to unlatch.

When she opened the box's door, Chip saw it wasn't for fuses, but had a computerized digital panel with space for inputting year, month, day, time, and location. Idunn typed in the information and pushed the aprons to one side. A portal materialized, opening to the Hollowells' wedding reception forty-eight years earlier. Idunn entered and Chip followed, taking time to observe the reception table, filled with lovely treats. Behind it stood a very young bride and groom, looking adoringly into each other's eyes, each giving the other a tidbit of cake.

"Don't let them see you," Idunn snapped at him.

They reached the kitchen and she motioned for him to keep to the wall. In a few moments, a waiter brought in the top layer of the wedding cake, then moved away, leaving it unattended. Quickly, Idunn snatched it and motioned with her head for Chip to follow. They retraced their steps to The Norse Star's pantry.

Idunn handed the layer of cake to him as she secured the portal and relatched the box. Then, she took the cake, made her way into the kitchen, and added some personalized touches to the icing.

"Get plates, forks, and a cutting knife," she said.

Before heading back to the dining room, she discarded the apple from her pocket. Chip noticed it had become wizened, like a miniature, prune-faced elder. He flinched as she reached into his pocket, then watched as she withdrew and tossed away another shrunken, crinkled fruit.

"Only one trip per apple. Let's go celebrate an anniversary."

Back in the dining room, without a word, Idunn placed the cake before the Hollowells. Chip set out the plates and forks and handed Idunn the knife. Mollie clapped her hands.

"The stolen top layer of our wedding cake."

"Now, Mollie," Earl said. "Theft was never proven. I'm sure it was just misplaced in all that was happening that night."

Mollie's eyes were misty with tears. "Aunt Trudy, who selected the cake herself and paid for our wedding reception, was furious we couldn't serve that missing top layer at our first anniversary. She said it doomed our union." Mollie reached to take Earl's hand. "But she was wrong, wasn't she?"

He squeezed her fingers. "Indeed, she was."

Mollie turned to Idunn. "How you could possibly replicate it is an amazement to me!"

"You described it well," Idunn replied as she cut the slices.

As Chip handed him a slice, Earl said, "The gift that just keeps giving."

Mollie cut a small bite of her cake to offer to Earl and he did the same. Both closed their eyes and concentrated on the flavor.

"Exactly the same, isn't it?" Mollie said.

"Just so," Earl replied.

"Please enjoy," Idunn told them. "The rest is for you to take home."

When they returned to the kitchen, Chip asked, "Did you change history?"

"They came to me with the story about the stolen cake."

Chip began pondering the timeline continuum. "But, what about the real thief?"

Idunn shrugged. "If it wasn't me, he's had his cake and eaten it, too, hasn't he?"

"How can you be certain? Maybe you snatched it before he did."

She reached for an apple from the box. "It's all lost in the sands of time."

"But, if you changed history . . ."

"Well, if I have, aren't we better for it? What the Hollowells thought they'd forever lost, returns anew each year." She took a bite of the apple. "Not a bad day's work."

"But . . ." Chip couldn't even express all the "what ifs."

Idunn pointed her apple toward him. "You can use the same method to procure the bread you and Zoe loved for a perfect proposal. Just remember to take an apple with you."

"Why?"

She gave him the whaler aiming harpoon stare again. "I'm not ready to reveal all my secrets to you. Yet. Suffice to say, the apple takes on the aging process, not to mention keeping any foods you retrieve from the past fresh."

The back door to the kitchen opened and Idunn's poet husband, Ymir Yngvar Bragg, entered, carrying his mandolin case. He kissed her on the cheek and said, "The crowd was floating on the waves of my words tonight. Never had a group so copacetic."

"And did their tips reflect their overflowing joy with your phraseology?" Idunn asked.

From behind Idunn, Bragg put down his case. He drew his arms around her and snuggled his beard against the place where her neck and shoulder met. "Darling beloved, lover-friend, how can you measure a moment of inspiration in coin and bills?"

"Very easily when it goes to fill my pocket and feed my stomach."

"Chip, are you such a challenge for your artiste?" Bragg asked.

"Probably," Chip replied.

"We're leaving now," Idunn informed them, tossing her half-eaten apple into the trash can. She slipped from Bragg's embrace and walked toward the back door, reaching for her shawl on its peg before exiting.

Bragg picked up his case, winked at Chip, and counselled, "Keep your chin up, man," before following her out.

Chip eyed the apple Idunn had discarded. What did he have to lose? Walking over to the wooden box, he picked out a luscious Golden Delicious. As he rinsed it, he calculated a date and time he and Zoe would have been together in Paris. Wiping the apple on his apron, then placing it in a pocket, he approached the pantry, entered, and unlatched the box. The information Idunn had typed in gleamed back at him.

He was ready to input his calculations when he heard Zoe's voice in the kitchen.

"I've got to talk with Chip. Have you seen him?"

A coworker replied, "He was heading for the pantry the last time I saw him."

Seeing the pantry door opening, Chip pushed aside the line of aprons, hoping to hide behind them. He forgot that he left the box open with its information from the last journey pulsing. As he pulled the aprons back as a shield, he fell through the open portal.

Landing on his hands and knees, he saw the carpet from the Hollowells' wedding reception hall beneath him. A female voice from a figure looming above commented, "How disgraceful. I certainly will report that staff was clumsy and very probably intoxicated on the job. And I shall demand that the cake fee be discounted accordingly."

Chip kept his face down. He remembered Idunn's warning: don't let them see you.

Young Mollie Hollowell called from across the room. "Aunt Trudy, I'm sure he just took a tumble. Come over and speak with Earl's family."

He felt Aunt Trudy's bulk moving away. It took a moment for him to get his bearings, to stand and look for the way out. Without Idunn guiding him, he felt discombobulated. Instead of retracing his steps to the restaurant, he ended up in the reception's kitchen. There, he came face-to-face with young Earl Hollowell, holding the top layer of the wedding cake.

Earl looked as horrified as Chip felt as they faced each other.

"You won't tell, will you?" Earl begged. "It tasted bad enough this evening. I can't imagine it will improve in a year."

"I suppose not," Chip stuttered.

"Please take it away. Don't make us ever have to eat it again."

"Okay."

Earl shoved the cake into Chip's hands, then struggled to reach the back pocket of his wedding trousers. "I'm forever indebted to you." He managed to find and open his wallet.

"No, sir, please no tip," Chip said. "It's my wedding present to you."

Earl's face relaxed into a smile. "I'll be owing you."

"Just keep your wife's Aunt Trudy preoccupied while I escape."

"That I can do."

Somehow, Chip found his way back to the portal, hiding the cake he carried. When he reached the pantry, he listened carefully. Entering the kitchen, he realized the restaurant was closed and discarded the cake in the trash.

Now he had found his nerve, he might as well return to get the bread. He entered the pantry, put his date and time calculations into the box, and pushed aside the row of aprons. Through the portal, he saw the Paris of his memories.

He arrived at the end of the day, not wanting to get a loaf of bread destined for a paying customer but hoping to snatch a remaining unsold loaf. He avoided detection, but still worried that what he procured was stolen from the mouths of a hungry family. Guilt had made him bring a handful of French euro coins left over from his internship trip. He'd planned to keep them as "seed money" for his next journey there, but he didn't want stolen bread to be the basis for his proposal. He placed an amount on the counter to pay for the bread.

As he left the shop, he passed by the courtyard to the theater and heard Zoe's voice. Her audition monologue. Leaning against the surrounding brick wall, he listened, captivated as always by her talent, knowing the moment well, even though he had not been present when it occurred. As she finished, he heard applause, then Tate said, "Isn't she exactly the actress you've been looking for to star in your next production, Dad?"

"I think you've picked a winner for me, son."

Zoe's gratitude spilled out like the inside of baked brie oozing from a puffed pastry. "Thank you, thank you, a million times thank you." Chip imagined her giving each man an extended hug and hated hearing their chuckles in response.

"Do you mind if I tell my boyfriend?" she asked.

Tate replied, "As long as it goes no further. We'll want to release information to the press strategically, as the show is in production."

"We can keep it secret," Zoe assured him.

Chip turned away as he heard the gate open. Zoe danced through on her way to see him. Fortunately, she headed in the opposite direction. His heart soared. In the moment it took before he was ready to depart, he heard Tate's Dad say, "She has the incandescent happiness down. I'm not so sure she'll be as believable portraying the grief."

"Don't worry, Dad. She's a big believer in this sense memory concept. I'm sure I can help her find an instance of grief from her own life that she can use to create the same emotion nightly on stage."

"Well, I bought your way into the internship so you could follow her here. I hope it taught you enough to be worth me taking a gamble on her in a starring role."

"You can count on it. It's sad really, but that boyfriend she adores will soon be out of the picture and his going will be the most devastating loss in her young life."

"Huh." Tate's Dad grunted. "Just don't return her to joy too soon by being there to pick up the pieces."

Chip's heart was pulsing like a blender. The adrenaline propelled him forward. Somehow, he returned to the portal and stumbled back into The Norse Star's kitchen. His legs were wobbly and his balance off kilter. He grabbed for the corner of a prep table. Gazing down at its stainless-steel finish, he saw the face of a very old man staring back at him. That was the last thing he remembered before collapsing.

When he woke, he found himself stretched out on the sofa in Idunn's office. She wouldn't let him talk until he downed two giant mugs of her hot apple juice.

Finally, when he was able to speak, he asked, "The bread?"

"It's a pile of crumbs where you fell on it."

"How did that happen?"

"Did you take an apple?"

"Yes, but I made two journeys."

Idunn listened as he explained about the mistaken return to the Hollowells' reception. She sighed. "One apple to a trip, I'm afraid. The apple juice has restored you to your youthful self, but there wasn't anything I could do for the bread."

Chip had no time to retrace his steps. The lunch crowd was arriving, including the happy Hollowells. Chip took a moment to check his face in the mirror, then changed into a new apron to take a tray with the Hollowells' order. On his way to their table, he noticed that Zoe and Tate were dining as well. Zoe looked up from her menu. Chip saw a warning in her eyes.

He meant to serve the Hollowells quickly so he could go to her, but Earl Hollowell recognized him.

"You're . . ."

Chip saw the fear in his eyes.

"He's the nice young man who assisted Idunn with our anniversary dinner," Mollie said.

"No." Earl began shaking his head. "He reminds me of someone I haven't seen since our wedding reception."

"Really?" Mollie looked pleased. "Do you think he could be related? Where are you from, young man?"

Before Chip could answer, Earl interrupted. "Mollie, I have to admit something to you. I took the top layer of our wedding cake. It was so awful. I didn't want it to sour our marriage by having to taste it again."

Mollie reached across the table to grasp his hand. "Oh, Earl, I hated it, too! I just told Idunn about it because I thought it was meaningful to you."

Earl reached to take her hand and give it a kiss. "It was, dearest. It meant we were free from your Aunt Trudy's schemes to separate us."

"Oh, Earl, you old romantic! Let's tell Idunn to never serve it to us again!"

"I can do that," Chip said. He put down their plates and turned only to bump into Zoe.

"Sweetheart, thank God you're all right!" She threw her arms around him.

At that moment, the police entered the restaurant. Zoe pointed to Tate Riddle. "Officers, I overheard a phone conversation where this man was arranging a hit and run accident to injure my boyfriend."

Tate tried to laugh the matter off, but Chip's co-worker spoke up about the car that barely missed Chip the night before. The co-worker thought it might have been a limo.

Several weeks later, Chip and Zoe were sharing wine and a baguette in Central Park, talking about all that had happened. Tate's father had arrived on the scene quickly and convinced the authorities it had been a publicity stunt gone wrong. After arranging for Tate to spend the next year cleaning stables on a dude ranch, he began promoting the show himself, ensuring he got credit for discovering Zoe and making her a star. Meanwhile, Idunn was giving Chip more responsibility at The Norse Star.

"What made you so brave, darling?" Chip asked.

"I remembered all those picnics in Paris, eating that delicious bread, feeling like we could do anything, as long as we remained together." She took a bite of the baguette. "You know, this tastes remarkably like what we purchased from the Paris bakery beside the theater."

Chip reached for the ring box and got on one knee. "I want to ask you a question."

MAN OF HIS WORD

Christopher D. Ochs

The automatic door slid open, and Chief Greg DeLanzo strode into Sioux Center's city morgue. His nostrils wrinkled from the hint of formaldehyde. The medical examiner paced like a sulking schoolchild between bright, stainless-steel sinks and a row of black filing cabinets. Greg raised an eyebrow, relishing the opportunity to needle the station's curmudgeon.

"What's the problem, Stanzy? One of your patients complaining again?"

"*If* you please, Chief DeLanzo," he shot back through gritted teeth, "It's 'Dr. Stanson' when entertaining official visitors." He unfolded his arms and nodded his head toward a dark movement in Greg's peripheral vision. "This gentleman says he's from the FBI. He wants to review my reports and examine the body from the Route 75 case." He folded his arms again, leaning against the filing cabinets, blocking their access. "Trouble is, he doesn't have any of the proper paperwork. And on *this* case, I want to see the paperwork."

The man in the far corner occupied himself with scrutinizing a freshly cleaned examination table. He straightened and faced Greg with an easy smile under piercing, no-nonsense hazel eyes, an aquiline nose, and pencil mustache.

"Good afternoon, Chief DeLanzo. I'm Special Agent Peter Freud." The glimmer of the visitor's grin vanished as he ambled over. His lanky frame flowed with the grace of a leaf on a lazy river. He planted himself between DeLanzo and Stanson. From within his suit, under a trench coat spattered with rain, Freud produced an open billfold displaying his badge and identification. "Regional Director Harrington should have notified you to expect me. The message must have gotten lost along the way."

Greg craned his neck forward to inspect the ID. "And a good afternoon to you, Agent Peter C. Freud, from . . . Special Profiles Division?" He squinted at the photograph showing hair slightly less tousled than that of the person in front of him. "How is Harrington doing? I haven't seen him since the Northwest Bank case."

"Other than a nasty cough, I really couldn't say," said Freud, snapping his badge shut at Stanson and slipping it back into his suit. "I caught the red-eye from DC and only spoke to Director Harrington during the drive here. If you check your email, I'm sure you'll find the 'paperwork' is in order."

"Sounds like Harrington still hasn't kicked his two pack-a-day habit." Greg scoffed to himself and nodded at Stanson. "Relax, Agent Freud. I checked my email after Stanzy phoned me. The notification from the Sioux City FBI office was there."

Stanson unlatched his arms but didn't unscrew his frown. A harsh yank on the end cabinet's top drawer, and he served up a folder inches from Freud's nose.

The agent's smarmy grin reappeared as he leafed through the report's pages.

"Special Profiles, eh?" said Greg. "I knew this case was going to be a royal pain, but I didn't expect it to raise eyebrows at the local FBI, let alone any muckity-mucks in Washington." He raised his hands in mock protest. "Don't get me wrong. Frankly, I'd be glad for the FBI to take this nightmare off my hands."

"Not until I verify some details," said Freud, his eyes flitting over the report. He closed the folder with a slap and shook his head. "This is much the same as the preliminaries our team received last night." He strolled over to the wall with three stainless steel doors. "May I see the body, please?"

Greg glanced at Stanson, who still aimed his glower at the intruder commandeering his domain. "Would you do the honors, Doctor?" He extended his arm as though he were inviting a date on the dance floor.

Stanson steamed across the room and heaved open the center hatch. Cold air spilled out of the opening and rolled around their feet as he trundled out the tray holding a shrouded body.

With a resolute expression that betrayed that he had seen this too many times, Freud snapped on a pair of latex gloves and flipped the toe tag. He took out his cellphone, tapped a short tarantella on the screen and placed it and Stanson's reports next to the cadaver's covered head. In a clinical tone, he spoke in the direction of the phone. "Jane Doe, Sioux Center, Iowa. Body discovered north of town on a private access road intersecting Route 75, one day prior. Time of death, two days prior."

After peeling the morgue sheet down to the neck, he twitched his needle-thin lips into a sliver of a frown. Leaning over the young woman's face framed by shoulder-length auburn hair, he scrutinized the cuts that spoiled otherwise perfect high cheekbones. "Confirmed, initials 'M' and 'R' carved into cheeks of the deceased."

Greg stood at the foot of the table, his thumbs hooked into his pants pockets. "There are no missing persons in Sioux or surrounding counties that match her description. And we checked the alibis for any locals with a rap sheet and those initials."

Exhaling a tired sigh, Freud lowered the covering to the woman's navel. Angry red slices in a goblet shape, ran from each shoulder joint, below the breasts to join at the sternum, proceeding straight down the length of her torso. Small holes puckered the skin between each suture holding the cuts closed. "I take it these incisions are not yours, doctor."

Stanson slipped into a professional manner to match Freud's. "Correct, although they follow standard autopsy procedures. They were executed by a professional's hand—no hesitation wounds. When closing, I avoided the puncture points from the original sutures."

Freud lifted the woman's shoulder, then examined the underside of one buttock. "Lividity indicates that the victim remained in a supine position after death." He ruffled through the papers in the folder, stopping at the biopsy details. "You're sure the incisions were antemortem?"

"Yes, there was swelling around the exterior incisions." Stanson swallowed. "Interior incisions as well, during the removal of the organs. Most of them, anyway. Before she succumbed to the vivisection."

DeLanzo's gut shuddered from the pit of acid forming in it.

Freud handed the folder back to Stanson. The agent prodded the left and right sides of the woman's abdomen from the rib cage down to the pelvis. He halted, then probed below her right rib cage a second time. He faced Stanson, his frown a little more pronounced. "Curious. You put the organs back in their proper locations. You *did* bag them before returning them to the thoracic cavity, didn't you?"

"Of course. That's standard procedure. I merely thought I'd afford her some small level of dignity, after what she suffered." Stanson's chin stiffened, baring his lower teeth. "Don't worry. I recorded the locations where they were found upon opening. Heart on the right, liver on the left, and so on. In short, the killer moved each internal organ to its mirror image side."

"Yes, I noted that," said Freud.

Greg shook his head, silencing the argument between his ears. Though he hoped to hand this case over to the feds, he yearned to dispense some Midwest-style justice on the psycho who tortured this poor woman.

"Dr. Stanson, you list the cause of death as a homicide, though I note you haven't signed off on the final report yet."

"Yes, we're still waiting for the toxicology analysis. We don't have the facilities. I sent blood and tissue samples off to Sioux City's ME lab."

Freud retrieved his phone from the table. "All right. I'll see if I can expedite the work." Freud turned to Greg and squinted. Crow's feet emphasized his bloodshot eyes. "Chief DeLanzo, do you have photos of the crime scene, or do we have to wait for the local Fotomat to develop them?" His jaw clicked shut with a sardonic bite.

Greg smirked at the shot across his bow. It had been a long day, and he didn't have patience for the high-handedness for which the feds had a reputation. Resisting the temptation to get into a pissing contest, he deflected the jibe with one of his own. "You sure you don't know Harrington? You sound an awful lot like him, but without the cough." His gaze locked on Freud, he asked Stanson, "You don't mind if I use your computer, Doc?"

Not waiting for a reply, Greg entered the side office and commandeered the chair. After a half minute doing battle with the keyboard, a parade of photographs popped up on the screen. He turned the screen toward Freud, shoved the mouse in his direction, and settled back in the chair. "Farmer Vanderberg nearly ran over her burial site while driving his harvester to his western fields," said Greg. Rocking back and forth, he interlaced his fingers while he watched the agent.

Freud's face, bathed in bluish screen light, was a study in concentration. His latex gloves seemed to glow like living neon. He clicked away, pausing at the occasional closeups of the shallow grave, and making verbal notes in his phone. "Body covered with quantities of lime, wrapped in a hardware store plastic tarp."

Click. "Surrounding ground raked to remove footprints."

Click-click. He tilted his head at the new screen shot. "Uncharacteristic deviation. Depth of grave, only four to six inches."

Click. "Body covered with similar amount of topsoil."

Click-click. Freud stopped at the full body shot.

Jane Doe lay naked on her back, ghostly white from a generous covering of lime. Small clumps stuck to the cuts on her cheeks and torso. Her hands were positioned flat to cover her genitalia. "Positioning of body matches MO."

Greg stopped rocking. "The body was scrubbed from head to toe before burial. Even with the lime, we still caught a whiff of bleach under the tarp. Whoever is responsible, they were quite thorough."

"So, no DNA or other forensics on the perp?"

"Afraid not. No stray hair or fibers."

Freud set the mouse next to the keyboard. "Did you find any paper? A business card, greeting card, any card stock with the body?"

Greg jerked his head straight, cocking one eyebrow. "Like I said, nothing."

Setting his bony shoulders square, Freud stuffed his cell phone into his trench coat and met Greg's inquisitive stare. "Take me to the crime scene, if you would."

Greg stood with an amiable nod. "Sure. What paper were you expecting?"

Freud turned his back on Stanson, who lingered outside the office in a clumsy attempt to appear busy. "Better if we discuss it along the way. Mind if you drive? Normally I would follow you to the site, but I'm exhausted. Our team burned the midnight oil when we received the notification about this case. In addition to that, I'm the type that cannot sleep on flights."

Exiting the morgue, Freud was about to rub his bloodshot eyes. With a click of his tongue, he said, "See? That's how tired I am, Chief DeLanzo. I almost forgot." He yanked off his latex gloves, lobbing them into a passing yellow bin, rolled along by one of the janitorial staff starting second shift.

Route 75 sliced due north through the center of the city. At a stoplight, Greg picked up the cruiser's radio mic. "Jannsen? What's your 101?" He drummed the steering wheel in time with the crosswalk countdown.

"10-106, Chief. Site is secure. Though Vanderberg's ticked that he has to drive his equipment five miles out of the way using the next access road."

"10-4, Jannsen. Ten minutes on-site ETA."

The moment Greg clipped the mic in its cradle, he sat straight in his seat, energized with anticipation of getting to the meat of the matter bugging him. The signal turned green. "Now, what's so important that you didn't want Stanson to overhear? It seemed like you already knew what the toxicology report would contain."

"No reflection on the good doctor. But until I verify my team's suspicions, the fewer who know, the better. I'm telling you now, so that you don't spend your time trying to second guess me. I expect the report to show cu-rare. In concentrations low enough to keep her conscious, but immobile."

Greg rapped his knuckles on the wheel. "I *knew* this case was going to be a headache. When a federal profiler shows up one day after the weirdest case I've ever seen, it doesn't take an Einstein to guess that you're tracking a serial killer."

"Correct. The portion of your reports we received had all the earmarks of our target. What ruled this case out as a copycat was Stanson's descrip-tion of the reversed organs. That is a detail that has never been released to the press. The Bureau will rely on your staff to ensure that it remains so." Freud pulled a paperback from his pocket. He thumbed through it while he continued. "The letters 'MR' carved into Jane Doe's cheeks indeed are initials, but not of a person's name. They refer to the killer's *nom de guerre*—Mengele Reborn."

"Mengele?" Greg's forehead corrugated when his eyebrows stood at attention. "The Nazi doctor?"

"Yes." Freud turned a page in his book, then rubbed his chin. "MR, like his namesake, is a doctor, or at least possesses a surgeon's skill. And like Mengele, he exhibits a fascination with identical twins."

"Twins? *That's* why you want to visit the crime scene." He slapped his palm on the steering wheel again, adding an exclamation point to his deduction. "You think there's a second body."

"Correct." Freud glanced away from his booklet, regarding Chief DeLanzo with a wry grin. "My colleagues have a somewhat low opinion of law enforcement in Iowa." He returned his attention to his reading and turned a page. "I must remember to inform them they are mistaken."

Greg chortled softly. "If that's your version of a compliment, I'll take it."

He brought the car to a halt at the last stoplight in town. "I can assure you, our techs scoured the surrounding acre looking for evidence. They couldn't have missed a second burial mound."

"Let's not jump to any conclusions yet. If I find what I'm looking for, I'll let you know."

"Is MR a blood relation to the 'Angel of Death'?"

"That was the first thing we checked. Mengele had a direct descen-dant in Chicago. His family spread across the nation over the years. Even though they all had alibis for the first set of murders, we double check their whereabouts with every new case." He ran a finger up and down his booklet several times, nodded his head and turned the page. "Don't you want to ask about the *other* family relation?"

"'Scuse me?"

"The question you've been nursing ever since my ID piqued your interest."

"Oh, *that*." Greg chuckled. "Since we've already touched on initials, I was wondering what the 'C' stood for—what your middle name was." The light turned and Greg gunned the engine. "I'm willing to bet it's Carl."

Freud lowered the book and regarded Greg with a mild bemusement. "Really? My *middle* name? Most new acquaintances ask about my surname, and if I have any famous relatives. The answer to the usual question is 'No, I'm not related to Dr. Sigmund.'" With a shake of his head, he brought the book close, his prodigious nose threatening to become a bookmark. "As for C, it's not an initial. C *is* my middle name, kind of like 'Harry S Truman.'"

"What kind of parents would give their kid a letter for a middle name?" said Greg through an incredulous smile.

"A father who was concerned about his family history. Despite our family name's reputation, mental illness had a tendency to skip a generation along my father's lineage. He wanted my middle name to be 'See.' As in, 'Peter, go and see Dr. Freud.' It was his best attempt at fatherly advice in case the Freud recessive gene manifested itself in me. But Mother would have none of Father's nonsense, so they compromised on the letter C." He turned another page in the paperback.

DeLanzo shook his head with a twitch. Pushing a wisecrack about family skeletons into a cubbyhole, he decided on a much safer remark. "Sorry I asked."

At the city limits, the cement road turned to asphalt. The hum of the tires dropped several decibels. Greg felt the urge to fill the relative silence. "How can you read in the car? Lotsa people get motion sickness after the first mile."

"I'm not reading, *per se*. Merely doing puzzles. It helps me relax."

Greg craned his neck and glanced over the front cover facing him. The pages inside were devoid of any written marks. "Hunh. I half expected it to be filled . . . in pen."

"I find it more of a challenge doing them in my head."

Greg rolled his eyes. "Why am I not surprised?" he mumbled.

Freud closed the booklet and tucked it back in his trench coat. He held his chin up a notch, exuding pride in his quirk. "Crosswords, acrostics, cryptograms, Sudoku . . . I go through a book like this in a day. I picked this one up at Reagan National, and I'm almost finished with it. My Achilles' heel, however, is anagram puzzles. Jumble, Wordoku . . . for some reason, I'm helpless against those." With a yawn, he added, "My apologies. I tend to ramble when I'm tired. I didn't mean to bore you with family history and personal idiosyncrasies."

DeLanzo felt the sudden urge to mitigate the awkward moment. "My colleagues think all feds are stuck up bureaucrats." His cheek bunched up with a half-grin. "I must remember to inform them they are mistaken."

Freud snorted with a mirrored expression. Mimicking Greg's Midwest drawl, he said, "If that's your version of a compliment, I'll take it."

Ubiquitous corn fields gave way to a parcel of land covered with wild-flowers, weeds tall as trees, and a host of noxious plants that would give a landscaper nightmares. Passing a pair of yellow metal posts, the cruiser slowed and took a sharp left turn. A rutted path meandered down the center of a wide, scrubby strip trimmed down to a mere foot. A dull red sun, low above the horizon, peeked between the approaching march of threatening clouds.

Past the first gentle hillock stood a pair of large white and orange sawhorses supporting hazard blinkers. A county police SUV cruiser hunkered between them, blocking the lane. An officer clambered out of the driver's side door and donned his hat.

Greg and Freud exited their car the moment its engine stopped. "Jannsen, this is Special Agent Freud. He wants to go over the crime scene again. Afford him every courtesy. He's an okay Joe."

Jannsen regarded Freud with his chin dug into his chest, a sure sign he was struggling with his ingrained skepticism. "How did Doc weigh in?"

"About as cranky as when he first sized you up," said DeLanzo.

"That bad, huh?"

Jannsen took the lead, turning left over the next rise. The trio entered a semi-circular clearing about twenty feet in diameter. Ringed by wooden stakes and yellow police tape, the region was carpeted with plants pressed flat by the passage of an army of shoes and boots.

Freud surveyed the grounds, snapping on another pair of latex gloves as he approached the grave site. Depressions in the ground along the way marked where a generator and light standards once stood. "Is there a shovel handy?"

"In my trunk," said Jannsen. "I'll fetch it."

Freud paced around the shallow grave. He halted every few steps to stick his index finger into the damp soil. Jannsen, a little winded soon rejoined them with a folding shovel in hand.

Jannsen handed the implement to the agent, who counted off five paces to the north and dug. Freud didn't break a sweat, despite his needing to break the soil, by placing his full weight on the upper lip of the blade.

Greg huffed out a small harrumph at Jannsen's and his own pants cuffs, wreathed with Virginia stickseed burrs, compared to Freud's seemingly untouchable bespoke suit.

"At least he had the foresight not to wear patent leather shoes with his fancy suit," Jannsen remarked out the side of his mouth.

Once the hole was a foot wide and a few inches deep, Freud stuck his finger into the exposed soil. Or he tried to. The underlying ground was obstinate as hardpan. Returning to Jane Doe's grave, he ran the point of the shovel along the grave's soil. "You stopped digging once Jane Doe was recovered?"

"Of course," replied Greg, trying not to sound indignant.

"Then why is the underlying soil so soft?" With one hand, Freud jammed the entire blade deep into the center of the grave with little effort.

In unison, Greg and Jannsen jumped forward, their palms outstretched. "Whoa!"

Freud stared at them, his expression one of confusion. "Is there a problem?"

"There's a reason we didn't go deeper. The same reason Farmer Vanderberg doesn't plow here." Greg gestured toward the highway. "Didn't you see the yellow markers when we turned off the main drag? There's a natural gas pipeline under here. One of the interstate transmission lines."

"Yes, I saw them." Freud exhaled an exasperated sigh that changed into a stifled yawn. Walking away from the grave, he left the shovel standing where he planted it. His shoulders slumped, and he gritted his teeth to hide another yawn. "It is my understanding that the interstate pipelines are supposed to be buried no less than thirty inches deep."

"On paper. Sometimes they're laid only eighteen inches down if the contractor wasn't on the up and up. Then there's soil erosion, settling, percolation and so on. Dig any deeper than one foot, and you take a big risk, my friend."

Freud pointed to the shovel behind him. A shadow of anger darkened his hazel eyes. "I believe Jane Doe's twin is under here, buried with one of

MR's calling cards—a new lead or one of his taunts. If it's there, and JD2's organs are on the correct sides, our perp is undoubtedly Mengele Reborn, and this becomes a federal case."

"Special Agent Freud," Greg pronounced in measured syllables, "You could be right about Jane Doe Two, and no one would be happier than me to hand this case off to you. But until I get notification from Harrington that the FBI is officially taking the reins, *I'm* calling the shots. And my call is, this is now my active crime scene. We're not digging deeper until the gas company gives us the green light."

Freud sniffed the air. "I don't detect mercaptan."

"Mer-what?" said Jannsen.

"The rotten egg smell," snapped DeLanzo, still glowering at Freud. "They only add that to the local pipelines. So, you couldn't smell a leak even if it was under your feet." Stepping over to the dig, he yanked the shovel out of the ground and lobbed it to Jannsen. Facing Freud, he said in a lower voice, "I'll have a crew out here crack of dawn tomorrow, along with CS techs ready to go the second we get the thumbs up."

Wide columns like rough brushstrokes were falling from the roiling western clouds. Greg glanced at the grave, then back at Freud, re-sizing him up. "Look, it's getting dark, and we have no lights. The rain's heading this way, but the weather calls for clear and sunny tomorrow. Jane Two is going nowhere, and Jannsen will re-secure the site."

The pitter-patter of water on the flattened grasses was joined by the growing chorus of splashes in the wildflowers beyond the clearing. Officer Jannsen shot an annoyed glance skyward. "I have a small tarp in my vehicle."

"Besides, you look like you're ready to collapse where you stand."

Freud peeled off his gloves and raised his right hand. "I give you my word. I will not return to the crime scene without your permission." He pulled out his puzzle book and shielded his face against the increasing drizzle. "Take me back to the station if you please. I'll collect my car, then check in at a local hotel."

The pair made it back to the cruiser in the nick of time. Spatters of drizzle gave way to a continuous drum roll of rain on the car's roof. With a hard right, the cruiser lumbered onto the highway. Greg clicked the windshield wipers from intermittent to constant. Rows of corn did a slow-motion hula in the wind until they abruptly disappeared after a crossroad intersected the single lane highway.

"What hotel are you staying at?" said Greg. "If your reservation's with any of the major chains in town, cancel it. All three of them have a bedbug problem."

He pointed down a second crossroad as it whizzed past. "Down that way's the Amber Land Inn, run by the Van Djik sisters. Sophie runs a tight ship, Mattie keeps the rooms spic 'n' span, and Zoe makes a breakfast stroopwafel that melts in your mouth."

"Enough with the hard sell, Chief DeLanzo. You had me at 'bedbugs'." Freud shook the dampness from his puzzle book and ruffled its pages before tucking it into his trench coat. "I hope I can relax enough to catch a few hours of sleep. All I have left in this book are anagram puzzles."

"If you need help, gimme a call," Greg snickered. "I'm fair to middlin' at Scrabble."

"Hey, Chief," crackled the dispatcher's voice, "Aren't you coming into HQ?"

"Nope, I'm heading to the Amber Land. Freud texted me last night to meet him there after breakfast." He turned his cruiser into the parking lot bordered with tulips of gold and red. "I'm showing up a little early. After all, I haven't had Zoe's stroopwafels for weeks. We'll be at the Jane Doe site in a half hour."

Greg hopped out of his patrol car onto the damp macadam. He exchanged polite waves with a man with thin salt-and-pepper hair, sporting a gray goatee and a pork-pie hat riding high.

The aging gent huffed as he tugged his roll-along luggage behind him then hefted it into the trunk of a white rental car.

Once out of hearing distance, Greg snickered, wondering how anyone could consider such a hat stylish. He swung open the front door to the Amber Land Inn and sauntered in with a sleepy smile.

Sophie Van Djik glanced up from the front desk, a moderate Chesterfield affair with all the accoutrements of business in their proper places. A small picture frame holding a much younger version of Mattie served as a paperweight for her inbox. She returned Greg's smile with one of her own and a nod. "Thanks for sending business our way again, Chief. Mr. Freud was the ideal customer—quiet and a good tipper."

"My pleasure," he responded with a satisfied grin. "The ol' bedbug story reels 'em in every time."

"My word, Greg." A mischievous spark in her eyes glinted at Greg. "Your little white lies are going to catch up with you one day. If a defense lawyer should ever cross examine me as your character witness . . ." She shook her head with a playful smirk.

Greg moseyed past the desk toward the dining room. "So where is our guest? In his room or having Zoe's stroopwafels?"

Sophie cocked her head at Greg unexpectedly. "Mr. Freud checked out a half hour ago."

"What?" Greg blinked with consternation. "That sonofa . . . Did he say where he was headed?" He clutched at his shoulder mic, intending to check in with Jannsen's relief.

"Ja, back to the airport."

Greg halted, clicking off the mic. "The airport? He didn't happen to say why?"

The scent of pine steamrolled over the breakfast aromas from the dining room.

"Oh, good," said a smooth voice from behind. Greg gave a start, twisting to face Mattie. She had maneuvered her cleaning cart, silent as a butterfly, between Greg and the front door.

The youngest of the Van Djiks, she had tied her apron snug to emphasize her hourglass figure. She cocked her hips at Greg as she dug in her apron pocket.

He smiled inwardly at her unflagging efforts to snag his attention. They certainly weren't failing this morning. If only she didn't wear her housekeeping bandanna like a frumpy babushka.

"Maybe you can catch him, and return this to him before his flight," said Mattie, handing Greg a cellphone. "Such a nice gentleman. And so tidy! He left the bathroom cleaner than he found it. He even put down fresh sheets—I could tell, because he made his bed tight with hospital corners, not straight corners like I do." A dainty pout marred her diamond-shaped face. "I only wish he hadn't helped himself to my cleaning closet."

"What do you mean?" asked Greg.

"He took my last bottle of all-purpose cleaner and a container of disinfecting wipes." She adjusted her bandanna as she scoured her mental inventory. "I think he nabbed an apron, too."

"I'll see if I can have an officer run this over to Sioux City, pronto." Greg rapped his thumb against the phone. His radar was knocking on the back door of his consciousness, but his attention, focused on Mattie, didn't want to let it in. "Strange that our meticulous Mr. Freud would forget something so—"

Greg's shoulder mic squawked to life. "Hey, Chief? Hendricks here. the feds just commandeered the Jane Doe site. They're crawling over everything and digging it all up."

"I *knew* it! Freud, you bastard . . ." He shoved the phone into his shirt pocket and clicked on his mic. "Is Agent Freud there?"

"I dunno, what does he look like?"

"Then who took charge? Is Director Harrington there? Put him on."

"Yeah, but he ain't in a talking mood."

Greg flashed Mattie an apologetic expression. "Sorry, Mattie. Duty calls."

Mattie leaned against Sophie's desk, folding her arms and pointing her bosom at Greg. She sighed and cocked an eyebrow at her sister. "What do you think, Sophie? Think I have enough rain checks to trade in for a free dinner?"

"Candlelit, at the very least." Sophie passed sentence by rapping a sheaf of papers on her desk.

With a wave, Greg beat a hasty exit from the lobby. Opening his cruiser door, he slid into the driver's seat. He froze just before turning the ignition key. Disinfectant laced with the tang of pine registered in his nostrils.

He scanned the cruiser interior by the glow of the dome light. A glint of cleaned plastic caught his eye. Taking out his utility flashlight, he flashed its beam across the passenger compartment. The entire seat, shoulder rest and door handle had been wiped down. Streaks of cleaner liquid evaporated before his eyes. An Amber Land Inn bandanna, folded into a swan, occupied the center of the passenger seat.

"When did Mattie manage to do this?"

Greg's radar knocked at the back of his head again. This time, he let it in. Jumping out of the cruiser, he scrambled to the opposite side and ran his light over the outside of the passenger door. The door handle was surrounded by an oval of clean, bordered with remnants of grime left by last night's rain. He jerked up his head and surveyed the parking lot. His cruiser stood alone.

Greg's stomach gurgled with fresh acid. "No, it *couldn't've* been him."

The shoulder mic chirped. "Chief, you better hurry. I think the feds found something."

Piling back into the cruiser, Greg revved the engine to life and screeched his way onto the service road. He flicked on the alert lights and skidded onto Route 75.

"Officer Jannsen," he barked into the cruiser radio's mic. He gunned the cruiser five mile per hour above the speed limit. "Dammit, Jannsen, what's your 10-20?"

"The HQ lot," he squawked. "Jeez, Chief. I just got in. Haven't even had my coffee yet."

"Get your ass to the Sioux City airport. Find and restrain Freud."

"Your fed buddy? What's up, Chief?"

"Just do it! 10-39 all the way, but lights only at the airport."

"On it."

Greg caught the tinny echo of Jannsen's engine roaring to red line over the speaker. He squinted against shafts of morning sun that sliced between the rows of corn.

Another five miles per hour higher.

Greg jumped at a "Dragnet" ring tone blaring from his chest. Digging the phone out of his shirt pocket, he frowned at the "Caller Unknown" message. He thumbed it to answer. "Freud," he snarled, "is that you?"

"I'm afraid you won't be seeing Special Agent Freud again, Chief DeLanzo," growled a voice lowered by an electronic scrambler.

Greg drummed the steering wheel with his thumb. He grimaced, doubt kicking gravel over his deduction back in the parking lot.

"And poor Mattie," the voice teased. "Did you know *she* was a twin?"

Greg's gut contorted into a wrung-out rag. He blocked the urge to yell a string of curses at the phone. "Mengele Reborn, I presume."

"Not to worry, Chief. Mattie shall not be required for my studies. She lost her twin sister in an auto accident over a decade ago." His electronic chuckle sounded like a bear emerging from hibernation. "But you had best hurry to the site. Ham-handed Harrington may destroy my message. One that you might be interested in." The phone flashed its "call ended" panel.

Another ten miles per hour.

A hard left, and the cruiser's tires squealed on dry asphalt before clawing clods of soil and grass, throwing them high above the wheel wells. Jannsen's relief officer flagged Greg down, to prevent him careening into two black vans that had replaced last night's blockade.

Chief DeLanzo exited his cruiser and stormed over the hillock. He was halted by a federal CSI tech in a clean suit. Greg bounced on the balls of his feet and shouted over the tech's shoulder. "Harrington! That you? What the hell are you trying to pull on me? Is Special Agent Freud with you?"

An overweight man in a dark suit, made even darker against his light blue shoe coverings, coughed and ambled toward Greg. The second he crossed the police tape, he lit up a cigarette. "De-e-e-Lanzo, right? Why have you been sitting on our case? We got a priority email from Washington, DC, in the middle of the night. A request from Special Agent Jannsen for a team to immediately exhume a second victim from your crime scene."

"*Agent* Jannsen? You got your wires crossed, Harrington. Jannsen's one of my officers. And I'm not sitting on anything. I tried to hand off the case to Special Agent Freud last night, but he wouldn't officially take it until he confirmed the perp was Mengele Reborn."

"How do you know about . . . Never mind." Harrington's countenance became darker than his suit. "There is no Special Agent Freud. Not in the Sioux City office."

"I know. He flew in from DC yesterday. I saw his badge and the email from your office informing us of his arrival. He's the one who filled me in about MR."

Harrington's eyes flitted back and forth, flickering with a taste of panic. With a lowered voice, he corralled Greg. "Dammit. We detected an unauthorized access on our local network two days ago. We're still trying to determine the severity of the breach." His chest heaved, and he let go a heavy sigh that ended in a hacking cough. "Looks like we were both played by your mystery man. But why?"

Greg's jaw dropped when he spied a suited team digging, shoveling spadefuls of dirt into the bucket of an idling backhoe. "Halt," he shouted. "Stop digging, you morons! There's a gas line under there."

Harrington placed his hand on Greg's shoulder. "Relax, Chief. We got clearance from the utility board, and our land sonar verified the line is thirty-six inches down. Moreover, it confirmed the presence of a second body, right where the fake Jannsen said it would be." He signaled for Greg to follow him to the dig.

They were a few paces from the widened hole when a tech waved to snag Harrington's attention. Through light-blue cloth headgear, she announced, "Director, we have the body. Under the plastic tarp and coated in lime." A second tech stood, holding between thumb and index finger the back portion of an oversized pulp paperback, torn apart down its spine.

The pages were stapled together along with a business card. She gingerly deposited them into a clear evidence bag.

Greg stood close to the dig and leaned over to view the body.

Identical twin, check.

MR on the cheeks, check.

Autopsy-style incisions, check.

Posed with her hands over her genitals, check.

Greg hissed out an empathetic sigh. "If Agent . . . if Freud was on the level, it's definitely MR."

Harrington took the evidence bag from the tech. He examined the contents through the plastic, then offered it to Greg. "What would your 'Agent Freud' make of this?"

DeLanzo accepted the bag. The back cover of a yellowed puzzle magazine was dusted with particles of soil and lime. He flipped it over. The magazine's section of puzzles devoted to anagrams stared at him, blank as the day they were printed. The business card was similarly barren, stamped with but a single line:

```
Mr Peter c freud
```

Greg looked at it suspiciously, then blew a soft raspberry followed by a snort. He shook his head and covered his eyes as his lungs forced out a jittery chuckle.

With a severe frown, Harrington tore the evidence bag out of Greg's hand and scrutinized the card within. "What's so funny?"

"Freud said MR's calling card would be a clue or a taunt. This is both." He inhaled and held his breath until the conflicting urges to scream or laugh out loud were quashed. "And Mengele Reborn called me on the way here. He said this message was for me."

Harrington's neck grew as red as the end of his cigarette. "For you? This has been buried here for three days."

"Don't you get it, Harrington? We've both been had. It's an anagram." Greg held up the bag by one corner in front of Harrington's face. "Freud, or should I say MR, was playing with me, dangling clues in front of me the whole time."

Harrington sputtered out a chain of smoke-filled coughs. "Wait. *You* were face to face with MR? What does he look like?"

"Tall with black hair and mustache. Old and bent over, with a graying goatee and a stupid hat. Take your pick."

"Talk sense, man. How do you know it was Mengele Reborn?"

"This *anagram!*" Greg stabbed his index finger at the business card.

Harrington ground out his butt with his shoe and glared at the card again. He shook his head, then stared at Greg. "Well?"

DeLanzo snatched back the plastic bag. "See the capital letters? There's only two of them. That should be your first clue." After a grunt of impatience, he added, "You still don't see it?"

"Enlighten me."

Greg's finger ran back and forth under the card's solitary line, dancing from letter to letter. He slowly enunciated, "Per . . . fect . . . Mur . . . der."

LAST BUT NOT LEAST

Courtney Annicchiarico

The sun always rose over Galway, Ireland, too early for Imogen's liking. Stretching her leg, she nudged the still sleeping lump of her husband. She snatched it back and held her breath, slowly exhaling when Callum's snoring resumed. Peeling back the covers, she forced herself out of bed. Padding across the floor, pulling on an old pair of overalls as she walked, she harrumphed in the bed's direction.

Standing a safe distance from the sleeping form, Imogen whispered, "Oh, you were such a strapping lad while you wooed me, weren't you, Callum McCallister?" Callum snored grotesquely. "So full of charm and promises until you took me to your bed," she whispered as she lightly touched the fading bruise on her cheek. *Five years of marriage to you has felt like fifteen.* Immy shook herself out of such dark thoughts. *No use dwelling on my fate,* she chastised herself. *'Til death us do part and all that.*

Feeling shameful for her reverie when there was so much work to be done in the morning, Imogen headed down to the kitchen. Yawning heavily, she made tea, let out their border collies and Shetland sheepdogs, and ate a quick breakfast of grilled tomatoes, bacon, and leftover colcannon. After downing her cuppa, Imogen headed out to the sheep shed and the chores that awaited her.

Twenty woolly heads lifted in unison the moment after the door opened. Lazy bleats filled the walls as Imogen visited each stall. "All right," she sighed as they walked past, "let me set to work cleaning up after ye lot." She raised her calloused hands and patted some heads, scratched a few muzzles, and playfully slapped a few backsides. "Go on now and stretch yeer legs a bit. It's a beautiful spring morning and there's a field of grass and forbs just waiting for ye." All the ewes ambled out, leaving Imogen to her work. While bent over a trough, she felt something bump her knee.

"Well, good morning, *a ghrá geal*." Imogen abandoned her work and gathered up the small, orphaned lamb in her arms. "How's my favorite girl?" Aisling laid her head on Imogen's shoulder. Callum had scolded her for bottle feeding the little Galway after its mother died during the lambing. "Give it time," he had said, "and another ewe will care for it." But no other ewe had, and the poor thing hadn't started grazing, so Imogen helped the fragile soul along. Naming her was probably a mistake, Imogen could concede, but it was too late to do anything about that now. Her Aisling had become her pet, she supposed.

"Well, I suppose you can come along with me for a short time. But you know," Imogen said as she fitted Aisling under her arm, "you're gettin' too big for me to be cartin' you around like some wee puppy." Gingerly, she placed the lamb down and it bounced and pranced around Imogen's feet.

At half-past eight, after all the stalls had been mucked and the water troughs refilled, Imogen checked on the rams and then made her way back to the farmhouse. She whistled for their dogs, fed them, and then allowed them to wander among the livestock. Immediately, she saw little Aisling match her pace, step by step, with one of the collies. "Maybe you are a puppy after all," she mused before going inside.

The house was quiet. All she wanted to do was settle down to her knitting, but Callum came lumbering down the stairs just as Imogen was removing her boots.

"Ahh, there you are, Immy. Are you settin' to make us breakfast?"

Can't say that I am, you lazy buffoon. An image of Callum's shocked face popped into Imogen's head and the giggle escaped before she could stifle it. She yanked off her second boot and smiled broadly "Of course. What did you think, man? Fairies would make your breakfast?" Imogen willed her smile to stay in place, even deepened it so it reached her eyes, as Callum glared. *Please, please, please believe that's why I laughed.*

Callum smiled back. Imogen raced around the kitchen, gathering ingredients and cooking his eggs and hash. "It will take some time, love. Why don't ye go hop in the shower while I cook?"

"Good idea," Callum said, but there was something in his tone that chilled Imogen. Twenty-five minutes later, Imogen served her husband. She placed the dish and a steaming mug in front of him and quickly hid her trembling hands behind her back. She sat down at the table across from him with her own tea.

"You certainly seem like you're in a great mood, *love.*" Imogen's heart tripled its pace as Callum spoke. "Somethin' *delightful* must have happened out there for you to go right ahead and make jokes and laugh at my expense. You're usually smart enough to not do that." Imogen gulped.

"I wasn't thinking, Cal. You're right. I do know better. But y-yes. I was just teasing because tendin' to the sheep put me in a good mood. That's all." As she stammered, Callum chewed the food he kept shoveling in his mouth. When he had finished, he wiped his mouth with his hand.

"Ah. Well, I can see that." He took a deep breath, stood, and gripped the table with both hands. He leaned in an inch. "Maybe you should sleep out there in the shed, then, so you wake up in a good mood, too." He shoved his plate at her. She didn't know if he'd meant to send her mug crashing to the floor, spilling tea onto her lap as it fell, but she didn't spare a moment in contemplation. She wordlessly sprang up, grabbed a dishcloth, and mopped up the mess as Callum went back upstairs muttering to himself.

Shame pinkened Imogen's cheeks. For a moment she sat among the shards of ceramic and cried, careful to do so silently, before getting to her feet+. The sound of creaking bed springs from upstairs meant that Callum had likely climbed back into bed. She blew her nose on a dishtowel, threw the broken mug in the garbage, and decided the dishes on the table could wait long enough for her to gather her wits and settle her nerves.

Still wiping at her eyes, Imogen walked into her sitting room and picked up her late cordwainer father's cast-iron shoe last, which had a place of honor on the mantle.

It was the only thing Callum allowed her to have from home after the funeral, and she had needed to beg for that much.

"Da, I should have listened to you when you told me not to marry him," she whispered. She settled into her recliner and cradled her heirloom, feeling comforted by the weight and solidity of it. "Nothin' is the way it should be, Da. You saw the man he really was, but I didn't listen." Imogen clasped her hands over her mouth to stifle her sobs, terrified that Cal would hear her. She cried at the thought of the children she wanted but would never have, as long as she had any control of the matter. *God, forgive me, but I can't bring babies into the world with that man.* She took a deep breath, closed her eyes, and was totally unaware as sleep overcame her.

Imogen woke up with a start. How long had she been dozing? Judging by the amount of light in the room, it was probably hours. She scrambled out of her recliner, returned the last to the mantle, and started toward the table to gather up the dishes. From outside, she could hear their dogs barking. She dumped the dishes in the sink and started scrubbing. She hadn't heard Callum come downstairs. *God be with me. Let him still be upstairs,* she prayed as she cleaned. Her hands shook. She fought to keep hold of each slippery dish, cup, and utensil.

"Well, look who it is. It's Sleeping Beauty."

Imogen froze, turned off the water, and slowly turned toward Callum as he loomed in the doorway. Behind him, the wind kicked up leaves and sent them swirling and dancing across their field. "I didn't want to wake you since you must have been worn out from all that work this mornin'." He slammed the door behind him.

"Well, you know, I'm just not made for it like you are, but I do the best I can." Her forced laugh sounded tinny and rehearsed. "I finished cleanin' up, so—"

Callum continued. "I mean, you must have been exhausted, sleepin' there like a lady of leisure, peaceful as you please. If you're having so much trouble keepin' up with the demands of this farm, we can always sell off some of the sheep."

"S-sell some of the sheep? They're not much of a bother, really. They're just about due for shearin'. No point sellin' them, sweetheart."

"Well, ya know," he jeered in imitation of Imogen, "Sellin' wool is fine, but we have a few ewes that aren't producin' a lot and gettin' outpaced by our rams. Then, of course, we have the lambs." He paused and grinned as understanding dawned on his wife's face. "We can sell them to a butcher and be done with them. Since you can't keep up."

"Cal, please, there's no need. We've never sold our sheep to be slaughtered. You promised me we never would. You can't."

Imogen didn't see Callum move before the slap landed on her cheek and spun her, head and body, around. She reached out to grab the counter in an effort to stay on her feet but missed. Her forehead made contact instead.

"I can't, can't I? Now it's you who decides, is it?"

Imogen crept away, dazed, and afraid. "Cal, please. I don't want to fight. I'm sorry I upset you."

But Callum wasn't listening. Imogen could see the last of her husband slip away as rage distorted his face. He kicked her, hard, and the steel toe dug deep into her ribs and stole her breath. Imogen cried out and struggled to her hands and knees, gasping and choking on her sobs. She could feel Callum's hands on her crown, his fingers brutally winding through her hair before a vicious twist and pull that catapulted her to her feet.

Imogen yawled and staggered as Callum dragged her through the house. Flashes of pain and panic heightened her senses. She could hear her husband's breathing and the sound of her shoes clopping and skidding across the floor. She could feel the wool of his coat as her hands groped his sleeve searching for stability rather than mercy.

Callum released her head and slapped her again. She crashed into the table but did not fall. Meaning to take full advantage of the new distance, Imogen turned and ran toward the back of the house, toward any door that could lock behind her and give her some, albeit temporary, sanctuary. But it was no use. Callum swallowed the distance, caught her wrist, and pulled her into the sitting room where she had just been sleeping a short time ago.

He shoved her up against the mantle and seized her throat, keeping her face tilted up so she had no choice but to look at him. "You think you make decisions in this house?"

He lowered his face until it was inches from hers. "And instead of bein' grateful that I'm willing to lessen the work, you start whinin' about those sheep. So, my mind's made up. I'll sell them in the morning. And we'll start with that blasted pet you were stupid enough to name."

Crack. Imogen gasped for air as Callum's eyes widened and his hand dropped. *Crunch.* "Oh, God," she sputtered as whatever her husband had been about to say was lost forever and replaced by disjointed syllables. *Squelch.* She stepped back as Cal crumpled to the floor after the third blow to his temple, her father's iron last still clasped in her hand.

"Lord, forgive me," she whispered as Callum vomited, seized, and was still. "But you are a horrible man."

She sat on the floor and, when she felt certain that he was truly gone, inched ever closer to the corpse that had been her husband. She reached out and touched his neck. Nothing beat under her fingers as she checked for a pulse.

"What am I going to do?" She examined what was in her hand and retched. *I've made this a murder weapon.* The room spun and sorrow swelled within her, more from the idea of contaminating her father's tool than from ridding herself of the soul that had animated what was rotting on her floor. *Good riddance to that.*

Her mind reeled. She struggled to her feet, holding her ribs where she had been kicked. She went out to the mud room to get Callum's old pair of hiking boots and brought them back to the body.

Callum's steel-toed boots were hard to remove, but it was far more difficult to cram his feet into the different shoes. She shoved the iron last into one of his boots, ran upstairs, and threw them in his closet where they rested among at least three other identical worn-out pairs.

Back in the kitchen, she snatched a cookie jar off the counter and heaved it to the ground. It splintered into chunks and sharp fragments. She took a deep breath and winced as she stepped on a few of the smaller, pointier ones. She called the Gardai station and wailed to the dispatcher. Someone had attacked her and her dear husband. "Come quick. I think he's dying."

She placed the receiver back in its cradle in slow motion, shock slowly giving way as a new thought dawned.

Where were the sheep? She limped to the window and swallowed hard as she saw they were no longer grazing in the field. *Please let them be back in the barn. Please tell me there was enough decency in that man and he didn't hurt the sheep and he just brought them back to the barn.*

She glanced between Callum and the window. *How could I ever explain leaving the scene of my husband's murder to check on some sheep if the Gardai arrive before I get back?* But she had to know. She threw open the door and ran to the stable. She could hear a chorus of bleats as she neared and offered up a prayer of thanksgiving. Still, she needed to see her Aisling, just for a moment. The wee thing bounded to the front of her pen and nuzzled Imogen's hand.

"It's all right, sweet girl. No one's going to hurt you now. The bad man is gone. No one's gonna hurt either of us now."

Sirens split the air forty-five minutes later. Gardai and three paramedics rushed in. Two went to Callum and the third, a young woman, knelt by her side to shine a light into her eyes.

No one shined a light for Cal. Imogen sobbed. They were both loaded into the back of the ambulance and carried away to a hospital where Imogen was treated for minor contusions and a nasty laceration on the bottom of her foot.

Imogen realized the concussion and bruises on her face helped sell her story to the inspector, and she was thankful for that. Someone had walked into their kitchen while she was doing the dishes. It was easy because most farming folk foolishly kept the doors unlocked, and Imogen and Callum were no different. Imogen had been so startled, she screamed, and the intruder struck her. Her head hit the counter and the last thing she saw before blacking out was her Cal charging at the man. No, she wasn't *sure* it was a man, but who else could have had enough strength to overpower her Callum? Only a man. When she woke up, her husband was lying where the paramedics found him, eyes staring blankly.

"Do ya know if anything was taken?"

Imogen swallowed hard, set her jaw, and raised her chin. "I wouldn't exactly do an inventory of my house with my husband bleeding all over my floor, now would I? I didn't leave his side once I got to him."

"And how did you hurt your foot?"

"My foot?" Imogen repeated. "Who cares about my foot? When I regained consciousness, I got up and saw my husband. I didn't notice the broken cookie jar until I stepped on it on my way to Callum. It . . . oh," Imogen paused. Eyes wide, she whispered, "Our petty cash was in that cookie jar." She took a deep breath and sobbed.

"And now, what? My poor Cal is dead for a few euros?"

Good riddance to that!

THE CATCH

Dianna Sinovic

Themeasure the wind whipped the trawler's flag, making the embroidered emblem of the Great Egret flap its wings in a frenzy.

"This storm popped out of nowhere," Andi said, frowning at the radar display in the wheelhouse. When Scoop didn't answer, she added, "Looks like we've got thirty minutes tops before it hits. Should we pull in the trawl net?"

Not a month into her first full season on the boat, Andi wanted to prove her worth. She had to. Her father, Neal, had grudgingly handed over the skipper's post when his arthritis made it impossible to keep up with the rest of the crew. "You're too much of a romantic," he pronounced. "The sea demands undivided attention. You never know what she'll throw at you."

Andi could almost feel his eyes watching her every move, even though he was two hours west, in Bridgewater Bay. And she imagined his voice a whisper in her head: *"This is all you can bring in?"*

Scoop moved to stand behind her, peering over her shoulder at the screen. "It's your call, but we've weathered a lot worse than this."

Scoop was in her corner, she thought, but maybe not. She took a breath. *I grew up on this boat.* She had learned to mend nets before she could read. *I know what I'm doing.*

The fifty-foot Great Egret was still solid despite its years in the fleet. Andi's father bought the boat nearly new from a wanna-be fisherman who didn't make a full season before bailing. "He said it was too much work," Neal often recounted. "What the hell did he think he was getting into?"

With the careful maintenance of someone whose livelihood depended on it, her father kept the flag flying through boom and bust. And now it was Andi's turn to make it a go. The lives of her crew were in her hands— and so was the heart and soul of the trawler.

"There's a chance of lightning," Andi said. "Let's pull up the net and batten down until this blows through. The catch sensor's going to go off any second anyway." She hoped she sounded more confident than she felt.

Scoop zipped up his oilskin and secured the hood. He stepped out onto the deck, the air alive with spray, to let the rest of the crew know the change in plans.

Would her father have pushed on despite the impending weather? They were well into day three, the final leg of their outing. Their hold was nearly full, so pulling up now would lose them some of their expected catch, but not much.

Andi powered down the engine as crew members Chez, Marlin, and Frey prepared to bring up the trawl net. How quickly conditions had turned. At five a.m., when they rose from their bunks, the sky had been clear with a steady breeze from the east. The day's forecast was a green light. Now the swells were growing, and the breeze had strengthened, the vast arc of the heavens full of scudding clouds.

"Ready." Scoop's call came through the deck intercom. Switching out of her pilot's chair, Andi moved to the trawling controls and turned on the winch. Gulls circled above the deck, hopeful of a free meal. The catch of herring would soon spill onto the deck and be rounded up for storage in the hold. The crew could then go below and ride out the storm.

The winching motor made a loud groan, and Chez signaled for Andi to stop the haul. The mouth of the long orange net had started to rise from the water, and she immediately halted the advance.

"What is it?" she called through the intercom. Through the rain-streaked pane, she saw Scoop and Frey step to the stern, but quickly step back. A tentacle snaked over the stern toward the two men. Then a second tentacle. Each was as thick as one of the men's legs. A third one appeared, and the men moved well back from the groping arms. Merlin climbed the rungs to the wheelhouse.

"Skipper, it's huge." Marlin, a seasoned fisherman who had reluctantly stayed on as part of Andi's crew, likely had seen his share of ocean phenomena. His hands were shaking as he gestured.

"A squid?" Andi guessed.

"A hell of a squid," he grunted, then shrugged. "Don't know what else it could be."

"Inside the net or outside?"

Marlin dug a handkerchief from his pocket and mopped the spray from his face. "Outside, as best I could tell. Almost as though it was riding along. Maybe it was after the fish."

"That's what I was thinking." A giant squid? Andi had only read about them; no one in the fleet had ever seen one. She watched Scoop conferring with Frey, his younger brother. Chez was halfway back toward the wheelhouse. "You've got more years on the drink than me. What do we do?"

Shaking his head slightly, Marlin looked away. "Open the trawl."

Andi was shocked. "And lose the catch?"

He nodded.

"That's crazy. We're so close to capping our run. Neal would . . ." She could imagine her father's anger at the news.

Scoop slammed open the wheelhouse door. "Skipper—"

"I already told her," Marlin said.

"Release it *now*," Scoop said, an unfamiliar edge to his voice. Andi knew it was fear, and she was suddenly afraid, as well.

With a deep breath, she released the winch brake, allowing the wire and rope to loosen, sending the net back into the waves. The herring, once freed, would likely disperse quickly, especially with the approaching storm.

No one spoke in the wheelhouse for several beats. The only sounds were the whistle of the wind and crash of the swells, and the deep growl of the Great Egret's engine.

Then a cry from the stern brought them back to attention. Another tentacle had reached into the boat and was wrapped around Frey's waist. Before any of them could react, he was pulled overboard, disappearing into the water.

"Frey!" Scoop shouted, pulling open the wheelhouse door. He rushed out.

Before Marlin could follow him, Andi held up a hand. "Take the helm and hold it steady." She zipped up her jacket and pulled on a thick wool hat.

"You're effing loony," Marlin muttered, but settled into the wheel seat.

On deck, Chez and Scoop stood at the stern. The spray was thick, and the thunder of the storm competed with the roar of the waves. Andi felt the rain pelting her face and inhaled the familiar scents of fish and salt. She saw only the roiling water behind the boat. No sign of Frey. No sign of the tentacled beast that had swept him up and away. But Andi noticed a warp wire and chain, still attached to the winch arm, were taut—and growing tauter. The otter board vibrated with the strain.

"Part of the net has snagged on something," she shouted to Scoop over the rush of the sea. "Or something's pulling on it."

She ran to the intercom. "Make sure the winch brake is off, Marlin. We're caught."

The speaker crackled with Marlin's voice. "It's off. Nothing more I can do in here."

The drag continued until Andi could sense the Great Egret's engine fighting it. Marlin must have noticed it, too, and kicked the engine into forward gear. Despite that extra power, they weren't gaining any ground. It was a tug of war.

"We'll cut the wire," Andi shouted to Scoop. A good eight hundred dollars in equipment, but jettisoning the trawl was their only hope of breaking free.

The engine throbbed beneath the deck as Marlin fought to keep the boat from being pulled backward. Rain poured from the low-hanging clouds, which seemed only meters above their whipping flag. Andi dug out a harness, but Scoop stopped her and strapped it on himself.

"I'll do it," he said. "Hand me the axe."

Chez tethered him to the boat. "Careful," he said. "Make sure you're balanced when you swing. You've probably got just one chance."

Andi put on her gloves and held another tether. Together, she and Chez would pull Scoop back aboard if he lost his footing on the gunwale.

"Quick now," she said. "We've got you."

Scoop leaned forward, steadied by their ropes, raised the axe, and brought it down, cleanly severing the wire.

With the load suddenly removed, the Great Egret lurched forward, throwing Scoop off balance. He fell overboard, but Andi and Chez quickly brought him back inside the safety of the boat. As Scoop removed his harness, Andi scanned the water. The trawl net was gone, likely for good. Was Frey still out there? He was twenty-six, just a year older than she was. She shivered. With the rain, wind, and fierce swells, his chances of survival were slim.

And then she saw it: a thick tentacle pushing up to the surface, still encircling Frey. Frozen in shock, she watched the suckered arm rise to the boat and lay the man just over the stern, at her feet. *Pop, pop, pop.* Sucker by sucker, it released him, uncurling and withdrawing back from where it came.

"Frey!" Andi said, quickly turning him on his back. He lay still, his eyes closed. His right cheek was ruddy and bruised with the outline of a sucker. She checked for a pulse, and Scoop knelt opposite her, starting chest compressions.

Within moments that seemed like an hour, Frey sputtered and gasped, his eyes wild until he took in the boat and the three crew members around him. Scoop hugged him hard.

"My god," Frey croaked. "Never saw—"

"Let's get you below," Scoop broke in. "Skipper, I think we're done here." He gave her a long look. "None of this is your fault." He and Chez flanked Frey, helping him walk.

Alone on the deck, Andi stood amid the spray and wind. *Like hell it's not my fault.* She ticked off the day's toll. *A haul lost. A trawl net abandoned. A man a hair's-breadth from drowning.*

She thought of the thick tentacle snaking over the gunwale, returning Frey. Had they witnessed some kind of signal between species? She didn't know what had happened out there, beneath the choppy swells. Frey might not know either. But the squid had brought him back.

"Thank you," Andi breathed.

Pivoting from the stern, she headed to the shelter of the wheelhouse. *Her* wheelhouse. Whatever the sea still had in store for her, she would be ready.

Barbara Jewel

Ralph Hieb

Jennifer Gritt placed a small pile of documents into her case files. Looking around the detectives' office, she shook her head at the other desks with stacks of paper cluttering the workspace. Coffee rings on their tops, spills on files and backlogged reports. *I guess the department runs on coffee and paperwork.* She sighed.

The desk phone rang. "Homicide," Gritt answered.

The voice was the captain's. "Just thought you might like to know that our 'Cupid Killer' is back. This time he got a jogger running through Bronx Park. Stole whatever she had on her and tore her throat out."

Please don't let it be him. The last time, the "Cupid Killer" had been her live-in boyfriend, Jonathan, who, like Gritt, was a vampire. *I don't think I can cover up his killings again.*

"Harris, looks like the 'Cupid Killer' is back," she said to her partner, whose desk sat across from her. "Another body with the throat ripped out."

He dumped used coffee grounds into the trash and started a fresh pot. "What holiday is our vampire celebrating this time?" He put air quotes around the word vampire. "Last time it was Valentine's Day. We're just past the Fourth of July. There's no holiday for weeks."

Gritt hoped her partner would continue to believe vampires were purely fictional, but she had to be sure it wasn't Jonathan. "Come on, Harris. There won't be time for another cup. Let's see what we can find," Gritt said. She pulled her holster from the desk drawer and strapped the weapon to her hip, before sliding her spare gun into her boot. "We're going to the north side."

"Good place for a murder," Harris said, grabbing his umbrella and weapon.

Rain pelted the unmarked car as they drove through the Bronx. Arriving at the park entrance, the two homicide detectives opened their umbrellas as they approached a cordoned-off area near a running trail. They flashed their badges to a patrolman who lifted the police tape and held their umbrellas as they passed under it. An officer on the scene handed Harris a clipboard.

"Hi, Margie," Harris and Gritt said in unison. Margie nodded as she wiped the rain from her glasses.

Gritt asked, "So, what's with this vic?"

"Terrible. See for yourselves." Margie walked away.

A canopy tented the body. The victim lay face down in a puddle of mud off the side of the trail.

Harris squatted to get a better look at the girl. "You would think this perp would have hidden her in the bushes. Keeping her in the open . . . this guy has some balls. Looks like it's the same guy, though."

"I don't know." Gritt crouched down and stared at the neck for a bit. "I don't see any sweetener on her. Our guy always left something on the wound." Standing, she added, "We'll know more when we get the ME's report."

What she'd left unsaid was that this perp had made a mess of this poor victim. Jonathan would never have shown her so little respect. She let out a long breath. *This isn't his work.*

Gritt moved away from the group and texted Jonathan. *On a case. Might need your help.* She shoved the cell into her pocket when the medical examiner arrived with her tools in two metal cases.

"Any ID?" the ME asked.

"Nothing. She has an armband to hold a phone but no cell. We'll get her prints to see if she's in the system," Gritt said, walking toward the police tape.

Harris looked from the ME to Gritt and back again before he asked, "Don't you think the ME is kind of young? Looks as if she just got out of school. Think she knows what she's doing?"

"You'd be surprised," was all Gritt said.

The next day

Harris dropped into the chair at the desk across from Gritt.

She sat staring at what little information they had on the victim, her lips pursed, her fingers tented. "I thought you were going to bring in doughnuts."

"I ate them already," he said as he brushed powdered sugar off his clothes.

With feigned shock, she said, "You didn't save me one?"

Harris just grinned. "What for? You never eat them anyway."

She pointed toward the folder with a pen and asked, "What's that note you have on the bottom? My vision is sharp, but that chicken scratch still looks like a scribble to me. Do we have anything to go on?"

"That's just a reminder to look for sweetener on the vic. Still waiting for the ME's report. Did you find anything else?"

Holding her notepad, she read aloud. "The uniforms canvassed the entire area, and no one saw or heard anything."

"Typical," Harris lamented. He tore a sheet off his pad, made a paper airplane, and threw it toward Gritt. It landed right in front of her.

She stared at the airplane sitting on her desk. "That plane is doing better than we are," she said.

The printer in the corner blinked on as pages spilled out.

Gritt grimaced. *You'd think they could send info through the computer.*

Harris walked over to it and said, "Our vic's in the system, picked up for prostitution a few times. Name's Barbara Jewel, no address, and the only thing we have is she works as a bartender at the Liquid Lounge." He passed the printout over to Gritt.

"Great," she said, scanning the sheet.

"An upscale dive bar," he said.

"An *upscale* dive bar?" she asked in an amused voice. "That's a new one."

"The girls are required to wear something besides shoes when on stage," Harris explained.

"How do you know that?" she asked.

"Never mind," he replied.

"Come on. That gives us a place to start," Gritt said, grinning.

As Gritt drove them back from the Liquid Lounge, Harris said, "Well, that was a waste of time. They didn't tell us anything of use." He checked his voicemail and tried to suppress a smile. "You're not going to like this much," he said, turning to her. "Listen to what my CI has to say."

He put it on speaker and grinned at her as the message played:

> Hey, Harris. I hear you and the boss lady went to the Liquid Lounge to find out about the girl in the park. You'll get more answers at Lucky's Dance Club. One guy who works there knows your girl. But they won't talk to the cops. You'd need a warrant to use the john there. But, hey, if Gritt went in by herself in a tight crop top, short mini, and four-inch heels, they might think she's looking for work. She has the body to pull that off. Don't let her hear this, or she'll kill me next time she sees me. Talk to you later.

"Very funny," Gritt said.

"He might be right. It's more than we got from the bartender at the Liquid Lounge." Harris grinned again. "Why don't I drive you over there tonight to see if you can get . . . Lucky's." Harris slapped his knee; Gritt scowled.

One a.m. the following day

An unmarked police car sat a few doors down from the entrance to Lucky's Dance Club. The bar looked to be deserted, but a patron walked in with his unbuttoned shirt hanging loose.

"Wait here," Gritt ordered. "There are a couple of our guys in there now." Opening the car door, she was assailed by the scent of garbage and vomit. Some trash blew down the street, and the heat and humidity didn't care that it was one in the morning.

Getting out of the car, she took a deep breath and tugged at her short skirt to make sure it covered her butt. As she walked into the club, she tried to ignore the odors of sex, stale beer, and smoke that permeated the walls.

The place was a small, dingy room. On one side stood a raised platform that served as a stage, with several tables and chairs by it. There were only a couple of genuine patrons, and one girl dancing onstage, who looked as though she might nod off. Gritt approached the bartender and pulled her shirt hem down to give the best view of her cleavage. She knew his name was Steve Fisher but didn't let him know.

"What can I do for you?" Fisher asked, eyeing her nearly exposed chest, as she leaned over the bar.

Standing straight, she drew back her shoulders and inhaled to get his undivided attention. "I'd like to speak with Barbara," Gritt said. "She owes me money."

"Ain't seen her in a few days."

Gritt said, "I need that money."

"Really? Sounds like you need a job, not Barbara."

"You offering?" Gritt asked.

"Boss is in. He might want to give you a personal interview," he said, jerking his thumb toward the back of the room.

He never raised his eyes to meet hers.

A guy, nursing his drink from down the bar, called for a refill. Gritt recognized him as one of the homicide squad, nicknamed Bottles. She knew he was her backup.

"I'll let him know you're here. Got to get this guy another drink." The bartender dropped the towel he used to wipe down the bar and walked to his customer, refilled the order, then disappeared through a door.

Gritt stood there for another minute before the bartender returned. "Boss said to head on back. He's in the office marked 'private.' And if you need a reference for a job, I'm willing to give you one for some consideration."

"No thanks," she answered.

A mirror on the wall gave an excellent view of the bar. Gritt glanced at it. Fisher was watching her body sway as she walked away. Then she knocked on the open door.

The man sitting behind the desk was skinny with unkempt hair and in need of a shave. He motioned for her to enter his office. "I hear you're lookin' for a job and want to speak with Barb."

"Mainly looking for Barbara Jewel," Gritt said.

"Don't know where she is, but if you want a job, you look as if you might do." He eyed her boobs, waist, legs, and then back up.

He took a sip from the glass of amber liquid sitting on the desk, then leaned back in his chair. The daily crossword, with some answers filled in pencil and what looked like a lot of erasures, topped his desk. The rest of the place hadn't seen a cleaning in years. Pieces of costumes peeked out from under the casting couch.

He turned back to the puzzle, bored with her.

Gritt knocked on the doorframe again. "We were supposed to split what was thrown on the stage when we danced together. She took off with my share of the night's dancing."

He glared at her. "I can guarantee she ain't gonna pay you what she owes. If you want a job, you can audition." He glanced at the couch. "Otherwise, stop wasting my time." He lifted the drink and swilled back the whiskey, slamming the glass on the desk.

"I'll think about that job . . . mister?" She hesitated, as if she did not already know his name.

"Name's Jake. If you want the job, ask for me," the manager said, barely looking up from his paper.

Gritt turned and stopped before closing the door. "Thanks."

Walking through the bar without a second look at Bottles, she shook her head. *How did Jake know Barbara won't be around anymore?*

Back at the car, Harris asked, "You learn anything?"

"Yeah," Gritt answered. "The manager confirmed his name is Jake, and he knew she's not going to pay back any debts. Seems he already knows she's dead. We haven't released her name to the press."

"Veeerrry interesting," Harris said, dragging the word out.

Two a.m.

The squad room was quiet. Even the custodial staff had left for the night. Only a few of the detectives were gathered, discussing cases they were investigating. Gritt sat at her desk, staring at her computer screen.

"See anything interesting?" Harris asked.

"Not really. Just checking on Fisher, that bartender, and Jake, the club manager. They both have enough priors to fill a book."

Taking off his jacket and hanging it on the back of his chair, Harris booted up his computer. He searched through the list of names he had for both bars' employees. Most had priors, a few came up as runaways. He noted them to give to the uniforms. He stopped and tapped his pen on the desk.

"Gritt, have you seen this?" he asked and pushed back as though the discovery would end all of their questions.

She'd been through the list three times tonight. If he had found something she hadn't . . .

"What?"

"A few years back, before all this 'vampire' stuff, a worker found the body of a missing girl. She was in a dumpster with her throat torn out. She didn't have any blood left." He looked up from his screen. "You think this guy started then, and we've only recently found out about him?"

"It's a possibility." Gritt walked around to his side of the desk so she could see what Harris saw.

He swiveled in his chair to look at her. "I believe our killer has come out of retirement."

"My guess is a copycat. The runaway had no blood, the seven 'Cupid Killer' victims had sweetener poured on their throats. This most recent one is just a bloody mess," Gritt said. *Don't connect this to the others,* she thought.

"So, you think maybe different guys?" Harris took a sip of his coffee.

"Yeah." Walking back to her desk, she sat down. "The last one could be an angry spouse."

"Why would he kill the girl?"

"Who said he?" Gritt replied, drumming her fingers on the desk.

"Okay. I'll start checking to see if we have anything on women doing this sort of killing."

Later that day at Gritt's apartment

"Jonathan," Gritt said to her boyfriend, "are there any vampires running around the city who might do killings for hire? Maybe a rogue." She knew he would know; he kept tabs on all the vamps in the city.

"I'm not aware of any," Jonathan answered. "And if there were, I don't believe that they would be so obvious as to leave their victims exposed and identifiable as vampire prey. It would go against the laws we follow, as in no advertising that we exist."

"I remember you left a lot of bodies in plain sight not so long ago." She teased.

"But that was to get you anticipating the kill," he answered.

"That's what I was thinking." Gritt walked to her refrigerator to pour herself a glass of blood. "But somebody killed her and made it look like one of us."

She stared at the nearly empty containers. "What happened to all the blood?"

"Most of it was getting too hard to drink."

Gritt winced at the thought of good blood going to waste.

Jonathan came to her side and rubbed her shoulders. "I'll ask around if any of the community has heard about a rogue vamp," he said.

"Thanks," Gritt answered, putting her glass in the sink and grabbing her jacket. "I better get going or I'll be late for work."

"Have a nice day," Jonathan said.

Gritt closed the door after her and walked to her car. *The blood was getting too hard to drink. I hope he hasn't gone back to killing for fresh blood.*

Later that afternoon

Gritt walked through the squad room, ignoring the others arriving for the evening shift. She sat at her computer and came across a file. She yelled, "Harris?"

"What?" he called from the break area.

"Have you read this guy's sheet?"

Leaning over to see the monitor, Harris whistled. "Whatever in holy? This might be our guy."

"Yeah," Gritt answered. "Seems he has a girlfriend, and they both like to play vampire."

"Let's see if the captain knows about this. It's from his old precinct."

They entered the captain's office, and Harris handed him the report.

Curious, Harris asked, "What happened?"

"They hung one armored car guard by his ankles, draining him, then drank his blood, before ripping out the throat of a second and beating the third guard and leaving her for dead. Fortunately, she survived," the captain said. He continued with his recollection. "Seems he wanted to rape her first, but his girlfriend, Darla, had an issue with that."

"You think this might have been a thrill crime?" Gritt asked.

"Don't know. We caught the two of them with help from the guard who survived."

"What happened to them?" Gritt asked, ignoring the rest of the file.

"Someone in the prison held Darla's head face down in a toilet," the captain continued. "While awaiting trial, her boyfriend killed himself after hearing about her death. The report is missing the DECEASED stamped on it."

"Couldn't have happened to nicer people," Gritt said sarcastically.

The captain hesitated, ignoring Gritts' remark, and continued. "I saw what they did to those guards. They died too easy."

Both detectives were silent until Gritt said, "Yup," before returning to her desk and computer.

The next day, at the precinct

"Hey Harris, did you find anything that might be useful?" Gritt asked, setting her briefcase on her desk.

"Nothing," Harris said.

"I've been thinking this guy wants to show off his work, which is why he left her out in the open," Gritt said. "It might be someone from out of town."

Harris shrugged. "Any ideas?"

"Not really. I've got some feelers out. I have a feeling the killer isn't a local." Gritt stared at her computer. *And not Jonathan.*

Sitting at his desk, Harris stated, "That's better than anything my CIs might come up with. They're only good for junkies." Kicking back in his chair, he asked, "What makes you think it's an out-of-towner?"

"Don't know. Just a feeling. And I think there will be more killings."

"Don't say that. It hasn't been a week yet." Harris picked up a paper clip and started bending it, as if he was going to make it into something.

Their captain called to them. "You guys want to come in here for a minute?"

"What's up?" Gritt asked, taking a seat in front of the captain's desk.

"Don't get too comfortable. We just got another torn neck victim over by Lucky's Dance Club. Looks like it might be the same bastard."

"Hope the vic is the manager," Gritt whispered to Harris as they left the captain's office.

"I never met the guy, but I guess he left a wonderful impression on you," Harris said, smiling.

"Yeah, wonderful."

Arriving at the scene, the detectives ducked under the police tape and were greeted by Margie. "You know the drill," she said, handing Gritt her clipboard.

After signing and being brought up to speed, they walked over to the body. It wasn't the manager.

"Who is he?" Gritt asked the ME standing nearby.

"Don't know," she answered.

"Guy over there said he recognizes him. Name is George Statery," a nearby officer said. "Nearest we can tell, just a customer at the bar. Would come here for lunch from time to time, and sometimes stayed 'til closing."

"See if you can find out more about our Mr. Statery." Gritt waved the officer toward the bar.

Looking carefully at the remains of the victim's neck, Gritt asked Harris, "Notice anything different about this guy?"

Bending over and looking closely at the wound, Harris said, "I don't see any syrup or other condiments on him." Standing, he added, "This looks like it could be the same guy who killed Jewel."

"I agree. But, why *this* guy?"

Later that day at Gritt's home

"Hey, hon," Jonathan said. "I've checked with everyone I can think of, and no one knows of any vampire in the city or from anywhere in the territory who would do the killing."

"I was afraid you'd say that," Gritt said. "Maybe there is a rogue that no one has heard about."

Jonathan shrugged his shoulders.

Gritt rolled her eyes. "I need some O-positive."

The next day

"Anything new?" Gritt asked.

"Yup. We found out something about our latest victim. He was a furniture salesman at Brown's Department store. According to some dancers, he would try to pick them up after their shifts. Offered them money."

"He get any takers?"

"Yup, once in a while Jewel would leave with him. Most of the girls said he was, and I quote, 'kind of creepy'."

"Think he saw the killer?" Gritt said. "The park is a shortcut from his workplace to the bar."

"That's my belief. I think a trip to his home and workplace would be appropriate."

Gritt stood up. "Let's go."

Once at the victim's residence, the two detectives split up.

"Let's start with the neighbors on either side of his apartment, then the ones above, then below him," Gritt said.

After knocking on every door, the two detectives stood at the building's main entrance.

"Well, that was a waste of time," Gritt said, walking down the steps of the apartment building.

"Bet the workplace comes up nil also," Harris stated.

"No bet."

Their next stop was Brown's Department Store.

"He was really creepy," said the salesgirl who worked in the same department as Statery. "You know, always giving these weird looks, like he would try to sneak into the ladies' room. Or if I wore something tight-fitting, he would stare at my chest all day, and I swear he tried to follow me home a few times."

"Anything else?" Harris asked.

"You can ask any of the girls here. V-neck sweaters or skirts above the knee, he was like a dog in heat," she continued, ignoring Harris' question.

"Thanks," Gritt said. "I understand completely."

As they walked to the car, Harris looked at his watch. "It's getting close to when all the regulars visit their local watering holes." He hit the remote to unlock the car doors.

"What say we lean on the barman at Lucky's? The way he sneered when he said 'the boss,' I have a feeling he isn't too fond of good ole Jake," Gritt said.

"Let's. What's the barman's name?" Harris asked.

"Fisher." Gritt checked her notebook. "Yeah. Steve Fisher. Looked it up before I went to Lucky's. And I ran his priors."

"Maybe you can wear something low cut again so he can talk to your chest," Harris said, laughing.

The dance stage seemed lonely, with no one working the stripper pole.

"Where is everyone?" Gritt said as she and Harris entered the deserted lounge.

"Someone had to turn on that disco ball," Harris said, pointing at the reflecting orb. Giving the room a once-over glance, he added, "This place stinks of trouble."

Gritt nodded.

Both detectives pulled their weapons and did a systematic sweep of the barroom, then made their way to the office at the rear of the building.

Stopping in front of Jake's office, Harris carefully opened the door as Gritt kept her gun trained on it.

The door swung open to reveal the manager sitting at the desk, leaning back in his chair, arms hanging at his sides. A large hole gaped in his chest where his heart had been cut out.

After a second of staring, Harris joined Gritt. They checked out the closet and the attached bathroom.

"Place is clear. I'll call it in," Harris said. "What happened to Fisher?"

"Don't know, but he might be in danger. Put out a BOLO on him." Gritt ordered. She turned to leave the room, catching the last part of Harris' *Be on the Look Out.*

Harris followed her out of the office to wait for backup and the forensics team.

About an hour later, while still at the crime scene, the ME walked over to the two detectives. "I'll know for certain how they did it after I do the autopsy."

"Thanks, Doc," both detectives said at the same time.

Harris said, "Don't think many people would sit still for someone to cut their heart out. I would guess this was done as some kind of message."

Ignoring Harris' comment, Gritt said, "I've run the info on Jake, and he lived in his office. So, I asked for a warrant for Fisher's place."

Gritt held up her phone, showing a picture of the search warrant they had requested while waiting. "Come on. We can check out Fisher's apartment."

"I'll run a check on Jake's bank statements. Living in his office means he could save a bunch."

At Fisher's apartment, they found the door unlocked. Both Gritt and Harris, after announcing their presence, entered.

"Am I seeing right?" Harris asked.

"Do you believe this?" Gritt answered. "There must be a thousand pictures of Barbara Jewel plastered around here."

"Looks like the guy had it really bad for her."

"Either him or someone who also lives here." Gritt was standing in the bedroom doorway looking at something. "Better call the ME and forensics."

She moved so that Harris could look in the room, revealing an unknown victim lying face down in a pool of blood.

"I'll check to see if there is anything on the computer and finish looking around until forensics arrives." Then she walked over to a table with an open laptop. After putting on gloves she always kept in her pocket, she touched the keyboard. The screen lit, not requiring a password.

Back at the station, Gritt punched her keyboard.

"Harris, I just forwarded the autopsy on the unknown. Looks like our boy Fisher did him in. Prints matching Fisher's are all over him. Bullet to the head after he smashed the skull with a blunt object."

"Not so fast. Fisher's journal was recovered from his laptop. I quote "Today they found Barbara. The bastard had her killed. He doesn't know it, but he just signed his own death warrant. But first, I need to get rid of the guy he hired to kill her."

"The dead guy?" Gritt asked.

"Guess so."

Gritt's phone rang. She listened, looking at Harris. "The captain wants us now."

Walking into the captain's office, they both stood in front of his desk. Looking at them, he said, "I just wanted to tell you personally that the dead guy is John Hardin, a professional assassin. Someone had to know him really well to get him into that apartment to kill him. Be real careful, but get the killer. Dismissed." The captain went back to doing paperwork.

Back at his desk, Harris continued to read the diary. "Jake will get a surprise. I'll cut out his heart and flush it down the john. I only hope he lives long enough to feel the pain." He stopped there. "There is some more but it only describes Jewel and how he loved her. He said they were going to start over again somewhere else. But he never mentions where."

The ME's report came over Gritt's computer.

"Seems our boy Jake had a real drug problem. He was a walking mixture of about anything illegal." Gritt said. "That explains where his money went."

Harris looked at Gritt. "I know that expression. You're onto something?"

"We have proof Jake hired Hardin to kill Jewel, or maybe even Fisher."

"How so?"

"The crime scene guys found info in Jake's office that Jewel was supposed to be picking up the drugs for Jake and some people he supplied. She was cutting the stuff and giving him less than he was paying for. My guess, he was really pissed about that."

"Okay. I can understand Jewel, but why Statery?" he asked.

"If you killed Jewel and now everyone concerned with the case was showing up dead except for her boyfriend, it makes sense to kill him, too. Especially if he knows who Jake's favorite hitman is, or was."

"Probably."

"Okay," Gritt answered. "I would say Jewel and Statery were killed by Hardin. Then Fisher killed Jake and Hardin."

"Sounds right to me."

Day five

Before Gritt got to the station, a broadcast came over the radio. "All available officers to Lucky's Dance Club. Officer down, suspect is armed and barricaded inside. Hostages taken."

She pulled up to the scene. Harris was already there and walked up to her vehicle.

"It's Fisher," Harris said. "One officer was shot trying to apprehend him. He's on his way to the hospital. His partner is over there." Harris pointed to one of several officers farther ahead of them, using their squad cars as shields.

"Do we know anything about the hostages?" Gritt asked.

"The owner of Lucky's and three of the dancers."

"Okay. I'm going to see if I can find out more." She walked to the command vehicle.

"Gritt," Harris said in a stern voice. "Let SWAT do their job and take out Fisher."

"I will," she said, over her shoulder.

Margie ran up and squatted behind the squad car next to Harris. "Where is she going?"

"To get herself in a shitload of trouble," Harris answered.

Gritt entered the command vehicle.

"We don't have time for chit-chat, detective," the SWAT captain said.

"Thought you might need an extra sniper. I'm qualified," Gritt replied.

"I can always use extra eyes and personnel," The captain said. "But only ones who are cleared to do so." Shaking his head, he said, "Sorry, Gritt."

Just as Gritt was about to leave, the radio announced, "Someone is coming out. It's a hostage."

The sound of a single shot came from outside the van. Over the radio, someone shouted. "I don't have a shot. I don't have a shot."

Drawing her weapon, Gritt jumped from the van and moved toward the sound.

"Shit." Gritt stared at a body lying in the street. Scoping out the building, she saw Fisher using a hostage as a shield. *How many are going to die? He's not going to stop killing until they're all dead.*

"Everyone clear out or this one is next," Fisher shouted.

She went to her car. Sitting in the front seat, she put on gloves, then reached under the seat and removed a .38 caliber revolver. Using her door as a gun support, she took careful aim and fired.

Fisher's head jerked violently backward; at the same time, his hostage fell to the ground.

Instantly, the SWAT team opened fire.

Everyone concentrated on Fisher and the girl on the ground. Making sure no one noticed she had been the first to fire, Gritt put the revolver into a nearby trash can. Removing the latex gloves, she put them into her pocket. They could be disposed of later. She didn't care if a search by the police found the gun. The serial numbers had been removed, and it was clean.

Members of special weapons and tactics moved closer to the body. Gritt was relieved to hear the girl only fainted when the first shot hit Fisher.

The SWAT captain collected weapons from his men to see who fired. Looking toward Gritt, he walked over to her. "I need to collect your weapon. I know you probably had it out."

She shrugged and handed her service pistol to him, handle first.

Putting his hand on the barrel, he asked, "Did you fire?"

"No need to," Gritt answered. "Your guys had it covered. Besides, I was kinda far back from the action."

"I still need to turn it in."

"Understood," was her reply.

Day seven

"You wanted to see me?" Gritt asked as she entered her captain's office.

"Yes," he replied, handing her weapon to her. "First, here is your gun. Not firing makes it easy to clear inspection. The dancer he shot in the back is going to live, don't think she'll be dancing for a while. But I also have a question."

Gritt looked at him.

"Normally you're pushy. Why not now?"

"Truth is, there wasn't time. Everything went down too fast."

Gritt was baking some cookies made with blood as its key ingredient.

"You know, Jonathan, I worried that the killer might have been you."

"Why?"

"You were the Cupid Killer."

"Don't you trust me? I promised you I wouldn't do that again."

"I know."

Jonathan reached into the bowl of batter, taking some, then licked his fingers clean.

She smiled. She trusted him.

Upon Seeing the Albino Buck

Paul Weidknecht

Pawdah, *powdah.*

Randy glanced over at Lucas for a clue, but his eyes were on the head mount of an albino buck fixed to the wall behind the old man filling out their camping permit. Light brown antlers, four perfectly matching tines to each side, a pure white head and neck, with pink eyes and nose. Odd-looking for certain, but striking, and Randy understood how someone could be taken by it.

Powder, Randy then realized, the old guy just said powder. He let out a breath. Some of these Mainer-accented words needed to come with a translation card.

"Yes, sirs, because of the drought, the roads back theyah ah like baby powdah. During the day when the logging trucks ah rollin', pull to the side and close the windows fast. Otherwise, you'll be in a wicked bad sandstorm."

They had gotten a late start, then doubled down by underestimating the length of Route 11 up to these north woods, but they had made the checkpoint shack in time to ask a few questions. Setting up camp in the dark wasn't going to be any fun. At least it wouldn't be in the rain.

"You like that albie," the old man said, without looking up.

"Excuse me?" Lucas asked.

"Our ghost deeah," the man said, pointing his thumb back over his shoulder. "The albino. That mount's oldah than both of you, prob'ly. Since ninety-two. Found wedged in the crotch of a tree, twenty feet up. A certified mystery. Of course, it's considered bad luck, too."

"Then why do you have it hanging up?"

"It's a kind of public service announcement, a caution to tourists. All right now, the campsite you two talked about wanting is twenty-eight miles away. It's the slow time, no one's huntin' now, so you'll have a good chunk of

Maine to yahselves." The man stapled the receipt to their copy of the permit and handed it to Lucas.

Randy and Lucas stepped out onto the porch, the screen door springing closed with a bang, the floorboards flexing under their boots. Insects haloed the shack's lone floodlight in a frenzy. The full moon was up, lighting the pale dust of the road that faded into the night forest.

Randy stopped a moment to ponder his little car. He grinned. The windshield and front passenger windows were the only windows that functioned as such, with backpacks, sleeping bags, camp chairs, fishing gear, water jugs, food boxes, the stove, the dome tent, and coolers—two of them—obscuring every square inch of remaining glass. And how the canoe had managed to stay tied to the roof was inexplicable. No question it had a very Grapes of Wrathy vibe; made Tom Joad's packing technique look downright fastidious.

The two slipped into the car, with Lucas tossing the paperwork onto the dashboard. "I figure twenty-eight miles over these roads will take us about fifty minutes, maybe a little longer."

As they began down the dirt road, Randy looked into the driver's side mirror to see the checkpoint shack's floodlight blink out, followed closely by the inside lights. He noticed Lucas looking into the passenger side mirror, his friend's profile unsettled.

They moved through the woods, dark on both sides except for where the moonlight washed through the shorn sections of clear-cuts. The fine dust under their tires was thin and easily drivable, but every so often they would hit a soft spot, where extra sand had accumulated around a bend, sending the car fishtailing gently as if they were in snow. The first time they felt the back of the car swing out a little, they'd flashed a look to one another, both knowing that getting stuck was unthinkable.

"Driving through here," Randy said, "you can see how the forest at night would work on people's imaginations, everybody thinking up their own back-woods tales. Werewolves. Chupacabras. Bigfoot."

Lucas nodded. "Yeah, something to talk about after the sun is down and the day's work is over. Adult version of monster-under-the-bed story. I think the old guy would have talked all night if he had the chance," Lucas said.

"Yeah, he saw your face and knew he had you."

Lucas turned to Randy and stared. "Had me what?"

"Well, you know, dude is telling tales to tourists for years and knows who he can mess with."

"I'm not scared."

"Didn't say you were scared."

"Not scared at all."

"But you are a worrier," Randy said, looking over to see how that one rode.

"Okay. I'll own that. But don't tell me you weren't creeped out by that wacky deer head. Thing had a bad aura to it. And I'd heard about that bad luck thing even before the old guy brought it up."

Randy shrugged. "But I've also heard it can be either an omen of something good or bad. You know, like with Native Americans, it's a special event when a white buffalo is born. We're on a camping trip to do some hiking, fishing, and canoeing; I'm thinking good omen."

After several miles the road flattened, and they picked up speed, at times the car momentarily floating over rises between the shallow dips before bouncing down hard. In the distance, the trail glowed dimly, and Randy flicked off the headlights.

"What are you doing?" Lucas asked.

"You can only get away with this during a full moon and a cloudless sky. See? The lighter the surface the better the effect. When I lived in South Jersey, we did this all the time on the white sand roads in the Pine Barrens. This isn't as white, but it's pretty good though."

"It does look cool."

Resting between the two, Randy's phone lit up. Lucas looked down at it. "It's Kelsey."

"I'll get back to her. She wasn't real crazy about this trip. I'll call back when I'm better prepared for the grief."

"She thought it was a waste of time and money?"

"Exactly, those were the reasons she gave. Not what she believed, of course. But what she gave."

"Pardon me for asking, but what will it be like when you two are married? Let's face it, Randy, she didn't want you going here because of me. I'm single and she had visions of us slipping back into town—yeah, a twenty-eight-mile skip across the street—looking for wild women we could ply with Wild Turkey. There's got to be some trust, right? Sure, I'm such a corruptor. I'm such a bad influ—"

Lucas shrieked. The same instant, he braced himself, his arms straight out, hands splayed on the dashboard and door, his knees jacking toward his chest. The scream cut through Randy so piercingly it made his scalp tingle and his chest seize in mid-breath. Then he saw it coming from the right. He white-knuckled the wheel and tried to turn left, hard, but it was too late; the moose was already falling in through the windshield.

A glimpse of its immense antlers, the dark mass blocking everything for a moment, rushed at his face. Randy turning away, wincing, waiting for the impact. Lucas' scream continuing. The spider-webbed windshield gone white, flexing into the car, glass dust blowing onto their faces. An explosion of tiny bluish cubes spraying over them, a brush of the moose's coarse hair through the jagged crater now opened in the center. Roof posts bending, driver side collapsing. Screaming, shrinking into his seat, still holding the wheel. The moose cradled in the windshield frame for a second, stilt legs kicking, then gone. A hollow bang overhead—*the canoe*—noises rumbling back over the roof. Wetness on his face. Gear rushing forward from the back. The car leaving the road, dropping down the low embankment, bucking over the uneven ground, dead-stopping into a tree.

Randy's head swam, lolling like a drunk's, like someone sitting up in bed, wobbly and flu-sick. His arms hung at his sides, palms up, heavenward. He slowly lifted a hand to his face, patting it with his fingertips. Wet and sticky; had to be blood. He touched his nose, broken. Each breath brought a pain from his left side. Ribs?

The car had caved in around them, tomb-like. The dashboard collapsed and the doors were hopelessly crushed shut. Climbing out through the cratered windshield would be the only way out, and that would be nearly impossible. He looked to the passenger side.

Lucas's window was gone, but he sat slouched, his head resting against the edge of the door and mid-post, the roof bellied between them, the car squashed. A vertical gash in his forehead bled in a line from the bridge of his nose down over his mouth to his chin, running in a syrupy string onto the front of his saturated shirt. Then he moaned. Alive.

"Luc, bud. Lucas." Randy reached out, placing his hand on his shoulder, shaking him lightly.

Lucas lifted his head a few inches, then let it fall back into the headrest. "Oh, my knee. Ah, this knee is killing me."

"Luc, we have to find our phones and pray we get a signal."

Lucas looked at him for a moment, his glazed eyes seeming to focus. "Bro, you're a bloody mess."

"We both are, but it's not pumping out, so it's not from an artery. We should be okay if we get help soon. Some of it might be from the moose."

Lucas' eyes widened in sudden recollection. "That moose was—"

"Yes, the moose's blood."

"The moose was running—"

"I know, it came out of nowhere."

"No." Lucas said, shaking his head, frustrated. "Stop it, just listen to me. That moose was being chased by something. I saw it."

"What?"

"The moose was spooked."

"What are you talking about?"

A large branch snapped in the woods across from them, followed by the crack of another. Lucas stared wide-eyed at Randy, shaking his head and putting a finger to his lips for them to keep silent. Weighty footfalls sounded through the ground litter, leaves pushed forward with each step. It exhaled in a kind of snort and stopped.

The moonlight glinted silver over the brown hair covering its body, falling across its domed head and wide shoulders—shoulders that had to be four feet across. Nine feet tall, easy. Six hundred pounds, probably more. Thick hands hung nearly to its knees. It turned its head slowly, looking where the moose had come to rest in the center of the road, less than fifty feet away. The creature plodded toward the moose.

The two sat frozen moving only their eyes to track the creature as it passed within twenty feet of the car, the odor of rotted meat trailing in its wake. They inched around to watch, a large patch of window now cleared away between their scrambled gear.

The moose sat in the road with its front legs tucked under itself like a cow in a pasture, its breathing labored. Blood soaked the fur at its throat, pooling in the dirt. Upon seeing the creature, the moose grunted in panic and tried to stand, but its back legs flailed uselessly. The creature stepped over the moose, with a leg to each side. It reached down, gripping the great rack of antlers in each hand, and twisted the moose's head until its neck broke with a dull snap.

Lucas let out a soft gasp. The creature whipped its head around. Releasing the antlers, it started toward the car.

"Don't look it in the eye," Randy whispered. "If we're not a threat, maybe it will take the moose and go."

"We're dead," Lucas said, whimpering. "We're just dead."

The creature slowed as it reached them, then bent down, peering into the crushed car. It sniffed the air.

Looking the creature straight into its red eyes, Randy and Lucas screamed like they had caught on fire.

The creature stretched out its muscular arms. Lucas recoiled from the door, squeezing under the dropped roof, pushing Randy against the driver's door. Randy tried opening his door to escape. No click, nothing moved; the handle was useless. Curling both hands over the edge of the buckled passenger door, the monster yanked violently, rocking the little car, opening a six-inch gap between the door and frame. The two shrieked, Lucas pressing Randy harder into the driver's side with his back. Randy turned, screaming from the shattered window, clawing for a way through the jamb. The monster ripped downward again, the gap now a foot wide, the door wobbly on its hinges. With both hands, one on the door edge, the other grabbing the inside panel, the monster pulled, snarling. The twisting metal moaned for several seconds before the upper hinge gave way with a ping. A moment later, the lower hinge tore apart, causing the monster to stumble backwards several feet with the wrenched door in its hand.

As Randy and Lucas cowered, the monster stood there, door in hand, its head tilted like a confused dog. It dropped the door with a thud and walked back toward the moose. Randy and Lucas did not move.

Reaching the moose, the creature hoisted up the animal, placing the carcass across its shoulders like a yoke. The creature threw back its head, bellowed to the stars in a roar the friends felt vibrate through their clothes, and trudged into the black woods.

Lucas shifted disjointedly back to his seat, grimacing. He backhanded the sweat from his brow and stared straight ahead. Randy, breathing through his mouth, looked back to where the creature had disappeared.

"You know what that was?" Randy asked.

Lucas did not answer, but only shook his head wearily.

"A thank-you."

Lucas made a face, a mixture of confusion and disgust.

"We helped get its meal; it helped us out of this car."

A sudden rectangle of light came on at Randy's feet on the floor mat, illuminating the car. Bending down, Randy winced, palming his ribs while reaching for his cell.

"It's a text from Kelsey."

"We have a signal out here?" Lucas asked.

"Full moon, Canadian radio towers, aurora borealis, UFOs. I'll give credit to anything at this point."

"You going to answer her?"

Randy scanned the inside of the car. "No, I'm not quite ready to brag about how much time and money I saved."

"I'll tell you one thing for sure," Lucas said. "When we get back to that shack, I'm slapping that albino deer right off the wall."

"Are you kidding me? We survived a collision with a bull moose and we're in tight with Bigfoot. Albie can't be anything other than good luck."

Author's Note: The author would like to inform any readers from New England taking offense at his mockery of the Mainer accent that he has been a loyal fan of the Boston Red Sox since 1977.

UNINTENDED CONSEQUENCES

Jeff Baird

I remember the exact day and time of the year when it became clear to me that I was in serious trouble with my on-again/off-again love affair with my arthritic knees. Nearly ten years ago, I had hiked up Hawk Mountain, an offshoot of the Appalachian Trail in Eastern Pennsylvania, and was scrambling up some hard-core rock faces. The fall foliage was both beautiful and distracting. This adventure happened long before Parkour freebase running and jumping, but I was bouncing on these prehistoric pebbles, just like, to name drop, "Ricochet Rabbit."

Hiking in Mother Nature brought out the adventurer in me as I vaulted and twisted and sometimes crawled up and down in what is lovingly nicknamed, Rocksylvania, in the appropriately named "River of Rocks." Up, up, and away, I leaped into the air and imagined the vibrato synthesized sounds of *The Six Million Dollar Man*. I landed spot on and began the simultaneous motion toward the next target. Unfortunately, my left leg collapsed when I tried to push off, and I rolled down Mount Olympus in a bloody mess of bumps, scrapes, and bruises.

Once at the bottom, I tried to catch my breath and clear the cobwebs out of my mind to figure out how much trouble I had gotten myself into. Slowly, I tried to push myself up from the rocky terrain, but it remained a no-go. My situation was not good. There was no one around to help, and I was out of cell range. As I looked up from the bottom of a ravine, blood continued oozing out of various cuts and bruises on my lower extremities.

Calling out for help garnered no response. I was left with the realization that I needed to work my way up to the main path all by myself. This struggle would eventually lead me back to my car in the, of course, farthest parking lot. Lucky for me, there was a downed tree limb with a crook in it that was about the right size to use as a crutch. So, I did the "Butt-Scooting

Boogie" over to it and picked it up and crawled/hopped/staggered up to the top of the ridge.

What should have been a short, ten-minute stroll turned out to be an over two-hour trail of tears.

Let's make a deal

Fortunately for me, it was mostly my left knee that was banged up and throbbing. At least I could still drive my car. Once home, I hobbled into my recliner, gobbled down several ibuprofen, and promptly passed out. The following day, I woke up, called my doctor, and got in early due to a canceled appointment. By then, both of my knees were black and blue, sore, swollen, and painful.

After the preliminary pleasantries, my doctor explained what my options were.

"Well, Jeff, it looks like it's time. I don't see any other way of addressing this issue. Unfortunately, that knee will have to be replaced."

"Yeah, Doc, I know, and I've been trying to push through the pain, but it's just simply getting worse. I have been researching knee replacements, and I want to talk to you about getting both knees done at the same time."

He just kind of sat there looking at me with a blank expression. After a few moments, Doc said to me, "Your left knee is absolutely a candidate for this procedure; your right knee, while it does have signs of degenerative arthritis, should be a couple years away from needing a similar treatment."

"Yeah, Doc, but I saw what my dad went through having separate operations on each knee, and I can't see myself doing that. I am now following the same path that he did years ago, and it just scares me. Watching his pained expressions and continued weight gain is not living. It's just surviving, and that is no way to exist."

As if in an old "Looney Tunes" cartoon, I could see the dollar signs appear above his head. He sat there in a doctorly pose; I suppose contemplating the enormous task at hand. Then, finally, he looked at me and said that he agreed. "However," he continued, "I will have to consult with the powers that be to get their permission."

At this point, he turned to his office manager and said, "Nurse Lori, connect me with the High Commander at the Masters of the Universe Insurance Company. You can reach them at 1-800-Omnipotent."

Fortunately for me, their office had been compromised by ransomware attacks. I snuck in under the wire before the Industrial Security Complex paid the ransom and restored their files.

In the good old summertime

Beginning in November, I counted down the days to my bilateral knee replacement scheduled for the first day of summer vacation. Since I'm a teacher, this delay would give me ample time to get my affairs in order and to get back on my feet before the start of school in the fall. It would also allow me to get back to hiking in time to see the fall foliage painting Mother Nature's landscape.

Baird, party of two

The appointed day, June 17, finally arrived, and I reported to the hospital to have my knee-replacement operation. I recall the questions and the forms and the drawings on my knees and the countdown while the anesthesiologist put the drug into my IV. A fog washed over me so quickly that it seemed just seconds until I woke up in the recovery room.

After surgery, I felt numb all over, but I stayed in la-la land as the attendants wheeled me into my luxurious suite that was my side of the hospital room. The nurses were quite attentive, getting all their equipment/IVs set up and making sure I was squared away before they moved on to the next patient. This preparation allowed me to go back to a welcome nanosecond of sleep. I awoke to all sorts of instructions. Maybe I was still in a haze and wasn't entirely understanding what the nurses were telling me, but it sounded like they said to get off my ass and walk to the bathroom.

"Sir, wake up, wake up."

A buzzing sounded in my ear. Again, I heard them say, "Get up."

You must be on drugs. No wait, that's me.

I finally realized what they asked me to do. "You understand that I just came back from major surgery, right?"

They answered, "That was then, and this is now. First, you need to get up and walk to the bathroom. Then, after you relieve yourself, you need to take a victory lap around the hallway."

Just a few hours ago, they had me in the operating room.

Okay, I got this.

With a bit of assistance, I swung my legs over the edge of the bed and carefully stood up. Then, using the IV pole as a steadying base, I inched my way toward the bathroom, step by step. Once there, try as I might, nothing came out. I figured that nature would call when it suited her.

Hopefully, it would be just a matter of time.

The miracles of modern science

The next morning, with my head cleared from the haze, I awaited the excruciating agony that I expected to follow. That turned out not to be the case as I not only awoke to no pain, but I could get out of bed and move around. My legs, and especially my knees, felt very stiff and tight but were relatively pain-free. *Yahoo!*

After being awake for a few hours and taking in some sustenance, I saw the doctors as they made their rounds. They let me know what a great job they had done. I relaxed for about seventeen minutes. To my surprise, that's when physical therapy showed up to start my recovery program.

I know it sounds silly and vain, however my ego prodded me to demonstrate the various ranges of motion to indicate the strength and flexibility of my knees and, to the best of my ability, show off. I guess my athletic background came into play. I was pushing myself to do as well as possible. After this initial visit, it became crystal clear that this would be my daily physical therapy regimen.

I have to admit that I looked forward to the following day. This ordeal was a necessary evil so that I could regain my life and be able to resume my love of hiking and chasing waterfalls.

Do I hear Niagara Falls calling my name?

Road to recovery

Did I mention the morphine drip?

Being a recipient of numerous outpatient surgeries in the past gave me quite a bit of experience. However, they were always accompanied by Tylenol Number Three, a mild pain killer. Morphine was a new experience for me, as the drip lasted for a day and a half. I felt stiff but reasonably comfortable and prided myself on a remarkable recovery. Of course, the drugs were probably speaking for me, but I'm going to say it was due to my outstanding physical prowess.

I awoke from my nap to cuddle with my newfound security blanket, "The Drip." *Oh no!* Nurse Shirley had disconnected my IV and was instructing me to get out of bed. The time had come to start my soon-to-be routine morning constitutional around the hospital's hallways which I envisioned as a stroll through Central Park. Again, I was pleasantly surprised at the ease of my strides and confident of early recovery.

They replaced the morphine with a medicine previously unknown to me, OxyContin. I received this medicine twice daily and, as with "The Drip," felt little to no pain anywhere in my body. Because of my meteoric improvement, I was given a gold star and told a transfer to a minimum-security rehab facility would soon be arranged to help me return to normalcy. Wow, it had only been a few days since I had entered their fine establishment.

I settled into a routine of a light repast in the early morning followed by a stroll on the veranda as I headed down to physical therapy for my twice-daily calisthenics. However, shortly after my surgery I began to notice a little pain which was to be expected, but also my stomach seemed slightly off. It wasn't that painful, just mildly queasy. I passed it off as a side effect of having my routine disrupted. I am nothing if not a man of habits, set in my ways.

Houston, we may have a problem

Once Nurse Shirley returned to my room, I mentioned getting some relief for my stomach, and the request then went up the chain of command. Shortly after that, the doctors game me medicine to settle my tummy, which even worked for a brief time. However, it soon became apparent that something was going on when my stomachache returned, requiring even more efforts to quell my nausea.

At last, Nursed Shirley got around to asking me what would turn out to be a prophetic question: "When was the last time you had a bowel movement?"

I had to think about this for a moment, and *Frankly, My Dear,* I could not recall.

"Well, we're going to give you something gentle to help you go."

Guess what? It didn't work. And while I managed to keep down the stomach medicine, it was a no-go in the Potty Mission Control Center.

Threshold of pain

Despite all the inconsistencies, I was making stellar progress with my newfound, six-million-dollar, titanium, bionic, artificial intelligence, neu-tronic-powered knees. As a result, they marked me for escape, um, I mean, release to the aforementioned recovery center.

"But what about my stomachache?" I asked plaintively.

"Well, we're going to give you some medicine to make you feel all bet-ter. After that, you can call us if you don't get any relief." Then, with a sug-ary-sweet, fake smile, my new attendant, Nurse Pouky continued, "Once you get there and are back on the road to recovery, we are sure that your symptoms will subside."

A Clockwork Orange meets *The Exorcist*

Despite the continued setbacks over the last few days, some good things were happening. While my stomach issues did not go away, my mobility had improved so much that I was soon sent on my merry way.

Off I went to my expensive retreat, otherwise known as my bedroom in the rehab facility. For the next day and a half, I slept on and off only about an hour at a time. During one of these catnaps, I'm not sure what woke me up, but I slowly regained consciousness. An agonizing feeling, like the torture scene in Stanley Kubrick's *A Clockwork Orange* overwhelmed me. I bolted for the bathroom, and by bolted, I mean a slow-motion crawl that turned out to be way too slow. You might think that the medicine they had given me to settle my stomach had kicked in big time. And you would be wrong. Projectile vomiting exploded throughout the hallway leading into my nearby, but still too far away, bathroom.

Danger, danger!

The next time I awoke from a restless sleep, the first thing that popped into my mind was not what you would expect. Nope, it was not the logical thought of my recent major surgery. It was not even the resultant pain from this procedure. It was the discomfort, nay the excruciating agony of my now predominant health issue: my stomach. It began in my tummy and would travel up to my chest, forcing me to hiccup and burp forcefully. I'm not talking about "excuse me while I turn my head to politely belch." It was a toe-curling eruption of gas that exited from my oral cavity, and any leftover gases escaped from another orifice.

Regardless of my ongoing predicaments, I was deemed to be low risk and able to continue my treatments as an outpatient and would be able to go home.

If I was low risk, I would hate to see what high risk looked like.

What a relief it is . . . not

Once home the only thing that gave me any relief from my stomach issue was taking antacids to help alleviate my massive, nonstop heartburn. Sadly, the duration of the accompanying relief grew shorter and shorter every day. I began to pop the pills like candy. But the acid reflux would always return. It grew so bad that I was considering going to the emergency room as I was in near constant pain.

I just love it when they talk technical

Several days passed with little relief which finally forced me to seek the help of the emergency room. I sat in the waiting room, doubled over to the point of tears, as I struggled to respond to the intake nurse's line of investigation, I mean interrogation, I mean inquisition.

"Can you tell me where it hurts? . . . On a scale of one to ten, what is your current pain level?"

Fighting the urge to throw up, I mumbled something like "seventeen."

"We're going to give you something to help you feel better, but first, we're going to have to run some tests to isolate the problem."

According to their blood analysis, my calcium level was extremely high. Apparently, popping antacids like Skittles can do the trick of mimicking symptoms of a heart attack. Because I had recently undergone major surgery, they hypothesized that the anesthesia gas was playing hide and seek inside me and could be the cause of my pain. Yippee, problem solved.

Once again, the hospital gave me something to settle my stomach, gave me a prescription for Oxy for the pain that now radiated all over my body, and then sent me on my not-so-merry way. After several days of little to no sleep and the inability to keep anything down, I was just too dang tired to argue with them. So, off I went to my comfy bed, where I collapsed from exhaustion, agony, and a growing sense of melancholy.

Lather, rinse, repeat

Whatever they had given me let me sleep a bit. I awoke feeling better, but my knees and legs ached something wicked! I took out my convenient stash of pills and popped the prescribed dose. I drifted off into another restless nap only to awake with that same tormenting triple-play combo (knees, stomach, and chest.) I became more depressed as the days wore on with no end in sight. All my plans of regaining my strength and endurance, and basically my life, were coming apart.

I was doing everything they told me to and just couldn't understand what was happening to me. I had mentally prepared myself for the pain and discomfort in my knees. I knew it would not be easy, but I thought my long-ago jock days had prepared me for the hard work that would put me on the road to recovery. So far, I wasn't even on the map.

During all this time, I tried to tough it out and go to outpatient treatment to revive my knees and my dreams. Regrettably, PT became increasingly difficult, if not impossible, due to the myriad problems that were my life at this point.

Where did I go wrong?

Downward dog, I think not

Try as I might, I couldn't perform even a fraction of the exercises or demonstrate the degree of flexibility that one would have expected at this stage of my rehab. In addition, I had altered my normal gait because I was overcompensating in my stride and tensing in anticipation of pains as I moved even in a limited fashion. To make matters worse, PT scolded me that this was my fault because I was slacking off on my exercises, evidenced by the various metrics they used to measure my strength and mobility.

It took all of a week of constant suffering to end up back in the emergency room with a now-familiar pattern of symptoms with a new twist of debilitating lower back and hip pain. Once again, in the darkness of the night that mirrored my pain and depressed state of mind, I returned to the scene of the crime. With tears flowing down my cheeks, I repeated the by-now memorized description of disorders to the medical personnel.

This time, they admitted me to the hospital. Again, I went through all kinds of tests to determine what was wrong with me. But, to a certain degree, the medical personnel made me feel like they thought I was imagining some of these issues or at least exaggerating them to gain attention or sympathy.

There were times where Nurse Retched downright yelled at me for throwing up right after taking several pills to, you guessed it, make my stomach feel better and alleviate the pain. There had been a change of shifts, and my new nighttime nurse arrived to check on me. In came Nurse Stacey, who took the time to listen to me when I tried to explain my issues before she perfunctorily gave me the medications.

A smorgasbord of painkillers

As Nurse Stacey and I talked, we both realized that two constant elements had followed me for several weeks. First was the obvious: Morphine, Oxycodone, OxyContin, Percocet, Percodan (you name it, they tried it). In one way, shape, or form, painkillers were present from day one. Of course, I expected this. The second fact was a symptom that had largely been ignored. So once again I was asked: "When was the last time you moved your bowels?"

I still could not remember, so she promised to discuss this with my doctor, and one of them would come back to chat with me.

No doctor came in, but Nurse Stacey returned with a new medication regimen, which included a laxative in my IV. Honestly, I had never taken a laxative in my life but was certainly aware of them and their effect. Finally, a breakthrough had been achieved and a small sense of optimism returned for the first time in several weeks. While still weak and unsettled, at last I was hopeful.

That morning, despite a familiar upset stomach, I forced myself to eat breakfast and then made a concerted effort to walk the hallways to put things in motion. A few hours later, I felt some rumblings in my digestive system and went into the bathroom in anticipation of activity that would soon be forthcoming. Time and time again, I felt on the verge of success, but all I could muster were a few small, dark-black nuggets. I could accurately describe them because I had to observe and report the result to the nurses.

It took me close to an hour to produce this small sampling. My legs and butt were extremely numb from the extended posture, but at least it was a start.

Not sure how I was going to fit all of this into my daily schedule.

Cost-benefit analysis

Despite this new insight into my multitude of symptoms, they discharged me the following day. It was with the understanding that I would continue with this new regimen of medications and go back to PT. I had minor success in mobility and digestive areas, but they were still few and far between.

Every time I would try to go the bathroom, it would be a lengthy battle, the cost of which, unfortunately, would outweigh the benefits as I continued to spiral deeper into depression. My recovery schedule of one to one-and-a-half months was not even close to reality. My two-month summer break was rapidly closing. Having to go back for the opening of school was an approaching nightmare.

It all came to a head when, after two days of faculty meetings and setting up my classroom, we all had to gather in the gymnasium for a faculty yearbook photo.

Sitting on the bleachers was excruciating. I couldn't bend my knees fully, and my back was spasming. I was close to passing out from the pain. The only saving grace was that it was the end of the day. I'd finally had enough and drove myself to the emergency room and did not take no for an answer. They were going to help me or else!

What was wrong with me?

Dammit, fix me

My return to the hospital was the third time I had gone to the ER in a month. After listening to me and seeing the look on my face, the tears in my eyes, the tone in my voice, they admitted me once again. So many parts of my body were affected by this agony that they did not know where to start. Naturally, they gave me something for the pain and stomachache while they figured out what to do. Don't get me wrong; they weren't forcing these pills down my throat. Instead, I wholeheartedly requested and received them. Once the suffering and spasms subsided, they started their tests again to determine the root cause of my agony and depression.

If only I knew then what I know now.

I can't study for this test

By now, they had run so many tests I had to remind myself to invest in this hospital system. They were making a fortune off me.

They repeated their ongoing scavenger hunt to cure me. Finally, they scheduled me to take another x-ray. This time the scan focused not on my knees or hips, but my stomach, which showed that I had an impacted colon. Then they set me up for another test, a barium contrast scan. A warm feeling washed over me which helped me to briefly fall asleep as they injected radioactive dye into my IV port to determine the extent of my colon's impaction.

I was startled awake by a team of nurses and attendants scurrying around me like busy bees as they instructed me to turn over on my stomach. I was still groggy from the tests and hesitantly asked the obvious question: "Wait, What?"

"Please turn over. We're going to give you an enema."

"Why, what's wrong?"

"Your colon is dangerously impacted. If you want to avoid emergency surgery, you'll turn over and let us do our job."

"Surgery? Are you kidding me?"

Being taken off guard, I took a moment to recover. Then, after realizing they weren't joking, I turned over and prepared myself for humiliation.

"Now, just relax." *Easy for them to say.*

I felt the tube go into me and the liquid release. I was lying in this exposed position, all the while listening to the nurses making small talk. "Did you see the leaves starting to change color?"

No. I was too busy playing ER Pinball.

Time seemed to stand still. Nothing happened. Everyone was standing around watching me while the clock continued to *tick, tick, tick.*

Nothing. Not a drop. The medical consortium told me they would give it time to take effect while they consulted with the doctor. When the brain trust returned, in a strangely foreboding moment, I recognized Nurse Retched from an earlier encounter. She was the same nurse that, in one of my recent trips to the ER, had yelled at me for throwing up all the pills they had made me swallow.

I wondered if she remembered me.

The sweet smell of success

Again, they instructed me to "assume the position." So once again, I turned over, and Nurse Retched began the procedure with, what I can only speculate was, a more potent brew.

As she stood over me delivering the magic potion, she scolded me again, "You'd better control yourself. Don't you dare let loose on me."

Magically, as if by the completion of an electrical circuit, my poop machine flipped a switch and, *thar she blows!*

I can only liken this to the movie Animal House when Flounder throws up unexpectedly on Dean Wormer after repeated being prodded to come "out with it." But, of course, there was a *slightly* different bodily discharge emanating from me, and it sure wasn't anything I could pop a breath mint to cure.

Months of emotions and pent-up pain and depression came, excuse the pun, pouring out of me. A volcano of the sweetest smelling poop exploded everywhere. It must have somehow reached you-know-who, because suddenly I also detected screams of. "Oh no!" Then I heard and felt Nurse Retched let loose with her vomit, which triggered my gag reflex that let fly. The floor, table, she, and I were covered in a mass of poop and puke. Despite the drama, I'm sure that was a Kodak moment. Smile for the camera. I hope they got my good side.

The end justifies the means

Now, several years later, I have settled with the Masters of the Universe Insurance Company concerning the cleaning costs and resultant lawsuits. I have also learned I am now a case study for the International Pharmacological Consortium Double-Blind Drug Trials and its effect on the addictive quality of painkillers and their (written in *teeny, tiny, small print*) side effects.

Unintended consequences that resulted from these events, and continue to . . . I don't know if "haunt me" is the right term, but I'm going to go with it.

Is that your final answer?

For three months, I went through hell. I went through uncertainty, pain, depression, and long-lasting physical and mental side effects. I still walk funny. I can only hope that, years from now, I don't relapse with the ailments that crippled me. My mobility deteriorated as a result of constant pressure in my knees and thighs, making me feel like they were ready to burst. The tightness was mainly due to the lengthy delay of meaningful physical therapy in my knees and legs to gain complete flexibility. They just kind of got set in a semi-locked position.

Please don't get the wrong idea; I am thankful to have resumed my life, including nature hikes and chasing waterfalls. Still, based upon what we now know about the opioid epidemic and how dangerous my situation could have been, I feel blessed that I could come out of this somewhat unscathed . . . but with unintended consequences.

NO ANGELS

Kidd Wadsworth

The night replayed itself, exactly like last night . . . and the night before . . . and the night before.

0400 hours. The phone rings. I drive in, park my car, get out, beep it locked—and the fog, great billows of it, rolls in, like my beep cued some film crew to start a fog machine at stage left. I approach Cortlandt Alley and the nearest streetlight flickers, twice, off and on, off and on. A cold wind hits my face, and with it comes the smell, overpoweringly sweet, of caramel and burnt butter. I'm an old cop, an old hound, and I bristle.

I duck under the yellow tape as Kris zips up the body bag.

"Nice to see you, Bill."

My reply is a what-time-is-it growl; she grins.

I won't need to read the report she'll drop on my desk at two p.m. I have three identical ones in the second drawer of my filing cabinet. Small puncture wound beneath the right ear where the drug was administered, probably by dart. Incision in the abdomen. Tissue removed from the pelvic bone. Bone marrow also removed. Left testicle swiped. All the vics were O'Malleys, including last night's who looked more like his Syrian mom than his Irish forebears. The lethal drug is still at the lab undergoing analysis. Seems they can't quite identify it.

0600 hours. I arrive at the office. I make the coffee.

Shamus, my partner, is still out. He's talking to the most recent O'Malley's mom and two sisters. I sit at my desk, ticking off the facts on my fingers, like I'm expecting some kind of revelation. Four dead. All New Yorkers. All O'Malleys. All males. All killed between three and four a.m., the bodies moved from their homes and dumped in random places across the city.

0800 hours. The captain drops a file on my desk. Seems Chicago has a dead O'Malley, and Honolulu, too. Same MO. That makes six dead O'Malley's.

0900 hours. I've graduated from counting on my fingers to an actual written list of facts. My cell rings. I tap it. A picture appears of a labor-exhausted woman with sweat-soaked hair and my eldest, three hours old, wrinkled and sleeping in her arms. I swivel around until I'm looking at a dreary Manhattan instead of a room full of ugly, exhausted cops.

"Hey, beautiful."

"Guess what?"

My heart stops. Thank the merciful Lord she keeps talking.

"I found something to help you."

I lean back—relieved. For the past sixteen years, "Guess what?" has been my wife's delicate code for "I'm pregnant." We've already contributed six new souls to the Earth's bursting population, all girls who love My Little Ponies. I live in Hasbro's magical world of Equestria.

"So, you're solving crimes?" I say, "Great! Can I come home?"

"Hey, you want some help or not?"

"Please God and the blessed Mary ever-Virgin. Yes, I want some help."

"They're all related."

"We've already run that angle. They're not related."

"Yes, they are. I used Sue's genealogy program. Those men all have the same ancestor: an Irish priest."

"Are you sure?"

"I'm sure. His name is Ronan O'Malley, born in Ireland in 1793. I Googled him. Ronan O'Malley supposedly had a vision in 1807, when he was fourteen years old. He claimed he was taken by angels into the sky until he could see the Earth below him like a huge blue-and-white ball. Everyone in the village thought the guy was crazy, but the local lord of the manor believed him. So, he paid for the guy to be educated. When O'Malley was twenty-four, he immigrated to America and married, had two sons, and later became a priest after his wife died. He was known as the Priest of the Clouds because he never stopped talking about being taken up into the sky."

"Babe can you run that program forward? Can you tell me who else is related to him?"

"Hmmm . . . I don't know." Keyboard clicks come over the phone. "Maybe not."

"It's all right. I can get the records."

"Wait!" she calls out. "Remember, it's only the male line."

"What?"

"The priest was the original O'Malley. To trace the lineage back to the priest, you move only through the sons."

I make to put down the phone but stop. I can't let her go so easily. It's always been like this. Sometimes I feel like a fool, but then I see her standing at the sink brushing her teeth or hear her laughing at a TV commercial—she loves commercials—and I get happy, stupid happy. "Thanks. I love you, you know."

"You want dessert tonight?"

That's code, too. "Oh, yeah."

I head across town to see Kris. Her lab is in the basement. Seems her boss isn't real pleased that Kris, fresh out of medical school, is constantly showing him up. I pass a dehumidifier on the way to her door. It can't keep up. The walls are leaking moisture. Overhead, half of the fluorescents are dead. She has the latest O'Malley on a table in front of her, his guts in trays. The dampness, one glaring light over the examination table, the gore . . . the scene has horror flick written all over it. I grin. "Having fun?"

"You betcha."

"Kris, I've got a genealogy program that tells me all of these O'Malleys had a common ancestor, Father Ronan O'Malley."

"Can't be."

"Why not?"

"DNA changes from father to son, because each child's DNA is a composite of his father's and his mother's. The exception is the Y chromosome." She begins weighing the stomach. "Women do not have a Y chromosome. Thus, the Y chromosome passes virtually unaltered from father to son. I put a rush on the DNA testing. The three O'Malley's tested to date all have different Y chromosome patterns. They could not have had the same great-great-great- however many greats-grandfather."

I lean back against the freezer. The unit looks like a chest of drawers. The gasket on one drawer doesn't seal properly. Arctic air finds the small of my back and creeps up my spine. Kris continues to work, paying extraordinary attention to her scale. I stay put, letting my back slowly freeze. She glances my way, and glances again, and again. I stifle the urge to ask her a question.

When I'm sure I'll never bend properly again, she takes off her gloves and says, "The DNA tests did turn up one strange thing."

"Yeah?"

"One thousand twenty-four Ts"

"Kris, I was born before people had DNA."

"All DNA is composed of four molecules: A, T, G, and C. Normal DNA code would look like a random string of those four letters." She thinks the old guy needs an example, "AATCGTGGCTT. . ."

"Okay, okay."

"In the Y chromosome of all of our O'Malleys there is a section of 1024 consecutive Ts."

"I thought you said the O'Malleys all have different Y chromosomes."

"They do, but the differences in their Y chromosomes appear to be limited to the 1024 base pairs adjacent to the 1024 Ts." She writes it out for me. "Their DNA looks something like this, only with more letters."

. . . TTTTTTTTTTTTTTTT . . . AGCTGGCCTTAATCGAT . . .

"Do most men have a bunch of Ts in a row in their Y chromosome?"

"No."

It's the volume of the captain's voice that tells me he isn't happy—that, and his colorful word choice. "How many effing birth certificates do you want me to request?" Shamus sticks up for me. "What else have we got, Captain?"

The next day, records pour in at three-thirty p.m. Last night produced another dead O'Malley. We're at seven and counting. The difference is that this time, the dead O'Malley's grandmother knows two of the other vics. She confirms: they're related.

Our records search produces eighty-two living male descendants of Father Ronan O'Malley. We rush warrants, divide the files, and get on the phones. My seventh call is to a Sean O'Malley. He picks up in LAX about to board a flight home. I run the names of the vics by him.

"No sir, I don't recognize them, but . . ."

"Spit it out."

"When I left, four days ago, I could have sworn someone was watching me."

"Mr. O'Malley, when you had this feeling, did you happen to smell anything unusual?"

"Yeah, candy."

My guts knot up. I hand the rest of the stack of names to Shamus—he isn't real happy—and assign two uniforms to Sean O'Malley's apartment.

I meet Sean at the airport, red-headed, skin so freckled he almost looks orange. He's twenty-two and running logistics for a production company making television commercials. He gets all puffed up, like a kid, excited and proud and wrapped in a cheek-bursting grin when he tells me, "Tomorrow I get to hire a helicopter."

For a moment I can't breathe. He's the spitting image of my first partner. It's more than his orange coloring. It's not his freckles that sucker punched me. It's the joy in his eyes. I remember Jimmy saying, "Do you ever think about it, Bill? We get to be the good guys, out here, every day, risking our lives for the citizens of New York City. I love this job."

Dread rumbles around in the pit of my belly. I don't want to bury Sean, too.

I give him the scoop on the murders and ask the usual question. "Your family have any blood feuds?"

He grins. "Both my older brothers are priests. The only feud I know about is between my mom and the archbishop. My brothers were supposed to give her some grandchildren. Now, she'll barely let the bishop in the house. She doesn't want him to recruit me."

I point to my car. "Get in. I'll drive you home."

He gives me a *you've-got-be-kidding* look. "You really think someone is going to kill me?"

"Son, we've got seven dead people all named O'Malley. How about you let me do my job?"

"And they say cops don't care." He grins again. "Hey, you want some dinner?"

"Bill, Bill, can you hear me?"

I wake, lying on a parking lot reeking of caramel. A frazzled Shamus is staring down at me.

"Did you see the perps? What did they look like?"

"Angels. I saw. . . angels."

During the four hours of debriefing, I almost tell the truth. "I saw a bright light and men who looked like they had wings."

"Wings?"

"Hey, maybe they were wearing Halloween costumes or something. You know, as a disguise."

They end the session with the requisite joke. "Angels, huh? And they let you live?"

When I finally get home, Joan's got the girls tucked in. Her eyes are puffy, her face wet. I pull her close. I can't stop shaking. She runs her hands over my head as if she has to keep touching me to know that I'm alive. Her warmth, her scent, her everything gets me talking.

"I saw this cloud. It was blindingly white, like something that's hot, incredibly hot." As the vision recreates itself in my mind, I act it out for her. I hold my hands up in front of my face. I shut my eyes, look away. "The light was so bright I could still see it through my closed eyelids."

She sits me at the table; puts a slice of hot meatloaf and a glass of cold milk in front of me. Damn, I'm hungry. As I wolf it down, she stands behind me with her arms wrapped around my chest. When the food is gone, she says, "I'll get you some more milk." But I don't need milk. I need to tell her all of it.

I grab her arm, bringing her to sit next to me. "They came out of the light. Dear Lord, Joan, they had wings—each one had six wings. They didn't walk, they darted about in the air, like gnats! What were they?"

I sleep with my arms wrapped around her; my head nestled against her neck.

The next morning, I put Sean O'Malley's picture on my desk and pick up Kris's autopsy report. The woman doesn't need a lab—just a Xerox machine. From across the room, the captain crooks a finger at me. I know what's coming. When I'm inside his closet of an office, the door closed behind me, he says, "You know I love you, but . . ."

". . . why didn't they kill me?"

"You've had some sleep. Any ideas?"

I say, "No, sir."

I think, *1024 Ts.*

Another victim (number nine) and Kris comes to see me. "Coffee, Bill?"

I look at the cup in my hand; she motions toward the door.

It's raining, the skies dumping water like we should be building arks. The local coffee shop is across the street, but she walks by it to the one two blocks south. She gets an artisan brew; I go for the cheesecake—with extra strawberries. She heads to the back of the room, where she fusses with her napkin. When she finally speaks, her voice is barely audible.

"Maybe it wasn't 'angels' that took Father O'Malley."

That knot in my gut cinches itself a whole lot tighter.

"You think I'm crazy."

She grabs her purse; I grab her arm and lean forward until we're an inch apart, my eyes staring into hers. "I've seen the 'angels,' remember?"

She's trembling . . . almost ashamed. "We're talking about—"

"Shhh . . . we're talking about DNA. That's all."

She nods, takes a breath, but the trembling doesn't stop. "Remember the Ts?"

I nod.

"Last year the new mass spec wouldn't talk to my computer. So, I called out the tech. She said the mass spec wasn't sending out a start code. Computers speak using only ones and zeros. Before the mass spec sends data, it sends out a start code to tell the receiving device, my computer, to pay attention. You know, like it's calling my computer's name. The mass spec's start code was a long string of ones." Her voice drops low. She puts her lips next to my ear. "I think those Ts are a start code. I think they mean, 'The message begins here.' I think whoever is killing the O'Malleys is looking for a message. I think someone hid a piece of the message in the DNA of each of Father O'Malley's great grandsons."

"Can you do that? Can you alter someone's DNA? I mean wouldn't they grow an extra toe or something?"

"Not necessarily. Whole sections of our DNA are not used. If one of those unused sections was altered, it wouldn't affect the person at all."

"How do you know the message was hidden in the great grandsons?"

She reaches down into her bag and pulls out a large, folded sheet of paper. "What clued me in was the genealogy chart." She unfolds the paper. "We've identified eighty-two male descendants of Ronan O'Malley. But within that pool, the killings aren't random. Look at the chart. Each of the vics is a descendant of a different great-grandson. What if the message was broken up? What if a piece was hidden in each great-grandson and then passed down generation after generation?" She takes a big gulp of whatever's in her coffee cup. "Bill, it makes sense. In every case, whoever is doing this is killing the oldest living descendant of each great-grandson."

I shake my head, "No, Sean had two older brothers."

She points to the chart. "Half-brothers. They were his mother's sons by a previous marriage. Sean's father died last year from a brain tumor."

Kris's words slowly sink in. She finishes her coffee and sits nervously drumming her fingers on the table.

"How many great-grandsons did Father O'Malley have?"

"Sixteen."

"So, you're saying that to find the entire message—"

"The perps need one descendant of each great-grandson."

I stand up, pushing back my chair, knocking it over. As I head out the door, I phone Shamus.

"I know where the perps will strike next."

Shamus and I assign extra men to the remaining seven oldest living male descendants of Ronan O'Malley's great-grandsons. Each potential vic now has four uniforms in their home. For the first time in a week, I see Shamus grin.

That night at 0400, the phone rings. Another O'Malley is dead (number ten). This time the perps kill some cops, too. They kill the four guys Shamus and I assigned to guard him.

1600 hours. The captain sends me home. I open my door and enter lasagna-perfumed chaos. Three of God's gifts are at the kitchen table doing homework while Stellie rides her tricycle in a circle—through the kitchen, through the living room, through the dining room, and back to the kitchen. My wife is making fruit salad. Her lips taste like pineapple.

I have only one rule: no My Little Ponies in Daddy's chair. I sink down into well-worn La-Z-Boy bliss and close my eyes. I shouldn't have. These days the backs of my eyelids are plastered with pictures I don't want to see, like Sean O'Malley so damn excited and Jimmy, my partner, lying dead, face down in the street.

I open my eyes, to see Emily, Stellie's twin, hiding Princess Celestia under my newspaper on the coffee table.

"Isn't that Shannon's pony?"

She jumps, then puts her hands on her hips and lifts her chin. Stubbornness and pride and sheer orneriness shine out of her fierce eyes. I smile. I can't help it. She's my favorite. I've never seen so much gall in one person.

"Shannon won't let me watch Nickelodeon."

"So, you're hiding her pony?"

She folds her arms across her chest. "She's reaping what she sows."

I should have told her about Jesus and forgiveness, instead I throw her in the air and whisper, "Thank you."

Out of the mouth of babes. Of course, Kris's hypothesis was a good start, but, basically, it didn't make sense. Why would the people—beings, aliens, whatever—kill the men to get the message out, when they didn't have to kill them to put it in? In my line of work the answer to that question is obvious: they got effed with, and they're effing mad.

I call out, "Joan, I've got to go back to work."

On the way in, I phone Kris. She picks up and I get an ear full of shower sounds, "Hey, Bill."

"Suppose, hypothetically . . ."

"Yeah, hypothetically . . ."

"That the message wasn't hidden in Father O'Malley's great-grandsons. Suppose beings from outer space, let's call them 'Ronan's angels,' hid the message in Father O'Malley's DNA, you know, when the 'angels' took him up into the sky and he saw the blue-and-white ball."

"Okay."

"Obviously, they hid the message expecting someone to find it. Let's call those people 'friends of Ronan's aliens.' Got it?"

"Got it."

"Now suppose that someone else came along, someone that didn't like Ronan's angels, and didn't like their friends. They decide to change the message. They know whoever is looking for the message will look for it in the living, so they change the message in Father O'Malley's living descendants—"

"—In all sixteen of Father O'Malley's great-grandsons."

"Now the 'friends of Ronan's angels' are back."

Again, she finishes my thought. "And they're searching for the message, a message they will never find."

"And they're pissed," I add. I'm pissed, too. I can't stop them from killing six more innocent people.

Or can I?

"Guess what, Kris?"

"What?"

"I know where the original message is. Get to the lab."

Priests are buried in the cemeteries of the church they pastored. Their graves are well kept. My wife had located the final resting place of Father O'Malley, The Priest of the Clouds, when she'd Googled him days ago. I don't wait for permission. I do the radical. I know a guy with a backhoe. He digs him up.

"Bill, you know this is the grave of a priest?"

"I'm trying to keep some people alive, and I don't have much time."

He nods. As he drives the backhoe down the street, I jump in the grave, pry open the coffin and chop up Father Ronan O'Malley. Leaning against his gravestone, I make necklaces, out of twine and Father O'Malley's DNA-laden bones. I recruit guys from the precinct, and we rush the necklaces to the living O'Malleys, to the guys stuck in their apartments waiting to die. The rest of the bones I put in a My Little Pony shipping box I have in my trunk. I give the box to Kris in her crypt for DNA analysis.

"Wow, you desecrated the grave of a priest?" she picks up a bone and whispers. "What if . . ."

"What if I get fired?"

"Well, there's that, but actually I wasn't thinking about you."

That's why I like Kris. She's all soft and mushy.

"What if we can decode the message?" she asks. "The department has some standard decryption software, and if it's numbers instead of a language—"

"Numbers?" I ask.

"Maybe it's the location of something hidden on the Earth, or the coordinates of their planet."

I exit the building, exhausted, heading home, looking for a bed. Overhead a streetlight flickers, twice, off and on, off and on.

The bastards kill again, but this time in addition to the testicle and the pelvis bone and the marrow, they take the necklace—and they don't kill the cops. I let Shamus work the crime scene. I need sleep. I pray it's over.

The next day I wake in time for dinner. Afterwards, I crawl wearily back to bed.

0400 hours. I wake. I phone Shamus.

"Everything quiet?"

"No one's dead, but . . ."

My guts are in knots again.

"Seems someone's been busy stealing all of those bone necklaces. Every last one."

Dread settles into the boiling, churning pit that used to be my stomach. The Pony Box . . .

"Where's Kris?"

"The last time I saw her she was at her lab."

"Find her!"

I hang up. She's on speed dial. "Pick up. Pick up."

"Hello, I'm cutting up a dead body right now and can't come to the phone. Please leave me a message, and, when I've cleaned the blood off my hands, I'll call you back."

Like a runner late out of the blocks, I race through the city. I enter the Medical Examiner's building, go down the back staircase, two flights down. The place reeks of caramel and burnt butter. Guys are standing around, everywhere. I push my way into Kris's lab. It's nothing but four scratched up white walls. Everything is gone: tables, benches, chairs, her computer—the My Little Pony box.

"Where's Kris? Where is she?"

No one looks at me.

"Have you traced her cell?"

"We found the phone on Lexington."

I can't tell a room full of cops that space aliens took Kris, so I don't tell them anything. Specifically, I don't tell them that the DNA-laden hammer I used to smash apart Father O'Malley's bones is in my toolbox in the trunk of my car. I present my badge at the armory. I go to the back, taking out our one and only Colt AR-15. I clothe myself in full riot gear, leaving no skin exposed. They'll have to come at me with something better than a dart. I sign out.

"Going somewhere, Bill?" the guard asks.

I raise two eyebrows. "Old" means everyone owes you.

He shrugs, and pretends his fingernails need attention. "Not that I care."

The place is dead. Everyone is down in the crypt, trying to make sense of Kris and her lab gone missing. Alone, I exit through the west door.

I slide a hand into my pants pocket.

Bring it.

I push the button on my fob. *Beep.* Right on cue, fog rolls in, great billows of it. Slowly, I walk down the row of cars. Ahead, a streetlight flickers, off and on, off and on. A cold wind hits my face, and with it comes the smell, overpoweringly sweet, of caramel and burnt butter. I stand next to my trunk, machine gun raised.

"What the hell?" Shamus comes out of the fog, gun drawn.

"Get out of here!"

A dart hits his neck.

"No!" I drop to my knees and pull out the dart.

I shout into the fog. "He doesn't know. He doesn't know."

The light blinds me. I don't turn away. They've killed twelve people. I fire. I fire again. They're too fast!

And they're not angels.

The Best Years of Her Life

Carol L. Wright

When in the shower, Jessie always found her mind drifting to the same thoughts. It wasn't that she couldn't get Chuck to help around the house that bothered her. It was that he sat around, doing nothing—including paying attention to her. She wondered if she nagged too much. *No,* she thought. *I remind him of things, but I don't nag.*

But it was no use. After thirteen years, he had checked out of the marriage. If it weren't for Jessie doing *everything* that got done in their house, they would never have a clean dish, clothes to wear, or food on the table. But fair is fair. He ought to contribute from time to time.

Theirs wasn't a big house. Two bedrooms, a single bath with no window, and a connected kitchen, dining nook, and TV room on a slab. Enough for two. Maybe enough for three or four. But even a small house needs maintenance.

They both had jobs. Chuck drove for a package delivery service, while Jessie was a nursing assistant. He made more than she did, and his job offered better benefits, but she knew men usually made more than women. That didn't make up for doing nothing around the house. They both worked long hours. When would it be her turn to just come home and turn on the TV?

Thirteen years. The best years of my life, Jessie thought. *If these were my best years, what will the rest of my life look like?*

She turned the water off and stepped out of the shower, dripping as she crossed the bare bathroom floor. Shivering, she lifted her robe from the hook and wrapped it around her, then grabbed the lone towel from the bar to wrap her hair.

As she passed the bedroom mirror, she turned to assess her face. She had to admit it was no longer pretty. She used to smile effortlessly, but now she had resting bitch face. Or maybe just resting sad face. She wasn't sure which was worse.

At thirty-eight, she still looked youngish. Chuck never wanted kids, so she'd kept her figure. Putting her hand on her belly, she wondered what it would have been like. *With a kid or two,* she thought, *I'd at least have some company while Chuck watches TV.* She was still young enough. Maybe there was still time . . . but not with Chuck.

Snow streaked past the window, and she shivered.

Her skin looked pretty good if you didn't notice her chapped hands from washing them so often in hard water. Chuck would never consider getting a water softener. He never wanted to spend money on anything he called a "luxury." No, he was way too practical for that—except, of course, for the sports package on cable.

They weren't rich; she understood that. But now and again, it would be nice to splurge on a dinner out, or even a vacuum cleaner that didn't break every time she ran it across the floor. Her vows declared she had married him for better or for worse, 'til death do them part. *Isn't this a kind of death?*

She knew Chuck wasn't having an affair. How could he? He was always either at work or in front of the TV. He had no interests, no hobbies, no friends as far as she knew. He worked alone in a truck most of the day, and they tracked him to be sure he didn't spend too long at any given stop. *No,* she thought. *He's just lost interest in anything other than watching sports.*

When the football season was over, he would move quickly to hockey, then to college basketball to hold him over until the baseball season opened. Then he would watch any game that came on, no matter who was playing. There was always a game on TV. He'd even watch games replayed from several years ago if that was all there was. If even that failed, he would watch golf. Always in his recliner, his stockinged feet propped up and a beer in his hand. *Anything's better than talking to me.*

As she dressed, she resolved that she had to do something soon, or she'd give up on life the way he had. Existing—not really living. She couldn't let that happen.

"That circuit breaker in the bathroom has gone out again." Jessie gave what she knew was an exasperated grimace.

Chuck, intent on his football game, gave a shrug. "Just push the damn button," he snarled.

Jessie balled her fists. "I *did*. It's the circuit breaker itself that's gone bad. There are no lights in the bathroom, and the outlet doesn't work. I can't dry my hair in there."

"First of all, it's not a circuit breaker. It's a GFCI switch. Second of all, use another outlet. I'm busy." Chuck's eyes never left the screen.

"That's okay. I'll call an electrician."

"We can't get an electrician out on a weekend—especially in a snowstorm. They'll charge an arm and a leg. It'll wait."

Jessie's frustration boiled over. "We don't *have* to call an electrician. I told you before, I bought a replacement breaker from the electrician the last time this happened. You can install it yourself and save money." *That, at least, ought to get his attention.*

Chuck waved a hand. "Nah. I don't want to mess with electricity right now. I said it will wait."

Jessie clicked her tongue and mumbled under her breath, "The directions are in the package. It shouldn't be that hard to do."

She dropped the conversation and went into the kitchen to start lunch. He always wanted the same thing. A tuna sandwich on rye. When they were first married, she would chop celery and onion and parsley and hard-boiled egg, with a touch of mustard and pepper and lemon juice, to mix into the salad. These days it was just tuna and mayonnaise. Chuck didn't seem to care. *I really could put anything in his sandwich and he'd never notice,* she thought.

As she worked, her thoughts went back to the circuit breaker. It was a small job, yet he refused to even try it. He was useless to her. She couldn't stand another day of it.

She handed him his sandwich.

"You didn't cut it in half," he said, handing it back to her and shaking his head as if at a naughty child.

Jessie felt her blood pressure rise and went to fetch a knife. *No,* she thought. *I'll just use a dinner knife. Anything sharper would be too tempting.*

She cut the sandwich in half and handed it to Chuck. He didn't even acknowledge her. Why did it matter whether it was cut in half or not?

She had to do something.

Returning to the kitchen, she opened her utility drawer and pulled out a new pair of rubber gloves. *These ought to be good for more than my chapped hands,* she thought.

After putting away the mayonnaise, she washed the bowl and utensils in hot, soapy water. Then she rinsed the tuna can and placed it in the recycle bin.

Hands on hips, she watched as her husband mechanically chewed, lost in whatever game glowed from the set. She strode to the pantry, peeking out a moment later, just in time to see the lights go out and hear the hum of the refrigerator cut off. The house was silent. The quiet calmed her jangled nerves, but only for a moment. Chuck was on his feet, remote in hand.

"What the hell happened?" He yelled as if he were in pain.

Jessie stared at him across the kitchen. "I guess the storm brought down a tree or something and the power went out."

"But the game was just getting good!"

Jessie felt a bit smug, enjoying his outrage at missing out on his game.

"I'll try to find the game online." Chuck patted his pockets in search of his phone.

"If the power's out, the internet is out, too," Jessie reminded him, trying to hide her glee.

Chuck threw down the remote, the force making the batteries pop out. "Well, now what am I supposed to do?"

Jessie shook her head. "I'm sure there are lots of other things you could do besides watch TV. Hey, you could even fix that breaker in the bathroom. Course we won't know if it works until the electricity is back on."

Chuck looked at her as though she were a madwoman. His anger burned too hot, she realized, to consider her suggestion. He looked at the dismembered remote and picked it up, collected the batteries, and put it back together. Sitting in his favorite chair, he took another bite of the sandwich. It was nearly gone. Just a corner remained.

"Oh, all right," he said, aggravation in his voice.

"All right what?" Jessie asked.

"I'll fix that GFCI outlet while the power is out."

Jessie's jaw dropped. She couldn't believe her luck.

She opened the junk drawer, withdrew the replacement, and handed it to him. He opened it and glanced at the directions.

"Looks easy enough," he said, and rummaged in the drawer for a screwdriver and a penlight. Jessie smiled for the first time all day.

She followed Chuck to the bathroom and watched him work. He held the flashlight in his mouth to find the screws for the switch plate, then removed them and placed them and the plate on the sink.

"You've left water all over the place in here," he groused after propping the flashlight on the counter.

"Oh, sorry. I couldn't see it in the dark," Jessie said. "I'll go get a towel."

She slipped into the kitchen and counted to ten before going back into the pantry to flip the main breaker back on.

She heard a zap. Lights flickered and the refrigerator clicked on before the main breaker slammed off and everything went out again. It sounded like a hippo landed on the bathroom floor. In a moment, the smell of scorched meat wafted through the house.

Jessie removed her rubber gloves and placed them by the sink. No sense making it easy on the cops by leaving her fingerprints on the switch. And to think she had come this close to putting rat poison in the tuna. No way they would have missed that. But this? Clearly a tragic accident caused by a man doing his household duties without taking the proper precautions. How sad. But at least his company's life insurance paid double indemnity for accidents.

She thought about when her grandmother died, summoning tears. When she was ready, she dialed 911.

Poor, poor Jessie. Thirty-eight and already a widow.

With the best years of her life ahead of her.

Seven of Hearts

Dianna Sinovic

On the threshold of his study, Thomas sensed without a glance that one of the hearts was gone. Then he looked at the shelf and saw that, indeed, only six hearts floated in their clear, glass jars. The seventh jar was not there.

"Who's missing?" Thomas said, adjusting his wire-rimmed spectacles to peer more closely.

The hearts shifted and bobbed in their vessels. A faint whispering: *Gold.*

"No!" Thomas said. "It *must* be here." Had he moved that jar to some other place in the room? Quickly he scanned the other shelves laden with flasks and vials, the nooks crammed with dried herbs and seed packs. No seventh heart afloat in its trans-ether anywhere.

He sagged into the hardback chair at his desk. This was unprecedented. Nothing had ever gone missing from his study—he assumed anyway. With so many objects in the room, it was possible that something had slipped away over the years. But a heart, and that heart in particular? He had spent years looking for the specimen. No.

Thomas moved the six remaining vessels from their shelf to his desk. Even that was a challenge, so covered was it with potion books, stacks of journals, and small trinkets he had collected. He shifted a few books to make room.

"What are we going to do?" he mused to the six. Six preserved specimens of human hearts, but with the bonus of the lilac-scented trans-ether, which gave them a kind of autonomy that wasn't possible as part of the human circulatory system. Braveheart and Proud Heart and Hard Heart, and the other three, carefully curated as only he could assemble them. The seventh heart had been his finale, the segue to his retirement, when he could simply potter about his garden and snooze in his chair.

The hearts continued to bob and shift, some coming to the edge of glass nearest Thomas, almost as if to stare at him. More murmuring: *Ask Ashtan.*

"Ashtan?" Thomas almost roared. "Has *she* been in here?"

But of course. She visits us often.

His housekeeper was a muse from the Old School. He had forbidden her entry to his study. Let the dust and chaos lie as they are, he'd said. I expect you to take care of the rest of the house, but not this room.

Evidently, according to his heart chorus, she had disobeyed his wishes. True to form for a muse. Still, if she came there often, she might have an idea of what happened to the errant heart.

A ruffle of feathers from the doorpost perch sent a lone piece of downy fluff spiraling through the close air of the study. "Look for Piper, methinks." The green bird with the orange beak then preened under its wing.

Thomas scratched his ear. "Piper, eh?" The young scallywag wasn't by the house much, but when he was . . . well, Thomas had to admit, things *had* disappeared. *Stolen* would have been more appropriate under the circumstances. The lad had a presence, an aura about him that Thomas couldn't quite pin down.

"Conure," Thomas finally said, "you may be right." He sighed. "But why would Piper want the heart?" Human hearts were only important to the humans who were kept alive by them. Once they were separated from the rest of the body, they were just body parts—of no use to anyone but pathologists and those like Thomas. Piper would have no connection to it, and the black market was not eager for spare hearts, especially those that had been severed from their original locations.

"Gold," Conure said, then fluffed her feathers.

"Yes, yes," Thomas said, with faint irritation. "It's the golden heart that's gone." He carefully placed the remaining six jars back on their shelf, caressing the glass slightly as he did so. "Don't worry," he said. "I'll find number seven."

Thomas located Ashtan in the kitchen brewing Peruvian coffee in the battered pot. She placed a mug flecked with red in front of him. He inhaled the scent of the dark roast overlaid with the aroma of baking bread. Ashtan returned to toasting slabs of rye over the open flame of the hearth. She was silent except for the dim humming that always enveloped her.

Clearing his throat, Thomas paused before speaking. It was always good to plan what you said to a muse. If not, the results could be painful.

"One of my jarred hearts is gone," he finally said. Best to keep it simple to start. No accusations.

Ashtan did not respond, intent on the toast, which was browning quickly.

"Not that I'm saying you're involved," Thomas said.

She slipped the toast onto a plate and put that and the marmalade jar on the table. Then with almost imperceptible motion, she was seated opposite him, blinking slowly.

Had he insinuated too much? He tensed, waiting for whatever punishment she aimed at him.

But she merely took a slice of toast and spread marmalade on it, covering every bit of the side of bread, and took a bite. "Seven has gone on a journey," she said.

"But . . ." he sputtered. "You were not to enter my study! And that would include not taking anything from it—especially not a heart."

Her eyes flashed black, an inkiness that he fought not to drown in. "I did not say I took Seven," she said oh so softly. "Nor did I say I breached the door of your study."

"Of course, of course," Thomas backpedaled, finally able to break his glance from hers. "I'm sorry I jumped to conclusions." He wanted to add: *But then who took the heart?*

They sat in silence for several moments, the crunching of crisp toast, the slurps of coffee, and the ever-present humming of Ashtan the only sounds.

"I will help you bring Seven back," she said at last.

Thomas smiled in relief. "You will?"

She nodded slightly. "But you must follow my instructions without a waver."

Thomas bit back his words, knowing they would not help matters. *But I'm a Hodden. I don't take orders; I give them.*

And so, Thomas slung a traveler's bag over his shoulder and set off down the rutted lane from Midtower to Thorn's Crotch and the tavern that sat at the far end of that hamlet. As taverns go, it wasn't the darkest, but the smells of sweat and ale and pipe smoke immediately infused any visitor, the odor remaining in hair and skin long after the visit.

His choice would have been a table in the back, where he could see the entire room, even if dimly, but Ashtan had made it clear he should sit at the rough-hewn bar, shoulder to shoulder with the local loghammers and pitmen.

"A dark ale," Thomas said to the bartender, who, after sizing him up, gave him a wink.

For the next hour, he nursed the ale, listening to the grunted exchanges on either side of him. It seemed hopeless, and he longed to be back in the quiet of his study, doing his research. A rustle in his traveler's bag made him start, and then a small furry head popped out of a pocket.

"Zeno," Thomas said, keeping his voice low, "I should have known you would sneak a ride." He pushed the brown rat back into the pocket. "You'll cause trouble if you show yourself in here." Not everyone appreciated Thomas' special talents, especially those who didn't do much deep thinking.

The bartender set a fresh mug of ale before Thomas, then gave a pointed glance down the bar. *The person you seek is at the far end.* The words floated into Thomas' ears, yet the bartender did not move his lips. *He's waiting for you.*

Thomas nodded. "Thanks," he said. The loghammers next to him paid no attention, ensnarled in an argument that seemed to be escalating. He made sure Zeno was well hidden, placed a coin on the bar for his ale, and walked to the end of the room.

A reed-thin man—or was it a creature?—leaned against the bar. His arms seemed oddly long, and through the translucent skin of his face shimmered the bones of his skull.

Thomas wished, not for the first time, that his talents lay along an extrasensory path for humans instead of an affinity with animals. *Who was this fellow?*

"Carpy," the man said, extending a hand. "Let's play cards."

Thomas offered his own hand reluctantly but remembered Ashtan's words: *It's the depth that tells the true worth of a person.* If only he could see into those depths.

Carpy led Thomas to a back room, even more dimly lit than the main bar. Two other men already sat at a table in the glow of an oil lamp.

With a flourish of his long jacket, Carpy took a third chair and motioned for Thomas to take the last.

"Hearts," he said, pulling from a pocket a deck of cards. "Hearts it is you're searching for, I hear," his voice both thin and needle-like.

"Yes," Thomas said. "One in particular." *But I'm not going to find it here at this card table.*

Carpy cut the deck and began to deal. "We play five games. You win, you get closer to what you came for. You lose and . . ." He let the words linger in the air, and they took on increasing malevolence the longer they drifted.

"What are we playing?" Thomas said, wondering if he could back out of the proposal.

Carpy's laughter boomed. "Hearts, of course!"

The two other men laughed along with him, their smiles suggesting that the opportunity to beat a stranger was one they had been waiting for.

It might have been two hours later, but it seemed like an endless night. Thomas had lost three games. He had two strikes against him: He was a green rookie in the game of hearts, and he knew they were cheating.

"Looks like you're not going to win today, bloke," Carpy said. "Too bad."

Thomas gently tapped his bag; it was time to call in the reinforcements. He felt Zeno scamper down his pant leg, and he looked at the cards he held. "You're right," he acknowledged aloud, laying down his hand. *At least not at cards.*

With a chattering that seemed to come from all corners of the room, rats swarmed to the table. The three other players shouted in pain as the rats bit them about the ankles and climbed their legs to nip in other places even more painful. Chairs fell back, the lamp was knocked over and quickly righted, and Carpy's twisted smile vanished.

"Call them off!" he said.

Thomas hoisted his traveler's bag and stood up. The scurrying of tiny feet continued, along with the cries and moans of the other players.

"I'll do that in exchange for the lead that was promised me," Thomas said. "Lead first, rats second."

Stomping and swearing as the rats overran him, Carpy reached beneath the table, drew out a playing card, and threw it at Thomas. "That's all I have. Now get out."

The card fluttered to the floor, and Zeno brought it to Thomas' hand: The seven of hearts. Thomas gave two brief whistles, and the rats skittered away, leaving only Zeno, who sat on Thomas' shoulder, carefully cleaning his paws.

If he weren't searching for a missing heart, Thomas would have walked back to Midtower that night. Instead, he pulled out a thin blanket and rolled himself up in it to sleep beneath a hazel bush. He longed for his chair before the fire, a mug of Ashtan's warmed spirits at his side. If he were a Merlin, he would have conjured a comfortable tent—even a cabin—in which to sleep, but Hoddens had lesser powers, so the best he could do was to make his form less visible to passersby—more of a smudge on the ground than a man in a blanket shivering in the cold and the damp.

By morning light, his blanket already tucked away in his traveler's bag, Thomas brewed coffee over a small fire—he could conjure fire, at least— and studied the playing card from Carpy. Seven hearts marked the face of the card. The back held an etching of several human skulls. He turned the card over and over. Where was the lead he needed?

With a slight wiggle, Zeno emerged from his favorite pocket. Thomas lay the card face up on his pantleg while he poured himself a mug of coffee. The rat nosed the card briefly, then started to scratch it with tiny paws.

"Hey, don't," Thomas said. He reached for the card, but Zeno gave his hand a small nip. "Ouch!"

Zeno kept scratching at the lone heart floating midway between two rows of three hearts. The rat stopped when he had removed all of the red, leaving a tiny word exposed. Thomas slipped off his eyeglasses and held it close to his eyes to decipher the script.

"Sandwich?"

Zeno sat back on his haunches, peering up at Thomas. Then chittered.

Thomas abruptly saw in his mind the card pulled apart, like pulling the two pieces of bread away from a ham sandwich. He gently teased the edges of the card, and it separated, peeling one side from the other. Inked on one interior was a map. Curiously, it started where they were, and showed a route through the next hamlet, along the Cataract River, and up the Twining Ridge.

"Blazes," Thomas said. "I'm getting too old for this sort of thing."

And all because of a missing heart. He had carefully tended to it, protected it, nurtured it, but someone had robbed him. It was vital that he find it. Only he knew the fine balance of trans-ether needed to prolong its preservation indefinitely. And he had sworn an oath, the oath of the Hoddens, that once collected, the organ would never be left to decay on its own.

"Why would someone take the heart?" Thomas said aloud to Zeno. The rat offered no mental image this time, just a wriggle of his nose.

A raven's rough caw sounded above Thomas' head, in the upper story of a beech tree. It hopped from branch to branch, moving downward, toward him, and giving its rough caw each time it landed on a new branch. Zeno dove into a pocket for safety. Then, no more than ten feet above Thomas, the raven dropped a small envelope, which settled on his lap. He opened it and removed a note, in Ashtan's handwriting.

"Go with speed, Thomas. The path is right. The six send their love, awaiting their companion."

He got to his feet, made sure that Zeno was still tucked away, and, with his traveler's bag over his shoulder, began the trek to Twining Ridge. He whistled an old sea chantey. Perhaps he wasn't too old for this after all.

It was dusk, and Thomas had just passed through the small hamlet marked on the card—a village so small, he could not find a name carved on any signpost—when three men emerged from a thick stand of bushes and trees. Immediately, he regretted not asking in the hamlet for space to spend the night.

"A lone man out on the paths at night," one of the men said. "He's probably up to no good."

"I agree with you, Will," another man said. "Likely a highwayman out to rob the innocent of their hard-earned coins." He laughed at his own joke, so obvious it was that the trio were highwaymen themselves.

"Then," said the third, "we'll need to take from the highwayman what he's he taken from others."

They stood blocking Thomas' way, and as the sky continued to darken, he pondered the odds of one against three, with knives. Not good.

"My good fellows," he said. "I'm but a weary traveler. I have nothing but my small pack, and no coins to spare. It's actually something stolen from me that I seek."

"Stolen," Will, apparently the leader, exclaimed in mock horror. "How much was taken?"

"A heart," Thomas said.

"Ah," Will moaned, again in melodramatic tones. "Your lady was swept away by some rake. More's the pity."

Thomas shook his head. "Not a woman, but a heart, the kind that beats in your own chest." *And yours would be shriveled with the crimes you've committed.*

"You're a grave robber?" the second man said, stepping forward with menace.

"No."

"A doctor then?" the man said.

"More or less." *Less, much less.*

Will, not to be upstaged by one of his gang, said, "The heart, is it valuable?"

"Not in terms of money," Thomas said. "Its value lies in the studies I make."

"And finding it," Will said, "would there be a reward?"

A clever man, Thomas decided. The question gave him the opening he needed to defuse the standoff. "There would," he said.

Will's broad smile was evident even as the day slipped into night.

"But," Thomas added, "it must be brought back safely, no harm done to it."

The three highwaymen consulted with one another briefly, and then Will pronounced their verdict: "We'll find it, and you'll pay a fine sum for it."

Thomas described the jar, the heart, how to carefully carry it. "I've been told to look on Twining Ridge, so that's where I'm headed," he said. "But I also suspect the thief was a young fellow named Piper." *If you can believe a parrot.*

"Piper," the third man said. "I hear he's as light-fingered as they come, so I don't doubt it."

And with that, the three highwaymen melted into the darkness, leaving Thomas alone again.

At sunrise, Thomas, with Zeno now perched on his shoulder, had his bag repacked, and a bite of bread and mug of coffee consumed. The day looked sunny, so he rolled his jacket up and carried it under one arm. Looking at the tiny map again, he tried to guess how far Twining Ridge was from where they stood. A day's walk? Two?

Through great fields of thistle and underneath stands of beech and oak, Thomas trudged, one foot in front of the other. The slight breeze carried on it a tang of citrus mixed with damp earth. The sky was cloudless, and even with intermittent shade, the day warmed to an uncomfortable degree.

He thought over his collection of hearts. He was no graverobber, but it was true that he had taken them from their owners. He knew of a Hodden who collected livers, and he'd heard of another who kept brains. He didn't see the reason. It was the heart that was at a person's core; it governed their sense of goodness or devilry. What could you divine from a liver? And as for brains—he knew most of them were wasted by their owners. Why be reminded of that? He had collected a heart of gold, the rarest find.

The sun had crested and was starting its slow descent when another traveler appeared ahead on the path. Despite the hours on foot, Thomas had seen no other soul on the hike. A kestrel called from overhead, and then stooped to reach the traveler, landing lightly on his outstretched hand. Even at a distance, there was something familiar about his pace, the way he carried his slight frame.

"Piper," Thomas called, pushing himself faster despite his weary legs.

Just as he spoke, three men swarmed out from the surrounding thicket and encircled Piper, shouting at him. The kestrel flew to perch on a nearby oak. It was Will and his small band of highwaymen.

Putting on an extra burst of speed, Thomas reached the group within moments.

"Master Thomas," Piper said. He was almost weeping. "It's not turned out as I thought."

Will turned and recognizing Thomas, pulled Piper by the arm to face the Hodden.

"We've found him," he said triumphantly.

But so did I, Thomas wanted to argue. *Or, was Piper on his way to find me?*

Instead, Thomas said, "So I see. Stand back, away from him. You'll not run, Piper, will you?"

No older than an adolescent, Piper was small and slim. The better, Thomas thought, to slip into places and take a thing or two. The boy shook his head and warily looked at the three highwaymen, who had taken a step back but still surrounded him.

"The main question is, do you have the heart?" Thomas waited with hope.

Piper patted a leather bag on his shoulder. "It's here, Master Thomas."

The highwaymen cheered.

"Our reward now," Will said. "We've done what you asked of us."

"But it needs your help," Piper said to Thomas. "I thought it would be easy. The hearts, Braveheart especially, whispered that I should do it; I should take number seven. I made it as far as the Twinings, but then it cried out . . ."

Thomas puzzled over the boy's words. *The hearts had spoken to him?* "Your pack. Open it gently."

Piper slipped the pack off and knelt to open it. Thomas reached in, taking out a package wrapped in wool. Within was the clear jar, and within that, a human heart that drifted slowly in the trans-ether, now tinged in a light brown.

"Blazes," Thomas said, frowning. "It's almost too late."

He meant well, the heart murmured faintly. *We were trying to help you find your way again.*

"No, he didn't mean well," Thomas said aloud. "He's a thief and a scoundrel."

As Thomas quickly thought through the next steps, Will moved close and grabbed the jar.

"If it's that valuable to you, then you'll pay up—now," he said. The two other men advanced as well.

From his traveler's bag, Thomas pulled out a small bag of coins. "Here," he said, tossing it. "Now hand it back. The thing I must do must be done with all speed."

Still Will held the jar, seeming to know how desperate Thomas was to save the heart. "And you," Will said to Piper. "Hand over your purse as well."

Thomas said later that he had no premonition about the next few moments, yet he should have. The hearts had known. Piper seemed to grow in stature, and his eyes flashed a brilliant green.

"Be gone," the lad said and flung his arms wide.

The jar was back in Thomas' hands, and the men had scattered with yelps and cries. Thomas' bag of coins lay beside his bag.

He eyed Piper cautiously. *Did Piper realize?* But the lad seemed only puzzled, looking around him as if the world had suddenly shifted.

"Master Thomas," Piper said. "What has happened?"

"There's time for that later," Thomas said gruffly to hide his astonishment. *The depth of a person's worth indeed.* "We must save the heart. I need your help."

The lad nodded. "I'm so, so sorry."

"Apology accepted," Thomas said. "Now let's get to work."

Ideally, Thomas would have tackled the delicate task in his study, mixing and measuring the elixirs and gases that made up the trans-ether. He was neither in his study nor within reach of his laboratory tools. But a Hodden does have special talents, and so he withdrew from his bag several small vials he carried with him when he traveled, because you never knew when you might run across another heart worth collecting.

With Piper holding the jar, Thomas infused its contents with the vials, one after the other, until the trans-ether was again clear.

The crisis has passed, the heart murmured again, shifting and bobbing once more.

Piper looked at Thomas, a smile widening across his face. "It will be all right!"

"So, you *can* hear it," Thomas said. "That's a fortunate thing. Few people can."

He carefully wrapped the jar in the wool and handed it back to Piper. "I'll trust you with it on our return journey."

Piper nodded. "Thank you, Master Thomas. I'll make sure it will come to no harm."

"And now," Thomas said, slipping his traveler's bag on his shoulder once more, "I have a proposal for you." They fell into a steady walking cadence, side by side, as though they had long done this. "How would you like to be my apprentice?"

The Last Deduction

A. E. Decker

Watson was away, visiting wife number two's (three's? four's? Watson was somewhat vague on the subject) relations in the country. But before he left, he must have given Holmes another lecture about his use of the cocaine needle. Otherwise, Lestrade knew, Holmes would likely have passed the time of Watson's absence sunk deep in a drug-induced stupor. As it was, he'd invited Lestrade over for brandy and cigars to while away the hours of ennui. Oh, and also to play the endless "see how clever I am and you're not, Inspector" game that he never seemed to weary of.

Lestrade hardly had time to clip the end of his cigar before Holmes started up this delightful pastime.

"I see you've been to Bristol in the past week," he said.

Lestrade's jaw clenched. He may as well have saved himself the trouble of clipping his cigar and bitten off the tip.

Holmes waited by the window, curls of blue smoke rising from the tip of his cigar. The expectant silence stretched like a bit of old toffee left over from one of Watson's surreptitious nibbles.

Lestrade gave in. "How do you figure that, Mr. Holmes?"

The vaguest twitch of a satisfied-addict smile flashed over Holmes's face before he composed it into his usual air of aloof boredom. "You were wearing that shirt when I saw you Tuesday last. I recognize the peculiar open chain stitching on the collar and the triangular nick in the top button. However, those ink stains were not present last Tuesday."

"And it's a type of ink commonly found in Bristol?" asked Lestrade, hoping to cut to the chase.

"I have written a monograph on the subject," said Holmes stiffly, and turned to gaze out the nicotine-stained windows. Nothing of the street below could be seen through the thick yellow fog roiling outside, but

Lestrade knew it was the pose that mattered. "I recognized three hundred and twelve distinct types," Holmes added, drawing on his cigar.

How many hours must one spend looking at drops of ink under a microscope to build up a catalogue of three hundred and twelve different types? And knowing Holmes, he'd have to test all those diverse inks against the God-knows-how-many kinds of paper—and cloth—he kept in his head. Lestrade was no mathematician, unlike the late, unlamented Professor Moriarty, but he reckoned the final tally would run to the hundreds of thousands.

Some people had a life, you know.

"I cannot compliment you on your handling of the Paxton Bowery case," said Holmes, still staring out the window, or rather at the window.

Yes, you could. Lestrade's fingers tightened around the fragile shell of his brandy glass. *You really, really could, just for novelty's sake.* He tried to relax back into the overstuffed chair and his ribs struck a hard object. With a hiss of pain, he reached back, drawing out a can of treacle secreted behind the cushion. Right; this was Watson's favorite seat, wasn't it? "Ah, well, we solved it in the end," he said, setting the treacle on the floor.

"Ah, no, no, no." Turning his head, Holmes did that combination tongue-clicking/finger-shaking thing that was so bloody irritating. "That won't do, Lestrade, it won't do. One look at Mr. Gregor Churchson's bootlaces should have ended it. Were it not for my timely suggestion—"

Lestrade stared at the mantelpiece as Holmes droned on, aware that his eyes were glazing. Odd. For all Holmes's much-trumpeted powers of observation, he seemed completely oblivious to signs of boredom in his listener.

"—while the frayed ends on his right bootlaces indicated they more often came undone. Moreover, the material they were made from was peculiarly slick—"

He's been hitting the tobacco heavily. Lestrade noted that only a small lump of the stuff remained in the toe of the Persian slipper. No cocaine bottle sitting on the corner of the mantelpiece this evening; perhaps Watson had spirited it away.

"—that, coupled with the flecks of gray-green mud on Mr. Churchson's left wrist—"

Perhaps Holmes fancied he was talking to the wax dummy of himself sitting by the far window, its white features molded into the picture of benign introspection. *Undoubtedly a far more attentive audience than myself.* Lestrade found himself incapable of taking his gaze off the thing. The bullet hole pocking its brow held a peculiar fascination.

"All in all, a most jejune little case," Holmes wound up. His sigh released another cloud of blue smoke into the air. "Mediocrity, I fear, is the mark of today's criminal class."

Yes, approximately twenty thousand instances of crime in London annually, and the Great Detective could only be bothered to show interest in perhaps six of them. *Too busy categorizing types of toothpicks the rest of the year, I imagine,* mused Lestrade. *That bullet hole. What a beautiful shot. You couldn't get it more perfectly between the brows if you measured.*

"I don't suppose you've heard of anything unusual lately, Lestrade?" Holmes asked, throwing his lanky body onto the sofa.

With difficulty, Lestrade tore his gaze from the wax dummy and ran his mind over the past few affairs that had been brought to his attention, searching for something suitably ridiculous.

"There's a fellow been pinching black cockerels from back gardens—"

"Pooh, pooh! That's Lord Barkham. It's part of his initiation into the Hellfire Club." Holmes drew on his cigar.

Don't ever say "pooh, pooh" in my presence again. Lestrade shifted uneasily. Presently he was working on a homicide case. Nearly solved, in fact, so long as he didn't let Holmes dip his fingers into the pudding and complicate everything. Aside from that, a couple robberies had recently been brought to his attention, but neither presented anything unusual.

The pressure of Holmes's eyes, locked onto his face, actually itched. Lestrade knew that every quirk of his lips, every flick of his brow, was being noted, parsed, dissected for meaning.

I'm going to crack and tell him about the Aldbloom murder case any second, Lestrade realized. *And then he'll either sneer at my weeks of work as something that should have been completed in a day, or he'll find some flaw in my reasoning and blow the whole mess apart. By the time he's through, I'll be browbeating myself for not noticing the number of spots on a rotten cucumber or something of the sort.*

The hawklike gray gaze hadn't wavered. Not once. Lestrade felt they were a pair of gimlets, not eyes, boring into his skull, seeking the luscious meat of information.

"Well, Inspector? I have heard tell of a little affair in Covent Garden. I don't suppose you thought to take a look at the canary."

Canary? What bloody canary? They hadn't found so much as a scrap of feather or handful of moldy millet in Aldbloom's apartment.

He's doing it. Lestrade's spirits sank like cooling lead to the soles of his shoes. Already he could envision it all: Holmes's sneers as he demolished piles of Lestrade's carefully compiled evidence. The tiny, overlooked clue upon which everything ludicrously balanced. Then, the denouement, when Holmes would triumphantly unmask the true malefactor—or let him go, if the whim struck him, Holmes never being one to allow the entire British legal system to overturn his own private verdict. For Lestrade there would be the backhanded congratulations of the papers for another successful case, which had never, not once, gone any way to making up for the routine humiliations at Holmes's hands.

Not again, not again, he begged, squeezing his eyes shut. But what else was there to do? His lips had actually parted to confess all when something else entirely burst into his mind. Like a divine light. An answer from God.

He smiled, opening his eyes. Holmes puffed, watching him expectantly. "Actually, I have recently heard of something more your style," said Lestrade.

Holmes cocked a brow. Lestrade allowed himself a sip of brandy, denying Holmes his fix for just that one second longer, then set down his glass. "Something so grotesque, in fact, we wish to keep it from the public eye."

The Great Detective sat up and pressed his fingertips together.

They met two nights later at Dobb's Tavern, a low-end dive in Lambeth, not far from the river. For attire, Lestrade contented himself with old clothes, a shabby long coat, and cabby's cap pulled low over his eyes, but of course Holmes had to indulge his love of disguise. He'd costumed himself as a pieman, complete with striped pants, gravy-stained apron, and thicket of ginger whiskers. A faint whiff of vinegar and pickled eel emanated from his coat, Holmes never knowing when to stint on effects.

Despite the disguise, Lestrade discovered him right away, sitting at the bar, a pot of beer he'd never deign to drink at hand. He never quite understood why Watson praised Holmes' powers of disguise so strongly. All you really had to look for were the razor-sharp nose and air of self-congratulation.

"It's happened again, then?" asked Holmes as Lestrade took a seat beside him, laying a plain heavy walking stick across the bar.

"Sergeant Whiting found them just four hours ago. Tracks larger than a man's spread hand leading away from the river. Tracks he swears he's seen the like of before, sir. The tracks of some prehistoric monster."

Holmes's lip curled in a faint sneer, revealing an ugly snaggle of fake buckteeth. Lestrade repressed a shudder. Where did the man purchase such items? "A monster, you say?"

"Yes," said Lestrade. "You can see why we wish to keep it out of the papers. Were the knowledge to become common, there could be a general panic."

A faint line creased the long stretch of skin above Holmes's brows for a moment as he acquired his far-off thinking expression, faintly ridiculous on the face of a ginger-haired, beaked-nosed pieman. All at once, he rose and threw a coin on the bar top.

"Let us have a look at these singular tracks before time and tide wash them away," he declaimed, as if ending the scene of a play. He strode out of Dobb's without looking to see if Lestrade followed. Taking up his stick, Lestrade glanced around the tavern. No one seemed to be paying the slightest bit of attention to their departure. Holmes would be disappointed.

A rotten damp night outside, the fog rolling in so thick one would be hard-pressed to see one's palm held up before one's face. Laughter and faint jeers echoed up and down the half-seen street; roughs and ladies of ill repute taking advantage of the atmosphere to ply unsavory trades.

Lestrade shut the door behind him. He could see the gray span of Holmes's turned back under the uncertain light of a flickering streetlamp. "Monsters, hah!" Holmes exclaimed, as if oblivious to Lestrade's footsteps, but obviously meant to be overheard.

"So I thought when I first heard of them." Lestrade motioned Holmes to follow him toward the river. "But I saw the first set. Five-pointed, like some sort of lizard's, and large as a bear's."

"You saw the first set, you say?"

"With my own eyes, yes. Gave me the shivers, they did. But they were some distance away, in Southwark."

"Hum!" Holmes said and fell silent.

The drunken cries faded in the distance as the street gave way to muddy ground. Lestrade rested his heavy stick on his shoulder.

"You came prepared, I see," said Holmes.

"It's a rough district," said Lestrade. "And if by some chance this creature is real and dangerous . . ."

Holmes did not say "pooh, pooh" again, but the curdled expression on his face carried much the same effect.

They heard the Thames before they saw it. And smelled it: a faintly oily, fishy stink laced with the sour reek of excrement. Lestrade paused to take a lantern from an inner pocket and light it. The yellow light pierced the fog just enough to show them the dark ripple of the river to their left. The crumbling façade of an abandoned glasswork stood on the rise to their right.

"Not much farther," said Lestrade. He grimaced at the feel of mud pulling at his shoes. Off to his left, the water burbled, hissed, rumbled, even sighed as a gust of wind passed over its surface. *Sounds like a living thing sometimes. And if even it's not alive itself, who knows what may lurk beneath its surface?*

Not monsters, if you asked Holmes. But not even Holmes knew everything about monsters.

In the sliver of lantern light, Holmes's expression resembled that of a sleepy cat waiting patiently beside a mouse hole. At least he'd divested himself of his whiskers, and hopefully those ghastly teeth as well.

"There," said Lestrade, pointing ahead to a strip of smooth ground sloping out of the water. He held the lantern to play over its surface. Five-pointed tracks pocked its surface, sunk deep into the mud. Uncanny things, like squeezed stars, the five clawed extensions biting into the soft earth.

Lestrade let out a whistle. "See the size of them, Mr. Holmes? Why, the creature must be taller than a man!"

A stronger breeze ran over the water, making a faint moaning sound.

Holmes pursed his lips. Taking the lantern from Lestrade, he advanced, his nostrils flaring. The Thames gurgled and giggled. Wisps of yellow fog curled into strange shapes over its surface. Lestrade followed Holmes, tapping his stick against his shoulder.

Setting the lantern on a somewhat dry strip of ground, Holmes knelt to scrutinize the tracks. He bent until his nose nearly touched one. "Ha!" he exclaimed after a moment. "You have been deceived. Again, I might add, my dear inspector."

"Have I?" *Tap, tap.*

"Indeed." Sitting up, Holmes laid his hands against his thighs. "These tracks are a mere fraud constructed from the discarded hooves of cattle, no doubt taken from the conveniently located Lambeth slaughterhouse."

"How very clever," said Lestrade.

"No doubt you would think so," said Holmes, his voice dry enough to absorb half the Thames. "Having ascertained that they are a fraud, the real question becomes whether they are meant for a mere prank or are the hallmark of something more sinister."

Lestrade's smile stretched his lips despite all his efforts to restrain it. "I believe I can answer that." *Tap, tap.*

"You can?" Holmes turned his head. In the yellow light cast by the lantern, his eyebrows were already lifting in disbelief.

Lestrade swung with all his strength. The crunch and collapse at the end of the blow frankly surprised him; he'd expected Holmes's skull to be thicker than that.

He paused to catch his breath, looking out over the water. The breeze sighed, gentling again. At last, Lestrade looked down. The Great Detective lay stretched in the mud, a baffled—and frankly, rather stupid—expression frozen on his slack features.

Taking a bit of string out of his pocket, Lestrade found a heavy stone and tied it to the stick. For a moment he debated tying those wretched false teeth to the rock as well—the world would be better off rid of those, but on balance he decided it would be more amusing if they were found on Holmes's person.

The rock and stick made a fine splash, far out in the middle of the Thames. Lestrade watched until the ripples subsided then turned away. The tide would wash away the strange tracks overnight. He'd checked.

Eventually Holmes's body would be discovered and all of London would undoubtedly break out their black armbands again. Dr. Watson would write a blubbering eulogy. Then someone, possibly even Lestrade himself, would have to take charge of the investigation.

If that happens, I'll pin the blame on that blighter Sebastian Moran. Damn Holmes. He barely resisted giving the Great Detective's body a kick. For all Holmes's bleating about how Moran would "trouble them no more," he had in fact gotten off scot-free for the murder of Ronald Adair. No witnesses to the crime, after all. Didn't Holmes have any idea how the legal system worked?

Oh right; this was the man who didn't know the earth revolved around the sun. Lestrade shook his head.

But perhaps some other detective would take up the sword to avenge Holmes. Perhaps Lestrade's crime would be unmasked, and his career come to an ignominious end on the scaffold.

Perhaps. But among all the future possibilities, there was an absolute certainty: the one person who would not be solving this case was Sherlock Holmes himself.

Lestrade smiled. Buttoning his collar, he struck up a merry tune. He whistled it all the cold walk home.

About the Authors

Courtney Annicchiarico is one of the original members of the Bethlehem Writers Group and is very proud to be a part of another BWG anthology. In addition to reading, loving on her fur babies, and knitting badly, Courtney is going back to school to fulfill some longtime dreams.

Jeff Baird is a natural redhead, a career educator at the secondary and post-graduate level, and a self-proclaimed computer junkie. He has presented at numerous state and national technology conferences and has published in the field of educational technology. He is a member of the Bethlehem Writers Group and has stories in each of its Sweet, Funny, and Strange® anthologies. He now turns his energies to publishing humorous memoirs about assorted topics such as Mother Nature (waterfalls and hiking), pets, and life's vagaries. Check out his Amazon Author page for his collection of titles.

Peter J Barbour has been writing for over thirty years. He published a memoir, *Loose Ends,* in 1987. A retired physician and now a full-time author and illustrator, his stories have appeared in many e-zines and publications. Barbour is a member of Bethlehem Writers Group and the Society of Children's Book Writers and Illustrators. He has written and illustrated three children's books. His latest, *Tanya and the Baby Elephant,* came out in 2021. Barbour lives with his wife in the Pacific Northwest. Links to his stories and illustrations can be found at https://www.PeteBarbour.com.

Paula Gail Benson is a legislative attorney and former law librarian, whose short stories have appeared online and in anthologies including *Mystery Times Ten 2013; A Tall Ship, a Star, and Plunder; A Shaker of Margaritas: That Mysterious Woman; Fish or Cut Bait: a Guppy Anthology; Killer Nashville Noir: Cold Blooded; Love in the Lowcountry; Heartbreaks and Half-truths; Once Upon a Time;* and Malice Domestic's *Mystery Most Diabolical.* In addition to short stories, she writes and directs one act musicals for her church's drama ministry. She's a blogging partner at the *Stiletto Gang* and *Writers Who Kill,* and her website is http://paulagailbenson.com.

A. E. Decker writes fantasy and has been published in numerous venues, including *Fireside Magazine, Beneath Ceaseless Skies*, and over half a dozen anthologies. She likes octopuses and chocolate, but not chocolate octopuses, and recently can be found hanging out on the aerial silks.

Marianne H. Donley writes short stories, funny romances, and quirky murder mysteries. She also owns and manages the multi-author blog, *A Slice of Orange*. Marianne is a member of Bethlehem Writers Group, Music City Writers, Sisters in Crime, and Charmed Writers. You can follow Marianne's various social media at: https://linktr.ee/mariannehdonley

Trey Dowell is an award-winning author of both short and novel-length fiction. His short stories have been or will be published in *Ellery Queen Mystery Magazine, Abyss and Apex, Intrinsick*, and *Mystery Magazine,* among many others. He won the 2022 Derringer Award, which honors excellence in the short fiction crime/mystery genre. His debut science-fiction thriller, *The Protectors,* was published in 2014 by Simon & Schuster. Dowell also teaches a seminar called *The Art of the Query Letter* at the Santa Barbara Writer's Conference each year. You can learn more at www.treydowell.com.

Judge Debra H. Goldstein writes Kensington's Sarah Blair mystery series (*Five Belles Too Many, Four Cuts Too Many, Three Treats Too Many, Two Bites Too Many,* and *One Taste Too Many*). In addition to winning BWR prizes, her novels and short stories have received an IPPY award and have been named Agatha, Anthony, Derringer, and Silver Falchion finalists. Debra has served on the national boards of Sisters in Crime and Mystery Writers of America and was president of the Guppy and SEMWA chapters. Find out more about Debra at https://www.DebraHGoldstein.com

Ralph Hieb is a short story author who enjoys reading and writing paranormal. His interests include travel and cryptozoology. He has taken a million pictures of things, but he can't remember where they were taken. He has been working on a novel for quite a number of years, hopefully to be finished this century, maybe. He is a member of The Horror Writers Association, The Pocono Liars, and The Bethlehem Writers Group.

Eleanor Ingbretson lives in Northern New Hampshire and busies herself with short stories, church, reading, gardening, and her family, not necessarily in that order but as the want arises. A compilation of her short, short fantasy stories, *A Baker's Half-Dozen*, can be found on Smashwords, Amazon, and BN.com. "The Tabac Man," first-place winner in the 2022 Bethlehem Writers Roundtable Short Story Award competition, is the first in a string of linked stories she hopes to have published someday. The second in the series, "Seven Women," recently won an Honorable Mention in the New England Crime Bake competition.

DT Krippene writes mystery, dystopian science fiction, paranormal, and alternate-world fantasy. His short story, "Hell of a Deal," appears in the Bethlehem Writers Group's award-winning paranormal collection, *Untethered: Sweet, Funny, and Strange Tales of the Paranormal*. He also appears in the 2020 Indie Award winning book, *Fur Feathers & Scales* with "Man's Best Friend." He's been a featured author with the Bethlehem Writers Roundtable with "Snowbelt Sanctuary," "In Simple Terms," "Hot as Sin," and most recently, "Desert Buzz." You can learn more in his Fall, 2021 interview on Bethlehem Writers Roundtable, on his website https://dtkrippene.com/, and on Facebook and Twitter.

Jerome W. McFadden is an award-winning short story writer whose stories have appeared in fifty magazines, anthologies, and e-zines over the past ten years. He has received a Bullet Award for the best crime fiction to appear on the web. Two of his short stories have been read on stage by the Liar's League London and Liar's League Hong Kong. His collection of twenty-six short stories, entitled *Off the Rails* was published in October, 2019, to great reviews.

Emily P. W. Murphy is a writer, freelance editor, and professional photographer, and a parent of the world's most amazing kids. Emily is a fan of the Red Sox, ampersands, and the Oxford comma. A Pennsylvania native, Emily currently lives in Maryland where the summers are far too hot, but the people are pretty great. Visit Emily's author/editor website at: https://EmilyPWMurphy.com, or photography website at: https://EmilyMurphyPhotography.mypixieset.com/

Christopher D. Ochs dove into writing with his epic fantasy *Pindle-bryth of Lenland*. He then crafted a collection of mirthful macabre short fiction in *If I Can't Sleep, You Can't Sleep*. His latest novel is a gritty urban fantasy/horror, *My Friend Jackson,* a Finalist in Indies Today's Best Books of 2020. His short fictions have been published in GLVWG and BWG anthologies and websites, and by Firebringer Press. His current projects include: the cosmic adventures of the world's most dangerous insurance agent; two sci-fi novels, "Sentinel of Eternity" and "No Place Like Home;" a prequel novella in the *Pindlebryth* saga. Follow Chris's daring-do at https://www.christopherdochs.com and Facebook @ChristopherDOchs.

Dianna Sinovic is an author, certified book coach, and editor based in Bucks County, PA. She writes short stories in several genres, including paranormal, horror, and speculative fiction. She is a member of Sisters in Crime, the Horror Writers Association, the American Medical Writers Association, and the Bethlehem Writers Group. Her website is https://www.dianna-sinovic.com.

Kidd Wadsworth has people in her head and likes to work in her pajamas. She found her career choices extremely limited: write or commit herself to an institution. You can find out more about this person, and her novel, "To Kill A Dragon," at https://www.kiddwadsworth.com/.

Paul Weidknecht is the author of *Native to This Stream: Brief Writings About Fly-Fishing & the Great Outdoors,* a chapbook collection of previously published short stories, essays, and poems. He wrote the short film, "Know Thy Partner", (IMDb), which is currently screening at international film festivals. His work has appeared in *Gray's Sporting Journal, Outdoor Life, Rosebud, Shenandoah, Structo* (UK), and elsewhere. He lives in Phillipsburg, New Jersey.

Carol L. Wright writes mysteries and more. Her debut traditional mystery, *Death in Glenville Falls: A Gracie McIntyre Mystery* was a finalist for two international book awards. Her short stories have appeared in award-winning anthologies and literary journals, and some of her favorites are collected in her book *A Christmas on Nantucket and other stories.* You can learn more at her website: https://CarolLWright.com

CPSIA information can be obtained
at www.ICGtesting.com
Printed in the USA
JSHW022142130922
30467JS00001B/33